My Name is Agnes

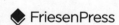 FriesenPress

Suite 300 - 990 Fort St
Victoria, BC, V8V 3K2
Canada

www.friesenpress.com

Copyright © 2017 by Kelly Brookbank
First Edition — 2017

All rights reserved.

No part of this publication may be reproduced in any form, or by any means, electronic or mechanical, including photocopying, recording, or any information browsing, storage, or retrieval system, without permission in writing from FriesenPress.

ISBN
978-1-4602-9234-1 (Hardcover)
978-1-4602-9235-8 (Paperback)
978-1-4602-9236-5 (eBook)

1. FICTION

Distributed to the trade by The Ingram Book Company

My Name is Agnes

by Kelly Brookbank

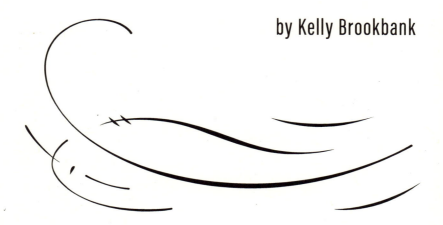

Chapter 1

It was a dark and stormy night…actually that's not true. I was in Arizona, what were the chances it was storming? I'll be honest, there are a lot of good books that start with that phrase so I wanted mine to also. Well shit, now I feel bad…first couple of sentences and I've lied already. Ok, let's start over. Hi. My name is Agnes and I am a witch.

I came to Earth about 25,000 human years ago. After exploring a couple of other galaxies and some very unfriendly and boring planets I dropped down here, saw how interesting it was, and have never looked back. Actually, I have gone back to my world a couple of times, but I try not to make a habit of it. It's not that I don't like everyone there; I don't feel it's my world any more. In human years I am just over 30,000 years old. In my world I am only three cycles, which is very young, if I do say so myself!!

So now I was here, living in Arizona, trying to keep to myself and stay out of trouble (really I was!) But I have to keep moving around as my situation keeps changing. You see, most of my "special gifts" I learn as I go. I don't have anyone to guide me (other than my best friend; a bat named Robin), or to tell me what is going to happen. So when I figure these things out…or more importantly — when the humans figure out what I can do, I have to cover my tracks and move on.

For example, when I first came to Earth (not what it was originally called, by the way — there are a lot of historical inaccuracies in the history books!!) But, it's not like I can say, "Hey — that is SO not how it happened!"

"Ummm, and how would you know that, Agnes?"

"Oh, never mind. I wasn't there. Carry on."

Anyway, I was living among the cavemen and women, minding my own business, when one of the men decided that he should "mate" with me. I was not about to be sexed-up by a caveman. First of all, he didn't speak my language because, of course, he didn't speak at all. And second of all he was about 5,000 years too young for me and had a really bad haircut.

He was getting aggressive and I was getting agitated. The more aggressive he got the more pissed off I got. Eventually I hit my boiling point and I pushed him (and by push I mean I used my eyes) and he fell (and by fell I mean he went flying about twenty feet into a pile of rocks). I also gave him a searing glare that shot fire out of my eyes turning this dumbass into a pile of ashes. Phew, that felt so good!

Even though I felt much relief, this was a pivotal point in my witch-iness. (Is that a word?) I had discovered I had two powers: 1) I could move things with my eyes and 2) I could burn shit up with my eyes. I am liking my eyes right now!! BUT, when I burned Dummy Dumbass up, I had unintentionally set some twigs on fire, which made the other caveman notice. Now, Doofus #1 and Doofus #2 were coming to see what this bright light was, dragging their knuckles behind them. Oh fuck! They had never seen fire before — quick, now what? I looked around, quickly put some twigs together with a bit of dry moss, and stood nonchalantly close to a pile of rocks, waiting for them to come closer. Great, now the fire mesmerized them. You try getting those no-minds to look away from this new bright light that had heat emanating from it! So there I was jumping up and down, making grunting noises. Yeah, that's going to distract them, like they've never heard grunting noises before. So, what else could I do? I just stood there and screamed at the top of my lungs.

Yes! They finally looked — I leaned on the pile of rocks, which showered down onto each other causing them to spark. (I may have helped with the spark....shhh). The spark hit the moss, the moss caught fire, which caused the sticks to catch fire — abracadabra, another fire! I pretended that I was seeing this for the first time, picked up two rocks, hit them together to create more sparks, then celebrated the sparks with more grunting. I gave Doofus #1 & Doofus #2 rocks and made them do it too. More celebrating sparks — we make fire! Yay us! Phew. I could now leave. Geez, this covering my ass was exhausting.

See how there are historical inaccuracies? You really think those idiot cavemen could've discovered fire? Nope, it was me. Whateves. I don't need the credit.

My Name is Agnes

Chapter 2

As I looked around my little store, Steamers and Dreamers, I couldn't believe it had been two years since I found this perfect spot. The Steamers part of Steamers and Dreamers was the Coffee/Soup & Sandwich Shoppe. We served homemade everything; breakfast sandwiches, chili, soups, etc. Our espresso drinks were delicious because there was a little something thrown in that no one could quite put their finger on…a little spell of happy juice. It might seem a bit corny but when you left my place you were a tad happier. A few hours later you turned back into the same grumpy ass you've always been, but there was not much I could do about that.

The Dreamers part of Steamers and Dreamers was the bookstore. We had all the mainstream books, of course, but I also prided myself in bringing in all sorts of eclectic books and authors. I love reading — the weirder the better. Humans have always fascinated me, so if I could have gotten a bridge-playing, marathon-running, true-crime writer in there, who only eats red meat and drinks only tequila, you bet I would have. We also had a daily "Read and Feed" where we fed and read to kids and their parents who were down on their luck.

I knew there wouldn't be any competition around me as I had put a spell on the land in all the vicinity. And I'd had a good feeling that this area would become a hub for urban families and young business types. loved all the people who came into my store and believe me I had all different kinds. Luckily I have a great memory so I remembered all of their names. I didn't call them all by name, of course, because that would just be creepy. Can you imagine coming into a store once, then coming in again five years later and the owner remembers your name? Ummm, crazy bitch.

This was my favourite time in the morning. No one had come in for their shift yet, but I had all the lights on and the coffee machines firing up and brewing the first pots. I made myself my ritual morning coffee — extra-large, non-fat vanilla latte. I was sitting in the most comfortable café bedroom chair, looking outside, and watching the traffic go by. I took in deep breaths, both to calm myself for the day and to take in the delicious smell of coffee.

I heard the all too familiar chimes-sound indicating that someone had come into the store. At first these chimes were annoying, but I had since learned to love them — it's like a new adventure was starting every time I heard them.

"Good morning Agnes," said Sarah.

She always amazed me; how she was both pleasant yet void of emotion at the same time. Sarah had dirty-blonde hair, but I had no idea how long it was because she put it up in a really messy kind of ponytail with a bandana. She always wore cargo pants with a jersey of some kind. She had really pretty blue eyes but never wore any make-up. I think she would much rather have said nothing at all, but she didn't want to be rude. Sarah was sweet though she failed in the common sense department, but we were working on it! "Good morning, Sarah. How was your night?"

"Not bad. I went to the movies. I found *Rocky Horror Picture Show* playing at the Adonis Theatre in Mesa, so that was kinda cool. Want me to start on inventory?"

Sarah wasn't much for chit-chat, but she was doing better than before. She used to answer, "I don't see how that's your business," whenever you asked her a question.

"*Rocky Horror Picture Show*? That's so cool!" I said. I thought about asking her to invite me next time. I made that mistake once before, though, and the look of terror on her face is still embedded in my

My Name is Agnes   5

memory, so I opted not to this time. "If you want to grab yourself a coffee first before you tackle inventory, go ahead. Or you can just wait until Bobbi gets here."

Bobbi is another employee, but she was chronically late. It was never more than fifteen minutes late so I didn't worry much about it. Besides, she was beautiful and people kept coming back to the store to see her, so I tended to look the other way. Bobbi had really long black hair with matching black eyes. She had flawless skin that was not really dark but not really light; it was almost as if it changed skin tone with what she was wearing. She was a tall girl with the longest legs you can imagine. Her arms were toned as well as her stomach, but she was one of those bitches who eats whatever she wants and you secretly can't wait for that to catch up with her.

"Yeah right," said Sarah in her monotonous tone. "I'll have half of it done by the time she gets here." She turned to the staff room to shed her "coat of many colors" and grab her dollar-store environmentally friendly coffee mug before heading to get started on the inventory.

I finished my latte and had filled my "Better latte than never" mug with regular coffee when Bobbi came in looking like she just finished a photo shoot.

"You are never going to guess what I did last night!"

I caught Sarah rolling her eyes as she filled her coffee mug and headed to the computer.

"Ummm, played tonsil tennis with Peter on a roller coaster?"

She looked at me with a very incredulous, but thoughtful grin like she was mentally putting that on her bucket list.

"No, but I like where your mind is — let's explore that later, Agnes. And BTWs, Peter and I broke up last week. My friends and I were totes bored, so we decided to go out line-dancing at a country bar. Problem is, none of us know how to line-dance! So we found this bar that had line-dancing lessons on. Well, the instructor was soooo cute..."

As I sat there listening to Bobbi, I was taken back to a time long ago when I had a best friend named Polly whom Bobbi reminded me so much of...

* * * * *

I was sitting uncomfortably on the marble, coliseum-type seating waiting for Aristotle to start his lecture. He was such a brilliant mind, I loved listening to him speak. It didn't matter what the subject matter was, I could listen to him talk about it forever. I actually had a crush on him. Well maybe not, I had a crush on his brain, not on him — he wasn't much to look at.

Out of the corner of my eye I saw Polly running in. She was always late. It annoyed me, but I didn't care, she was my best friend and I loved her to bits. She had a great sense of humour, and was generous to a fault with a fiery temper that was matched only by her wits. What they say about red hair and tempers is true! It made her unpredictable but that was part of her charm; I never knew what she was going to do next. Polly's red hair was long and beautiful. Her deep-black eyes were mesmerizing. She was very tall with extremely long legs and she hadn't quite realized how beautiful she was yet.

"Philosophy," I said to Polly.

"What?" she asked, out of breath.

"Before you ask what subject we are about to learn I thought I would just tell you."

"Oh," she sighed. "Thank you. Traya had me so annoyed this morning I am surprised I even made it here."

Traya was Polly's younger sister. They had learned to get along as they grew older but at the moment Traya was the bane of Polly's existence. "That little weed stole all of my brooches, so I practically had to beat it out of her where they were. My hair has not even been done!"

Polly's thick, beautiful, curly hair didn't need to be done at all, it looked stunning naturally.

In this era (Grecian times) we wore dorics, which were basically white sheets with the arms cut out. The men had one shoulder held with a brooch and the women had both shoulders held with brooches. Around our waists we wore fancy belts made out of different types of materials. Of course Polly could pull this look off because she had those crazy long legs. I liked the look because the men always had half

My Name is Agnes

7

their chests showing.

"I know she is a pain but shhhh, he is about to start," I said. We listened to Aristotle's dreamy voice and I started to daydream about becoming his brain's wife when, almost like clockwork, we felt the pebbles being tossed at us. Almost every day, the pair of us would be listening intently, taking notes periodically when BAM, one of us would feel something hit us in the head or arms, which would be followed by the incessant giggles. I usually ignored it but Polly didn't have the restraint I had. Today, at the end of the lecture, she threw the pebbles back at them. Unfortunately, because of her lack of athletic ability they hit an innocent bystander, who turned around with a "What are you doing?"

Polly, aghast, said, "Throw me to the Gods! I am so sorry!!!"

SHHHHH!!! Everyone else around us was spewing, as the annoying pukes who started the whole thing were laughing their asses off.

"Oh, I am going to poison them one of these days," Polly said to me after class.

That could be arranged, I thought to myself. "Ignoring them would be prudent," I said.

Polly's teeth clenched. "But they annoy me so!! We need to teach them a lesson."

"How do you propose…wait, what do you mean we??" I asked.

"Well I cannot do it by myself and besides, doing it together would be so much more enjoyable!" Polly said with her little sideways mischievous grin. I just rolled my eyes as she intertwined our arms, walking me out to the common grassy area.

We were lying on the grass waiting for our next class when I said, "They are fond of you. That is why they are irksome to you."

She sat up. "Pardon me? Are we children? If he favors me why does he not just tell me? No, this has been going on for too long. I am here to learn and it is unfavorable enough for us!!" She laid back down in a huff.

Polly and I were the minority here when it came to women. She got in because her parents were rich and very important. I was here because I'd put a spell on the administrators. There were a couple of other women here too, but it was hard to tell if they were women at all, (if you know what I mean), so the men didn't pay much attention to them. As we walked to our next lecture you could see wheels turning in Polly's head, so I tried to defuse the situation a little. "Why do we not have a conversation with the professor?" I implored her.

"I do not think so. And look like we have tattled? We will look weak. Never," she nearly hissed at me.

I said, "Well maybe ignore Jordan or just smile sweetly at him, perhaps he will think you favour him and he will no longer bother you."

Her facial expression changed slightly..." Hmmmm, pretend that I like him. I like your way of thinking! Thank you Agnes!"

Polly was pretty quiet the rest of the day. We usually hung out at her place after school, but she made up an excuse about her aunt and uncle coming over for supper and that she had to help get ready for them coming. That was such a bad excuse because they had servants who did all that for them. I wasn't sure what she was up to but I was hoping that her sister Traya would annoy her and she would forget all about Jordan.

The next day at school Polly was there before me, which never happened. I guess she hadn't forgotten about getting back at Jordan. "Agnes, come hither — I need your help."

"Why do I feel you are being mischievous, Polly?"

"What makes you think that?" Polly said, with a naughty grin.

I said, "Well, firstly you are here early, which I have never seen before. And second, you have that look in your eyes that gives me pause. And thrice, that satchel you are holding is very concerning. And fourth..."

She cut me off. "All right, stop it. Now listen — all I am suggesting you do is give this satchel to Jordan."

Confused, I said, "You are proposing for me to saunter up and hand this over to Jordan?"

Polly rolled her eyes. "Tsk, no — I do not want you to just give it to him. I would like you to sit down near him in class and I will give you a signal. Then I would like you to set it down beside him. Come

My Name is Agnes

along, class is starting — let us go."

Well maybe this wasn't going to be that bad. Maybe she just had a note in the satchel that explained that she didn't appreciate that he was interrupting her studies and she felt that she was being victimized by his behaviour…Oh who was I kidding? As if she would write him a note. Besides, the satchel was way heavier than just having parchment paper in it.

"Aha, there is Jordan and the rest of the behemoths. You go sit over there and I will sit in our usual spot. Now, when it is the correct time I will look over at you and nod my head? Then you set the satchel down and back to your seat you will go. Understand?" she ordered.

"I understand. Well, not fully but I have heard what you are saying."

Class started as usual and we were all listening intently. But as I was listening, I watched Jordan and Polly out of the corner of my eye. Sure as the sun goes down, Jordan turned around and threw a pebble at Polly. But this time, instead of getting angry, she smiled and throws a pebble back at him, which actually hit him! He threw another pebble back and she kept throwing them back at him — laughing and giggling.

Were my eyes deceiving me? Was she actually flirting with him? Maybe I had it all wrong –maybe she actually liked him! Maybe she had changed her mind after all! Maybe she was going to start dating him, then break his heart or maybe she was going to…Oh, there was the nod. I got up and put the satchel down beside Jordan. *Who knows what's in the satchel?* I said to myself as I started to listen to the lecture again. Maybe it was full of Jordan's favourite fruits and nuts, or maybe a new bowl, who knows? Anyway, I'm glad Polly decided not to do something sinister.

All of a sudden there was a blood-curdling scream in the room! Everyone looked at either Polly or me because they assumed it was coming from a girl. Polly and I looked at each other, like *I do not know what is going on.* Then everyone realized that Jordan had jumped about two rows back and was in a foetal position. One of Jordan's friend's picked up a snake that had mysteriously gotten loose in the lecture hall, and started laughing hysterically, pointing at Jordan. Everyone else realized what had happened and started laughing.

Jordan looked through the fingers that were covering his face to see that everyone was laughing at him for screaming like a girl at the sight of a snake. Utterly embarrassed, he went sprinting out of the room.

Benjamin, who was holding the snake, yelled after Jordan, "Do not forget your new acquaintance!" and shook the snake at him. The whole room erupted in laughter again.

Chapter 3

"Phew, that was a busy morning!" Bobbi said, exasperated.

"And it's only ten o'clock," I said, looking up at the clock. "Why don't you go take a break and I'll clear the tables. Can you tell Sarah she can take a break too?"

"Sure, I bet she'd love to hear all about my night!" Bobbi said over her shoulder as she skipped off.

I'm sure she will, I smirked to myself as I started to clear the tables.

"What is that little grin all about?" A masculine voice had come from a table by the window.

Startled, I banged a couple of the cappuccino glasses together and looked up to see where this mystery voice was coming from.

"Oh, Hi Stuart, sorry I didn't notice you there. I was just thinking about what's going on in the back room. I'm sure the girls are…oh never mind. How are you doing today?"

Stuart is a regular. He had been coming in every day for the last six months or so. Admittedly I didn't know much about Stuart, but I assumed he was a businessman as he's always dressed very nicely and carried a briefcase. He's (I would guess) in his mid-thirties and good-looking. Not drop-dead gorgeous, but definitely good looking. Let's just say I wouldn't have kicked him out of my bed for eating crackers. Yes witches can have sex. What? Do you think we have pumpkins down there?

We were having a nice conversation when I heard someone clearing their throat. Actually I might have heard it a couple of times, but it didn't really register with me the first time. Or the second. When I finally clued in, I looked over to see Bobbi and Sarah standing behind the counter staring at me. Apparently Stuart and I had been chatting for over twenty minutes!

"Oh wow, look at the time. I should probably get back to work. And I shouldn't hold you up any longer either," I said to Stuart, embarrassed that I had been talking his ear off.

"No problem Agnes, I enjoyed our talk. We'll see you tomorrow," Stuart said as he gathered up his computer and papers.

I grabbed more of the empty glasses and put them on the trolley to take back to the sink. When I got back to the counter, Bobbi and Sarah were still standing in the same position they had been in when Bobbi was clearing her throat.

"What?" I said, "Don't you have work to do?"

"Screw work! What was going on with you and cute briefcase guy?" Bobbi said with the biggest smile I have ever seen on her face.

I tried to squeeze by them to get to the sink. "What do you mean? We were just chatting."

"Ummm, I have never seen you "chat…" (Yes, she actually used air quotes.) "…with someone, let alone a man, for twenty minutes before," Sarah said, with the most emotion I've ever heard from her.

"Don't be silly, we were just having a friendly conversation, it's really no big deal," I said. And it really wasn't, it was just a nice conversation. I'd really never even noticed him that much before.

"No big deal? Of course it's a big deal. He's obviously totally into you. Haven't you noticed he's been coming in here every day, like, for the last year? And when he does he's always checking you out. I have been waiting for one of you to make the first move. It's about time! So when are you going out?" Bobbi said without taking a breath.

Shocked, I said, "Going out? Are you crazy? It was just a friendly conversation. You are blowing this way out of proportion. Now, come help me clean these dishes and get ready for lunch. Sarah, get ready for story time read and feed. Jeremy will be coming in soon."

My Name is Agnes

Holy Bobbi took things to the extreme. She was so much like Polly — it's just like the snake situation...

* * * * *

"That went exactly as I had planned!" Polly said as we met up after our lecture. Professor Aristotle let us go early as everyone was so distracted.

"Any better? Do you not think that was a bit extreme?" I said under my breath.

"Extreme? Blasphamy! That chamber pot deserved what he received. Now Jordan knows I am a force," she said through grinding teeth.

"That is an absolute. Where did you find that snake, anyway?" I asked.

"Oh, that. My chambermaid and her family go to some strange religious cult where they sacrifice snakes. I knew I would have to go to a meeting with her in order for her to give me one so that is why I was not being myself yesterday. My apologies. That place is not normal. You should see what they do to the poor snakes." She shivered.

Witches are very used to snakes, bats, and spiders. They are our pets and guides back home. I didn't bring any of my pets with me to Earth but I did bring my guide, my bat named Robin. A lot of my time spent on Earth I have been alone so I'm not sure what I would have done if I hadn't had Robin. Only we witches can communicate with them. My guide taught me how to make spells and he also comes in handy by spying for me. Other than that he is just a very good friend. He's my bff — Bat Friend Forever.

The next morning at school, Jordan was obviously missing. Didn't bother us though, he was a pain in our ass. At the end of the class Polly and I looked at each other.

"Did we just enjoy sitting through an entire class without being accosted by an object?" Polly asked me.

"I feel as I should throw something at you, strangely enough," I said, looking around for something to throw. "It does not feel right leaving here without something in our hair." I kept searching my locks

14   *Kelly Brookbank*

as a handsome young man came up beside Polly.

"Excuse me," he said.

She was still laughing at me as she turned around.

"Yes?" As Polly turned around her facial expression instantly changed from laughter to fright. It was still in the shape of a smile, but it was stuck there like stone. Polly has only dealt with immature young boys, she hasn't really met any older men, especially none who looked like this.

"Hello, my name is Philip. I witnessed what you put that poor young man through yesterday and I knew I had to introduce myself," Philip said with his hand stretched out in introduction.

As soon as I heard the deep voice I turned around to see who it was. He was very handsome. I looked back at Polly — she was obviously very taken with him because she looked absolutely hilarious. She couldn't move. She looked like a complete idiot. I thought about freezing everyone and sketching her but I'm not sure I even would've been able to draw her because I would have been chuckling too hard and crying with laughter on the parchment. But being the best friend that I am, I had to rescue her.

I bumped into her hard to wake her from her stupor as I introduced myself to Philip. "Hi, my name is Agnes and this is my best friend Polly." I looked back at Polly, as she was shaking herself out of her dreamland.

"Ummm, yes. Hi, Polly," stumbled out of her face.

"Apologies. An explanation, please? What you witnessed yesterday? We did not do anything." I crossed my arms.

"Ladies, ladies, I have caught you," Philip said sternly.

My Name is Agnes   15

Chapter 4

"Good morning my lovelies!" Jeremy announced/sang as he made his entrance into Steamers and Dreamers at about eleven that morning. Jeremy was another one of my fulltime employees. He had very feminine mannerisms (but swore he was heterosexual), had a great sense of humour, would give you the shirt off his back and always smelled great. He was slim, about 5'11", and blonde, with dark skin and blue eyes.

"Good morning, Jeremy!" Bobbi and I answered.

Then all three of us glared at Sarah. "Oh right. Hi, Jeremy," Sarah reluctantly said from across the room.

"Any juicy gossip this morning?" Jeremy put his elbows on the counter and his head in his hands as he looked at Bobbi and me behind the counter. Bobbi whipped around so fast I almost lost an eye from her ponytail.

"OMG you are not going to believe it!! Agnes and cute briefcase guy actually talked today for, like, forever!"

"Well it's about freakin' time, girlfriend," Jeremy said as he made his way behind the counter to make himself his double-whipped, double-cap, double- whatever with a cherry-on- top drink before his shift started. "When can we expect our wedding invitations?"

"Ummm, about the same time Sarah starts greeting everyone who comes in with a big hug and a kiss on the lips," I said as I rolled my eyes. "Seriously you two, it was just a friendly conversation. Geez."

"Uh huh," they both said in unison, as they giggled together.

Oh they're insufferable, I said to myself, jokingly. My staff didn't always get along but we were all like a little family. Besides Robin, they were the closest thing I really had to a family on earth. I really did love them all dearly…even if they drove me up the wall some days.

"Sarah, can you come here for a second?"

"Ok," I said to Bobbi, Jeremy, and Sarah as soon as she got there, "Bobbi and Jeremy — you two look after the lunch counter, the prep is almost done. And Sarah, you look after Dreamers cash, ok? A couple of the part-timers will be coming in at 11:30 so I will send them to wherever needs the most help. Sarah, did you get done the inventory?"

"Yeah, there's just a couple books that aren't in the system yet — I left them by the second till."

"Ok, thanks. Anyone have any questions?"

"Yes," Jeremy said, "where are you and cute briefcase guy going on your first date?"

"I thought we'd go to your place and ask your mommy to cook for us. Now get to work before I put you over my knee," I said as I snapped him with my towel.

We usually ended our "staff meetings" laughing as we went to our stations. I noticed people starting to trickle in, so I thought I had better get those last books in the system before it got really busy over the lunch hour. I went to the computer, logged myself in, and looked down to see the title of the first book. It read: *Pet Snakes.*

* * * * *

Polly and I looked at each other. I think Polly's eyes welled up with tears. I furrowed my brows.

"Another explanation, please sir. What have you caught us doing?" I dropped my arms and took a step closer to him, feeling my neck getting red as I furrowed my brows. "Exactly who is it you think you are?"

"My apologies." He stepped back with his hands up. "I am having

My Name is Agnes

fun with you." He started to laugh.

"Oh." I looked down and started to wipe off some imaginary stain on my doric.

"Myself, I thought it was quite hilarious," Philip said with a smile and a wink at Polly.

Polly looked down at the floor and then back up at him out of the corner of her eye, twisting her body like a monkey trying to get that last gnat out of its side.

I rolled my eyes. "It *was* very hilarious — the snake thought it particularly amusing as well. I am sorry to end this stimulating conversation early but we have another lecture we must get to." I grabbed Polly and started to walk out.

"What is it you are doing?" Polly whispered to me as she looked back at Philip and tried to lift her arm to wave. I batted it back down.

"You must pretend like you are not interested," I whispered back at her.

"But what if I am interested?"

"Just act like you are not, silly."

"I would like to speak with you again," Philip called after us.

"You did not have much trouble finding us in the first place," I yelled down at him as we left the room. Polly and I giggled together.

"Why did you say we had to leave so suddenly?" Polly asked as we headed for our next lecture.

"You need to find out how willing he is to seek you out." I intertwined our arms together. "I have an idea, let us go lie in the sun in the common area instead of going to the lecture."

"Why Agnes, what has gotten into you? You have never missed a lecture!" She turned to me in shock. "But we have just told Philip we were going to our lecture."

"Like I said, you need to find out how willing he is to seek you out." I pulled her in the direction of the common area. Truth be told, I had a bad feeling about Philip. Something about him told me to stay away. I was hoping that missing our lecture would be a sign that Polly wasn't interested.

What a beautiful day out. *Maybe I should listen to Polly more often when she suggests we should ditch school,* I thought. The sun was shining and there was just the slightest breeze. I heard a band of woodwinds playing in the not-too-far distance.

I had just fallen asleep and was getting to the interesting part of the dream where Mr. Starofmydream was going to show me why he was the star of my dream when…

"My, my, my ladies…."

My head popped up.

"What? Huh?" I looked up. *Oh. It's you.* I looked at Polly; she was all smiles. *This fool better be worth missing out on Mr. Starofmydream.*

Philip knelt down. "Firstly I catch you two embarrassing a fellow student with a serpent and now I catch you missing a lecture? I believe something must be done about you two."

My Name is Agnes

Chapter 5

"Well that was a fairly uneventful lunch," said Bobbi after the lunch rush was over.

Jeremy rolled his eyes. "I know. How boring! No hysteria, no drama, no nothing. Why did I even come in here today?" He dramatically launched himself onto a table and pretended to sob. Bobbi ran over to him just as dramatically, soothing him, rubbing his shoulders and said, "Don't worry darling, hopefully somebody will slit their wrists during the supper hour."

Jeremy looked up hopefully, "You really think that might happen?" He slumped back on the table again, "Oh I could never be that lucky," he started sobbing again.

"You two are terrible!!" I said to them as they laughed and slapped their knees, quite enjoying their little dramatic display. Was that a snort or two I heard? I was proud that they enjoyed working there. I gave them the freedom to fool around but they also knew I expected them to work. Rewarding my employees was something I loved to do, but I had also been known to fire people on the spot, with no question. Humiliation wasn't a tactic I used but there were certain things that I just did not tolerate.

"All right my little drama queens, show's over. Bobbi, you can help me clear up the tables and Jeremy — can you go look in the fridge and coolers to see if anything inspires you for a special tonight?" Jeremy really had a culinary gift. If he had a toothpick, a pine-cone, and a brick he could probably whip you up a five-course meal.

"Chef hat is on," Jeremy said. He pretended to put his chef hat on, did an about turn with his feet and marched into the kitchen.

"So, how are you doing, Bobbi?" I asked as we started to clear the tables.

"Actually, I'm glad I finally got you alone," Bobbi said in a hushed tone. She stood beside me with her back to the rest of the store so no one could hear her talking to me. "You know Peter, the guy I broke up with last week?"

"Yeah…" I said, in a go-ahead kind of tone.

"Well, he's really starting to creep me out."

"What do you mean, "Creep you out?""

"Well…he was getting really clingy when we were going out, like he always wanted to be with me. He would show up here all the time."

"Yes, I noticed that but I thought it was sweet."

"It was at first, but then after a while it just got on my nerves because it wasn't just at work. He would be here after I was done work to pick me up, even if I hadn't asked him to and even when I had driven my own car — he would follow me home, or to the store, or to my hair appointment or wherever. He had to be with me all the time! I just couldn't take it any more so I broke up with him, which he didn't take very well. He said he would change, blah, blah, blah, but at that point I couldn't stand him any more, so I just flat out said that we needed to break up."

"Ok, so that should be it, right?" I said, confused.

"That's just it. He keeps showing up at places, just standing there — looking at me. He'll be looking at me through a window. Or if I go to the movies he'll be in the same movie theater watching me instead of the movie. Last night when we went line-dancing he was at the bar watching me. He is a SUPER freak and I am getting really worried!"

"Did you go to the police about it?" I said, getting angrier and angrier.

"Yes, but they said they can't do anything because he hasn't actually done anything to me yet."

My Name is Agnes

"Yet," that was the operative word, wasn't it? Well, you could bet he wasn't going to be doing anything to MY Bobbi!! "Well, I tell you what. If the police won't do anything about it, then I will. I'm not going to wait until this psychopath actually does something to you for them to act. My uncle Robin is very intimidating; I will ask him to go have a little chat with our Peter. Believe me, you won't be seeing him again."

* * * * *

Still groggy and a bit pissed off I didn't get a chance to find out why my dreamboat was so dreamy in my dream, I said, "Who, swimming in Hades' sea, are you?"

"I am Philip, did I not introduce myself earlier?"

"Yes, you introduced yourself, my meaning is: why are you here? Are you a student? In which case, be off — you are bothering me. Are you a professor? As I do not recall seeing you in any lecture halls before. Therefore I must repeat the question. Who are you?"

He chuckled a bit. "Ahh, I understand your question. No, I am not a student."

Damn it!

"I am an assistant to Professor Aristotle."

I thought Polly's cheeks were going to burst her smile was so big.

"Oh, that must be so fulfilling." She looked up at him with her big eyes.

"It really is." He sat down beside her and they gazed into each other's eyes.

"Whoa, whoa, back up the manure cart, if you please. Two seconds ago you were putting the noose around our necks. What do you want?"

"Your friend has misplaced her funny bone," Philip said to Polly.

"No, she is just very protective of me," Polly said to Philip and then glared at me.

I gave her a *What?* look and shrugged my shoulders.

"Well I do not know who you are. You keep showing up and threatening us. You need to explain," I said with an annoyed look.

"Truth be told I have been watching your friend for a while, the snake incident gave me a good opportunity to approach her." He looked at Polly with a red face. Ok, that was kind of cute, but I still had a bad feeling about him.

"You have been watching me?" Polly said with a sheepish smile.

"I am embarrassed to admit it, but yes. That could be why I did not excel in my studies when I was a student. I am easily distracted by beautiful things," he took Polly's hand, "such as yourself."

She was eating this up!

"I did not have the great Aristotle as my professor but Mother thought if he was my mentor maybe the subjects would be more relatable. I am afraid it is not the teacher but the student that is at fault here. I am just not able to concentrate when I have someone as gorgeous as you so close to me."

Things will certainly be less beautiful when they start wiping off the contents of my stomach from their dorics. I had to stop this. "So you are not a scholar then?"

"I am afraid not."

Shit, he even made that sound sexy. I grabbed Polly. "Apologies, we have to go."

"Pardon?" Polly looked at me as I kept pulling her up.

"Not really? Ummm, fine. May I see you again?" Philip asked.

I pulled her towards her house. Polly began to say something but I talked over top of her, pulling her away and talking over my shoulder. "Thank you Philip, it was very pleasant speaking with you Philip. See you again." I hurriedly pulled her away.

"What in all the God's lands are you doing?" Polly said to me in a very hushed but irritated voice.

"I am trying to stop you before you get too involved."

"I do not understand."

"Polly, he is obviously not very bright and you have always wanted to marry a scholar. Do you really think your family would let you be involved with someone less than that?"

She looked back at him. He looked like a child who'd had his favourite candy taken away from him. "I suppose not." She looked

My Name is Agnes   23

away reluctantly. "I had such immediate feelings for him though. I have never felt that way before."

"Well that could just be lust, Polly. That does not necessarily mean you have feelings."

"You think I do not know the difference between horn...."

"Excuse me ladies…"

We stopped and turned around. Philip had caught up to us and was not even out of breath. "I have to ask the question, have I done something to offend?"

Polly looked at me with an accusatory look on her face and crossed her arms. "No, Philip, you have not offended…"

"Perfect." He took both our arms in his. "Then I would like to take you both out for a glass of wine.

I started to object but Polly quickly said, "We would love to."

Chapter 6

"How about gumbo?" Jeremy proudly suggests as he comes out of the kitchen.

"Sure," I said as I dried my hands on the towel by the sink.

"Ok, here's the list I will need from the store, boss."

"Great, I will head to the store. Jeremy — you help Bobbi finish cleaning up here, and then you can head out Bobbi." I took off my apron and threw it in the dirty laundry basket in the back room. I brushed my hair to make sure I didn't have any food in it and grabbed my purse. As I was heading out, I made my way over to Sarah. "How did it go today, Sarah?"

"Pretty good."

"How are the part-timers doing?"

"I think they'll work out fine. They are catching on to the till pretty fast. Brenda is really interested in leading the reading groups."

"Oh that's great to hear. Ok, cash-out of your till and drop your bag in the safe then you can head out for the day. I have to head to the grocery store. Have a good night."

"Bye Agnes," Sarah said with almost a grin.

As I walked over to the deli counter, I told Jeremy I was heading to the grocery store so he was in charge after Bobbi and Sarah left. "You can cash out and drop your deposit bag in the safe when you're done, Bobbi." As I leaned a little closer I said in a softer voice, "And I will

25

handle your problem, don't worry another second longer." I gave her a wink. "See you tomorrow," I said louder, and then I was off with a wave.

When I walked outside I took as many normal steps as I could, looking around the corner of my eyes into the trees for Robin. I was trying hard not to run, but it felt like forever to get around the corner so as no one in Steamers and Dreamers could see me. As soon as I was "home free," I furiously looked around until I spotted him. We locked eyes (we had been together long enough for him to know I needed to talk), and he followed me into a dark alley.

"What's up, buttercup?" Robin said when we met. I filled him in on Bobbi's creepy ex.

"Oh he sounds just lovely. Ok, so how do you want this to play out?" Robin rubbed his little wings together as he always does when he's about to get up to no good.

I smirked at my little best friend. "I think for now, we will do just as I said — my Uncle Robin (I exaggerated my wink to Robin) will go have a talk with Peter the puke, then we can do some more digging into his history later. He sounds a bit fishy to me. I don't understand how he has all this time to follow Bobbi around — doesn't he have a job? Is he independently wealthy or what? And B) is this the first time he's become a stalker? I know Bobbi is great and everything but to become SO obsessed after such a small amount of time? I don't think this is his first pride parade, if you know what I'm trying to lay down on the down low."

"Agreed. I think he has plenty of experience in the creep department. So I will get myself all buffed up. How will we meet up with Mr. Wonderful?"

"Bobbi is getting off work soon so you can go get a smoothie and hang out outside Steamers and Dreamers. I'll make myself invisible and watch for him — I imagine he will be stalking her somewhere around there, ok? Maybe hang out a little too close to Bobbi...perhaps open her car door for her, have a chat or something, be overly flirty.... maybe Pete Superschmuck will get a little jealous and want to have a chat with you?"

"Have you been stalked before, my dear Agnes, because I've known you for a long time and it seems to me that you are relating much too well to this Peter guy and it really pains me to hear this…"

"Oh knock it off, Robin." I cut him off before he transformed himself into a psychiatrist complete with glasses and lounge chair. "Come on you wing-nut before I have you committed to a zoo."

Robin turned himself into a typical beefed up, gorgeous gym-rat, complete with fake tan, cut-off jeans, peach muscle shirt, sunglasses and eighties blonde frosted hair. He went to get himself a smoothie and hang out until Bobbi came out. I made myself invisible to everyone except Robin and flew above the scene so I could see and hear everything.

Bobbi and Sarah came out and talked for way longer than I ever thought they would, said their good-byes, and went in separate directions. Sarah took the transit system because — big surprise — she didn't believe in depleting the ozone by riding in automobiles. Bobbi — big surprise — didn't give a shit and was heading towards her car. Robin was pretending not to pay attention and "accidentally" ran into her, it was actually really funny, and hovering over the whole scene I found it very hard to contain my laughter. Robin was apologizing profusely with an over- abundance of arm rubbing. Bobbi was totally falling for it saying, "No problem, no problem," and I'm pretty sure she put her hand on Robin's chiselled chest. The ensuing flirty conversation commenced — Robin is so good at that.

After watching those two, my eyes hurt from rolling them, so I flew around to keep an eye out for Mr. Prick. I couldn't see him out skulking around anywhere so if he was there, he had to be in his car. If I was right about his being independently wealthy then he wouldn't be in a junker, so I flew in close to check out the more expensive cars. About five rows back from Bobbi's car, I saw him sitting and steaming in his Lexus. He was watching what was going on between Robin and Bobbi. His face was so red I thought it might explode.

When their conversation ended, Robin opened the door for Bobbi and she got in. As he stood there waving to her I swooped in to let him know where Peter Poophead's car was in case our plan didn't work

My Name is Agnes   27

and Poophead didn't come over to warn off this hunk who was zoning in on "his" woman. Robin stayed waving as I kept an eye on Peter Pinkeye. No sooner than Bobbi was out of sight, that Lexus door was open and Pete's beet-red face was bee-lining it for Robin.

Robin got a tapping on his shoulder followed by an, "Excuse me sir, but I don't appreciate you talking to my girlfriend." Robin whirled around with blood-red eyes, got right in Peter's petrified face, grabbed him by the shirt and said, "I don't appreciate you stalking defenseless girls and scaring the shit out them."

* * * * *

Philip took us to the campus phatnai (like our modern day pub). I had been to many phatnais in the years before I showed up in Donemacia…this was no phatnai. This was a bunch of pompous kids drinking in a very civilized establishment. If I had taken Polly to a real phatnai I am pretty sure that upon entering it she would swallow five flies while gasping for air. Then she would shriek, jump back, and run away. Wait — she might trip first. Yeah, she would probably trip and then run away. No wait, she would be frozen in shock. Ok, first the flies, then she would be in shock, then after coming out of her state of shock she would trip and run away….that's definitely how it would go. Yep, I can see it now. Really funny wearing a doric too. Hee, hee. Hey! That's my best friend, don't laugh at her, it's not her fault!

Growing up in a wealthy family, Polly had been protected from the realities of the poor. I don't think she even knew what a brothel was. If I had tried to explain what it was I'm pretty sure she wouldn't have been able to understand the concept. I guess it's kind of sweet to be that naïve, but it's also kind of scary. Just a couple of wrong turns on a moonlight walk and she could be in serious trouble….then be scarred for life! It would be like taking a three-month-old puppy, fresh off the tit, and throwing him into a pit-bull fight. Sad and scary.

"Do you enjoy being Aristotle's assistant?" Polly asked Philip, her arm bent with her elbow on the table, and resting her chin on her hand.

"It is very interesting, I have to admit. Aristotle is very patient. I can see how the students are consumed by everything he says. But I am afraid that is what I find most interesting, how the students are interested...not in what he is teaching."

"Wha..." I started to say, but every time I started to say something Polly cut me off.

"That is fantastic," Polly said. "You are so compassionate."

Compassionate? Is she crazy? This guy is a twit!

"Have you spoken to Aristotle about this?" Polly asked.

Aristotle will have you committed if you tell him this. I dare you, go ahead and tell him!

"No I have not. I am not sure what his reaction would be."

"Ha! I know wh...Ow!" Polly kicked me under the table.

"I believe you would be surprised at what Aristotle would reply. He is a very remarkable and sensitive man. Just like you." Polly smiled up at him. Philip took her hand.

"I think I need some air," I said as I stood up.

Polly said, "Are you ok?"

"Yes, I am feeling nauseous suddenly. I will not be long." *Whoa, I cannot take much more of that! That was painful.*

As soon as I stepped outside and the sun hit my face, it was as if the sunny smiling sun bitch slapped me. *Why am I being so hard on this guy? I should give him a break. I owe that to Polly.*

I took in another deep breath, spun around and just about ran right into Polly.

"Feeling better?" Polly asked with no sympathy whatsoever.

"Yes. Thank you. Listen...."

"No, Agnes, I think you should listen. I do not know why it is that you are giving Philip such aggravation, but I think you need to resist. He is lovely and I enjoy him."

"I have realized and I apologize. I had an uneasy feeling about him, but it may have been indigestion. When I emerged outside I inhaled fresh air and but I also gained a new perspective, thank you to the sun."

"Pardon?"

"Never mind." I took her arm and we turned towards the pub door.

My Name is Agnes

"Come, I will get us another drink."

We walked back inside. "I am sorry Polly, I will give Philip a chance. I will try my best." We went to the table. Polly sat down. I flashed my best smile.

"I think I shall fill our glasses. Does that sound agreeable?" I looked straight at Philip.

"That is an outstanding proposal." He slightly nodded at me. He could tell I was apologizing.

I made my way up to the barkeep. "Three glasses of wine please, sir."

"Of course, ma'am." He filled the glasses. "I see you are accompanying Philip this evening." I was a bit taken aback. "Oh. Are you familiar with him?"

"Of course," he said with a chuckle. "Everyone is aware of Philip."

Oh great. Not only is he an idiot, he is a boozer as well.

Chapter 7

Peter was visibly shaken after Robin's little talk with him and we were pretty sure that's all it would take to scare him off from Bobbi, but I wanted to dig into his past anyway. I magically made the ingredients I needed from Jeremy's list appear in Fry's grocery bags and headed back to Steamers and Dreamers.

"Here you go," I said to Jeremy as I plunked the bags down on the counter. "Do your damage."

"With pleasure, madam. Let me just finish this drink order and I will start on the most fabulous gumbo you've ever tasted."

"Remember, I *am* from New Orleans," I said, with my one eyebrow raised.

"What? Really?" he said, with a look of shock on his face.

"No," I said. Jeremy made like he was fainting. I smiled, "I just have to go check something on the computer, I'll be right back, Jeremy." I wanted to see if the book order had been placed for next week. It had been, so all was good.

When I got back there was a bit of a line-up at the coffee counter. I took over for Jeremy so he could get started in the kitchen keeping the drink orders flowing as Amanda and the part-timers came in. They jumped in where they thought they were needed the most as there were people lining up to buy books as well. I was going to be leaving soon but there were people browsing around in the book aisles looking like they needed some help, so I decided to stick around until the rest of the staff came in.

I was walking around asking people if they needed help or had any questions, when I ran into a familiar face. "Wow, twice in one day, should I be flattered or frightened, Stuart?"

"Well, I sure hope you're flattered. If you're frightened then I'm doing something very wrong and I need to re-consider my conversation techniques."

"I can assure you I'm not frightened, I was just looking for a word that went smoothly with the word flattered. Honestly, frightened was the first thing that popped into my head. After today, it's really quite fitting....forget I said that. So was the rest of your day productive?"

"As productive as I needed it to be. We have something in common; I have my own business. I got some work done and then remembered that there was a book that someone told me about that I should really check out. I was told that it was a good summer read. I think Ellen Degeneres recommended it or *People* magazine or something. Do you know which one I'm talking about?"

"Hmmmm, you might have to be a bit more specific. Do you remember what type of book it was? Murder/mystery? Love story? Cook book?"

"I believe it was a suspense novel, at least that is my favourite genre so I think that's the reason why it piqued my interest."

"Well, follow me to the new releases — maybe something over here might tweak your memory."

"I have a funny feeling I could follow you anywhere."

"I have taken a lot of different paths in my life so if you like adventure, then following me would be of benefit to you..." I said with "fuck me" eyes, then realizing that I had divulged too much information about myself and been WAY too flirty, I stammered, "So, ummm, yeah, this is the way to the new releases," and knocked over some miniature teddy bears. "Those needed to be re-arranged anyway," I said, as I was trying to compose myself. Why was I being so stupid? Maybe because I hadn't been laid in 200 years? Maybe because I hadn't felt like this in 300 years?

We finally made it over to the "New Releases," which felt like we walked a hundred miles. I don't know if it was just me or if there was actually an awkwardness between us but I had to break the silence. "Here are the books."

That came out really loud, so loud that the people around us looked at us and then looked at the books as if they were special books written by Gandhi or something.

I put my hand on Stuart's shoulder and leaned in close to him. "I'm really sorry, this has taken a weird turn between us. Just to be clear, before I knock over every display in my store — are you flirting with me?"

"Me? Flirting? No...."

* * * * *

I took the drinks back to the table and tried to be as pleasant as I could. As soon as we were done with our drinks though, I made an excuse about my father coming home tomorrow and insisted we leave.

"Why did you excuse us again?" Polly asked as soon as we were out of earshot.

"Apologies Polly, but I am afraid that Philip is not who you believe he is."

"What are you referring to?" She looked at me funny.

"I had a conversation with the barkeep. I am afraid Philip is well known at that phatnai."

"Oh," Polly said, with a look of disappointment. "That does not sound promising, does it?"

"I am afraid not. I am sorry, Polly," I said.

"Well, he is not aware of where I live. I was bemoaning the fact that I did not tell him. I guess now I know that was fate."

I felt terrible, Polly looked so sad. "Do not feel bad, there are a lot of gorgeous men out there just waiting to take your hand." I was trying to make her feel better.

"Yes, I believe what you say," she said.

"I know there are. In fact, I heard your father say just the other day that General Thracian was willing to take your hand if you had not married by the age of thirty. Even if you were fat and cross-eyed by then."

"Beg pardon? Why would I not be married by thirty? And who says I will be fat?"

I looked at her with a smirk. She hit me in the shoulder.

"Why Agnes, I swear you are Hades' daughter!"

We giggled. I always could make her laugh and cheer her up. She seemed in a better mood as we walked the rest of the way home.

As we neared Polly's villa there seemed to be a lot of commotion going on outside.

"What is going on at your place?" I asked Polly.

"I do not know but it seems to have everyone in a dither."

"Polly, is that the royal colors on that carriage?"

"Holy shit! Let us hurry!" We picked up our pace to just short of a sprint. When we got up closer we confirmed it was definitely a royal carriage but who was standing by it was what shocked us.

"Philip?" Polly asked, "What are you doing here? How did you find me?"

"It really was not that hard. There are not too many beautiful women who attend university. Only a few inquiries had to me made." Polly blushed.

"What is this royal carriage doing here?" I asked.

Now it was Philip who was blushing. "I apologize. I did not introduce myself by my full name. I am Prince Philip Dracas."

"So that would be why everyone knows him at the phatnai," I whispered to Polly. She smiled at me.

"Pardon?" Philip asked.

"Nothing, Prince Philip," I said.

"You can refer to me as Philip."

"Thank you. OH! This makes sense — why your mother has you assisting Aristotle," I hit my forehead with my palm. "I should have picked up on that. Not too many people can be Aristotle's assistant."

"That is correct, Agnes," Philip nodded at me. The arrogant way he did it made me want to pull his eyelids down and pin them under his nose. I really needed to know more about this guy.

"Polly, I was wondering if you would like to escort me to a meal tonight?"

Without hesitation, "I would love to!" came out of Polly's mouth in a voice that was just a notch below the sound only dogs can hear. "I need to change, I will not be long!" She grabbed my hand and pulled me into her villa and up to her room.

We quickly changed her hair, she changed her doric and her brooches, and then she was off. I pretended I was excited for her, he was a prince after all, but until I knew all I could about him, I was going to reserve all judgements.

I went outside the back of the villa and walked down the street until I came to the nearest alley. Robin was there immediately.

"Polly met a prince, that is fantastic!!" Robin gushed.

"I do not think so," I grimaced.

"I could tell he was a vomit bag. Wait, what? He is lovely and hot. Did I mention hot? Why do we not like him?" Robin asked, confused.

"I do not know. I have a feeling."

"Damn your feelings." Robin scrunched his little bat face up. "Your fucking feelings suck ass, you know that?"

"I know. Sorry." I shrugged my shoulders.

"I just wish, for once, your feelings were wrong." Robin glared at me.

"Me too."

"All right, you want me to find out all there is to know about Prince Philip?"

"Yes please."

He rolled his eyes.

"I love you, my little Batty!"

"I know you do, crazy." He flew off.

I walked back to Polly's. I wanted to talk to her before heading home. I was like family in Polly's house so it's not like it was strange that I was hanging out there by myself. It also wasn't weird that Polly's parents had no idea she was out to dinner with a gentleman. In fact, her parents had no idea that she was out with a man at all. I actually

My Name is Agnes   35

didn't know where her dad was — probably off at some war or something and her mom was probably lounging around being fed grapes and fanned with large plants by gorgeous, chiselled young men.

Later that night, I knew they were home by all the commotion outside. It's pretty obvious when a royal carriage pulls up. Polly and Philip stood outside talking for a while before coming in. Polly's close chambermaids were more interested in her budding relationship than her own family, other than her younger sister Traya, whom we had to restrain after catching her on the way to the front door with eggs in her hands. The gods only know what she planned to do with those. Once we had her firmly restrained, we continued to listen as closely as we could through stone walls. Of course the other girls couldn't hear a thing, but I could hear everything. The conversation was pretty tame (boring!) but they did agree to meet again.

As soon as we heard the door opening we all scattered and pretended like we had been doing something else the whole time. I don't think Polly even noticed because she was so elated from her dinner with Philip. She grabbed me by the arm and we ran to her room. "All my prayers have been answered! I think I have met my true love. He is so handsome and he has this air about him, I just cannot believe it!"

Polly went on for a lot longer and I was truly happy for her, but I just couldn't shake this feeling I had about Philip. I was so confused by this weird feeling. I wanted to be happy for my friend. He seemed like the perfect man for her — I mean, for the gods' sakes he's a prince! She was so happy...but this feeling I had just kept nagging me. I simply had to know what Robin turned up about him.

Chapter 8

"Oh holy night, I am so embarrassed! I guess I was reading the situation wrong!" I said to Stuart with very red cheeks, I turned and said, "This is the way to the new releases…"

He grabbed my arm as I was heading to go. "Of course I was flirting with you, Agnes….you're not the only one with a sense of humour."

I could have hit him. "Holy shit, I don't think I've ever been that embarrassed! Ok, now that we're on the same page, continue following me over here!" I was kind of pissed but I was also relieved that he had the same sick sense of humour that I had. "Oh, right, we're already here!" I said and then burst out laughing.

Stuart started laughing too. After I shook off my laughing-fest, I gathered my composure and said, "Geez, I feel like I'm twelve years old!"

"Oh good, I feel the same way, I was hoping it wasn't just me."

Wiping away a tear of laughter I said, "No, you are definitely not alone. Damn, my stomach hurts! I don't think I've laughed that hard since…you know, I can't really remember the last time I laughed that hard!" That wasn't true, I laugh that hard with Robin all the time but I couldn't really explain my talking bat friend to Stuart. "So here are the new releases, any of them look familiar?"

Stuart looked them over. "Hmmmm, I kind of recognize this one, is it any good?"

37

This must be fate. "Well, as a matter of fact, this happens to be one of my favourite authors. He isn't very well known, but this — in my opinion — is his best book yet. I'd be very curious to see what you thought of it. I'd only want your honest opinion, of course, [in my best Russian accent] and believe me — I have ways of making you talk," I said, with my one eyebrow up and pointing my pinky and pointer finger at him — I'm not sure why….I guess in that moment I thought pointing my fingers in a U shape was more menacing.

He put both his hands up in the air holding the book up, "Ok, ok, I promise — only honest opinions!"

As we were heading to the checkout, I said, "So now that your distraction is taken care of are you heading back to work?"

"I'm not sure, I think I will call in and see how everything is going, but I have a feeling that I will be distracted by something — or should I say, someone — else anyway, so there's really no point going back to work."

That was funny, I didn't remember eating fireworks, but there were definitely some going off in my belly.

"You've put in a long day, do you ever go home?" he asked.

"Actually, I was just thinking of heading out before I ran into you, I was going to wait until it slowed down a bit before clocking off though. Will that be cash or credit, sir?"

Stuart pulled out a money clip, "Cash please, ma'am." I gave Stuart his change and handed him his book.

I came around the counter and said, "Well, hopefully your distraction doesn't keep you from ruining whatever plans you had tonight," shocking myself at how bold I was being.

"I actually didn't have much in the way of plans, but now that I have become a book critic, I guess I should get cracking on that. But if I needed some help with the big words or needed to take a break and the only thing that would distract me from my distraction was a familiar voice, how would I be able to get a hold of you?"

Damn those fireworks again. "You mean like, perhaps, my cell phone number?" Acting all coy and shy (back to twelve years old again).

"Ummm, I believe they have done away with the telegraph, so yeah, your cell phone would work," he teased me.

"Yes, that would probably work — it's (878) 555-1973." I heard a ping in my back pocket. I took out my phone to see a text from Stuart that read, "ARE YOU BUSY LATER?"

* * * * *

"Nothing is sinister about him? Seriously, Robin? You could not find anything? Are my senses off?"

"No, my lovely. He is a prince and I mean that literally. He is Prince Philip of Mathesdon and he is a great warrior also. He has fought many a battle. He also competes in the Olympics with his horse and in the 200-meter race. Everybody loves him, that is probably why…"

"Why what?" I said with my eyebrows furrowed.

"Well, the only — I guess — thing that could be considered a negative about him is that he has been married a couple of times."

"What? Married a couple of times? And you do not think that is a bad thing?" I said to Robin, outraged. How could he not think that was a bad thing?

"Now, Agnes, do not get all twisted in a knot over this. The first marriage was an arranged marriage, and we all know how those work out. And the second one was for political reasons. I do not think it is really anything to worry about."

"Nothing to worry about? Have you lost your mind? This is terrible! Oh, I hope Polly will not be too disappointed when she finds out."

"Listen, Agnes — I think all Philip needs is to find the right girl and then everything will be fine. He just needs to find true love."

"Or he could break Polly's heart."

"It is really not as bad as you might think, marriages are more like business deals around here."

I calmed myself down a little bit. Took some deep breaths in and out. Paused and thought about it for a minute or two…

"Well, I will trust your judgment on this one and hope you are right. Maybe if he is actually in love and not marrying for "business"

My Name is Agnes   39

then it will be ok…" I still wasn't sure about this, but I guessed I would just have to see what Polly thought about it all.

The next day I was over at Polly's house bright and early (about noonish — that was early for rich people), after I had gone on a little fact-finding mission of my own. I had flown over to the township of Mathesdon and turned myself into a soldier of Prince Philip's to find out for myself what kind of a man he was. His last marriage was over; it had just been a business deal to gain more land and more soldiers, which was very common for that day and age. He was a great soldier and an even better leader. All of his soldiers adored and respected him. Shit. Ok, now for his personal life. Let's find out about that.

I walked around the township to hear what people were saying about him. No one was saying anything bad. They all admired his athleticism in the Olympics and they all thought he would be a great king one day. Grrrr.

I flew over his palace to hear what was going on in there. I could hear him talking about Polly to his brother and he was only saying nice things, and how this was different, he never felt this way, blah, blah, blah.

Why did I have it out for this guy? Why was I looking for something bad? Maybe I was just being jealous because he was getting in between my best friend and me. I guess I just had to put on my big girl panties, realize that he was a good guy, and be happy for my friend.

I went into Polly's room and she was still smiling from last night. "So what are your plans? When are you seeing him again?" I said, being the new and improved, happy and delighted for my best friend, with the biggest smile on my face-Agnes. Note to self — tone down the smile.

"First he is training this afternoon. Then he will pick me up and we will go for a stroll," she said gazing out to space.

"Oh? Training for what?" I said, like I didn't know anything about him.

"That is right, I did not inform you! He is an Olympian! Can you believe it? He races his horse and he is also a competitor himself. I believe he is a runner or something, but is that not amazing? He just

40　　　　　　　　*Kelly Brookbank*

gets more and more impressive!!"

"He sounds great, that is for sure! What else do you know about him?"

"What do you mean?"

"Well, what else do you know about him? I mean, what does he do to earn coins? What trade does his family do? How many relationships has he been in? What is his favourite color? Does he like animals?"

"Geez Agnes, why do you interrogate me? We have just been introduced! I am sure I will learn all that information in time but I do not need to be asking the questions immediately!!"

"Do you not think the information prudent?" *Stop it!* I said to myself. *What is wrong with you*???

"What is wrong with you?" Polly asked.

"I just believe you should know who it is you are dating before time gets passed you."

Why can't you just be happy for her??

"Are you jealous or something?"

"Beg pardon? Me jealous? No, I am concerned about you."

Polly looked at me with a funny look. "Look, Agnes, I appreciate your worry about me but do not. I am a big girl, I can take care of myself."

I gave out a sigh. "I know that Polly. Maybe I am jealous, but I am also worried about you. I do not want you to get hurt. I am sure Philip is a great man and you two will have the best lives together. Now, how will we do your hair for your dinner tonight?"

Polly gave me a big hug, "Thank you Agnes, I love you too."

The rest of the day we lounged around and planned out what Polly was going to wear and how she was going to do her hair. We made sure she ate small meals so she wasn't too bloated. When Philip came to pick her up she was primped and perfect and absolutely ready for her date. I hung out with the staff until Polly got back. I had actually become quite close with some of them, they were — after all — like my family since I spent so much time there.

Way before I had expected her to come back, I heard Polly come running in, and go up to her room. I ran in after her. She was lying on

My Name is Agnes   **41**

her bed crying.

"What is wrong, Polly?"

"I am never seeing him again!!" she said between tears.

I am going to kill him...

Chapter 9

Stuart and I had agreed to meet at around seven, for an early drink at a little sports lounge both of us knew, which was walking distance from my place. I was opening the door into my condo when Robin just about knocked me over.

"I have found out quite a bit about our furry little friend Peter and believe me, he is no saint!! You were right, this is not his first trip around the stalker merry-go-round, he has had obsessions before and a few of our poor victims have taken out restraining orders against him. But whenever ol' Petey gets himself in hot water, Daddy comes swooping in and saves the day. This is where the money comes in. Daddy is a partner in the prestigious law firm of Digion & Getsifrize, Daddy being Digion. Mommy is an heiress with a rubber band fortune. From what I've found out, Daddy is sick of saving Peter Cotton's tail, but Mommy keeps insisting that he does.

"Hmmm, so I was right about him," I said making my best evil face.

"Ahhh, but that's not all…our little friend's got himself a bit of a habit. Like a $1,000-a-day habit. And his drug of choice is heroin."

"Oh my. So he's a real prince! Well I'm glad we rid Bobbi of him, she doesn't need him around her a second longer! Ok, I need to eat and get ready."

"Get ready for what?"

"I have a date!"

"Like the dried fruit?"

"Yes, I need to eat and get ready for a dried fruit. No, a real life, boy and girl date. He's been coming to the store for a while now but I never really noticed him. We talked a couple of times today and he asked me to go for a drink tonight. We're going to meet for an early drink at Padre's."

"Well don't let me get in your way…"

I quickly heated something up that was leftover in the fridge then jumped into the shower. I wasn't much for doing my hair so I just blow-dried it and straight ironed it. I was kind of a minimalist when it came to make-up too, so it was eyeliner, mascara and lipstick for me. Now clothes…shit, this was soooo not my forte. It was a hot one out so we'd probably be sitting on the deck. *Jean skirt — ok good. I've got some wedge heels that will look nice with that. Now for a shirt, probably something sleeveless. I've got a black and white layered number that will do just fine. Ok, outfit done — doesn't look too bad.*

I called a cab to take me to the lounge so he wouldn't know that I live nearby. "Bye Robin, wish me luck!"

"Good luck, Agnes. You know I'll be right outside, don't you?"

"Of course, I just thought I would act normal for a second." I winked at him as I closed the door.

Stuart was already there when I walked into the pub. It wasn't too busy in there. That's why I loved this pub, it was never too busy but there were always people in there. They had every game that you wanted to watch on TV and great beer on tap. We both wanted to sit outside so we found a nice table in the shade with some comfortable chairs.

The conversation flowed easily and never felt awkward. We just felt like old friends. We ordered a couple of appetizers and didn't have any trouble deciding what to order. We were munching away on our appeys when I got a phone call from Bobbi.

Before answering I said to Stuart, "Sorry about this, it's just one of my employees — probably calling to say she's going to be late tomorrow," I rolled my eyes. "Hey Bobbi, how are you?"

"Ummm, not very good, actually."

"Why? What's up?" I said, getting a bit concerned

"I don't think your uncle's talk did the trick."

"What do you mean?" I sat straight up.

"Peter texted me, YOU CAN'T GET RID OF ME THAT EASILY. Ummm, yeah, he's standing across the street and I think he's holding something shiny in his hand."

* * * * *

I could hardly contain my anger. Polly was crying so much, she could barely talk. "Polly, my dear, I beg, take a deep breath, calm yourself. Now make known the reason for your distress."

Polly sat up, did the whole good air in the nose, bad air out the mouth thing, then began. "The evening was going along swimmingly, we were strolling around conversing and then the thoughts you remarked earlier ran through my head so I began to ask him some questions. Everything about him is great! He is an amazing soldier – he is actually a general! Can you imagine? A general at such a young age!"

I was waiting for the punch line so I could go put a stake through his heart. "So in what way did he harm you?"

"Harm me? He did no such thing. He was a complete gentleman the whole evening."

"I am confused. I do not understand the problem."

"He is married, that is the problem. And he has been married before!"

The knot in my stomach just untied itself. "Is that it?"

"What do you mean, 'Is that it?' Did you not hear me? He is married!"

"Ummm, please do not get angry, but when you were away I went out and made some inquiries about Philip myself," I lied, sort of.

"Pardon? You did what?" Polly stood up from the bed.

"Wait, wait, wait — just sit down and listen to me for a moment." I pulled Polly down to the bed with me again. "I wanted to find out for myself if he was good enough for you, in case you were not going to ask him the important questions. So, I admit, I actually knew all

My Name is Agnes   45

about the soldier thing, the Olympics thing and…the marriages thing. But, what I also found out is that his first marriage was an arranged marriage. His second marriage was to gain lands in Dandier. As soon at they were married, Mathesdon invaded Dandia and captured their lands in a coup. So obviously that marriage is over. He has never actually married for love, because he has never found love."

Polly looked at me with a scowl but then her scowl turned to a look of sadness and then her look of sadness turned to a smile. (This girl does NOT have a poker face.) She jumped on me and gave me a big hug. "Oh thank you, thank you, thank you, Agnes!" She pulled away from me then, with a shocked look on her face. "Shout to the gods, what if I have made a huge mistake? As soon as he told me about his marriages I told him I never wanted to see him again and was away running!"

"He has been married twice before I am sure he is used to women's erratic behaviours."

Polly glared at me.

"Oops, too soon?" I said with an apologetic face.

"Uh-huh."

"Well, it has not been that long, let us just go and see if we can find him," I said as I started leaving her room. Polly followed me. As we were heading to the front door we decided that Polly would jump in one of her family's chariots and head to his house. Since she hadn't actually met his family, when she got there she would send a messenger to fetch him so she could talk to him outside.

I would take another chariot and head to the beachfront where they had spent most of their evening. Hopefully he was still there, brooding. We would meet back at Polly's later to update each other.

When I opened the door, I looked outside then turned to Polly. "Change of plans. You may have to think of your apology sooner, rather than later."

With a confused look, she said to me, "And why would that be?" and walked out the door. She all of a sudden stopped dead in her tracks when she saw Philip standing there with a dozen white lilies.

"Polly, I know you are upset with me, but please, I implore you, let me explain."

I could almost hear his heart breaking. I think I actually said, "Aw" out loud but no one noticed because everyone else was thinking it anyway.

Polly walked straight up to him, took the lilies out of his hands, looked up at him and said, "Philip, it is me who owes you an apology. I jumped to the wrong conclusion without giving you a chance to explain. I am sorry. I will try to never do that again. Forgive me?" Polly looked up at Philip and batted her eyelashes.

I've never really understood that or thought it looked particularly flattering but I guess men like it or at least this man did anyway. Maybe it's just me that makes it look ridiculous or it looks like I have something in my eye...That's probably it.

"Thank the gods!" Philip said and gave Polly a big hug.

"Now, tell me about these wives?" She looked up at him.

Philip kind of squirmed, which I took notice of, and said, "When I was young, I was taken hostage because I was the son of a king."

We gasped in shock.

Philip shook his head and waved his hand. "No, no, it's not like you think — I was not tortured or anything, actually it was very good for me — I was taught by some great scholars and had second to none military training." We both relaxed a little. "I was still, after all, a king's son — it was in their best interest to keep me alive. So after seven years my father negotiated my release with the condition that I marry Pammenes daughter, Audra. Obviously I felt nothing for Audra and it was a marriage of convenience, the convenience being it was a lot better for me to live at home rather than being held captive!

"Once I returned home we were in the throes of battle, and I had a lot to learn at such a young age so I was not paying any attention to my wife. We were in many battles and I was learning a lot about the political side of being one of the hands of a king, alongside my older brothers Alexander and Percius. We still had our father to guide us, but we were very engrossed. We were gaining a lot of land but we had such vision for Mathesdon. The only thing that stood in our way was the land of Dandia, ruled by the Ilurias. We had managed to negotiate

My Name is Agnes　　47

a type of treaty with the Ilurians and my father had even negotiated, again, for me to marry the King of Ilurias' granddaughter, Badriane."

"Ouch!" Philip and Polly looked at me. "Thorry, go ahead!" I was listening so intently with my chin on my hand, atop my crossed legs, that my arm slipped and I'd bitten my tongue.

"Anyway, our plans had been orchestrated so well with the Ilurians, they were astounded when our troops attacked the day after the wedding. We marched in on them and they lost most of their troops. We gained Dandia. Needless to say, that marriage did not last."

"I guess not!" Polly said. "Oh, Philip, apologies for doubting you." Philip leaned in for a kiss.

I looked around and it suddenly felt really awkward. Slinking away I made my way inside, leaving these two to "discuss" the matter further.

Chapter 10

I told Robin about the text. "Looks like Peter didn't get the hint."

"Fuck."

"Fuck is right," I said as I headed towards a dark alley. Stuart had completely understood and I'd told him I would call him the next day. Once we got to the back alley, I transformed into a bat and Robin poofed us above Peter. "That's definitely a knife in his hand. I doubt if he would actually use it, he's too much of a chickenshit, but we're not going to take that chance," I said in a voice only Robin could hear.

"I agree, I don't think he would use it but who knows when he's going to snap! Let's take him home and have a chat with this dipshit." We poofed Peter home.

When we got him back to his home he still thought he was in the alley, but then he realized he was in his doorway and we were standing in front of him. His face went from menacing to shock as he looked around. I suggested to him that his legs not move. I love doing that to people. It's really funny when people try to walk but can't and then just about double over.

"What the fuck? Who are you?" he said to me. He looked at Robin, who was back in his bodybuilder body. "What the fuck are you doing here?" Robin and I started laughing as Peter folded in half and dropped the knife. Robin picked up the knife and stepped back beside me.

"Can't move? Aw, tough shit. You also can't lie. Were you

stalking Bobbi?"

His shoulders slumped. "Yes."

"Were you going to kill her?" I asked him as I glared at him.

He looked at the ground. "Yes."

All traces of smiles left Robin's and my faces as we looked at each other.

"Well, he's got to go. Do you want to do the honours or would you like me to?" Robin was practically drooling at the thought of ripping this asshole to pieces.

"Just wait," I said. "We have to be smart about this. It's not like he's some homeless person with no family, friends, or job. This guy has a father with an important job. AND he's rich. I think we should make this look like a drug deal gone bad or he's had an overdose or something."

"Ok," Robin said with a pouty face, "but can it still be painful?"

"Of course! Who do you think I am? Mary Poppins?"

"Who is Mary Poppins?" asked Robin.

"Never mind. Do your thing."

Five minutes later I texted Bobbi I was outside her door. After I knocked she said, "Who is it?"

Good girl. "It's Agnes." I saw the curtains pull back, and then the deadbolt clicked and she opened the door. She quickly pulled me in and gave me a huge hug.

Bobbi's apartment wasn't as I expected it to be. She had a very western theme to the whole place. I hadn't realized that she was into horses as much as she was. Most of the décor was horseshoes, cacti, and paint-horsehide. She had dark-brown, leather couches and chairs, and rustic pine coffee tables and end tables. Her dining room furniture was a beautiful metal set with a glass-top table. She had some really gorgeous paintings of horses hung up and beautiful pictures of horses displayed. Most of the pictures were of her with her horses but some were just of horses in fantastic landscapes.

"How are you doing?" I asked her.

"I'm a complete mess!" she said through tears.

Other than swollen eyes and running mascara, she still looked adorable. Somehow she looked like one of the "big eyes" paintings. Even though I felt sorry for her, I still kind of wanted to strangle her for looking cute in this situation…

"I've been pacing back and forth in the kitchen ever since I saw him outside!" she said. "I keep looking out my bedroom window every couple of minutes to see if he's left yet."

"Is he still there?"

"Last time I looked he was."

"Let me go get you a drink, I've brought some wine to calm your nerves, and then I will check to see if he's still here, ok?" I poured two glasses of wine. "Drink this, I'll be right back." I went to her bedroom to "check to see if he was still there."

More horse stuff! Wow, this girl was into horses! I grabbed my glass and went to the kitchen "I didn't see anyone out there."

"Really?" Bobbi took her wine glass to the front window and slowly pulled the curtain to the side. "Oh thank God, he's gone!"

"Ok, now sit down and tell me about this creep."

"Well, I volunteer at this rehab center because my sister was an alcoholic so I like to give back, you know? Peter had been in rehab before and now he is a mentor himself, so…"

Oh shit!

* * * * *

"Your time has been monopolized by Philip as of late, has it not?" I said to Polly one morning as we were having a soak.

"I realize and my heart is full of regret that I have been ignoring you. I have been such a donkey. Please forgive me?"

"I did not mean it like that. I am happy for you. I just mean… is it becoming serious between you two?"

"Oh, I do not know. The thought has not crossed my mind. It has been such a dream between the two of us, I do not want things to ever change. I want it to remain as it is forever. To tell you the truth though, But I really do believe I am falling in love with him!"

I went over and gave Polly a hug (even though we were naked in

My Name is Agnes

a huge bath — it meant nothing in those days...well it would've for some women, but not Polly and me). "That is fantastic! I am genuinely happy for you!"

"And in all seriousness, I am remorseful that I have not been including you. You are my best friend and you need to be more involved. After all, when Philip is absent during battles, you will be here with me. You need to gain friendship with him. I am going to witness his training this afternoon and then I will gather with his family afterward, I beg of you, join me."

"That sounds awful, but you know I would do anything for you."

Polly gave me a playful punch in the shoulder. I really wasn't kidding. Meeting his family? What if they hated her? That would be so awkward. Oh well, it could also be very entertaining...Robin was going to love it.

The Olympic training center was awesome! It wasn't exactly a center, it was just a huge park cordoned off strictly for the Olympians with all the equipment they needed, but it was so unbelievably grand. On the other side of the park was where the stables and training centre was for the horse events. When we arrived, Philip was helping to train some of the wrestlers. Polly was completely enraptured by the whole man-on-man action. I had to admit it was pretty awesome... Both of us nearly missed our seats as we went to sit in the grandstand because we were gawking at the muscles and sweat on these gorgeous beasts of men.

I had never seen wrestling before but I was quickly becoming a fan. I couldn't really tell who was the better wrestler or who was getting more points, but I can tell you that I really didn't care. I think I definitely agreed with Polly when she said I needed to be more involved in their relationship!

Watching Philip train for running was not as exciting as wrestling. Don't get me wrong, running is interesting, the Olympics were based around the running and a few other sports, and it's one of the peoples' favourites, blah, blah, blah...let's get back to the half-naked men rolling around with their muscles bulging and glistening! I got bored of watching the men running around the track soon after we starting watching Philip, so I decided to people watch, as I love to do.

I noticed that most of the men competing were the same soldiers I met when I was on my fact-finding mission about Philip. I suppose that makes sense since only the brave, tough, strong men would be in the Olympics. I also noticed that we were the only women watching the men. Wow, these men were really dedicated! If they weren't training for whatever event they were in, then they were standing around lifting weights. Phew, these men were serious!

Just in the corner of my eye, I saw Robin in the tree fluttering back and forth trying to catch my attention. "I am going to venture over to the other side and examine the horses," I said to Polly.

"Uh-huh." She had no idea what I had said; she was too wrapped up in Philip.

"Actually, I am going to go see where they scoop all the horse dung and take a bouquet of it to Philip's mom's when we go meet her tonight."

"Sounds lovely."

I giggled to myself as I started walking away. Wouldn't that be funny? I could actually see her face, not that I've actually met her, but really anyone's face when they got a pile of dung as a gift. Wait a minute…actually that's not funny at all, only an asshole would do that. Never mind.

I had made my way over to the horses' grandstand to see if I could find a dark place to talk to Robin when I saw quite the commotion. There was this hunk of a man, well — what I surmise was a hunk of a man anyway, demonstrated by all the women that were surrounding him. No wonder there were no women in the training center, they were all out here drooling over this guy. Something about this guy seemed familiar to — "Hey, what the hell?" Robin actually swooped down and flew right in front of my face!

I said to him in my witch/bat-witch voice that no one else could hear, "I am trying to find a place for us to talk. This is a very wide-open spot. Give me a minute."

I kept looking around, but couldn't help but look back at the man surrounded by all those women…something about him was just

My Name is Agnes   53

so familiar.

"Are you kidding me?? I know you have something you need to talk to me about, you do not need to poop in front of me! I am loo…."

And that's when I made eye contact with the man in the circle of women.

Robin rolled his eyes and said, "This is what I was trying to tell you."

"You are not serious!" I snarled as I walked straight towards him.

The women parted as he stood up and took a couple of steps towards me.

"Hello Agnes. Big hug and kiss for your older brother?"

Chapter 11

I had two glasses of wine with Bobbi, and I put a spell on the second glass so she would have a good night's sleep and wouldn't be up all night worrying about that idiot Peter.

As soon as I left Bobbi's I walked into the nearest back alley and poofed my way home. "Asshole was a drug rehab mentor!"

"Shit."

"Yeah, that's what I said. We need to get back over there and leave some more evidence to make people think he had been off the wagon for a while now."

"Good idea. Let's be maids this time. I'll even be a girl," Robin said all giddy.

"Now, *you're* having the good idea."

"Aw, we make such a good team. Maybe we should go in a cleaning van or something."

"Brilliant! Let's go, I'll drive," I said, as we poofed our way close to Peter's place in a maid's van.

Pulling around the corner to Peter's place, we saw police lights everywhere! We drove up to the police line because we had already turned the corner. Running now would look too suspicious.

"What's going on, Officer?" I said with my most innocent voice and face. How you can make your face look innocent, I have no idea.

"There's been an incident, ma'am," the officer said. He was quite

55

young, but he looked like he thought he was more important than he was. Obviously if he was actually important, he would be inside the house, not on guard duty.

"Oh my goodness, that's awful. We are here to clean a house, if we don't get it cleaned we will be fired. Can we get through to get the house cleaned, please?" I pleaded with the officer, grabbing his hand, tears in my eyes — I was really pouring in on. Robin was crying in the passenger seat too.

"Uhhh, well, what house is it? If it's far enough away from the vic's house, maybe I can sneak you in."

"Oh my goodness, thank you, thank you," I said shaking his hand. "Thank you, sir! Thank you, sir!" Robin grabbed a tissue and blew her nose. "It's Mr. Peter's House. Mr. Peter Digion."

"That's the vic's house!" the officer said quickly before he realized what he'd done.

Robin and I gasped, then hugged and started bawling. "Not Mr. Peter!" "Oh my God, no!" "How could this happen!" "He was such a good person!" We were shouting out in between sobs.

The officer was trying to calm us down and shut us up before anyone heard that he let it slip who had died. "It's ok ladies, it's ok. Calm down, calm down."

Sniff, sniff. "What happened to Mr. Peter?" Robin was blowing her nose again.

"If you quiet down, I'll tell you." He frantically looked around to see if any other cop was around that could hear him.

"Ok." Waterworks turned to off.

"I've heard it come down the pipe that it's an open and shut case of drug overdose. The vic was a known drug offender."

"Mr. Peter? I thought he was diabetic with all the needles and such. Oh my goodness. That is terrible." We started bawling again, really loudly. The officer was really nervous and not really sure how to deal with us, so he just politely asked us to pull over and try to compose ourselves. The damaged rookie police officer hurried back up the street once the windows were up and no one could hear the crying any more. We then transformed ourselves into detectives and walked right into the crime scene.

"Excuse me, you can't be in here," some tired officer said to us.

Robin went on to plant some evidence and I stayed to talk to Mr. Officer.

"Oh hi there, yeah, my name is Detective Violet Strange. I'm new here. What was your name, Officer Collins? Hi Officer Collins. Lieutenant Baker sent me here. Can you tell me what we have here?"

"Who sent you down here?" Officer Collins said.

"The lieutenant, now can you tell me what we have here, Officer Collins? Phew, is it always so hot here?" I waved my notebook at my neck to cool off my chest and undid a couple of my buttons. "I'm not used to all this heat here in Arizona. I'm going to have to get used to this. Phew! Now, Officer Collins, can you run me through the crime scene?" I took some pictures of Pete's dead body with my cell phone.

"Well, there really isn't much of a crime scene, ma'am. It's just your basic overdose."

I saw Robin coming.

"Well, I thank you, Officer. I think I might have to go get some water and cool myself down. I'm not used to all this heat and all these good lookin' officers around here." I gave him a wink.

I rolled my eyes as we left. Robin and I got into an empty police car and poofed ourselves back home.

"Did you get the drugs planted?" I asked.

"Yup, I put some extra syringes in his bathroom and kitchen drawers. What kind of drugs did we use?"

"I don't know. Heroin and some other street drugs. You know you men are all the same. Show a little cleavage and you completely forget what you're doing. I mean my cleavage is exceptionally nice and every…"

Robin was already asleep. Whatever. Bats need sleep, witches don't. I don't usually go out without Robin and if he had to he could go without sleep, but he likes his sleep.

I poured myself a glass of wine and lay down on my bed. Grabbing my laptop, I opened up a network server and logged on to my favourite anonymous email website. I typed in the email address rittenwrdash@

My Name is Agnes   57

sundaily.com into the TO spot and "scoop 4 u" in the subject line. I typed in "Peter Digion dead. Suspected overdose," then attached the pictures I'd taken of Pete's corpse. I was hoping the story was going to be in the morning newspaper, so Bobbi didn't have to worry about it any more. At the very least, I was hoping I could show her something on the Internet about it.

All I wanted for Bobbi was for her to put this all behind her and get on with her life. I grabbed my book off the stack of books beside my bed and started reading. This had been a long, eventful day and I needed some downtime.

* * * * *

"What are you doing here, Winny?" I said to my brother.

"Nice to see you too, Agnes," he said with a sly look out the side of his eye.

"Don't give me that shit, what are you doing here?"

"I can see why you chose to live here, these humans are so easy to enchant," he said as he played with the faces and hair of the women around him.

As soon as we had locked eyes, everyone around us was enchanted and couldn't see us or hear us, so Robin was able to speak.

"How did you find me?" I said, annoyed.

Winny laughed. "Did you really think you are that hard to find, sister? We've known where you were the whole time."

"So no one cared that I left?"

"No and I don't want to be here now, but mother made me come to check on you. But now that I see how easy it is to play with these humans, maybe I'll stick around…"

I spun around and did my fire glare on him.

Dancing with one of the mannequin girls, he nonchalantly put his hand up to stop my fire glare. "You didn't really think that would work on me, did you little witch? But since Mom is watching, that will be your one and only gimme. Try anything else, though, and you'll be sorry."

58   *Kelly Brookbank*

Robin flew down and stood between us. "Don't try your bully shit down here, Winny, you know I'm much older than you are." Robin moved closer to Winny.

"Ah, yes, Robin. How are you, you little rat?" Winny moved closer to Robin.

"Don't push me Winny or you'll be going home with one of your eyes in a jar on my shelf." Robin and Winny were practically touching noses at this point.

Winny broke away, waving his arm, "You know, this place is a little boring for me. I think these humans would be a bit tedious — I need a challenge." He turned to me, "I'll tell Mom you're as bratty as ever and still up to your old tricks, but other than that you seem to be doing ok."

Winny started to walk away. I thought I was going to burst into flames. I was still in shock. "No. Wait. What did I ever do to you, Winny? Why do you hate me so much?"

He turned around to glare at me. "You really don't know? You're really that thick?"

"You're such a pot of piss. And what do you mean I'm still up to my old tricks? I didn't do anything to you at home!" I shouted at him.

"Have an awful life, Agnes." And he was gone. Everyone was back to normal and I was standing there dumbfounded. I looked around, started running to the grandstands, and kept running until I found a door. It was locked but I unlocked it and went inside. I made a fire with my hand until I found something I could transfer the fire to.

"Grrrrrrrrrrrr, Robin I could just rip him in half!!! I do not understand! What in Hades' gates did I ever do to him? And what does he mean "up to my old tricks? Wait a minute, did he say that no one cared that I left?" I felt like I'd been kicked in the chest.

Robin transformed into his normal-man self so he could give me a hug. "No, Agnes, no. That was just Winny being nasty. Obviously they care that you left or they would not be coming to check up on you." He took my hands

"Well, if they knew where I was the whole time, why has it taken so long?"

My Name is Agnes

"Honey. I hate to be the one to break it to you, but you told them you wanted to go find yourself, didn't you?"

I pouted. "Yeah, I guess so." Robin still didn't have me convinced but I felt a little better. Man, I hated my brother, at least that one anyway. Why would my mom send that one when she knows we hate each other? Maybe he's the only one left at home. Maybe he's driven all my other brothers and sisters away too.

Oh, who cares about them? I'm not going to waste any more time thinking about them. I left that place for a reason. They know what they did to me.

Chapter 12

Ahhhh, back to my favourite chair, which I enchanted over to my favourite spot in Steamers and Dreamers. I was sipping my full-fat (Don't give me that! I deserved it after yesterday!) vanilla latte out of my huge black and white *Starter Fluid* cup, which I got from this adorable little boy and girl that came in every weekend in the summer. I was sitting with my feet up, sipping my drink, and waiting for the whipping cream to melt into the drink. Oh, did I forget to mention the whipping cream? Whatever, screw you, you Nazi calorie counter — I was planning on working out that day. I don't actually remember when that part of my conscience developed because I didn't used to care about how I looked. It must have been when I bought the store and started putting the magazines out. I thought maybe I should have put those magazines behind the counter along with the XXX magazines. I could put that on my honey-do list and go back to not caring any more. I felt better already. And damn, that whipped cream was good!

The familiar noise of the newspaper van was pulling up. I was so anxious to see if Ashley Taylor's story hit the press in time! I didn't know what it was about this Ashley Taylor that I'd taken a liking to, but for some reason she was the one I chose to give my "scoops" to. Whenever Robin and I had to put our "skills" to work, I always had this feeling that I should tell Ashley Taylor about it to help her career. I guess because we were both in the literary field I felt like I should give back and help a sister out? I don't know, I just had this gut feeling that I needed to help her out.

I saw her in passing one day at the farmer's market. I was going to the next vegetable stand, and she was passing me going the opposite way. I didn't really see her face, but I almost turned around to stop her, because I knew that I knew her. I told myself I was being silly and chalked it up to having seen her before in my store.

Then again that night, I was meeting my friend Megan from my condo for appetizers and drinks at our favourite restaurant, Lombardini's, and she was there. Again, I couldn't really get a good look at her face. She was assisting the food critic. You could tell she was terribly bored. I felt so bad for her. I read in her bio that she was thirty-five so she was pretty old to be an assistant, but she was definitely younger than the food critic. Lombardini's was a very high-end restaurant. (Megan could never understand how I could always get a table. I had enchanted the hostess to have a table for me whenever I called. Being a witch sometimes has its perks!) To be critiquing this restaurant is quite an accomplishment, and I suppose being his assistant was too, but she seemed to be wasting her talents. I just knew I had to help her when I could.

The first time I sent her a scoop it catapulted her into the category of investigative reporter. I watched her career blossom from that day. It felt good to help a total stranger, and I wondered why I felt I needed to do it. Who knows, I might have needed a favour from her one day.

After my chair was back in its original place, I opened the door to greet the driver. "Hello Giorgio."

"Agnes! Buon Giorno! How are you?"

"I am well. Tall Americano, double cream to go?"

"Agnes. Grazie, grazie!"

I liked Giorgio so much. He was always smiling and never missed a day of work. He always appreciated everything. While he was delivering the papers I went to get his coffee. Just because I was in a good mood, I grabbed him a muffin too.

"So what's the weather going to be like today, Giorgio?"

"Oh, Agnes, I tell you. It's going to be bery bery bad today."

"Is that right? Why do you say that?"

"I see ze donkey in ze pool!"

"What the hell is that supposed to mean?"

"I do not know! I bring ze paper to you!" We had a good laugh over that. I gave him his coffee and muffin. He tried to pay for the coffee and muffin and I refused. We went through this every morning. I never accepted his money, but he always tried to pay. He was so funny.

Giorgio kissed the back of my hand as he went to leave. "Grazie, Agnes! Ciao, Bella!"

"Bye, Giorgio. Ciao!"

"Buon Giorno!" Giorgio said to Sarah as he held the door open for her.

"Good morning Giorgio." Sarah said with a half smile.

"Look at you, Sarah. That was almost a smile you gave to Giorgio!"

"Can't help it, it's Giorgio."

Couldn't argue that.

The door opened and Bobbi came in. She gave me a smile. "Thank you for sending your uncle to escort me to work this morning. I'm not sure if I could have made it on my own."

"No problem. Go hang your stuff up in the back room. I'll make you a coffee, and then we need to talk about something." Bobbi looked at me, confused, but turned to go to the back room anyway.

I went behind the counter to make our drinks. Sarah came behind me. "What would you like to drink, Sarah? I'll make your coffee, and then can I ask you to watch the store for a bit while I talk to Bobbi?"

In her monotone voice, Sarah said, "Sure, I guess."

"Here's your coffee, Sarah." Bobbi came up on the other side of me. "I'm going to make our coffees then sit down with Bobbi. Can you look after any customers?"

"Yup," Sarah said as she went to the register.

As I was heating the milk, I could hear the door chimes and Sarah in the background, "Can I take your order?"

Then there was a deep voice: "Actually we're here to speak to Bobbi Lea."

My Name is Agnes   63

Bobbi looked up. I turned around and two police detectives flashing their identification were standing there. I guessed I wouldn't be the one to break the news about Peter Digion.

* * * * *

In a poof I was back to the other arena, thanks to Robin. Oh, that reminds me — I really need to practice my traveling spell. Last time I tried to get somewhere I ended up in someone's lavatory and when I landed there I knocked over the woman's perfume powder. That's why I call it my poofing spell — thank the gods no one was sitting on the toilet at the time!

"Did you see Philip's speed? He is just so impressive! No one else was even close to catching him! And the way he burst out of those starting blocks, is he not magnificent, Agnes?"

"Oh yes, magnificent," I said as I looked back at the horse stadium. "Probably could have been a cannon if he wanted to."

"You are in a mood. What is astray?"

"Nothing, I guess I am just nervous to go with you to meet Philip's family," I lied.

We were waiting outside the athletes' rooms waiting for Philip before we all got in his family's chariot and rode to his estate. After being all sweaty and playing around in the dirt and sand, the athletes needed a good scrubbing off.

"Why in Zeus's name would you be nervous? I am the one that is meeting my future in-laws."

"I do not know. They are a powerful family — what if I knock over the olives and they decide to cut off one of my hands? I have grown quite fond of having all ten fingers."

"For an offence such as that you would surely have both arms skinned and your toes plucked by rabid geese," a deep voice growled in my ear. I whirled around prepared to do my worst spell and looked up to see Philip grinning down at me. My face turned ten shades of red. I should really find a spell that prevents my face from doing that. It's so embarrassing.

"You are too much, Philip!" Polly flirted with Philip as she walked around me to give him a kiss.

I was just relieved it wasn't Winny. "Yeah, uh, ha ha…too much," I uttered.

"Well, shall we? We would not want to be late to Mother's party." Philip gestured to the carriage. He held his hand out to assist me up, and then did the same for Polly.

The inside of the carriage was a deep mahogany wood with red, velvet- covered seats. The windows were covered with white silk drapes held back with beautiful white ropes. Above the doors was what was Philip's family crest, I assumed. Everything had gold trim. I was afraid to sit down for fear of creasing or tarnishing something.

"So what was your impression of the training today, Agnes?" Philip quizzed me.

"It was quite impressive. You have got great skill." I couldn't help looking out the window in case I saw Winny. I was pretty sure he was gone, but the shock of seeing him that day and the fury he riled up in me kept me on edge. There wasn't much I could do against him. He was a lot more powerful than me since he had been living in Riesmpire this whole time, learning about his witchcraft and his skills. But I had a lot more rage so I'm pretty sure I could have damaged something on him.

"Have you ever been to the Olympics?" Philip asked me.

"No actually, I have never."

"Well, I will be delighted for you and Polly to be my special guests tomorrow. You will love it! It is quite a grand show!"

"Why is that, Philip?" Polly asked.

"They pull out all the stops for the Olympics. The stadium is filled to capacity. Wine is flowing freely. The bands are playing at every entrance. The air is filled with the smell of horses, corn-cob vendors, and sweaty men. The people are excited and cheering for their favourite athletes. The announcers are hurriedly commentating on all of the events. You can hear the hooves of the horses, the stomping of the men racing, and the thumping of the cannonballs landing. The fireworks explode after winners are declared. It is just a magical time."

My Name is Agnes

"It sounds brilliant! I can not wait to attend and watch you win," Polly gushed. I had to admit it did sound pretty awesome.

"Of course you two will be in our family's private seating area, so you do not have to endure the commoners spilling wine all over you and be crowded and uncomfortable. Food and wine will be delivered to you. You will be fanned if the temperature is too hot and you will be covered if it is raining."

"That sounds wonderful, Philip. Thank you so much," Polly interjected.

"Yes Philip, that is very gracious of you. Thank you." He was kind of being a pompous ass, but he probably didn't know any different. I was perfectly ok being in with the "commoners" as he puts it, but I knew Polly would be uncomfortable. Polly can be tough at times, like she is with the snakes, but she'd been spoiled all her life. I can't see her being squished in between a stinky, sweaty man spilling wine all over her and a woman on the other side with her boobs falling out of her doric, pleading her love for Philip and all the other athletes competing. No, I think a private area would be best.

"So give us an introduction to your family, Philip," I asked. I wanted to know something about them beforehand so we weren't going in blindly.

"I have two older brothers, Alexander and Percius, and a younger sister, Eunice. All my eldest brother Alexander has ever hoped is to take over the throne, but he always seems to disappoint Father. Percius has always been stronger, faster, and a much better warrior, and he takes much joy in throwing it in Alexander's face. He teases Alexander incessantly. Alexander is constantly practicing his skills; lifting weights to make himself stronger, or throwing his swords at targets. Percius has never done anything to improve himself, his only goal in life is to fool around or go out on the town to bring different girls to his bed. But if Percius happens to see Alexander practicing, he chooses to pick up a weapon – no matter how much wine he has in his belly – and challenges him to a duel, just to show off to whatever trollop he happens to have hanging off him at the time and embarrasses Alexander. And unfortunately for Alexander, Father is always overlooking the moment when Percius humiliates Alexander.

"Alexander has never been able to beat Percius at anything and he is incredibly jealous, but he knows he is infinitely more mature than Percius and the throne is rightfully his. Even though they have their problems, they are still brothers and will always have one another's back. We are bound by blood and that is the strongest bond there is. Alexander is the more intelligent of the two and Percius is too impulsive.

"Now Eunice is a different sort! She is the light of all of our lives! She is absolutely beautiful, and has a big heart and delights us all with her sense of humour. She just lights up the room whenever she enters it. Everyone loves her…except Mother."

Chapter 13

"Bobbi, these police officers would like to speak to you," Sarah said to Bobbi.

"I'm Bobbi Lea," Bobbi said with a croak in her throat.

"Maybe we could sit down at one of these tables, if it's all right with your boss?"

"Yes, yes of course. Can I get you anything, Officers?" I said.

"That's very kind, ma'am. Two cups of coffee would be appreciated."

"Coming right up." I went and got two cups and started filling them up with coffee.

"What the hell is this all about?" Sarah asked me in a hushed voice.

I looked at Sarah. "I have no idea. I guess we'll find out after they leave. You don't want to go to the book department, do you?"

"Um, hell no!" she said too loud, and then covered her mouth.

I whispered, "I didn't think so." I grabbed the coffee cups and delivered them to the table, where Bobbi and the policemen were sitting, then walked back to the coffee counter.

"What??" I heard Bobbi say.

I guess they got to the point of their visit. I turned to see her head in her hands. I don't think she was actually crying, I think she was just processing the information. Her head popped up again, hands out wide. I couldn't quite hear but maybe she said, "You're serious?"

We probably should have stopped staring at them.

"Ok, let's make ourselves busy, we're going to have customers pretty soon. Since Brad [the morning kitchen helper] has called in sick, we have to do extra morning duties. I need to get the muffins in the oven, and you can cut fruit out here plus all the other morning duties."

"Right, quit staring, work to do. Gotcha," Sarah uttered.

I went into the back to get the fruit so Sarah could cut them out front. I put a bunch on a big tray and brought them out to her. "Here you can start cutting these so you can "keep an eye on the door." Yes, I actually used air quotes.

I went into the back to put the muffins in the oven. I usually did everything by hand, measured everything that the recipe told me, and did everything by the rules, but I was in a hurry this time so I cheated. I used my magic and got them done fast. Luckily Sarah didn't usually work on this side so she couldn't know whether we did them the night before or not, so that's what I went with.

I heard the door chimes and I went to go deal with the customers. As I was taking the order I spotted the two officers and Bobbi standing up from the table and shaking hands. They were all smiling, so I assumed everything had gone well.

I took drink orders and Bobbi and Sarah made the drinks and talked about Bobbi's interrogation. I got a bacon breakfast sandwich order, so I ran to the back to take the muffins out of the oven and get the order going. I was dying to hear what the officers said to Bobbi, but the customers kept coming. I had texted Jeremy earlier to see if he could make it into his shift ahead of time but he wasn't able to come in until 9:00. Thankfully, the book department of the store didn't open until 9:00, so Sarah could help out until then. I couldn't believe I would have to wait until 9:00 to hear what the cops had to say to Bobbi!! The till sent the order directly to the kitchen, so I couldn't even grab Bobbi for a second to ask her what happened. I should have just put a spell on the door to keep everyone away. *Hmmm, I thought…* *No, no, no, I can't do that! I can have patience. Come on Agnes, you can do this!*

The orders just kept coming one after the other. Man I hated bacon grease! I was going to smell like a fried pig for the rest of the day. I

My Name is Agnes

thought *Maybe if it's slow I can sneak to the gym for a quick workout and a shower off.* That's wasn't usually how it went though, in my experience if the morning was busy, the rest of the day would be busy. Lucky me! *Guess I will stay in the kitchen all day — best for everyone, really. I don't really want to subject everyone else to my bad pig smell.*

Jeremy poked his head in about 8:30 a.m. "Hey gorgeous!"

"Jeremy! Thank you so much for coming in! I thought you wouldn't be here until nine?"

"Oh, your little hero was able to do some manoeuvring and 'Tah dah!' Here I am!" he said with his usual flair.

"You are the best! Can you help Bobbi out front until it slows down and send Sarah to the book department to get that opened up?"

"Your wish is my command."

"Thanks Jeremy!"

I love food but I do not like working with greasy food. I feel like my face is going to burst out with acne any second it's so greased up. The skin on my arms did kind of feel nice though, but that could have been because the palms of my hands had a layer of grease on them. *I bet I could do some fantastic things with my hair right now, though.*

You should have seen Eunice's hair the first time we met her...

* * * * *

She was beautiful, just like Philip said. Eunice came running down the lawn as the chariot pulled up. Her blonde hair had at least twenty braids in it from the bottom up then twisted around with a huge bun on the top and flowers everywhere. I don't think I could've have done that even using my magic. She had three long, flowing, gold necklaces around her neck and one large wooden bracelet, plus two smaller diamond bracelets on each wrist, large gold hoop earrings, and a wide leather belt with a dangling silver hoop belt attached to that. She was holding two bundles of white daisies for each of us. You could hear her giggling and see her skipping as she made her way toward us.

Both Polly and I were very confused when Philip told us his mother didn't like her own daughter, but then he explained the situation.

Philip's mother, Ina, had been the only woman for many years. She was this beautiful, intelligent woman whom her husband adored. She was absolutely stunning. She had long blond hair down to her waist, which flowed into gorgeous waves. Although she had natural blond hair, she had deep brown eyes with long, black eyelashes. Her legs were long and athletic. Her breasts were very full although she was always thin. Philip's father, Andias, fell in love with her the moment he saw her. Even though she didn't come from money, they were soon married. Not long after the marriage, she and her husband had three boys. All four of her men loved her and basically worshipped her for over thirty years. Then this little girl came along who took her place.

All of a sudden there was this adorable little happy child whom everyone adored. Ina was now number two and she was not happy about it. The boys and her husband tried to re-assure her that they loved them both, but she saw how Eunice lit everyone's face up when she entered the room and she just let the jealousy consume her. Eunice still tried to gain her mother's affection, but Ina just couldn't get over the jealousy and the spite she felt for her daughter all those years. Philip and his brothers didn't blame their mother; they blamed themselves. They felt they shouldn't have doted on their mother, so much so they tried to keep Ina and Eunice separated from each other as much as they could. It wasn't a stretch in these days for the servants to raise the children anyway, so the servants and the boys raised Eunice and Andias worshipped Ina. They always had a game plan during family functions and did the best that they could.

Still doesn't excuse a mother for hating her daughter in my books...

Breathless, Eunice came up to the three of us as we came out of the carriage. "You are here, you are finally here!"

Philip's smile was from ear to ear. "Eunice, may I introduce Polly..."

Eunice instantly gave Polly a hug. "I have heard so much about you, I feel as if we are sisters already. I have always wanted a sister. You can not know how excited I am to meet you." She looked over at me, and then at once gave me a hug as well. "Agnes! We are going to be best friends as well — I just know it! Oh, I almost forgot, I brought these for you."

My Name is Agnes

She handed each of us a bundle of daisies. Many of the petals had come off with the force of her hugs, but it was a lovely gesture. We were quickly learning why everyone who met the spunky Eunice fell instantly in love with her.

She linked her arms in both Polly's and mine and directed us around the grand mansion. "I can not wait to introduce you to Mother, she is going to adore you both!" We looked at each other and then at Eunice, but she did not notice the concern on our faces, she just kept going. "You have to see the spread we have laid out for you. The cooks have been in the kitchen for days preparing for this afternoon. We even have three ice sculptures. I have been checking them all day because I have feared it was too hot and they were going to melt, but they have not melted yet. I do not know how that works, you would think they would have melted by now, would you not? And the flowers Mother has decorated with are just beautiful. I love flowers. Do not worry, they are nothing like these silly daisies I have brought you, I just found these when I was exploring down by the water this morning."

"All right Eunice, can I have my girls back now?" Philip grabbed Eunice before we got to the back yard.

"What? I was about to introduce them to Mother," Eunice pouted.

"Thank you, Eunice, that would have been delightful of you, but the girls have had a very long, hot afternoon and I think they may be interested in a drink before they meet Mum, do you not agree?"

Eunice looked at us, "My apologies, how selfish of me. Of course you need a refreshment. I am so foolish for not offering you one in the first place! Let us be off to get you some wine! Follow me!"

I followed Eunice as Polly took Philip's arm. We headed toward the tents just as a medium-height man, who looked quite important and had very good posture was coming towards us.

"Eunice, darling, cousin Julia has been looking for you, can you please seek out why she is in a dither?"

"Of course, Alexander. Excuse me, Polly, Agnes, I will return as soon as I am able." Eunice skipped off.

"Alexander, you have saved us. We were near disaster. I had imagined Eunice introducing the girls to Mother!" Philip said to Alexander.

72 *Kelly Brookbank*

"Well then, my appearance was fortuitous, was it not?" He took Polly's hand and kissed it. "Polly, I presume?" I think I heard her giggle.

"Yes, it is." Why doesn't her face turn an embarrassing red?

"I am Philip's much more handsome older brother, Alexander." He turned to me and kissed my hand as well. *There goes my red face...* "And who is this beauty?"

Philip replies, "Alexander may I introduce to you Polly's best friend, Agnes?"

"Pleasure to meet you," I said, still with my mug as red as a brick in the face.

"It is my pleasure, Agnes. As much as I would love to stand here exchanging pleasantries, you had best go and meet Mother while Eunice is detained. Cousin Julia wasn't really looking for her so she will be returning forthwith."

"Thank you, brother. We will meet up shortly." Philip nodded to Alexander.

"Shall we ladies?" Philip held his hand out to Polly and she laid her hand in his. They walked into the tent and I followed behind. As soon as we walked in I could tell who she was. She was a beauty. She certainly didn't look her age. Her hair was flowing freely with a simple string of diamonds around her forehead. She looked more like her sons' sister than their mother.

Of course Andias was right by her side. He was no slouch himself. He was a very commanding man. Although he was older, he still had a great deal of muscle. He still had a full head of hair, but there were definitely grey hairs amidst the dark ones. His head was large as were his neck and hands. You could see the scars all over his body from various war wounds. Definitely an impressive man. It was clear from their body language that he was more in love than she was.

"Mother, I would like to introduce to you, Polly."

Polly curtsied and said, "I am very pleased to meet you, ma'am."

"Well, let me glance at you." Ina put her hands on Polly's shoulders, turned her around, then put her hands on her hips. Polly had a very shocked look on her face! Ina turned her around and with a stern face, she said, "So...tell me why you believe you are good enough for

My Name is Agnes　　　73

my son."

Chapter 14

"It's about time! I've been so anxious to hear why the policemen were here. Are you ok? Is everything ok?"

"Yes," said Bobbi with a slight smile on her face. "It's actually good news, in a way."

I tried to let on that I didn't know what she was talking about so I put on my best confused face.

The breakfast rush was over so the kitchen had slowed down. I did the fastest clean-up possible — Mr. Clean's Magic Eraser took on a whole new meaning! I went out front to help with the clean-up and, most importantly, talk to Bobbi.

"Peter Digion is dead," Bobbi whispered to me like it was top-secret.

"What?" I gasped, falsely shocked. "What happened?"

"He overdosed on drugs," she said with her brows furrowed. "Which I find really strange, but I guess it happens all the time. Lots of people relapse. I just didn't think it would happen to Peter." She shrugged her shoulders, "Oh well, at least he won't be terrifying me any more."

I could tell that she was trying to find a silver lining but she was also sad. She had such a big heart; only a person like Bobbi would feel bad about a stalker, who was threatening her life, being dead. She'd get over it; she was just in shock. Nothing a little wine wouldn't cure.

"So the policemen were just coming by to let you know he

was dead?"

"Well, I think they were here to rule me out as a suspect, but they could tell by my reaction that I had nothing to do with it. I still have to go to the police station to give my statement though. You'll have to come to the station to give your statement too. I still can't believe he's actually gone."

She turned to go get the trolley to collect the empty cups.

She's such a nice girl to st...did she say I had to give my statement? I went to the kitchen and started filling the sink to do dishes. The dinger by the till went off — it was a sensor under the mat to let us know someone was standing by the till. I could have had a bell there that people rang, but I can't stand those.

I came through the doors to see Stuart standing at the till. I let out a sigh. "Stuart, I'm sorry, I forgot to text you. There has been such a shit storm, you have no idea!"

"You left in such a hurry last night, I thought I would come by to see if everything was all right. Plus you're the only barista that can make my caramel cappuccino just right."

I smiled. Was he really real or was I being punked? Considerate, kind men like him didn't happen to me. Maybe it was my turn. Maybe it was finally my turn.

"Sit down over at your table, I'll bring your drink over. I can fill you in. Just don't mind the smell."

"The smell?" he asked

"I was on fryer duty this morning, I smell like an onion ring now."

"Mmmm, I've always said they should make that into a perfume." He winked and took his newspaper to his table.

I had started making his drink as Bobbi came up behind me with empty drinks on the trolley. "Oooooooh, cute briefcase guy again? Are you two an item yet?" she teasingly said.

"His name is Stuart, and no we're not an item. We're just friends. Hey, Bobbi, what do you mean I have to go give my statement to the police department?"

"Oh, they just need you to verify my alibi, that's all." Relief. That made sense. Soon this would all be over and Bobbi would be much better off. I finished Stuart's caramel capp (with a little extra whipped cream) and took it over to him.

"It's been a crazy few hours since I saw you last."

Stuart folded his paper and said, "Do tell."

"Bobbi texted me last night, when you and I were out for supper, that her ex-boyfriend, who had been stalking her, was across the road from her apartment with something shiny in his hand. That's when I went over to her place."

"You did what? That wasn't very smart! The both of you could've been hurt!"

"Oh, I don't think so. From what I've heard of this guy, he's more of a talker stalker than someone that would actually inflict pain. He's all spit and no fire. Besides, I have an uncle with a pretty bad reputation, who is pretty protective of me. Anyway, I went over to Bobbi's to calm her nerves with some wine, and by the time I got there he was already gone. Then this morning, two policemen show up to talk to Bobbi. Apparently her boyfriend was found dead of a drug overdose!"

"This doesn't happen to be the Peter Digion case, does it? Stuart asked.

I was completely taken aback. "How did you know that?"

"It's all over the Internet."

Oh, yeah, I suppose it would have been. My leak to Ashley Taylor would have made it onto the Internet a long time ago.

"And he's my nephew."

* * * * *

The astonished look on Polly's face was stuck like a mask for at least fifteen seconds. The only thing she moved was her eyes, looking from Ina to Philip to me, back to Ina again. She stammered and said, "Uhh, well."

Finally, after what felt like an eternity, Andias laughed, "Oh Ina, do not torture the poor girl."

Everyone around sighed and laughed slightly.

Ina smiled and hugged Polly. When they broke apart she said, "My

My Name is Agnes

apologies Polly, I must make sure a potential wife for my Philip has a sense of humour. He is quite the jokester himself."

I could tell from the smirk on Polly's face she wasn't sure if she should cry or laugh.

Eunice came running up. "Mother, is Polly not fantastic?"

Ina just looked at Eunice and her smile faded. She wound her arm inside Polly's. "Come Polly, let me show you the grounds."

Polly and Ina led the procession, followed by Philip and Andias, Alexander, who had caught up to us, and Eunice and me trailing behind. As soon as Eunice saw Alexander, she swatted him and hissed, "A million thanks to you, brother. Cousin Julia was bewildered as to what I was talking about. I looked like a complete jester."

"Apologies, Eunice, you know how she is getting on in age. You must forgive her forgetfulness." He winked at us.

I tried to suppress my smile. Eunice gave him a playful slap.

He fell back in line so he was walking with Eunice and me. "So tell me, Agnes. How long have you and Polly been friends?"

"My father and I made the trek to Mathesdon about three years ago." Argh, I hate when people start asking about my life. My trick is to immediately ask them questions about themselves. People always love to talk about themselves! "I did not see you at the stadium today, are you training for different events than Philip in the Olympics?"

"Oh no, my time is far too monopolized with Father, learning all the different facets regarding taking over the throne than to be bothered with the Olympics. There is much to learn. There is the political side, which is varied and multi-faceted in itself. Then there is the historical side, learning all of the culture of the lands and families. Then, of course, leading the troops. We have grown up learning how to fight, but leading all of these brave soldiers is another thing altogether."

All of a sudden, Alexander's skirt flew up to reveal his under garments. This was followed by raucous laughter. We turned around to see what was probably the most handsome yet obviously irritating man I had ever seen. He had sandy-blonde hair with a natural wave that found you dreaming of ocean tides, as did his eyes that sparkled like only the deepest tropical sea-green could. I pictured him standing under a fountain of tears from the gods, bathing his gorgeous, chiselled body as only this earthly god deserved to be touched by the heavens themselves…Whoa! Where did that come from? I looked around to see if anyone else had noticed my little venture into fantasyland and thank the gods, they hadn't.

Between belly, or should I say fine-looking-abs laughs, Alexander chortled, "Are you trying to convince yourself or these ladies that you are taking over the throne, Alexander?" He laughed again. The rest of the group had gone ahead. "Because we all know that Father will be bestowing the throne on me." As he was quite a bit taller, he patted Alexander on the head. My fantasy was starting to lose its lustre. Then he noticed me standing there and took my hand, ooooooh, he did make me tingle though!

"And who, may I ask, is this beautiful lady?"

As he kissed my hand, I either curtsied or my legs gave out a little, I'm not sure which.

"This is Agnes, Polly's best friend!" Eunice interjected, "and she is just delightful!"

"Well then, Agnes." He took my arm in his. "I am Percius, Philip's much more entertaining brother. Let me give you the real tour," he leaned in close, "but first, let us get another drink." He steered us toward the tents.

"Umm, I think I should probably…" I pointed towards the others. Percius kept me on path towards the tent.

"Oh do not worry about them, Mother will keep Polly occupied for the foreseeable. We can sneak away and they will not know otherwise."

I knew I should probably stay with Polly, but Percius was so damn cute! "Well, all right, if you say so." I batted my eyes at him, then, because I was so bad at flirting, I lost control of my eyes and looked like I could see both right and left at the same time. Trying to save face I batted away a make-believe mosquito. Up in the tree, Robin laughed at me.

Percius made no notice and gave me his extra glass of mead. "I believe there is never a family gathering where one should be without a glass of mead in each hand…or any gathering, I should say." He

My Name is Agnes   79

cheered me with his glass.

Mmmmmm, this was going to be fun!

"So what kind of tour shall you take me on?" I asked of the hunky Persius.

"Oh, I can not reveal any of my secrets until I have whetted your appetite! Ah, here we are! Darsuvious, my good man, please fill us up with your finest mead!" We had just come up to the first tender of the alcohol. Apparently Persius was on first-name basis with all of the tenders.

Now that I had a few meads down my throat I was a bit cockier than before. I said to the mighty Persius, "How do you propose we might carry another glass, as we have already two in our hands?"

"An easy solution to a common problem, my love…" He wound our arms around each other. "We must down a drink or two." And with that, the obscene amount of drinking began.

Chapter 15

I stared at Stuart as I registered this information. Peter was Stuart's nephew? "He's your what?"

"Peter Digion was my nephew. It's a bit surreal that I'm saying his name in the past tense, but I had resigned to the fact a long time ago that Peter would die young. You can't live that lifestyle and expect be around a long time. I wasn't surprised when my brother called to let me know."

I was completely in shock. I was trying to think of what I would say if I hadn't known Peter before this morning. If I hadn't known Peter? What was I saying, if I hadn't murdered Peter! *Come on Agnes, think quickly!*

"Uh, are you sure you're ok? I mean, are you sure you should be here — do you think maybe you should be with your family right now?" *Real cool, Agnes...real sensitive.* I felt like punching myself in the face.

"Nah, it's ok. My brother and I aren't that close. We used to be when we were young, but we've kind of grown apart."

"I'm sorry," I interrupted. "Let me go get myself a coffee, you a refill, and tell my staff I'm taking a break. I'll be just a second, ok?"

I needed a minute to digest this information. Holy crap, I could not believe this! *Ok, settle down Agnes, breathe.* I started making the drinks, going over in my head what I was going to say.

"Agnes!"

I snapped out of it and turned around. "Geez," Bobbi said, "I literally said your name three times!"

"I'm sorry, I just have a lot on my mind." In a very hushed tone, trying not to move my lips, I said, "Stuart is Peter's uncle."

"What?" Bobbi said, confused.

Ok, that was clearly not going to work. "I'm going to take a little break to talk to Stuart. His nephew was murdered this morning." Then I stared at her intently until the "light bulb" over her head went off.

Once she figured out what I was talking about, her eyes just about bugged out of her head. "His who?"

"I know! I'll fill you in when I know everything."

I set down the coffees as I pulled up my chair at Stuart's table. "Here you go. Sorry about that. So you and your brother drifted apart? How come?"

"Growing up we were inseparable. We were only twelve months apart so we were like twins. We did everything together. We were on the same sports teams, we had the same friends, we had the same interests…we were best friends.

"Then when Thomas went to university, everything changed. We had always planned to both become lawyers and open a practice together, but that plan all went to hell when he met Angelina. I went to Stuart's university to visit, and I knew as soon as I saw them together that she had changed him."

"What do you mean by that?" I couldn't believe a woman could change such a strong man so suddenly.

"We met at an on-campus bar. Thomas and I had been excited to see each other and catch up so we ordered a beer. We were having a great time and we were going to order another beer, but Angelina put her hand on Thomas's and gave him the look, as if to say "That's enough," and that was it. Our night was over. I guess Angelina was feeling left out and she couldn't handle it."

Stuart looked down at his hands. "I could tell how sorry he was, but that had been clouded by all that she and her family could do for him. All he was seeing was dollar signs and prestige. You see, Angelina

82   *Kelly Brookbank*

was an heiress to a rubber-band fortune."

I clenched my lips together. Stuart stopped talking and looked up at me. We both burst out laughing. "Rubber band fortune?" I said.

Through his laughter, Stuart said, "I know…I can never say that without laughing!"

I guess when Robin had told me about it before, I was so angry I never thought about it. Or maybe we just needed to break the tension, I don't know, but damn did it sound funny now!

I wiped away a tear. Stuart took a deep breath, "Anyway, after that I applied to a different university, changed career paths, and focused on work. Thomas and I saw each other on family occasions and talked occasionally, but that's about it. My mother kept me informed of everything that was going on with Thomas and Angelina — basically, their relationship was a sham. They were both so busy with work they didn't care about their kids. Thomas had his law firm and Angelina was taking over the rubber-band business."

We both giggled.

Bobbi came over with a refill on our cappuccino and latte and water for both of us. "Thank you, Bobbi," I said.

"Sorry to hear about your nephew," Bobbi said to Stuart.

"Thanks Bobbi. I hear you were connected to him, too?

"Yes, I dated him briefly. Then he kinda wouldn't leave me alone," she said as she looked down at the ground.

"Listen, Bobbi. Don't feel bad about it just because he's dead. Peter was not a good person. He stalked you and probably would have seriously hurt you, since he was back on the drugs. It doesn't matter now that he's dead; you don't have to change your opinion of him."

"Thank you Stuart, that's so nice to hear." Bobbi smiled back at him and went back to work.

"Anyway," Stuart continued, "just because Thomas and I weren't as close as we once were didn't mean I was going to let my niece and nephew suffer. I started taking them out on weekends and school holidays. I took them on school trips, I did everything I could for them. Isabella turned out to be wonderful. She was always on the honour roll, valedictorian, got an athletic scholarship, volunteered at an old

My Name is Agnes

folk's home; she's just a sweetheart of a girl."

"Peter, was a great kid until he hit about ten or eleven, then I think he must have hit puberty or something, but he developed a nasty streak in him, no matter what I tried to do. And I mean nasty. I even caught him pulling legs off frogs one time."

"Seriously?"

"Yeah. I know. I debated talking to Thomas about it once, but how do you tell someone their kid is a possible psychopath? I tried everything I could think of but every time I thought I was getting through to Peter, his parents undid everything by buying him off. It seemed like they wanted him to fail. Then he fell in with that gang." Stuart shook his head. "I basically kidnapped him for a weekend and took him camping. By the end of the weekend I thought I had him convinced to ask his parents to transfer him to a different school. I was so relieved you have no idea!

"The next weekend, Isabella called me bawling her eyes out because Thomas had come home high as a kite, bragging that he'd shot someone in a drive-by shooting, as a hazing in this new gang he was in. I immediately told Isabella to get out of the house and come to my place. I called Thomas and told him what was going on and that he needed to kick Peter out for the safety of his family. What he did next shocked me."

Stuart took a drink of his cappuccino.

"Oh, don't leave me hanging like that!" I smacked his arm.

"Just had to make sure you were still listening." Stuart raised his one eyebrow.

I rolled my eyes.

"Thomas covered up Peter's crime and allowed him to stay in their home. Isabella was in her senior year of high school and didn't need the added stress, so she moved in with me. I severed ties with Peter. I told him if he ever wanted to get help I'd be there for him, but I wouldn't support him in his current lifestyle.

"Of course, Thomas and Angelina continued ignoring him so he just spiraled out of control. He kept having run-ins with the law and Thomas kept covering them up. Peter repeatedly OD'd and ended up in the hospital. He would promise that was the last time and that he would clean up his act. This would last about a month or so and then he would be back into the drugs again. I guess this was ultimately his fate. I thought Thomas knew that too."

"What do you mean?" I asked, confused.

"Well, there were two reasons that Thomas called me this morning."

Still confused, I said, "To tell you that Peter had overdosed and what else?"

"He asked me to look into his death. He seems to think it might not have been an overdose." He took my hand in his, "And I was wondering if you would help me?"

* * * * *

The next morning when I got to Polly's, she jumped up from her bed. "And where did you sneak off to last night?"

I hugged her, "Oh, you know," I walked towards the settee. "We just went for a tour around the grounds and time seemed to slip away from us." I looked at her sidelong as I lay on the bed.

"Us?"

I was wondering if she would catch that.

"Who is this 'us'?" She jumped on the settee with me.

"Well, Percius seems to have kidnapped me."

"EEEEEE!!!" she shrieked. "What?? That is amazing! We are going to be sisters-in-law!" She hugged me.

"Oh my heavens, do not get so carried away, Polly. I am not one of his little trollops! Give me a little credit!"

Polly looked like the air had just been sucked out of her balloon.

"But, we did have a lot of fun."

"Yay!!!" She was smiling again. "How much fun?" she pried.

"Why Polly, I am not a girl who kisses and tells! I think Percius actually enjoyed that I did not just jump into bed with him. We had conversations. He showed me around the grounds and told interesting stories about the lands. He is very humorous. Besides, he was quite inebriated and in the mood he was in, I suspect he would have put a

My Name is Agnes

85

damper on your night, so I thought getting him away from your affair would be best for everyone." I had no delusions that Percius was going to fall in love with me nor did I want him to. I wanted someone to fall in love with me, for me, and to be faithful to me. It would have taken all the magic in my power for that to happen with Percius. Plus, if something ever happened between Polly and Philip, that would leave an awkward situation between Percius and I. Nope, too many factors I didn't need. But what I did have, was an ally. In fact, I had two allies — Percius and Eunice.

"How did everything go with Philip's parents?"

"Grand! They love me and I really adored them. Even Philip declared on the way home that they have never enjoyed any of his wives as they did me! Oh Agnes, I am just so happy!" She hugged me again.

"I am really happy for you, Polly." I still didn't trust Philip, but seeing Polly so happy really warmed my heart. *I am going to have to get over myself and jump on Polly's silver cloud.*

"So when do we depart for the Olympics?"

"Not long from now, but we have time for a soak…"

Later, as we got out of the chariot and looked around at the Olympic Center, I said, "Wow, I can not believe how this place has transformed in just one day!"

"There are so many people here," Polly said, almost afraid. She grabbed my arm. "Where do you imagine Philip's balcony might be?"

We both looked around and started walking, having no idea where we were going.

"Agnes!" Percius broke through a cluster of women and headed towards us. He gave me a hug. "How is this day finding you?"

"I am well. How are you this fine day?" We both started laughing.

"Oh, Agnes you are too much." He gave me a wink. "Polly, love." He kissed her hand. "Are you ready for this glorious event?"

"I believe I am, Percius."

"Well then, beautiful ladies," he put his arms out so we could take them, "let me escort you to your seats."

"Why thank you, Percius." I nodded to him.

Percius leaned over to me, "Agnes, I beg of you, do not leave my side during the events. I feel I will not make it through if you do."

"Of course, it will be much more enjoyable with you." I smiled. *I am getting much better at this flirting thing*, I commended myself.

Percius brought us to a guarded and much more secluded area, at a grand set of stairs. You could just see the relief on Polly's face. It seemed with each step closer there, the color returned to her face. Percius and I looked at each other and laughed at the sight of her.

She looked at us and was instantly annoyed. "What are you two laughing at?"

"Oh, nothing Polly. Let us make our way up." I giggled.

"What in Hades' gates were you two up to last night?" she grumbled as she made her way up the stairs.

Percius and I laughed again. He grabbed my hand and we walked up the stairs together. It was too bad he had such a wandering eye, because we really understood each other and had a great time together.

With a smothering hug, Eunice was the first to greet us as we got to the top of the stairs. She had a strange look on her face when she saw Percius and me holding hands and I got the impression she didn't want anyone else to see that; ergo the huge and very fast hug. I made a mental note — *Talk to Eunice about Percius's and my friendship*.

Philip was there to see Polly for a short time before he had to go and get ready for the ceremonies. Even I had to admit it was sweet of him to come and get some "good luck" from Polly before the games.

"Oh for all the stars in the heavens, this is stifling. Let us get drinks. Eunice, are you coming?" Percius sighed.

"Oh, I should go see if Mother needs anything."

Percius rolled his eyes at her.

"Oh, do come keep me company." I grabbed Eunice's arm. "Let us get some wine and have some fun while we watch the events," I said to her as we followed Percius. Polly was by Ina, doing her diligent girlfriend duties.

We went to the food and beverage table to fill up our plates and glasses.

"Eunice might you know anyone else who is here?"

My Name is Agnes

Eunice's face turned pink as she looked down at the ground. "No, I do not believe so."

Percius and I looked at each other with a puzzled look.

Percius poked at her. "Why Eunice, are you keeping something from us?"

She slapped his hand away from her. "No, I am not Percius. Never mind." Some music began and Eunice looked relieved. "The ceremonies are starting." She practically ran towards the seating area.

"That was suspicious," I said under my breath to Percius.

"My thoughts exactly." Percius rubbed his chin. "A very suspicious notion. Well, not to bother. Wine will be flowing today! Let us take our seats, we would not want to miss a thing." Sarcasm dripped from his words.

The ceremonies were spectacular. Andias had been building onto the Olympic grounds for years, so there were many people who were seeing the beautiful, completed grounds for the first time. All the wars at the time had called a truce and people had come from all over the country and brought gifts to present to King Andias. Beautiful monuments, which people had spent months and years crafting were unveiled. Previous winners and heroes were there to share in the event. It was one big group hug. If there was one dry eye in the crowd that was one too many. Even Percius felt the magnitude of the event.

The day started with the smaller events, which didn't take up as much space, going four at a time; each in its own arena. There was wrestling, boxing, long jump, and pankration wrestling (a mixture of wrestling and boxing where pretty much anything goes except eye gouging and biting — I had a feeling Percius and I would have fun watching that one). They presented the wreaths to the winners then those athletes were done. Once those events were finished they split the arenas and had the discus and the javelin at the same time. Then it was on to the foot races. It started with the most boring, the 2000 meters, followed by the 400 meters and finally the 200-meter races. Now if that wasn't exciting enough there was an event called the hoplitodromia, which was a 200-meter sprint wearing a helmet, calf armour, and shield. I imagine a lot of wine was involved at the origin

Kelly Brookbank

with whoever thought of that event.

After the individual races, the horses were invited to play. First were the chariot races. The tethrippon had four horses pulling chariots running twelve circuits around the racecourse, which was about fourteen kilometers long. The synoris had two horses pulling a chariot about half the distance of the tethrippon.

The horse races were the most popular events of the Olympics, mostly because of the danger of the event. There were no saddles or horseshoes used, so basically there was nothing to hold onto, with the horses running as fast as possible.

Because of the danger factor, the owners didn't participate. It was usually hired jockeys (slaves). The horse events were only for rich people. They were the only ones who could afford these horses, and they were the only ones who could afford to travel around with them. It was going to be a long day, but an exciting one.

"Agnes," Percius leaned over and pointed to the nearest arena, "keep your eyes on this arena. This is one of my favourite sports." He had a sideways smile on his face. 'It is called pankration, you are going to love it."

I'm sure Percius thought I was going to be shocked or appalled, but it was nothing I hadn't seen when I was living with the cavemen. Actually, I had seen it on a daily basis. I certainly didn't think they would make an Olympic sport out of it. Percius kept looking at me, expecting a reaction, so I figured I might as well have some fun with him.

The men were in a basic wrestling position in the arena so I said, "You know, if the man on the bottom were to just sweep his leg around and grab the other's arm, straighten it and pull it behind, he would have him." I used my magical power of suggestion on the wrestler to do just that.

Percius furrowed his brow as he looked at me and looked back at the arena where the wrestling match went just as I predicted. His jaw dropped.

I nudged him. "Oh my! Would you look at that! It is as if he could hear me. Maybe I should go down and coach them?"

My Name is Agnes

He was still looking at me confused. "How in the heavens?"

I shrugged my shoulders. "Maybe I was meant to be in the Olympics?"

He shrugged his shoulders too. "Maybe you were." He took a drink of wine and looked back at the arena.

I smirked and started watching again. "Perhaps a wager might be placed?"

"I think not!" Percius laughed. "With your suspicious talents revealed, I refuse to lose money to you." As if a lightening bolt had hit him in the back of the head, he turned to me and grabbed my shoulders. "But! We could lay bets with my nemesis, Nefarius. With your strange knowledge we are certain to take his coins! What do you say, Agnes?"

"Of course, as long as you explain why he is your nemesis."

"Oh, just the small matter of him stealing the only woman I ever loved."

"Well then, let us go take his purse!" I got up and headed for the door.

"Splendid!! Eunice, are you coming? We are going to visit an old friend of mine, Nefarius of the Prodicus house."

She gasped and her face went red. "Why would you want to visit him?"

"Oh, you never know when you might want to bury the hatchet." He looked sideways at me.

Confused she said, "All right." And followed behind us.

Chapter 16

"Now before you freak out, let me explain," Stuart reasoned with me. "I think Peter did die of an overdose, but it doesn't hurt to do some more digging around to appease my brother, and I thought it might be fun if you and I did it together. Honestly, what better way to get to know one another than investigating a murder?"

Stuart made those puppy dog eyes at me. How could I resist? And I couldn't really argue with his logic, it would be a good way to get to know one another. It's not like I would let him figure out who actually did it. "Ok, it actually sounds like fun. I've got enough staff who can handle the store for me for a while during the day." The more I thought about it… "Yeah, let's do this! Wait, won't the police be annoyed with us snooping around?"

"Well, I haven't actually figured everything out yet, Thomas only asked me this morning. I'm sure he will smooth everything over with the cops, but if they've ruled it an overdose I don't know if there will actually be detectives or what-nots still at Peter's place or not. I guess we'll find out. We have to get the funeral out of the way first off before we do anything. We're having a family gathering at Thomas and Angelina's this afternoon, so I should probably put an appearance in there. I want to give Isabella my support anyway. Mother is probably a wreck too. Actually I hope Mom doesn't go. There's going to be a lot of talk by a lot of insensitive people, and I don't want her to be in earshot of any of them." Stuart looked like he was in deep thought.

"You mean at the funeral, not at the family gathering today, don't you?"

"Oh Agnes, you don't know my family very well… well my dad's side anyway. My dad managed to escape and did very well for himself, but the rest of the clan are a bunch of back-stabbing, lowlives. Most of them will be more concerned about what food they're serving and the free booze than the fact that anyone has actually died. I swear my dad died of embarrassment, not of a heart attack. Although I do enjoy seeing Angelina squirm around my part of the family. I think I will take Isabella and my mother, say our "How do's," then be off."

Geez, I figured his family might even be more dysfunctional than my family. Holy shit, I just about spit out my coffee, that was so funny. Man, I am so witty, I should really write these things down… oh wait…

Stuart got up from the table. "Ok, I think I'm going to be off, I have to get in touch with Isabella and Mother to make arrangements. So you're good with this whole detective agency thing?"

"Yeah, sure. I think it might be fun. I've never been a detective before." Actually that was a lie, but that's another story for another time…"Let me know how this afternoon goes. I'm kind of afraid for you now that you've given me such frightening, vague information."

"Oh, don't worry about me. I can always manage to get out of situations quickly for some reason. Must be my stealthy, quick reflexes." He showed me some really bad ninja moves as he tried really hard to keep standing vertical.

"Mmm, yeah, that must be your secret weapon. Try not to use that on your mom, she might not let you down gently…"

"Ok." He put his head down in shame and then looked up at me like a dog that got caught eating out of the garbage. "I admit it's not my ninja skills, I have to use my quick wits."

"Whatever you have to use, just get out safe!" I pretended like he was going to battle or something. I dropped down to my knees, put my hand up to my forehead, and looked like I was wincing in pain.

He looked at me, bit his knuckles, and then ran out the door.

Gawd we were drama queens. Not two seconds later he came back in, grabbed his phone, gave me a wink and said, "I'll call ya tonight, baby."

As I stood there and everything kind of hit me at once, I thought, *OH MY HEAVENS, WHAT HAVE I DONE?*

I immediately froze everyone in the store — I needed a minute to think. Robin came in and I looked at him. "What do you think?"

"Well...I actually think it might be a good thing."

"Oh, thank the gods. I was hoping you would think so."

"You could hide evidence that we may have left that we didn't know we left."

"Right? And it might be fun. It might be a lot of fun! I can make it fun, right? I can make it lots of fun? I think it will be a good thing. He already hates Peter, I can make him hate Peter more? It will be a good thing! Ok, let's do this! Thanks Robin. You like Stuart, don't you?"

"I really do."

"Have I told you lately that I love you?"

"No, but I know that you do."

I winked at him and off he went. I unfroze everybody and took our coffee mugs up to the counter with a big smile on my face. Until I looked at Bobbi who, by the way, did not have a big smile on her face.

"WHAT. Do you. Have. To be smiling. About?"

And might I add that there was a nod or two of attitude in between those statements? Did I mention that she was not smiling?

"Oh, Bobbi, ummmm, I am trying to think of a word like relax, but there really is no word that I can say to you right now. So all I can say is, don't worry. It's all good. Stuart is Peter's uncle, but he knows he's a bad seed, ok? Chill? Take a breath. Ok? Breathe in. Breathe out. Ahhhhhhhh. There we go, gooooood."

"Seriously?" She looked at me sceptically.

"Yes. He told me the whole story. He tried to tame the beast that was Peter, but evil Pete got the best of him so Stuart washed his hands of druggie Petey. Stuart hasn't spoken to him for years. He offered him help but he said he wouldn't support him unless he was drug free and Peter never was, so he hasn't been in contact with him for years. He actually kind of convinced himself that Peter was already dead. He

My Name is Agnes   93

knew it would happen eventually so why postpone the inevitable?"

"Oh thank goodness, oh my God, I was over there worrying my head off, thinking about just horrible things. I thought he was blackmailing you, I thought he wanted me as a sex slave, I thought he wanted your business…" She put both her hands over her eyes and started crying.

"Holy shit! Stop. Bobbi, stop. It's nothing like that." I hugged her. "Hey Zeus. It's nothing like that." I felt so bad. "I am so sorry I took so long to come and explain this to you." Fuck now I felt like an asshole. "No, Stuart is a good guy. Peter and his dad are bad guys." It just dawned on me we were two complete messes in the front of the store. "Ummm, how 'bout we go in the back room?" I ushered her to the back.

I took her head in my hands to look her in the eyes, and she tried to talk, but I said, "Zzztt," which apparently in my language, means shut your face, then I put my hands on her shoulders, keeping eye contact…running my hands down her arms until I was holding her hands. I pulled her hands up to our chests and said, "I'm taking you out to the bar tonight for shots."

* * * * *

Obviously the house of Prodicus was a wealthy one because Percius said their balcony was just beside ours, so we would only need one drink to take with us. I suggested he might go ahead, and Eunice and I would be right behind. He looked a bit curious as to why.

I tried to look a little ashamed, so I looked to the floor and said, "I do not think I have the correct walk of royalty, so I am trying to have Eunice teach me a thing or two."

Percius looked confused and bewildered at the same time. "I would not think you the type to be concerned with those things, but if you need the time, take a few minutes." He still gave me a questioning eye but went on ahead.

Eunice rolled her eyes and said, "What was that all about?"

I stopped and looked at her. "Why are you concerned about your brother and me?"

She stammered, "What are you yammering…"

"Oh, do not be coy, I saw your reaction to our hand holding. Your brother and I are just friends. I know it is hard to think of a woman being that to Percius, but that is all that we are. I know what he is and I could never be anything but a friend to him, I am afraid. I know I will grow to love him very deeply, but I could never be in love with him, do you understand?"

She nodded her head and hugged me. She bit her lip. "I think you will be very good for him!" She hugged me again.

"Now let us catch up with him before he causes a disturbance!" I said and we ran to catch up with him, giggling away. We were such dorks.

There was not much difference between the two balconies. We caught up to Percius just as he was making his way to the food and drink table. He had already attracted the attention of a couple maidens. Eunice and I were slowly making our way up to the drink table when a good-looking man bumped into me.

"Oh, pardon me, do excuse my clumsiness."

"No harm done, sir. I have not a drink yet," I said matter of factly.

"Well, let me rectify that situation for you," he said coolly.

That was really smooth. Not being very tactful, I said, "Wow, that was very smooth, sir, well done."

"Excuse me, miss?" He looked at me like he had no idea what I was talking about and, to add to that, that I was quite beneath him.

Not to be outdone I gave him a gold shilling and said, "Bring drinks for my friends as well, will you?" And turned around and walked away.

Percius was just about throwing up he was laughing so hard when he came up to me. He could not believe what I had done.

"Who was that horse's ass?" I said, strumming my thumb in the jerk's direction.

"That, my darling Agnes, would be Nefarius Prodicus," and Percius started laughing once again.

"Well," I said, "I can see why you do not favour him."

As soon as Percius regained his composure he said, "Eunice, you

My Name is Agnes

take Agnes and retrieve seats – I must talk to Nefarius beforehand," he said with a mischievous smile and a little hop to his step.

Just as Percius promised, in no time, I felt a tap on my shoulder, "Agnes, I would like to introduce you to….Oh, that is right — you two have already met, have you not?"

"Not formally, no," I said with as much of a smile as possible.

"Well, Agnes, this is Nefarious." Percius swung his hand in presentation. He was enjoying this a little too much.

Nefarious gave me a wine glass and bowed. "Here is the wine I promised, my lady."

"Thank you, good sir," I said with a curtsy. Thank the gods, I really didn't want him to kiss my hand. *All right, we have made nice, now let us take this fool's purse full of money.* "Shall we sit and watch the events?" I urged the others.

Eunice and I sat down with the men behind us. Every time a match came up, Percius said their names out loud, and I said something or asked a question about one of the athletes. Then I either slightly nodded my head "yes," or slightly shook my head "no." Percius made his bet accordingly. At first, Nefarious thought Percius was just getting lucky, but then he started to get annoyed and then he started to take it personally. It was like it was his mission to get his money back, so he started to make double-or-nothing bets. Of course he lost those. Then he was getting absolutely furious. Of course Percius did not help the situation (he was not a gracious winner). I had suggested we leave a few times, but Nefarius would not let us leave. It was fun for a while, but eventually, even I was feeling sorry for Nefarius.

I stood up. "Thank you for your hospitality, Nefarius, but I feel I need be with Polly. She is, after all, the reason why I am here. I do believe that Philip's event is coming up soon, is it not?" I looked at Eunice, pleading.

She looked at me with a sad look on her face but then, dejected, she agreed and stood up. "Yes, it would be best."

"It is a shame to leave you without coin, Nefarius, the time has come for us to make our departure," Percius announced and bowed to Nefarius.

"What? You can not. I have not a chance to redeem myself," he snarled.

I put my hand up to his chest with some "extra force" behind it. "I think it is best if you retire at this point, with a semblance of dignity. Do you not think so, as well?"

His face changed from furious to quizzical. "Maybe you are right, Agnes. I shall not keep you any longer. The best of luck to Philip tonight." He turned around to watch the games.

I almost had to close Percius and Eunice's mouths for them. "Come on you two, let us be off!" I both growled and whispered at the same time.

When we burst through the doors after running down the stairs, Percius was the first to say, "How in Hades' gates did you do that?"

"What ever do you mean?" I sung.

"I have never seen anyone talk to Nefarius in that manner. Or Nefarius listen to anyone for that matter!" Eunice mused as we walked back to our balcony.

"I suppose I just have that effect on people. I can be very sensible at times, you know."

They both shook their heads.

We filled up our drinks and ate some more before heading back to our seats. If we hadn't gone over to the other balcony, this definitely would have been a boring day! They were just finishing up with the 400-meter race awards, and then it was time for Philip's first race.

I had to admit it was pretty exciting seeing someone out there that we knew! There were eight heats of eight runners. The top runner in each would move on to the last heat.

After the seventh heat, I noticed everyone was grimacing. "Percius, what is going on? Why has the mood dampened?"

"It is not 'what' is the problem, it is 'who' is the problem. The fellow that won that heat is Trevario, son of Plennsenous of Aphlios. Aphlios happens to be the land we seek to conquer at the moment."

"Oh, I see. I do not know anything about war. Why do you pursue their land? Why can you not leave it as is?"

"Their king and queen are greedy and brutal. They tax the people

My Name is Agnes   97

to squalor until they are forced into slavery. I have seen what they do to them. The people of Aphlios are all dirty and disgusting. Most of them either starve to death or die from disease. The streets are riddled with dead bodies."

I was dumbfounded. I could barely bring my head back around from staring, mouth gaping at Percius, but Philip's heat was up. If he ran into some trouble, I would give him a little "help." Turns out he didn't need any help at all. The guy could really run fast!

Now Philip and Trevario, the disgusting filth from the horrible Aphlios, were going to be running side-by-side.

Chapter 17

"You can call your friends and ask them if they want to come, I don't care, but we're going out tonight. You need to release some of this stress. Have I ever showed you my Elaine dance? Oh you're too young, Google it. I'll show you my version tonight. I'm going to go invite Jeremy and make the obligatory invite to Sarah. And just so you know, I'm inviting Stuart so you can get to know him. We all good?"

Bobbi gave me a hug. "You're the best boss ever!"

"I know, right? Now get to work." I gave her a wink as I turned around and went back out to the floor.

First I walked over to Sarah. "Sarah, Bobbi needs to let off some steam so I have invited her to go to the bar tonight. I am going to invite Jeremy as well. Would you like to come?"

There was the deer-in-the-headlights look I was expecting. "Oh Gawd, ummmm. Thanks but yeah, I can't."

Exactly what I figured. "No problem. I just wanted to ask." I turned around. Then stopped. I turned back around again. "You know, Sarah, I would love to go for drinks with just you sometime, maybe in a quiet lounge or maybe somewhere that you like to go?"

She thought about it. "Yeah. I'd like that."

Breakthrough!! I smiled at her. "I'd like that too." *Ok, don't make this awkward, Agnes.* I turned around and walked over to Jeremy. "Jeremy, we're going for drinks tonight. You down?"

"Yup. Time and place?"

"Nine at 'The Joint.'"

Bobbi and Jeremy exchanged looks and then laughed. As soon as Jeremy could catch a breath, he took his apron off. "I guess I should get there now to stand in line if we expect to get in before last call... tomorrow!!" He started laughing again.

Oh how I loved proving these kids wrong. I loved calling them kids as well, even though I was only technically eight human years older than they were...they thought. "Oh behave. Meet me there at nine...Ok, I'm heading out. Bobbi is too. We've both had trying days. I've called all the night shift, they're coming in early and should be here shortly."

Bobbi looked at me with a stunned look on her face.

"Well don't just stand there, get your stuff. Let's get out of here," I said to her on the way towards the back room.

"Oh, um, ok. Let me just finish up here," Bobbi said in a flurry.

I went to the back room, called "The Joint," and asked for the manager. I "suggested" that my friends and I would be allowed in that night, no questions asked, and there would be a nice table waiting for us when we got in. He thought that sounded like a great idea. I texted Stuart as well.

As soon as Bobbi came into the back room, she grabbed her purse and said, "I can't tell you how much this means to me, Agnes." Her eyes started to well up. "You're not only a great boss, you're a great friend too." She gave me a hug.

What a sweet girl. "It's my pleasure, Bobbi. Now, you better text your friends or they'll miss out on the party!"

We started walking out. "Ok, guys. Take care. Jeremy, feel free to bring your friends and your girlfriend." I almost choked on that but held in my laughter.

"Will do!" he said cheerily. He was such an enigma!

"Okey dokey. Over and out!" I shouted as we headed out the door.

"All right, missy, how about you and I head to a patio somewhere and have a drink to calm your nerves?"

You could see the relief drain from her shoulders. "That sounds like heaven."

Funny thing, now that I knew she liked horses so much, I could almost hear a slight drawl in some of her words. "There's a nice pub right by my place, hop in my car."

"What about my car?"

"Don't worry, I'll have it all taken care of. It'll be back at your place tonight."

Bobbi shrugged her shoulders. She was starting to trust that I just took care of things.

I loved this little pub. It was almost like coming home. I had spent so much time there just sitting back, drinking wine and reading, or people-watching or whatever.

"Hey Agnes!" George said from behind the bar.

"Hey George. This is Bobbi."

"Well hello there!" He was an insufferable flirt.

"Behave yourself." I pumped my fist at him.

"What would you like to drink, Bobbi?"

"Just a Budweiser."

"Ok and I will have a Captain's and coke, with two tequila shots on the side, you know how I like them. Can we have them on the deck?"

"You bet, I'll bring them right out."

We took our seats outside in the sun — both of us liked to soak up the rays whenever possible. "We should probably eat. Want some appetizers?"

"Sure, that sounds good. What's good here?"

"They have some amazing wings and their spinach dip is delicioso." I made that motion when you kiss your fingers then splay them out in front of your face. I have no idea where that came from and why that would mean something tasted good.

"Sure, sounds good to me."

"Here you go, ladies," George said as he placed our drinks down in front of us. Then he stood there and waited.

"Oh right!" I said, "George likes to watch."

"Huh?" Bobbi looked mortified.

"George waits to watch us do the shots, then he takes the empty

My Name is Agnes   **101**

shot glasses away."

"Oh! Makes sense."

"Ok, lick the back of your hand, pour the salt on it, shoot the tequila, lick the salt, then suck the lemon. Got it?"

We both made the twisted face with the crossed eyes.

George chuckled. He was clearing the glasses as I stuck up my finger as if to say 'just wait,' but couldn't talk because I was still sucking the lemon. "Phew, ok. Damn, those are good. Anyway, can we get a pound of Salt and Pepper wings and spinach dip, pretty please?"

"You bet." He turned and walked away.

Standing right behind him was Stuart. He stopped George. "I think we'll need another round of those and a scotch for myself, please." He sat down heavily. "Well I've solved the mystery. Peter killed himself because he couldn't stand his family, and frankly, I don't blame him."

Both Bobbi and I stared at him with blank looks on our faces. Neither of us knew whether to laugh or console him. After I came to my senses, I said, "That bad, huh?"

"Yup, they're all a bunch of assholes."

"I think I'm missing something," Bobbi said, confused.

"Sorry," Stuart said to her, "I have just come from a family gathering for Peter's wake, and it was the most atrocious spectacle I have ever been to. My side of the family was acting like they were mourning while at the same time asking if there was anything in his will being left to them. It was absolutely disgusting.

"And Angelina's side was acting like they were being held there against their will. They were all stuck together in groups looking down their noses at everyone. I personally wanted to line them all up and bitch slap every single one of them. The only entertaining thing was watching Angelina run after my side of the family making sure they weren't stealing anything. That was good for a chuckle. After about half an hour I had enough and took my mother home. She lives a couple blocks from here, actually. I happened to see you two out here and thought I might join you for a drink. You don't mind, do you?"

"No, of course not," Bobbi said.

"Sounds like we all had shitty days," I said, just as George came up to the table and put down the shooters and Stuart's scotch. "Well then," as we licked our hands and poured the salt on them. We raised our shot glasses and clinked them together. "To shitty days!" all three of us said.

* * * * *

As the athletes were stretching and lining up for their heat, you could see Philip and Trevario glaring at each other. It was quite evident that they did not like each other and the fans all knew that these two mighty athletes were from two battling kingdoms. The tension was mounting with every second before the horn sounded.

The way they lined up was in order of the heat they won, so Trevario was in line seven and Philip in line eight. It was only 200 meters so the men were lined up beside each other, instead of along the curve of the track. They could start off any way they chose, either with their hands on the ground or standing up — whatever their preference. Philip chose to start on bended knee with his hands on the ground. Trevario chose to stand.

The crowd was hushed. "On your marks." Trevario "pretended" that he lost his balance and knocked Philip over onto his legs and ass, scraping them up. "Get set." Trevario quickly regained his stance while Philip was still trying to get back into position. "Go!"

Luckily Philip was nimble, got back into his position in time, and got a great start, out of the "gates" even faster than Trevario. Being on your hands, low to the ground and knees bent gives you more traction and allows you to start faster, so Philip was ahead right off the bat.

Philip was the odds-on favourite to win and he was not letting anyone down today. Even with blood running down his leg, he was ahead of everyone by a horse-length. Trevario was in second place and after what I'd seen of him that day I couldn't let that happen. Mysteriously, a fair-sized rock appeared in front of him and he tripped over it, causing him to fall from second place to last.

Philip blew the rest of the competition away and won the 200-meter dash in fine fashion. When he won and accepted his medal

My Name is Agnes   **103**

he turned and blew a kiss to Polly on the balcony. She was absolutely thrilled.

Now to the hoplitodromia. This was the craziest thing I had ever seen!

"So clarify for me," I said to Percius. "Four grown men, dressed in armour, will run the same race that Philip just ran?"

"That is correct, my dear. It is quite entertaining, to say the least!"

"But, they can barely walk, let alone run!"

"Yes, indeed. That is what makes it even more enjoyable. You will see. Oh, here they go."

Right away, three of the four fell. It was very hilarious to watch them trying to get back up again also. The other one took three steps and then fell himself. One man tried doing cartwheels all the way down but he got way off-track. Another man kept doing the same thing over and over; he would try to go too fast, fall down, and then take too much time trying to get up. The third man tried to crawl, but that was not working the way he had planned, I don't think. The man who was successful, was the man who went slow and steady. He didn't fall, therefore he didn't have to worry about dealing with that horrible business of trying to get back up again.

Oh my, that was quite the sight. My stomach hurt after watching that event, that was for sure. Philip had made it back to the balcony by the time the hoplitodromia was over so he could watch the horse races with everyone.

The horse races were very intense. No wonder the owners of the horses didn't ride in the chariots themselves, because it was extremely dangerous! Basically you had nothing to hold onto, you had no way to slow the horses down, and you had no way to steer them. They just got in and went and hoped they didn't crash. There were four in each heat of the tethrippon and they started staggered across the racetrack, I guess they didn't want them running into each other right off the bat. When the horn blew, each of the men in the chariot snapped their whips at the horses, which spurred the horses on to start running... and they were off. The men kept snapping their whips with one hand and holding on for dear life with the other. The four horses of each chariot charged around the track as fast as they could, lashing the chariots behind them this way and that; each chariot getting closer and closer to the others at every turn.

As one horse team gained speed on another, the closer they came side-by-side; the horses not being smart enough to know to stay far enough apart. As the chariots gained on each other, the charioteers had no control. They thrashed back and forth and couldn't help but bang into each other. Inevitably the wheels touched and both wagons smashed apart, throwing their passengers into the air to roll onto the ground. If they were lucky the men were thrown far enough to land off the track, or behind the other chariots. If they were unlucky, they landed on the track, the other teams of horses couldn't get out of the way in time, and they got trampled.

The tethrippon had four heats and the winner of each faced off in a final heat to determine an overall winner. If there was no winner of a heat (if everyone crashed and died, thankfully that didn't happen this time!) the second fastest runner up would compete in the final.

Finally the last event was up, the synoris. Philip's horses were in the second heat. I wasn't sure about anyone else, but I had had enough of this very long day of Olympics. I hadn't talked to Polly all day, but she had looked over at me several times and rolled her eyes at me as if to say, "Get me out of here!" Percius was getting quite intoxicated also. I still thought he was funny, but you could tell his parents were getting annoyed.

The synoris wasn't quite as dangerous as the tethrippon because there were only two horses, so it wasn't as fast and erratic, but it added another element of danger because the gladiators in the chariots were allowed to use swords against the other gladiators.

Again, this one started with the horn, the whip, and the chariots being staggered. The second heat with Philip's chariot was fairly uneventful, with Philip's horses taking an early lead, and no one else able to catch up. The other events had clear winners also, but were a bit more bloody.

At last, the final event of the day. The mood had certainly changed from that of the morning. It had gone from long anticipated

My Name is Agnes   105

excitement and good sportsmanship, to drunken hostility and fierce rivalry. Everyone was out for blood and no mercy.

The four chariots lined up, the men cursing and jibing their fellow competitors the whole way. Philip's chariot was in lane two. Somewhat of a hush fell over the drunken crowd (those who didn't know what was going on were still singing), the horn blew, and the chariots were off. Philip's chariot was in second but he quickly closed the lead by half right away.

Philip's horses ran like might and closed the gap even more. One snap from the whip and they jumped forward just enough that Philip's gladiator could reach the leader's gladiator. Philip's gladiator, in a brilliant, but disgusting move, used his whip to lash the leader's left hand, which brought it down and into his chest, throwing his right hand up — exposing it. Philip's gladiator was close enough that he used his sword to cut off half of the other man's arm! The crowd let out an uproarious cheer. It didn't matter if they were applauding for Philip or not, the crowd just liked to see blood and guts. I think some of them could have been throwing up because they were so drunk too.

Obviously this gladiator did not stay on his chariot for long, being that he no longer had a hand and he was losing blood at a furious rate. Once the gladiators fell off, the organizers around the track waved their hands furiously and threw themselves at the runaway horses to stop them and get them off the track. After all, the owners of the horses were more concerned with their expensive horses than they were with the hired help.

Philip's horses now had the lead so he continued to charge ahead. They were ahead by a full horse-length.

The trailing two chariots were only apart by a chariot-length, but the last chariot was catching up. Because the chariots were so close, the front chariot's gladiator was able to threaten it by swinging his sword. The crowd realized what excitement was about to ensue so they voiced their encouragement.

The trailing chariot continued to gain and also to avoid the sword of its closest competitor. It was obvious as to who was more intelligent. The leading gladiator continued to swing his weapon at his opponent,

106   *Kelly Brookbank*

who pulled his chariot in the opposite direction of his horses, visibly slowing them in the process. The latter chariot wasn't defending against the sword, he was just avoiding it, which wasn't that hard to do. The charioteer was biding his time until the opportune moment that was quickly coming upon him, as they were almost side by side.

Dummy gladiator could barely hold his sword up any longer he was so tired. He rested his sword on the chariot and poked it at smarty-pants in an effort to look threatening, but it really wasn't fooling anyone.

"You do not believe what he is doing could work in his favour, do you?" I asked Percius.

Percius just laughed. "If he lasts another lap I would be surprised!"

With the tired gladiator no longer a threat, the smart gladiator whipped his horses to start pulling away from the idiot. The crowd could not believe what they were seeing. Were they actually going to be deprived of seeing a man being stabbed to death? *You mean no blood? No guts? You can't be serious?* It took them a while to catch on, but once it sunk in the shouts of disgust started emanating from the stands.

Smart Stuff was almost half a chariot length ahead of Doofus now. A resounding "Boo" was rolling from the grandstands. Dumb Dumb was getting his strength back now, and he picked his sword up again. The crowd threw things onto the track. Smarty-pants looked up and around into the masses realizing what they were upset about. He was so focused on what he was doing that he hadn't even heard the crowd. He had been keeping an eye on the nitwit, who still hadn't been a threat so he wasn't a concern. Because of the crowd though, Smarty-pants turned and looked at the nitwit, picked up his sword and cut off his sword hand.

Elation erupted from the crowd as the hand separated from the arm and fell to the dirt, still holding the sword. Even though the crowd was cheering for this act of gruesomeness, Witty One thought they were cheering for him and he hammed it up for the crowd. He held his sword and other arm up and pumped them into the air. The crowd cheered and laughed at him, although all he could hear was noise so he assumed it was all cheering.

My Name is Agnes

He swung his sword and cut the chest of his opponent, who was having a hard time standing upright at this time. The crowd cheered again, which spurred another round of air pumps to his "adoring fans." This time, to entertain them, he thought he would poke his opponent, á la fencing. You could tell his opponent was losing a lot of blood and close to falling out of his chariot. His head bobbed up and down and he leaned farther and farther back and forth.

The brainchild wasn't paying any attention though, he was bowing to the crowd. Wise-Guy stood up, and in one valiant effort with his only free hand holding his whip, he lashed his competitor catching him around the neck, and taking him to the ground with him as he fell out of his chariot.

I guess he wasn't as smart as I thought he was. He was just a nobody who got caught up trying to be a somebody!

We were completely stunned. No one said anything until all of a sudden Eunice quietly said, "Philip has won, has he not?"

We all started yelling and screaming, "Philip won!" "Oh my heavens!" "He really won!" We hugged each other and cheered each other; it was a great celebration. Then all of a sudden we looked over and Philip was on one knee beside Polly. Everything went dead quiet.

"Polly, will you make me the happiest man for the rest of my life?"

"Of course!" and the celebration continued.

Chapter 18

As soon as Bobbi went to the bathroom, I said to Stuart, "Ok, here's the plan. Don't be a lightweight tonight. We're on recon duty. We'll get Bobbi drunk and ask her questions about Peter, like if "The Joint" was a place he ever went to, what kind of a guy he was, if she ever suspected the drug use, etc. Then when we meet her friends we can ask them questions too. Ok?"

"Ok, sounds good. Wait, what do you mean lightweight?"

"Oh, here she comes. So then the frog said, your lily pad's too slimy!" I slammed the table and laughed like I was telling a joke. Stuart started laughing because what I said was so stupid.

"Were you telling a joke? What was the joke?" Bobbi said.

"Oh it was a joke my ex boyfriend used to tell all the time. Speaking of ex-boyfriends, I hope it's ok that we're going to The Joint, that's not somewhere that you and Peter used to go to all the time, was it?"

"Oh no, that place is so hard to get into. We tried one time, Peter thought we could get in for some reason, but of course we couldn't and he was so embarrassed I never brought it up again. Are you sure we can get in tonight?"

"Yes, we'll be fine," I said.

Stuart looked at me funny. "So where did you guys hang out?" he queried.

Bobbi started opening up to Stuart. I tried to flag down the waitress to order more drinks. It had become busier in there, so George wasn't able to look after us any more. I wanted to order some drinks then go to the restroom to put my anti-drunk spell on myself. I liked to give myself a bit of a buzz and then apply the anti-drunk spell. I finally caught the waitress's eye and gave her the "round" signal. I also gave her the shots signal.

"Sorry you two, I'm just going to the bathroom. I ordered another round then we should probably get going, don't you think?"

"Yeah, probably," Stuart said.

"I'll be right back." I went to the bathroom to do my businesses. When I got back our drinks were there.

"Well," we licked our hands and poured the salt on them. "What should we drink to this time?" Bobbi said.

"How about a good time tonight?" Stuart suggested.

"A good time tonight!" we all said and downed the shots.

When we finished our drinks, I asked for the tab. "So Bobbi, you'll just come to my place to get ready. And Stuart we'll meet you there at nine, how does that sound?"

"Sounds good to me," Stuart said with a smile and a wink.

Mmmm, that totally gave me butterflies!

"Hold it," Bobbi said, "I have nothing to wear at your place and what am I supposed to do about my car?"

"I have it all taken care of."

"What?"

The waitress came with the bill. "I'll take that," Stuart said.

"No you won't!" I argued and took it. "This was my idea, not yours." I got my wallet out of my purse and gave the waitress my credit card.

Stuart put up his hands, "Sorry, sorry."

"I guess," I looked at him, disgusted.

"Umm, excuse me," Bobbi interrupted, "what do you mean you have it all taken care of? How could you have something for me to wear and have my car taken care of?"

"Well, I have a friend who is a personal shopper so she went and got you an outfit, and my uncle and his friend will have your car at home for you."

She looked dumbfounded. The waitress came back with my credit card and receipt.

"Ok, let's go. Bye George!" We waved as we made our way outside.

"Ok, so we'll see you at "The Joint" at nine?"

"You betcha," Stuart said as he bent down and gave me a kiss. That took me by surprise, but a pleasant one at that.

As Bobbi and I got ready at my place, we kept drinking but slowed down a bit. The first glass of wine that I gave her was actually a potion to sober us a bit so we could last the night. I kept asking her questions about Peter too.

Bobbi loved the outfit I got for her. It was a beautiful, fitted red dress with a halter-top neckline, bunched fabric coming across the shoulders and down across the ribs, with diamond-shaped cut outs at the waist. It was nicely fitted but still classy as the hemline came down almost to the knee. The shoes were black Jimmy Choos. The jewellery was a simple diamond bracelet and necklace. She looked absolutely gorgeous.

I just wore my skinny jeans with my tall, brown riding boots and long socks above the boots for the elf look, a cute beige tank, and long gold necklaces.

I invited a friend of mine, Julie, over from down the hall (it was really Robin), who was a stylist and she did our hair and make-up while we all drank wine. Before we knew it, it was 8:30 and the car was here to take us to "The Joint".

It would've been rude of us not to invite Julie so she came with us. We took our wine with us, as this was a car service I used all the time — I told Bobbi, really I "suggested" to the driver that he not care. By the time we got there it was five minutes to 9:00. Pretty much everyone who was invited was there, except for Stuart who texted that he would be fifteen minutes late. The line-up to get in was obscene. I couldn't believe that people would wait all night just for a chance to get into a bar!

We all gathered near the door. I saw Jeremy and Bobbi saw her friends. "Ok, is this everyone?" Everyone agreed. "Ok, come with me."

My Name is Agnes   111

I went up to the bouncer and tapped him on the shoulder. He looked at me, like I was an annoying bug that needed to be squashed. He probably gets people doing this all night, trying to sneak in. I looked at him and tilted my head slightly. "Hi, I'm Agnes, I talked to your manager earlier." He looked at me for a second and then, as if a light bulb went off, "Oh right, come on in everyone," he said with a smile as he opened the door. You could hear the groans from the people in the line-up.

I thought Jeremy's eyes were going to fall out of his head! "How on this side of Hell did you do that?"

"Oh, I can be very persuasive when I want to be. Now come on, I believe they have a table for us."

I walked up to the hostess to tell her who I was, and she promptly showed us to our table. We settled in and ordered some drinks with, of course, a round of shots. Man, this place was massive. It was two floors, just huge. The first floor was the DJ booth/stage, dance floor, some tables and the main bar, then behind the half-wall was the shooter bar, another bar, and some more tables. The second floor had another bar, pool tables, and some more tables.

As soon as the drinks and shooters arrived, Stuart did as well. He came behind me and gave me a kiss. It was really loud in there so he had to talk into my ear. "How did you get in here?" he said to me.

"I can be very persuasive when I want to be."

"I see that, but you got everyone else in here too?"

"What can I say? I have the power of persuasion, I guess. Do you want a shooter?" I started to give him the shooter and then put it back down. "Wait a minute, how did YOU get in here?"

"I own the place."

* * * * *

The next four months were a whirlwind — good thing witches don't need to sleep. The wedding planning was boring as shit. Polly's mother just followed Ina around like a lost puppy and agreed with everything she said. Polly and I walked behind them and listened to Ina say what she wanted and where she wanted everything, followed by Polly's mother saying what a wonderful idea that was.

Polly did one of three things: 1) Liked the idea and did nothing. 2) Hated the idea and spoke up, at which Ina would just laugh and make a comment to the effect of, "Oh, darling you do not mean that." Or 3) Said nothing, rolled her eyes at me, and complained to me that night. On occasion 2 or 3, I got up early in the morning and met Ina for breakfast, to discuss the previous day's wedding plans and "suggested" she change her mind, which she always did, so Polly got what she wanted.

As we walked around on those days, Ina would completely change her mind and mention something that Polly actually wanted, but Ina clearly had not the day before. Everyone looked at each other, confused. The first time someone questioned Ina she was quite indignant and very offended, so we learned early not to question her. It was quite amusing to me how she made it seem like her own brilliant idea.

When Ina wasn't around one time and the rest of us talked about it, we just decided that she was getting older and confused. That explanation certainly worked for me.

The men spent their time in the war room, deep in the throes of war and hostile takeovers. I hardly ever saw Robin because he either hovered above the war room or transformed into General Thracian to keep me informed of their daily meetings. To tell you the truth, I was more intrigued with what the men were doing than all this wedding plans rubbish.

The first night we moved into the palace we realized we couldn't have gotten there sooner. Philip looked so dejected when he came in from the war room, Polly immediately ran to him and gave him a hug. "Philip, my love, what is the matter?"

"It is not a worry for you, my sweet." He kissed her. "How was your day?"

"Do not avoid my question. Why are you so terribly sour?"

"I do not want to worry you," he said looking to the floor.

I felt sad for the guy.

"Shall we retire?" Polly asked.

My Name is Agnes   113

"All right."

Polly looked at me. "See you in the morning." She shrugged and gave me a look like, *I will give you the details tomorrow.*

I waved. I had just filled my wine so I was going to finish my glass and wait to see if Percius was coming in. I had hardly swallowed my first gulp when Polly came to fetch me.

"Agnes, your assistance is requested."

Polly had a smirk on her face I had never seen before. I got up and followed her. "Now what could you two possibly be up to?" I stopped. "Wait, this is not about to cross a line, is it? You know my feelings about lines."

"Oh Agnes, stop your teasing and come along. You will enjoy this." We had reached Philip's bedroom.

"I feel I must repeat myself and my line aversion..."

"Oh just get in here, silly."

We walked in to Philip's bedroom, which was the size of most regular folks' villas. I was pleased to see him fully clothed and off the bed. He was sitting at the table with a glass of wine and a map of the lands spread out on the table. Polly brought me over to the table and invited me to sit down.

Philip was obviously embarrassed so Polly elected to explain the problem.

"The reason we have asked you here, is because we believe the three of us can put our heads together to help Philip. Well, honestly, I think mostly you can help Philip. He does not exactly have the mind for coups and takeovers, so he is feeling quite inadequate in the war room."

"Well I do not know if I would quite use the word 'inadequate,' Polly," Philip chimed in.

"Apologies, Philip. How exactly would you characterize it?" She looked at him.

Philip thought for a second or two, sat up, then opened his mouth to speak.

"Go on." He slumped back down and looked at his fingers.

Polly continued to look at Philip until she shook her head out of the stupor she was in. "To continue, I thought if Philip explained to us what was taking place maybe we could make some suggestions for him." Polly looked at me with a twinkle in her eye.

"That is a brilliant idea," I said. How I kept myself from rubbing my hands together and laughing wickedly, I will never know.

Philip tried to explain, the best he could, what the current situation was but he didn't have the best recollection and he was an idiot. Luckily, because I had been so interested in what the men were doing rather than the wedding plans rubbish, I'd had Robin transform into General Thracian to keep me informed of their daily meetings and I already knew what the situation was.

We needed to take down Aphlios before they took us down, but we needed more men, hence a bigger army. Aphlios had all but secured the lands to the south. Wherever they turned up, all the men and women were so terrified that they never resisted or they would be slaughtered on site.

All the lands that we had secured were heavily protected and impenetrable. It was a clear case of brawn versus brains. They muscled their way through without thinking of the consequences or having any plans. But to their credit it seemed to be working so far...Our men were determined to break their streak.

Their fierce leader was Philip's Olympic competitor Trevario's father, Plennsenous, a particularly gruesome fellow who had no morals and felt no regrets. He had one agenda and one agenda only, and that was to rule at all costs. It didn't matter if there was a treaty or not, he was out for blood. He would invade a town, kill the leader, take the men in the land to join his army, then send them, chaperoned, to scout the next invasion. While they were doing that, in celebration for their victory, he allowed his army to go into town to rape and pillage whoever and whatever they chose.

Plennsenous built his army until the day that the Aphlios army met the Partisian army in an open field battle. It was a grand battle that was talked about for ages, but in this battle, Plennsenous killed the Partisian king himself, and the Partisians left hanging their heads in an unprecedented defeat. After that victory Plennsenous began to dismantle the Partisian dominance.

My Name is Agnes

When King Andias heard what Plennsenous had done he knew he and his sons had to do something about it. It was now or never, or soon we would be under the rule of Plennsenous as well....and most likely raped and killed.

Chapter 19

What a fun night. It was exactly what everyone needed. We danced a lot, we played pool, we drank a lot...we just had a lot of fun. I put an enchantment in the last round of shooters that would remove everyone's hangovers. I had a hangover once in 1903 BC and I'd never wish that on my worst enemy. Actually that's not true. Some of my enchantments are based on that hangover, but that's when I really want them to suffer.

The whole night it just kept bugging me what Stuart had said, or at least what I thought he'd said. He owned the place? He couldn't have said that. I must have heard that wrong. It was really loud in there and Bobbi grabbed me to dance as soon as he said it so I couldn't ask him to repeat it.

Oh well, it was Saturday morning and we were going to meet for breakfast and start our investigation. I was actually quite excited. We weren't meeting at Steamers and Dreamers, we were going to a restaurant closer to Peter's house, somewhere I'd never been before. I wasn't actually sure what I was supposed to wear. What is the appropriate attire one wears to be a super sleuth? I was sure my go-to boy-shorts cut-offs, doubled-up muscle shirts, flip-flops, Toronto Blue-Jays baseball cap, and aviator sunglasses (just in case we needed a quick disguise) would do the trick.

I drove to the restaurant and saw Stuart outside on the patio.

117

Feeling all dangerous and bad-ass, I hopped the barrier to go meet him. I'm pretty sure if someone had given me shit I would've apologized profusely, but at that moment I felt it was something I needed to do.

"You know they have doors here," Stuart chastised me as he folded his paper and sat it on the table.

Sitting down I said, "I don't need no stinkin' doors," in a terrible Brooklyn accent.

"My, my, aren't we all rebellious this morning." He smiled at me. He was wearing loose 7 For All Mankind jeans and a Chanel t-shirt.

I must admit, he looked pretty hot. "You know, I do feel pretty bad-ass! I'm not really sure why, it's not like we're breaking any laws or anything, but it feels like we're doing something wrong, you know what I mean?"

"I do know what you mean." He leaned in a little closer. "Going into someone's house to go snooping through their things just feels..."

"Icky!"

He pointed at me. "Exactly! Icky!"

We both laughed. I leaned in closer and so did he. "I've had..." We both leaned back in our seats as the waitress came to our table.

"Oh I'm sorry," she said. She looked confused. "Did I forget to bring you a menu?"

"Yes you did and may I have a coffee and Baileys, please?"

"Yes, right away, sorry about that." She still looked confused as she walked away.

"You're terrible," Stuart said with a chuckle.

I winked at him. "Anyway," I said as I leaned in, "I've had butterflies in my stomach all morning thinking about today." I hunched my shoulders up like I was a stupid little schoolgirl. I'm surprised we both didn't start clapping and shouting "Hercules, Hercules!"

Stuart leaned back. "I suppose we shouldn't get ahead of ourselves. This "investigation" of ours could produce nothing."

Sitting up straight, I composed myself as I looked at the menu. "That's right. This could just be a glorified snooping mission. Two busybodies poking around in some druggie's personal stuff."

"Here you go," the waitress said as she sat down the coffee and Baileys. "Now what can I get you?"

"I'll have the Eggs Sherlock Holmes with some Watson on the side." I set my menu down.

She looked at me funny. "I'm sorry, where did you see that on the menu?"

"Oh pardon me, must be my Canadian accent, I'll have the Eggs Benedict with some hash browns on the side."

She stared at me way too long, "O…k…" There was a pleading look in her eyes when she looked at Stuart. "And for you, sir?"

"I'll just have two pancakes, two eggs — over easy, and two slices of ham. And may we have two mimosas, please?"

With a sigh of relief, she said, "Yes sir [heavy on the sir], right away."

"You would think someone in the service industry herself would be kinder to the wait staff," Stuart said to me with one eyebrow raised.

"I wouldn't be in the service industry if it weren't for people like me. I thrive on people with a sense of humour. That's what I live for. Dull people are what I can't stand. If you can't make your job fun then you should be in a different industry. Anyway, did you get any intel from any of Bobbi's friends last night about dear ol' Peter?"

"Umm yeah, but let's wait for the mimosas first. Oh there she is, I see her coming, I wouldn't want her to interrupt our conversation." He pointed to the waitress heading towards us.

I looked at him like his lips were exploding.

"There ya go, can I get you anything else?" The waitress asked us.

Stuart looked at me very strangely and then asked her, "Can you bring us each a shot of tequila with two lime wedges, please?"

"You bet." She turned away.

Stuart watched her walk away with an inquisitive look on his face. "Huh, I thought she would've been more shocked at that. I guess she's seen a lot in this line of work." He looked at me and saw that I was glaring at him. "Oh, right! Ummm, yes. I talked to all of Bobbi's friends about Peter, and they all basically said the same thing. I can't remember all of their names, but you know that one that tried to get up on the speaker to dance but she was too drunk?"

My Name is Agnes   119

"Oh yeah, that was sooo funny! Plus her dress was too tight so there's no way she would've gotten up there without splitting it right up to her belly button!"

We laughed and laughed.

"Anyway, before she got too drunk, she told me that Peter just gave her the creeps, that's what they all said — he gave them the creeps. How she described it was he just looked right through her. He wanted to know all about her, but it was as though he wanted to use the information so he could get closer to Bobbi. It wasn't because he actually wanted to get to know her. Of course she hated him, but she always had an uneasy feeling about him. She didn't want to talk about him very much. I think she felt guilty she let Bobbi date him as long as she did."

I took a drink of my mimosa — I knew how she felt.

"Then the one that ended up sucking face with that guy who had the tattoo of his mom on his forearm also said Peter was creepy. She described him as having "dead eyes." Peter asked her to tell him all about Bobbi, but she told him he needed to figure that out for himself. He didn't like that, so being the spoiled little rich bitch that he was, he pouted and never talked to her again. She figured she got a lucky escape. I agreed with her."

"They all said the same thing except the one girl. That one that broke her heel trying to do a country line dance."

I pointed at him. "To a rap song? Yeah her name is Amanda — you know… Amanda Hugginkiss?"

"I don't get it," Stuart said confused.

I rolled my eyes.

"Anyway," Stuart continued, "she was the only one that didn't have anything to say about Peter. All she said was he was fine and then changed the subject."

"That's weird…" I said.

Our breakfasts appeared. "Mmmm, this looks delicious. Thank you," I said to the waitress.

She looked shocked and stammered, "Y…you're welcome? Enjoy…"

"Oh yeah!" Stuart spit a bit of his pancake out, "that girl that spilled the beer on Jeremy?"

"Yeah, yeah?"

"She said something interesting...." He took another bite of his eggs.

I looked at him as he sat there chewing. "Seriously? You're going to say something like that and then not tell me?"

He swallowed. "Sorry. So they were all at Peter's house early on in Peter and Bobbi's relationship, because that was the only time that Peter allowed her to see her friends. She got lost in his house but she had to go to the bathroom really bad. She found his bedroom and used his bathroom. She snooped a little and looked in the medicine cabinet and saw there was flunitrazepam in there, of course among other things. She's studying to be a pharmacist so, of course, she recognized it."

"Ummmm, so I'm not studying to be a pharmacist, so what is flew-new-try-zu-pee-pam or whatever the hell you said?"

"You might recognize the other name for it — Rohypnol."

"The Date Rape Drug????"

* * * * *

"The debate is where we want to strike." Philip pointed to the map. "Percius wants to come from the top down because that is our strongest area. But Alexander believes they will be expecting that. He wants to come from the east, off the water, because they will not be looking for us there and we can take them off guard."

"And your opinion?" I asked Philip.

"I agree with both of them."

"Of course you do. So basically you were of no benefit to either of them?" I crossed my arms and looked at him. "You were the tie-breaker yet you chose to abstain?"

"I did no such thing!" He sounded quite indignant.

"Will you promise to never be an abstainer again?" I asked of Philip.

"I promise." I looked at Polly, who was glaring at me now.

"That is much to ask of you and will cause you great discomfort, so

My Name is Agnes   121

I must ask again, will you promise to never abstain?"

Philip looked down at his fingers. "I am afraid I do not know the meaning of the word." His face turned red.

"I realize that, Philip. I am trying to prove a point." I let my arms down. "I am here to help you, so you are going to have to do a few things for me. One is to let down your guard. The other is to treat me as an equal. Can you do that for me?"

"Apologies. I will try."

"Thank you. Now," I went over to the map, "let us have a look at this. I think I may have an idea."

The next day I saw Percius on his way down to the gladiator-training centre, so I excused myself from the nauseating wedding plans and went to meet him. "Hey you."

Percius turned around "Well, are you not a relief to see. I have been looking at the ugly faces of my father and brothers for far too long!"

"I would trade you in the beat of a heart. I will come and strategize the fate of Mathesdon and you can plan the wedding of the year."

"As long as I have a glass of wine in my hand it does not matter," Percius said.

"And does your father allow you your favourite beverage while you are planning the fate of the world?"

"Well played, my lady, well played."

"So where are you off to, kind sir?"

"Down to the dungeon of sweat and muscles. Would you like to accompany me?"

"I would. Anything for relief from silk and flowers. Any longer in there and I am afraid I will turn into a decoration myself!"

"We could not have that, now could we? Stay close to me, I would not want you to lose your way with these heathens about."

"How goes the war plans today?" I was anxious to hear how Philip had made out executing my plans. We had rehearsed for hours how he would make the proposal and discuss the different scenarios that might come up. I was just hoping he hadn't fucked everything up too much.

"Surprisingly well, actually. Philip shocked all with a brilliant idea." Percius looked at me with wide eyes. "Two brilliant ideas, in fact.

Silence befell everyone."

"Huh," I said. "Will wonders never cease!" *Thank the Gods, he pulled it off. At least he can be a parrot when he needs to be. He is good for something.*

We made it to the dungeon. The place was wretched with the stench of sweat and ale. The men lived down there as well as trained for battle. Luckily I did not have to go into the trenches, we had a balcony to look over the soldiers, where thankfully there was circulation of fresh air. The men were training so hard, you could see a sense of pride in their faces.

Percius rang a bell and General Thracian stopped and looked up to the balcony. He waved someone over, gave him some kind of order, and then he made his way up to where we were. Once he got up to the balcony, he saluted Percius until Percius saluted him back and said, "At ease."

"General, discussions have occurred up at the house and we need to inform you of some decisions. Would you please find your way to the war room as soon as possible?"

"Yes, sir." Robin saluted again, turned and walked out.

"He must be fun at parties," I said to Percius. We both laughed. "Well, I must get back," I said.

"Yes, I suppose we should." We both looked like our puppy had been stolen.

"Well, it was nice to take a little break," I said, always looking for a silver lining. We made it back out to the fresh air, as I took in a deep breath. "I do not believe I have ever appreciated fresh air as much as I do right now."

"Oh I apologize, I have grown used to it. I have forgotten what the stench is like."

"Well, what a useful talent. Does that apply to all distasteful scents or just that terrible combination?"

"Just that one, I am afraid. It is quite a specific tolerance."

"What a shame. Thank you for the distraction."

"You as well." He stuck his tongue out the side of his mouth and made the hand gesture like someone was hanging him by a noose as he

My Name is Agnes

entered the door.

He opened the door. I looked back at him as I walked away and saw the strangest look on his face. I hadn't seen that look before and I had no idea what it meant...What the fuck had Philip done now?

Chapter 20

"No one said he used the Rohypnol on them though, right?" I said shaking.

"No, no, nothing like that."

We finished the rest of our breakfast in silence, swirls of thoughts whistling around in my brain. *Why would he have that drug in his possession if he wasn't using it on someone? Was he using it on Bobbi? Was he using it on other people? Was he stashing it for someone else? Surely the police would've found it. If they found it, wouldn't they have investigated that more? Is the date rape drug used for something else? I'm full, why am I still eating?*

I wiped my mouth and threw my napkin on my plate. "Ok," I got my phone out, "I'm going to search to see if Rohypnol is used for anything other than date rape."

"It's prescribed for anxiety, insomnia, sleep disorders, and seizure disorders, they are also used as skeletal-muscle relaxants."

I put my phone down. "Did you already look that up?" I asked in awe.

With a red face, Stuart said, "I'm in the pharmaceutical industry."

"Oh, that makes sense then." I guessed he mustn't have said he owned The Joint then! That answered that question....sort of. I shivered. "I feel gross talking about Peter."

"That's why I got these shooters, to cleanse us before we have to go digging through his stuff." We licked our hands and poured salt on them, lifted our shooters and Stuart said, "To a successful investigation."

I parroted him, "To a successful investigation." And we shot them.

"I texted my car service," Stuart said. "They can drive us over to Peter's house. I think we've drunk too much to be driving."

Even though I can enchant myself to be sober, I didn't want to argue with him — I had no problem driving over with Stuart.

"I agree, thank you, that's sweet." *So he's in the pharmaceutical business and has a car service. He can't just be a pharmacist, he must own his own pharmacy. That's how he can take time off when he wants to.* I didn't want to do any digging on Stuart and I had forbidden Robin from doing any either. I wanted to find out things the old-fashioned way. I could get hurt easier that way, but who cares — I'm a witch, I can just turn his penis into a turnip or something. Just kidding…sort of.

We got into the back of a Lincoln Town Car. Wow those things were comfy! "So you think we should be writing this stuff down that we find out? Or just make sure that we take pictures of everything?" I asked.

"I'm thinking just take pictures of everything. I don't know."

"So you've got all the security codes and everything, we have carte blanche on the place?"

"Yes, police have done all their fingerprinting, dusting, and whatnot. Although Thomas told me there wasn't much of an investigation, they said it was a clear case of a drug overdose. Thomas was quite pissed that they didn't do a more thorough job of investigating, because he thinks there's more to this case. He's convinced it's not an overdose. You would think after all these years of constant disappointment you would become more jaded, not more blinded. For such an intelligent guy he can be a real dipwad."

"I've known a couple of those types in my day," I said, thinking back.

"Is that right? You, in your great many years on this earth?" Stuart said.

"Yeah," I said seriously, then realizing what I had said, I explained,

"Well, you know, I...I just mean the many people that have come through the doors of Steamers and Dreamers. I have met a lot more people than the average Joe." That was weak, but hopefully it would be enough of an explanation......

Stuart was still looking at me funny when the car started to pull into a driveway. "Well, looks like we have arrived."

Not a minute too soon! I thought. Any longer and he might have wanted a less lame explanation.

We got out of the car and stood out in front of the house for a minute. "Just looks like an innocent, regular house, doesn't it?" I said to Stuart.

"Yeah, kind of surreal. Doesn't look like someone just died in there."

We stood there for another minute.

"Well," I just about jumped out of my skin. "No time like the present," Stuart said as he walked towards the door.

Why was I so jumpy? Get a hold of yourself, Agnes. Don't act like the last time you were here you helped kill a stalking, drugged-up, psychopath or anything.

I followed Stuart to the door as he checked his phone for the code. I looked behind us to make sure no one was watching us, which was ridiculous because we had permission. I laughed a bit.

"What's so funny?" Stuart asked as he was punching in the code.

"Oh, I'm still acting like we're doing something wrong. I just surveyed the area to make sure no one was watching us break into the place with the security code!" I rolled my eyes.

"Well, you have to admit what we're doing is pretty weird. It's kind of hard to shake that "dirty" feeling." The door buzzed and Stuart opened the door. "Ah ha! Success!"

We walked in and took a look around. Obviously the cleaning crew had been here. Not a coaster was out of place. It certainly didn't look like the police had just finished an investigation here. Peter's house was the typical rich kid's house decorated by his mommy. Hardwood floors throughout, beautiful oak cabinetry, stainless steel appliances that probably had never been used, furniture from Ethan Allan.... basically a "show home."

My Name is Agnes

"I think Angelica's been here," I said.

"Somehow I can't see Angelica with rubber gloves and a mop and bucket. More like Angelica's minions have been here," Stuart said.

"Somehow I can't see Peter living like this. He didn't strike me as the Martha Stuart type…" I waved my arms around.

"No, me either. Let's take a look around." We went into the kitchen and looked into the cabinets. Everything seemed normal. There were four settings of dishes and cutlery. He had everything he needed. There were even muffin tins.

"So how long did Peter live here?"

"I think about five years or so."

"Hmmmm."

"What are you thinking?" Stuart looked at me quizzically.

"Well, I just think it's strange that he has exactly four of everything."

"I don't get you." Stuart looked at me sideways as he kept looking through the cupboards.

"Well, I know he's rich and everything, but do you really go out and buy a whole new set of dishware when you break something? I mean, he had to have broken SOMETHING in the five years he lived here."

"That is pretty odd that he has an exact set of everything. And the price tags are still on everything." He picked up a pie dish and showed me the bottom of it.

"Well, I really didn't think he was a baker." I smiled at Stuart. I looked into a cupboard. "Aha!!" I said for dramatic flair and yanked out a jar of nutmeg. "None of these things in the cupboard have been opened either!"

"Ok, now that's odd. Well, not that the nutmeg isn't open, I don't think I even have nutmeg at home, but the fact that nothing is open is pretty odd. Let's look in the pantry."

We both looked in the pantry — nothing was open in there either. "How old is all this stuff?" I asked as I grabbed some cereal. "The expiry on this is three years ago. Now that brings me to two questions."

"Shoot," Stuart said as he leaned back on the pantry shelves.

"Ok, number one: Why aren't these dusty? Somebody has been cleaning this food? That's weird. Number two: Cereal has an expiry date? Since when?"

"Both excellent questions. Let's keep exploring the house and see what else we come up with," Stuart said as he shuffled me out of the pantry.

We made our way into the great room, opening drawers and cupboards as we moved along, finding nothing as we went...meaning literally nothing — there wasn't anything in the drawers and cupboards. Who lives in a house and doesn't have anything in the cupboards and drawers? We went through the living room, family room, whatever else those rooms are called, then we got to the spare bedrooms, and they were decorated like everything else — as if Angelina had decorated them.

Stuart went into the ensuite to check it out and I opened the closet expecting to find nothing, just like everywhere else.

"Uh, Stuart, can you come here for a second?"

He popped his head out of the bathroom. "There's some weird stuff in here..."

"Kid's stuff?" I asked.

"Yeah, what the hell?"

I left the closet door open. "Is the stuff hidden away and the decorative stuff displayed?" I asked Stuart.

"Yup, I take it that's what you found in the closet?"

"Uh-huh." I sat down on the bed. Stuart came and joined me on the bed too.

We sat in silence for a bit. "What are you thinking?" I asked.

"That my nephew was even more fucked up than I originally thought?" Stuart said.

"Besides that."

"I really don't know what to make of this. I really don't want to think the worst, I can't go there."

"I wasn't a big fan of his either and even I don't want to think that of him. Maybe it's not that — maybe it's just a psychological thing. I think we can both agree that he was pretty messed up. Maybe he just liked to decorate this room up like a child's room? I'm going to get the stuff out, see what it looks like."

My Name is Agnes   129

I got the bedding out of the closet and unfolded it onto the bed. It was Spiderman stuff, definitely boy stuff. It looked clean, at least there wasn't any blood on it. That was a good sign, anyway.

"Ok, here's what we'll do — I have a friend that works in a laboratory," I lied. "I can have her test this stuff to see if there's any, ummm, DNA on this bedding so we can find out for sure what kind of a sicko Peter really was; if he was a first class or just a regular sicko."

"That sounds good." Stuart looked shaken but a bit relieved by that.

"I'll fold this stuff up, get a garbage bag and find us a drink. How about you go to the next bedroom and check it out?"

"Um, yeah. I'll do that."

I thought he needed to take a breather, he was obviously upset by all this. He had resigned himself to the fact that Peter was a drug addict a long time ago, but to find out that he might be a pedophile was a whole different ball game!

I was folding Spiderman in half when I heard, "Ummm Agnes?"

I walked to the other room. "Yes Stuart?"

"You might need two garbage bags." He held the closet open full of Strawberry Shortcake bedding.

"Hey Zeus."

"What?"

"Never mind, let's go find that drink. I'm sure this show home would have liquor in the liquor cabinet," I said. We walked downstairs to the liquor cabinet in the den in silence.

"Ah, here we go. I knew it. Full to the brim. I'll go get some ice." I grabbed two glasses and filled them from the ice maker in the fridge. As I walked back into the den I tried to be more cheery and said, "I wonder if that's the first time…" I stopped walking because Stuart was standing there beside another man in a really bad suit, "Agnes, this is Detective Lester."

* * * * *

Eunice came running up to us late that afternoon as everyone sat in the garden discussing lace or tapestries or something equally as boring,

130   *Kelly Brookbank*

and she announced Andias wanted to have a formal dinner that evening. I barely heard her as I was deep in thought, thinking about the look on Percius's face and what it could mean. Everyone looked at each other in surprise, but also delight, as we hadn't seen the men in such a long time.

Sergeant Ina decided we could break early to get ready for the evening's dinner. Or maybe she realized we all had bags under our eyes, which simply wouldn't be presentable, and thought we should all take a cat nap. Either way I was thankful for the early exit.

Ina went to get the kitchen organized for all the guests. Polly's mother and sister were there, as well as other close relatives, the General, his right and left hand men, and other key people whom I had no idea who they were would be there too.

After we were all refreshed and looking our best, we met in the front room for drinks before dinner would be served.

"Have you a notion what this is all about?" I whispered to Percius.

"I might have an inkling," he said without his usual wink or sideways smile. Something was off. I looked at him to see if I could telepathically get anything from him. (I don't have that gift, by the way.) I wasn't able to sneak away to talk to Robin either — Polly's idea of perking up was bitching about Ina.

"You are not going to inform me though are you?"

"No." Finally, a smile!

Dinner was served so we made our way into the dining room to seat ourselves around the table. Even though all the women were anxious to hear what this special dinner was about we still had to have manners. We probably had to wait for the soup course to be over before any announcements would be made. Stupid manners. Percius was starting to lighten up and become more himself again.

Soup was delicious…I'll give it that. *Bring on the main course, damnit!! I am not a patient witch.*

Finally main course was served. Duck. Wow, must be a big deal! We started digging in; it smelled so good we almost forgot about the reason we were there. A tinkling of the wine glass came from Andias. Finally!!

My Name is Agnes   **131**

He cleared his throat. "You might be wondering why I have gathered you all here tonight. I have made a decision and I wanted to share it with all of you as it will affect your lives as well. I have been pondering this for a while now and I feel the time has come for me to step down as king and to leave this country in the capable hands of my son…Alexander."

All of the women let out a gasp and then started clapping, saying "Congratulations", "Good for you", etc… and then, "I cannot believe you will be stepping down!" "You will not be king?" To Ina: "Does that mean you will not be queen?" "I just cannot believe it." Ina just sat there smiling and nodding.

We finished supper and then moved out to the garden where we all celebrated. Everyone was in a grand mood. I understood now why Percius was in a funny mood before. It was a lot to take in for him.

After supper we all stood around talking because it seemed we hadn't seen the men in such a long time.

I cornered Percius with our usual glasses of wine. "How are you truly feeling about all of this?"

"It is all so surreal. Father has been king for such a time, it will be awkward calling Alexander king, not that I will, but you know my meaning. It is truly hard to believe, but I suppose it will take time to get used to. Alexander deserves it, he has been grooming himself for the position since he was born."

"That is not what I meant — how do you FEEL about it?"

"Oh." Percius looked at his glass. "You are suggesting that I am jealous? Of course not. I am the middle child, he is the eldest, why in all the lands would the position have been bestowed on me? He is obviously the right choice. Besides, I am not the right man for the job and I would hate it."

"It still must have stung though, did it not?"

He looked up at me, almost sternly. "How can someone who has known me for such a short time know me so well?"

I shrugged my shoulders.

"Of course it stung. I know I would be the worst person to be king but there is a silly part of me that always hopes one day I will sit on

132 *Kelly Brookbank*

that throne with the crown on my head." The tears welled up in his eyes. I put my hand on his shoulders.

All of a sudden he took a deep breath, closed his eyes, shook his head and said, "But that would mean growing up and I do not plan to do that for a very long time!" He playfully elbowed me. "How are things progressing in wedding central? Are you nearing the end?"

"I would not know. I just do as I am commanded. But I do not believe we are anywhere near the end." That was a strange question to ask as the wedding was months away…"Why would you…" I heard some raised voices coming from the water fountain.

"Ahh," Percius said, "I believe the proverbial ball has dropped."

"Beg pardon? I am officially confused," I said, looking in the direction of the water fountain.

"Well Agnes, as you know, my mother is always a part of any decisions that are made in this house, but I believe this one was made by Father and Father alone."

"Oh…that is not good. Why would he do that?"

"I am not sure, exactly. Maybe because Mother would not have approved of father's choice?"

"Oh?"

"Everyone knows Philip has been Mother's favourite ever since he was born. She has always said he was destined for greatness."

"Really?" I thought I heard some other raised voices, but before I could discover where they were coming from I heard the tinkling of the glass again.

"May I have your attention, please? Please, will everyone gather over here in the middle of the garden?" Alexander bellowed.

We all shuffled our way over to King Alexander.

"As king, I have my first announcement. As you are all aware, Plennsenous is a loathsome and detestable excuse for a human being, but what you might not know is that his army grows stronger as he nears our lands. If we do not act swiftly we will no longer be able to call these lands our own and we will be forced to bow down before Plennsenous."

We collectively said, "Pardon?" and looked at each other and

My Name is Agnes   133

the men. When I looked over at Polly, I noticed she sat there with a stone face, not saying a word. I tried to get her to look at me, but she wouldn't.

Alexander said, "Please, calm down, calm down. We have kept such things from you women because we do not want to worry you. Now do not fret, we have a plan to stop him. Mark my words, he will never own these lands."

We all let out a sigh of relief. Ina said, "Well now, what is this plan of yours?"

I still couldn't get Polly to look at me.

"I will not bore you with the details but we are going to align with Carnacias and Attica, then take our weapons and men to an area they would never suspect, and attack them from behind," Alexander said proudly.

Ina hugged him. "That sounds brilliant, my son."

Ina, being used to sending her husband off to war and knowing how long wars can sometime take said, "All right, we must move the wedding up two months so we can have it before you leave. You will need a few months to prepare for battle anyway. I believe we can have it ready in two months if we really dedicate ourselves." She looked around at all of us. "Right ladies?"

We nodded our heads in acknowledgement,

"I appreciate the sentiment, Mother but I am afraid you are going to have to be ready sooner than that." Alexander looked at her and tried to be as strong as he could now that he was king, but you could still see his legs shaking, because no matter what, she was still his mother.

"And just when do you propose this wedding shall take place, Alexander?"

"In two Saturdays from today."

Polly finally looked at me with a tear rolling down her face.

Chapter 21

I put the glasses down and extended my hand. "Hello, Detective Lester. How are you?"

"I'm fine, thank you."

"I was just making us a drink, would you like one?"

"No thank you, I'm on duty. I was just explaining to Mr. Digion here that I was the detective that was working on Peter's case."

Stuart made a gesture to the chairs. "Why don't we all have a seat?"

"Would you like anything else to drink? Water? To tell you the truth, I don't really even know what else is here other than liquor." I opened the bar fridge. "Ah, there's bottled water in here."

"That would be great," Lester said. I handed him the water with a glass and made Stuart and myself a drink.

"So what brings you by, Detective Lester?" Stuart said.

"Well, to tell you the truth, this whole case doesn't sit well with me."

Stuart and I looked at each other. "What do you mean by that?" Stuart asked.

"I don't mean to cause any offense here, Mr. Digion, but your brother for one thing."

"Oh? And what was odd about my brother?"

"Well." Lester squirmed in his chair a bit. "He didn't want us to do more of an investigation when we suggested we could look into it further. After we initially ruled it a drug overdose, he jumped on

135

that like a woman at a shoe sale. I told my boss that I wanted to look into it some more but your brother obviously has some pull with the superiors in the police department. My boss said it came down from Jesus himself that the investigation stopped there. I was told if I did any more investigating I would be ticketing people for stealing shopping carts."

Stuart and I shot each other a look when Lester wasn't looking.

"I know I shouldn't be here at all but something just doesn't sit right with me."

"What's that, Detective?"

"When we arrived on the scene, your brother was already here and it looked like he was searching for something. He didn't look like he was a grieving father."

"Really?" Stuart said. "That does seem odd. Is there anything else, Detective?"

"It isn't anything in the evidence, it's just a feeling that I get and my hunches are usually pretty accurate." Lester looked at his water bottle.

"What is it, Detective?" Stuart pried.

Lester looked at Stuart, "Usually in these drug addict cases when you have absentee parents, something traumatic has usually happened to an addict as a kid. I'm not trying to give Peter an excuse or anything, but I bet if you do some prying you'll find there's a story there. This one looks like a textbook case to me."

We all sat there lost in our own thoughts for a second or two.

"Well." Lester stood up. "I have taken up enough of your time."

As we were walking to the door, Stuart asked Lester. "So, since Peter is dead, it wouldn't hurt to look at his records, would it? Hypothetically speaking? He was my nephew and if I could clear his name in some small way, then I would like to do that for him."

"Well, of course physical files can't just walk out of police stations, people would notice that."

Stuart and I snickered. Lester did not. Wow, talk about a dry sense of humour.

"But computer files can leave in people's pockets every day... hypothetically. Of course, I'm not allowed to look any further into this case, but if I can help you out in any way, I would be happy to. Sure, I can get you all of his files. They weren't much help to me, but maybe you might recognize some names. There's lots of room on those memory sticks, I'll put whatever I think might be useful on it for you. Have a great day."

After he left, we sat down to finish our drinks. "He could be a great asset," I said.

"What the fuck is up with my brother?"

"Oh yeah, what's his deal? I thought you said he was pissed they didn't do a thorough investigation?"

"That's what he told me. So why would he want the actual police to wrap up their investigation right away, but he would want me to look into it?"

"Maybe there is something incriminating in this house that he didn't want the police to find, but he thinks if you find it you won't tell anyone because you're Peter's uncle and you'll keep it under wraps."

"Like Peter being a pedophile," he said as he took a drink of his scotch.

"We better get that bedding to my friend sooner rather than later." I took my phone out and pretended to text my "friend." Robin texted me back right away. "She can do it tonight after hours. We better get it out of here before Thomas changes his mind and gets rid of the evidence or something!"

I went to the kitchen and got some garbage bags, then we headed upstairs to wrap up the kids' bedding and bath stuff.

We checked out the other rooms upstairs, but nothing was out of the ordinary with them other than they too were bare. Even the master suite upstairs was cleaned out.

"We are obviously missing some part of the house. What's that door?" I said to Stuart. I had assumed it was part of the utility rooms, but I opened it up and it was a bachelor suite. I looked at Stuart and we both smiled. "Now this looks more like Peter."

The whole place was carpeted and it had a huge TV screen on each wall, a great big leather couch, a big coffee table, two leather gaming chairs in front of one of the TV screens, DVDs stacked everywhere on

My Name is Agnes   137

one wall, video games stacked on the other wall, a pool table, and a fooseball table. In place of a kitchen table there was a queen-sized bed, and across from the bed was a fully stocked bar, an apartment-sized kitchen with a breakfast nook and bar stools, and across from that was a three-piece bathroom. Everything a bachelor could dream of.

"I think this would be a good place to start looking, don't you?" Stuart asked.

"First thing tomorrow, you bet!" I said. "I think we should get this bedding to my friend and then I think we should eat. I'm getting hungry. What do you think?"

"That sounds like a good plan."

We left Peter's house and locked it up. I gave the address of the laboratory Robin had texted me to the driver when we got into Stuart's car service. He had enchanted a woman there into testing the linens for us. He also gave me a full description of the woman and enchanted her into thinking that we were old friends.

Stuart said, "Where do you want to go for supper?"

"How about Japanese?" I said.

"Great. I'll pick you up about 7:00, does that give you enough time to get ready?"

"That sounds just perfect. I'll text you my address."

"So how long will it take to get the results from the bedding?" Stuart asked.

"She's doing it on her own time, so I'm sure she's going to want to push it through as soon as she can. I'm not sure if this is exactly "kosher." (I love making air quotes.) "She'll probably have it done tonight."

"I wonder if your friend would have any CSI type kits we could use for our investigation?"

"What do you mean CSI kits?"

"You know, like the ones they use on TV?"

"Oh! Those ones."

"You don't know what I'm talking about do you?"

"Of course I...yeah I really don't. I'm a reader, not a TV watcher. Did you want to stop the car right here and let me out? I can find my own way home." I inched over toward the door.

Stuart laughed. "It's really ok that you don't watch TV. I prefer books over TV too. It's just when I can't fall asleep sometimes, TV helps me to shut off my brain."

"Oh, phew." I moved back over towards him and brushed my forehead with the back of my hand. "I was starting to like you!" I hit him on the arm like we were in junior high school. *Holy shit, did I just say I liked him?* I looked at him wide-eyed. He smiled and looked at me. I looked down at my lap, "Ummm...I mean.....you know....we get along and..."

He cut me off with a kiss.

"Oh! That was nice," I said in my flirty voice.

The driver snapped us back into reality with, "We have arrived, sir."

"Ok," I said.

"Well," Stuart said.

We both looked around like we were looking for something. "Comforters." I pointed to the trunk.

"Right," Stuart said.

I started to get out.

"I'll help you with that," Stuart said as he got out of the other door.

We reached into the back of the car to grab the garbage bags and our hands touched. I felt the electricity between us now. I looked up at him and my face instantly went red. Why had I never done anything about this? I could not have my face getting red all the time! Too embarrassing! We'd have to chat about this on the ride to the cars.

We walked up to the receptionist in the lab. "Hi Meagan?" I said shakily. I thought this was my "friend" but I wasn't absolutely sure. I knew it was after hours, but who knows how late the receptionist stays?

"Hi Agnes!" She came around the desk to give me a hug. "It's been a while, we should go for coffee soon."

"Yeah, definitely. Hey, thanks for doing this for me, I really appreciate it."

"Oh don't worry about it, anything for you. Are these the specimens?"

"Sure are." Meagan took them from us and started to leave. I said

My Name is Agnes   139

as she turned, "Thanks again and I'll text you about that coffee."

"Sounds good. Bye Agnes."

Stuart and I gave each other a weird look as we started to leave. "That was strange," Stuart said.

"Even for Meagan," I said. "I guess she wants to get it done as soon as possible." We left the laboratory and headed for the car.

Once we got in the car Stuart said, "Ummm, so about that kiss."

"Yeah, I know. Ummm."

Then at the same time, we both said, "Can we just forget it happened?"

We both started laughing. "Oh good. I didn't want it to get weird between us."

"Me either," Stuart said.

"Plus my face turns red all the time and I look like a total weirdo, so I'm glad we worked that out! So, hey, on a totally unrelated note — you said you were in the pharmaceutical business, right?"

Stuart looked sheepish, "Uh, yeah, why?"

"I could've sworn you said, "I own the place" when I asked you how you got into The Joint yesterday..."

"Close. I said, "My buddy owns the place.""

"Oh, ok — that makes sense. There are our cars. We still on for Japanese tonight?"

"You bet, I'll pick you up at 7:00."

"I'm texting you my address right now," I said as we got out of the car. "Text me when you're close and I'll come down," I said to Stuart as we were both standing outside of the Town Car.

"That sounds great. I'll see you in a little bit." He leaned down and kissed me and we both got into our respective cars. *Wait a minute, did that just happen?* I got out of my car. Stuart got out of his.

"What was that?" I said to Stuart.

"I don't know! Seemed pretty natural though."

"It did, didn't it?" I shook my head. "Weird." I shrugged my shoulders.

"Whatever, see ya later."

"Yup." We got into our cars again.

As I was driving home I realized I'd given out my address...I never did that! What was happening to me? When I got home, Robin tried to take my temperature. He was shocked at what I was doing too.

I got ready in half an hour and Stuart texted that he was near so I went down to meet him.

We went to the restaurant and things were just the same as always, like we were best friends. We were having a great time — it was the perfect restaurant for us because the restaurant owner was crazy. Our chef was great, but the owner kept going around scaring the shit out of everybody. A family that was at our teppenyaki had been coming there every year for eighteen years on the mom and dad's anniversary. Stuart had been frequenting that restaurant for the past five years, but this was my first visit. The owner, of course, picked up on this and often snuck up behind me with various forms of loud instruments.

While we were eating, Stuart's phone went off so he took it outside to answer it. I was obviously quite entertained on my own inside the restaurant. When Stuart came back in, he said, "Just as we suspected. Thomas wants us to look for something." And he took a shot of sake.

* * * * *

There was an uproar from the women as well as laughter from Ina. "Alexander, my son, may I have a word with you?" Ina sternly said to her king.

With, I'm sure, the most amount of balls he has ever shown, Alexander said, "No Mother, you may not. We cannot put this battle off any longer than two weeks. There is just no other way to avoid it. You women will just have to do your best. Now if you will excuse us, we men have much work to do."

I looked over at Polly as Philip leaned down and kissed her on her cheek and then walked away. He did look sorry, I'll give him that. I immediately walked over and sat next to Polly, who broke down in tears and fell into my arms. All the other women started crying as well, I think Ina was still in shock from her son speaking to her that way for the first time in his life.

My Name is Agnes

I pulled Polly away from me and said to her sternly. "Now listen to me. I will fix this. Dry those tears. You will have your wedding in two Saturdays from now and it will be the most beautiful wedding you have ever seen. Do you understand me?"

I stood up. "All right ladies, stop your weeping. We have a job to do. We are going to have this wedding and it will be grand. My father is an adventurer and he just happens to be in Boneapia right now, where they make the most beautiful silks and have an abundance of beautiful flowers. I will get word to him and he and his crew will be here. Until he gets here, we need to make sure that everyone knows that the date has changed. We need to alert the chefs, gardeners, all the help! Come on ladies, we are capable of doing this for Polly."

Every one of them was staring at me with her mouth agape. Once what I said sunk in, Eunice was the first to stand up. "You are right, Agnes. We can do this!"

Ina stood up. "That is most gracious of your father and will be the utmost help." Ina started giving directions to everyone, basically mimicking everything that I had just said.

Polly took my hand and pulled me to the side. She gave me a big hug. When she looked at me there was a tear rolling down her face again. "Why are you crying now, Polly?"

"The tears I shed before were because I thought my world had come crashing down around me. My dream wedding was becoming a nightmare and I thought Philip was going away to war before I could fully commit to him and show everyone how much I loved him." I wiped the tear from her face. "But the reason I cry now is because I am so grateful to the Gods for giving you to me. I could not have asked for anyone so special in my life, Agnes. You are the best friend anyone in this world could ever have." She hugged me again.

I felt a strange feeling just then. I had never cried before, but I think that was the closest I had come to it. "I love you too, Polly. I would do anything for you. Now, I need to go get word to my father or your wedding will be full of rags and lily pads!"

It took two days for "my father" to get there. Robin wasn't too happy about being out of the war room but it was necessary. Once

142   *Kelly Brookbank*

he got there with his friends and his tickle trunk full of supplies, the wedding plans went smoothly.

I had to act like I hadn't seen my "father" for a long time, and Robin was hamming it up, like usual. I think he was punishing me for pulling him from the war room. Once we had retired for the night and I showed him to his room we finally had a moment to ourselves. "You are really enjoying this, are you not?" I said, playfully glaring at him.

"You know me, always make the most of every situation!"

"Just a few weeks, Robin, then you can go back to normal," I said as I started walking out of his room.

I nearly ran into Percius as I walked out into the hallway. "Geez, Percius, you could have broken my nose or more disastrous — spilled your wine!"

"Sorry, darling." He looked shaken and confused. "Who is Robin?"

"My father," I replied. Trying to think quickly I said, "You see, we do not have the traditional father — daughter relationship." I grabbed his arm as we started walking downstairs. "He is away a lot exploring and I had to grow up earlier than most girls should, so I started to call him Robin instead of Father. I know it seems silly."

"Not at all, actually."

Phew, I think my story may have convinced him. "Were you looking for me?" I asked.

"It was nothing," he said, "I must get some sleep." He kissed me on the cheek and headed to his house. Since Percius "entertained" so much he had his own house built on the grounds.

The day of the wedding was a bit strange for everyone. It was a happy occasion but it also had the feeling of impending doom, because the men were going off to war the next day. Mixed feelings were an understatement. We were all trying to forget about the war and concentrate on the wedding. As a distraction, there was more wine flowing than usual, which lead to more strange things. Ina was actually being pleasant. That threw everyone a curveball! And Percius was drinking less than everyone. I was probably the only one who noticed that because no one notices a sober person when you're drunk.

The nuptials went smoothly, dinner was delicious, and the

My Name is Agnes   **143**

reception was beautiful. I kept noticing Percius looking at me funny and he still wasn't drinking like he usually did. Had my story about Robin not convinced him? Was he putting the puzzle pieces together about me? Betting, that day at the Olympics? Robin showing up as my dad? *No. This couldn't be happening.* Come to think about it, he wasn't even flirting with women like he usually does. He must have really been upset. *No, this can't be. There must be some other explanation. He's probably just upset about going to war. But that would make him drink more. If I know anyone, Percius would be drinking more! Shit, what am I going to do? I need some air.*

"I need some air," I quietly said to Eunice, as I grabbed my wine glass and headed outside. There were quite a few people outside so I maneuvered my way around them and headed to the war room. I figured there wouldn't be anyone in there. As I got closer, just as I suspected, the room was in darkness.

I reached for the handle of the door, but before I could open it, someone else's hand turned the handle and opened the door for me. "Ladies first," Percius said.

"Oh, if you wanted to go in there alone, I can go elsewhere."

"Do not be silly, I have wanted to see you all day."

"Oh?" My heart started racing. "Why is that?" He shuttled me inside the door. It was dark inside the war room, there was just the reflection flowing in from the moon and the light coming in from the house.

"Would you like some more wine?" he said.

"My glass is full," I lied. "Where is your glass?"

"I have not been drinking that much today."

"I have noticed, why is that?"

"You look stunning, Agnes."

"Thank you, Percius." How many women had he said that to? "Why are you not drinking today? Is everything all right?"

With a glare in his eyes, mouth slightly open, and front teeth grinding, he started slowly walking closer to me, studying me from my feet to my head, eventually landing on my eyes.

My back was leaning against a wall with nowhere to go.

He stopped with inches between us. "My mind has been thinking of nothing but you lately, Agnes."

"Well that is natural, you are…"

"Shut up."

I pressed my lips together and nodded.

"I have always enjoyed the company of many women."

I opened my mouth to talk. Percius closed his eyes in annoyance. I shut my mouth again.

"But since I have met you, I have not been able to stop thinking about you. I have not thought of another woman. I have not wanted another woman. Just you, Agnes. And it is not only because you are the most beautiful woman I have ever seen…" He took a step back to look at me, shook his head, and made an "mmmm" sound. Now he stepped in closer so our bodies were touching and he held my hands. "It is because you understand me, you get my sense of humour, *you* have the best sense of humour, you just…"

He tilted his head and kissed me, slowly at first, then he parted my lips with his tongue and kept kissing me. He dropped my hands and took my head in his.

When he stopped kissing me he had tears in his eyes. "Agnes, I have never felt this way about anyone, I swear to all the gods. I just could not go off to war without telling you."

"I know," I said, "me too."

He started kissing me again, then dropped his hands down to my waist, and lifted me up so my legs could wrap themselves around his waist. He walked me over to the desk, sat me down on the edge, and started kissing me down my neck until he got to the clasp that held up one side of my doric. He undid the clasp and it let go to expose my breast. As it did, Percius let in a gasp. He looked at me and gave me that little mischievous grin. I smiled back at him. He kissed me softly as he cupped my breast and played with my nipple. I bit his lip a little. He gave me a bigger smile this time.

He pulled me off the desk so we were standing, our bodies pressed together again and undid the other clasp, exposing both my breasts. I undid his belt and it fell to the ground, and he did the same to my

My Name is Agnes   145

belt, except when my belt let go so did my doric. Without thinking I crossed my arms in front of my stomach as I stood there naked.

He took my hands and put them out to the side. "Why do you do that?"

"I do not know. Perhaps because you look like a god?"

Percius looked down at my naked body. He took one breast at a time in his mouth and gently kissed it, biting it slightly before doing the same to the other breast. He kissed his way across my collarbone and up my neck. "You have no idea of your beauty, do you?" he whispered as he started kissing me gently again, his hands slightly caressing the curves of my back sending shivers up and down my body.

Oh I had had enough of this! I pushed him away and took his doric up and off his head. This man had to have been made by the gods themselves. I took my fingers and ran them across his defined abdomen then up across his chest. I sure hope I wasn't drooling, that wouldn't look good, but I really didn't care at this point.

I heard Percius growl and he said, "Agnes, I can not stand it any longer." He picked me up and walked me over to lay me on the settee. He started gently kissing me down my torso and down around my belly button, his hands caressing the insides of my thighs. I thought I could feel something wet on my stomach. I lifted Percius's head up. "Are you not happy, my love?" I said confused.

"I do not believe I have ever been this happy in my life," he said with tears falling down his face and landing on his smile. That gorgeous smile.

"Then why the tears?" I kissed him.

"Because I have to leave you tomorrow."

I kissed him again. I ran my fingers down the side of his body, over his buttocks, then inside his thighs. He shivered. I felt for his hand with my other hand and put it between his legs to navigate him inside me.

He looked at me, "Are you sure about this?"

"More sure than anything."

We fit together like we were made for each other. We moved together like we were built for each other. Every time he moved made

146   *Kelly Brookbank*

me feel even better, which I didn't think was possible. When I kissed a different part of his body he got even more excited. It was complete ecstasy. We went on until we were completely exhausted. Then we just lay there looking at each other and holding each other.

"I bet you would like that wine now, would you not?" I teased Percius.

"If I thought my legs could function, I most definitely would fetch us some, but that would mean leaving you so no, I do not." He kissed me.

"I suppose we must go back to the wedding once we have our breath," I said with obvious disappointment.

Percius laughed. "You have false thoughts if you believe I am to spend any of my last moments before I leave for war anywhere but naked with you."

I thought about it. "You are correct. But we must vacate, we do not want to be discovered like this in the morning by your father and brothers."

We got dressed and I tried to make my hair look as presentable as I could. We both grabbed wine glasses and filled them up from the bar in the war room then headed outside. It's not like it was strange to see the two of us together, after all. We took a wide berth around the wedding and headed to Percius's house.

Once we were out of earshot and away from prying eyes, he grabbed me and kissed me hard, pressing me up against a tree. Before we knew what was happening, both our dorics were up and he was taking me against the tree. Our bodies were so in tune, we both came at the same time and groaned into each other's necks.

"Holy shit, that was a first for me," I said.

"Me, as well," Percius said, as he grabbed my hand and we continued to his house. I looked at him suspiciously.

He looked at me, "I am serious." I could tell he was telling the truth. "I have never wanted anyone like I want you, Agnes." We stopped in front of his house and he kissed me. "I love you, Agnes." I smiled at him and we went inside.

"We are in need of new wine glasses," Percius said. We had left ours

My Name is Agnes   **147**

at the tree. "The bedroom is up the stairs and down to the end of the hallway. I will get some wine and meet you there.

I was standing outside the bedroom when Percius came down the hallway with the wine and glasses. "What are you doing out here, gorgeous? And more importantly, why are you not naked?"

"Well," I said, "See for yourself," as I opened the door. Percius looked at me oddly as he went in the bedroom. I followed him and we both stood staring at the naked woman in his bed.

Chapter 22

As we got to Peter's place the next day, we set our coffees down in the newly found "man cave." "So, explain this to me again? What did Thomas say last night?"

"He wants us to look for an antique, hand-painted pin from Angelica's mother that she kept in a little case. Peter swore he didn't steal it from Angelica, but Thomas thinks he did and he was going to give it to Bobbi. Thomas said it would've broken Angelica's heart if she found out her son stole it from her."

"What do you think?" I asked Stuart.

"I'm not sure, it's a pretty elaborate story," he said.

"That makes it even more suspicious," I said as we finished our muffins. We had stopped by Steamers and Dreamers to stock up on coffees and muffins…ok, I wanted to check on the store too. "Well, should we get started?" Stuart asked. "I'll start at this end and you can start at the entertainment end?"

"Now that sounds like a deal, I did not want to deal with the bathroom!" I wiped my forehead.

"Yeah, I figured as much." He looked at me out of the corner of his eye. Just as he got into the bathroom, I got a text from Meagan.

I shouted to Stuart, "Meagan just texted me — the linens are clean. So at least your nephew isn't a pedophile."

"That's the best news I've heard in a long time," he said as he poked

149

his head out of the door. "So why have the kids' linens then?"

I pointed at him. "Now that's a good question."

I went through the movies, opening them up to make sure there wasn't anything hiding in them and to make sure there were the actual movies inside. Once I started getting down the stack there started to be two movies in each case, and the other movie was always a cartoon.

Stuart came out of the bathroom. "Nothing out of the ordinary in there, other than everything is vanilla."

I looked at him.

"What? I like vanilla."

I told him about the movies.

"Well maybe he likes cartoons and he's embarrassed about displaying them?"

"Could be," I said.

Stuart opened up the first cupboard in the kitchen. "Holy shit."

I stood up. "What?"

"Come here, does this look strange to you?"

I walked into the kitchen and looked into the cupboard. "Holy shit." The cupboard was full of kids' candies, and most of them were vintage types; there were Tootsie Rolls, Candy Charm Bracelets and Necklaces, Laffy Taffy, Caramel Apple Pops, Big League Chew, Runts, Curly Wurly, Baby Bottle Pops, Pop Rocks, Good & Fruity, Gummi Worms, Tart n' Tinys, Air Heads, Push Pops, Gummi Cola Bottles, Bottle Caps, Sour Patch Kids, Cow Tales, Lemonheads, Big Red Gum, Fun Dip, ICEE Squeeze Candy, Mint Julep, Scooter Pie, Nigger Babies, Megalollies, Hubba Bubble Gum Tape, Chiclets, Ring Pops, Astro Pops, Chupa Chups, Jelly Bellys, Cherry Sours, Nerds, Twizzlers, Buckeyes, Rock Candy, Gobstoppers, Gummi Blue Sharks, and Zotz. The cupboards were packed with candies.

"Where the hell did he even get some of these? I haven't seen these candies since I was a kid!" Stuart said as he pulled the Scooter Pie out.

"I don't even recognize most of these," I said.

"What?" Stuart looked at me like I was growing a plant out of the side of my head. "Didn't you eat candy as a kid?"

"No, my parents didn't allow us sweets when we were growing up,"

I lied. Truth was, since I was never a child on this earth I had never really tried any of this!

"Oh you have got to try some of this stuff!" Stuart suddenly turned into a child; he was downright giddy! He turned around and looked into the fridge. "Oh my God!"

I spun around, "What?" I thought there was severed heads in there or something.

"This is full of my favourite old pops growing up too! Crush, Fanta, Sunny Soda Pop, Frostie Soda, Jolt Cola, A&W Root Beer, Slice, Mello Yellow, Tab!"

"Shit, you scared me Stuart!"

"Sorry, but this is awesome!" He pulled out a bunch of different kinds of pop and put them on the counter then turned around and directed his attention to the candy in the cupboard once again.

"You sure this is ok?" I said, feeling a bit awkward.

"I don't think Peter will mind."

I shrugged my shoulders, "That's true."

"Ok, what will we start with? Ah, I have it — Fun Dip. Ok, rip the top off and pull the stick out and suck on it like so."

I copied him. "Simple enough," I mused.

"Now dunk it in the other side and suck on it again."

I copied again. "Genius!"

He opened a Frostie Soda for me. "A Frostie Soda for you madam, to cleanse the palate."

I tipped my head, "Thank you, sir." I took a drink. "Ohhhhh, now that's a tasty Frostie Soda!"

"I hate to be bold this early in our relationship but I would like to give you something…actually two things, but they're a matching set." He pulled the wrappers off. "In case you get hungry in between tastings." He put the Candy Charm Bracelet on my wrist then the necklace over my head and onto my neck.

"They do look lovely together. I shall never remove them…Unless I have eaten them all or unless I take a shower, whichever comes first."

Stuart put his hands together in front of him. "I knew you would love them."

My Name is Agnes   **151**

He looked into the cupboard again. "Oh you have got to try these! I love these. Thankfully they're still on the market. Or they have come back on the market, I'm not sure, but anyway, you can still get them. They're called pop rocks." He ripped open the package and put some in my palm. "Now you just pop them in your mouth."

"Ok," I said. Immediately they started exploding in my mouth. "What the hell?"

Stuart started laughing and threw some in his mouth. "Aren't they awesome?"

I let them calm down. "You could've warned me."

"That wouldn't have been any fun! Here, have some root beer." He handed me the A&W and I took a gulp.

"That is fantastic! I love that drink! Mixed with the Pop Rocks is even better!" I took some more pop rocks, threw them in my mouth, and shot the root beer. "Oh my gourd, that is bliss! Are there Root Beer-flavoured Pop Rocks?"

He looked into the cupboard. "No, I don't see any."

"Well they should make it, that would be awesome."

This went on for a while, with Stuart wanting me to try all his favourites, which seemed to be all of them until we were on a sugar high.

"Hey! I have an idea!" I said (or most likely yelled).

"What?"

"Let's take the rest of these to the entertainment side of the room with some pop and try them while we play some video games?"

"That's bbbrrrilliant!" We stuffed our cheeks with Big League Chew, put a ring pop on each finger, and then pulled the bottom of our shirts up to carry the candy to the other side of the room. Then we had to make a second trip for the pop.

We looked at the videos then looked at each other. The games were titled: *Assassin's Creed, Mortal Kombat, Dark Souls, Castlevania, The Witcher, Metal Gear, Plants vs. Zombies, Destiny, TitanFall.*

"I'm not sure these games are going to be up our alley…" Stuart said.

"Well let's try this one." I grabbed the video game named

Middle-Earth and opened it up. Just like the movies, the right video game was in it but there was another video game in it also, which was *Sonic the HedgeHog 2*. "Check it out! Just like the movies! Oh thank gourd, 'cause I was not about to play *Dagger Daddy* or whatever those games are."

"Let's see what else there is," Stuart said and we started opening up the videos at warp speed.

"Holy Crap. I found Pokemon!" Stuart shouted.

"Is that good?" I tried to sound excited.

Stuart looked deflated. "Don't tell me you didn't play video games either."

"Sorry, sheltered childhood, I guess. I found *Legend of Zelda*?"

"Awesome sauce!" Stuart grabbed it. "We're putting that in the jersey for suresy pile. Oh. My. God. Super Mario World," he said in a high-pitched girly voice.

"Jersey pile?"

"For suresy!!"

"*Banjo-Kazoo...*" I looked squint-eyed at the game I found, trying to read the title.

"Banjo-Kazoozie?" He grabbed it and started dancing around. "We're playing this first!!" He grabbed an Astro Pop for us both. "Here, suck on this!"

I jumped into the gaming chair, crossing my feet as Stuart put the game in the machine.

After we played at least six different games stuck in our chairs, we found *Dance Dance Revolution* and played that for about half an hour, falling down and laughing our asses off before Stuart all of a sudden went running for the bathroom.

I stood up. "What's wrong? Are you ok?" I thought it was kind of weird as he went whizzing past me, then all of a sudden I felt a bit light-headed myself. I needed some air! I went out the back by the pool area. Oh that felt better, there was a bit of a breeze today. But it was still really hot out. Too hot...*Oh, I'm not feeling good!* All of a sudden I threw up in Peter's pool. Hmmmm, that kind of looked cool, some really psychedelic colors! I was not cleaning that up. I looked

My Name is Agnes   153

around to see if Stuart was coming, and he wasn't coming yet, so I just "got rid" of it myself.

I can usually make myself feel better when I'm not feeling well, but that had really snuck up on me quick-like! I knew I should probably go check on Stuart and see if he appreciated his throw-up as much as I did. I walked into the house and he was still in Peter's bachelor pad, so I decide to make us my healing Cuba Libre and order us some food.

I was sitting on the couch when he came out of the bathroom. He had obviously been throwing up and did not look well. I could not help but laugh. He covered his face with his hands.

"Aww, I'm sorry, come here and have a drink."

"Oh Christ, I could not even think about having a drink right now, especially something with pop in it!"

"Trust me, this will make you feel better."

He looked at me warily. "Ok, if you say so." He took a sip and sat back.

"We're so stupid. We shouldn't have eaten all that sugar and then danced." He looked at me. "Why do you still look gorgeous?"

"I don't think Peter's pool echoes the same sentiment...I just yacked in it. It was really pretty though."

"Did you just say you thought your puke was pretty?"

Did he just say he thought I was gorgeous? "It was! It was all these really cool colors. Maybe it just looked that way because it was floating in the pool," I said embarrassed.

"You're gross."

"I know."

We drank some more. Stuart was looking better already.

I broke the ice. "So Peter had children's bedroom linens in the upstairs bedrooms, fridge full of old sodas, and cupboards full of children's candy. Children's movies and vintage video games hidden down here. What does all this mean?"

Stuart groaned. "I don't know. Seems like he was trying to hang onto his childhood or trying to be a child. I know he was a happy kid. When I took him and Isabella out we always had a great time, then all of a sudden he changed. Seemed like overnight he was a different kid. Started getting into trouble, couldn't be controlled, he turned into a little monster. Maybe Detective Lester was right, maybe something happened to him. You know what? Let's get out of here. I've had enough for today."

"I've ordered some food but I can cancel it. You're looking better, are you feeling better?"

"Yeah, I feel way better, thank you."

"Ok, let's clean this place up and get out of here."

I called to cancel the food and Stuart started to clean up our wreckage. He cleaned the kitchen and I picked up the empty wrappers in the entertainment area. I was picking up the wrappers around the couch when I felt something down in the cushions. I reached in and it was a cell phone.

"Stuart, look at this."

"Is that Peter's cell phone?"

I fiddled with it, "I don't know, it's locked."

"Here let me try." He tried Peter's birth date and Isabella's birth date.

"I'll try," I said. I tried Bobbi's birth date and that didn't work, but then I plunked in four other numbers and it unlocked.

"How did you get it open?"

"The numbers spelled BOBI."

"You're so smart." He put his arm around my waist and kissed my forehead. "Now let's check out who Peter's contacts were."

Just then I got a tingle in my stomach. I was definitely developing feelings for Stuart. But I'd just met him! Maybe I was just horny…

We both looked down at the phone and scrolled through the contacts, which took us about twenty seconds.

"Wow, I think I've made that many contacts in the last week," I said.

"No kidding. I knew he was a weirdo, but holy…! Maybe if we drop this phone off with Detective Lester he could do a background check on these contacts for us?"

"He did say 'anything we need,'" I said.

"Doesn't hurt to ask. I'll go give him a call." Stuart went into the hallway to call Lester, and I finished cleaning up.

My Name is Agnes

"Yup. He says to drop the phone off and he'll run a check on all of them."

"Sweet."

"What about you and me take a night off from detective work tonight?"

"Oh, sure," I said, a bit hurt. "I've probably got some stuff to catch up on."

"Well, if you must. I just thought we could finish that date we started a couple of nights ago."

That tingle in my stomach started again. "That sounds great! What did you have in mind?"

"I saw a picnic basket in Peter's garage. I thought I would grab a blanket from his closet, we can walk to the grocery store around the corner, then head to the park across the street?"

The tingle was starting to grow. "That sounds perfect."

* * * * *

"Oh for the burning gates of Hades! This is Kordinia. I have told her over and over that I do not wish to be with her, but she can not understand this!" He went over to his bed. "Kordinia." He shook her. "Kordinia!!" She began to wake up. "Come on Kordinia, you have to leave." He threw her doric at her. "Get dressed, you will go at once."

Kordinia started to realize where she was. "Percius, my love. Come to bed. I will pleasure you."

Percius grabbed her arm and pulled her off the bed. "Kordinia, get up and get dressed. I have told you I do not wish to be with you. I have met my true love. Now go."

Kordinia looked at me and grabbed her doric to put on. She laughed, clearly drunk. "Percius with one woman. What a funny tale."

Percius said in a stern tone, "It is true. Leave."

She grabbed her wine glass and glared at Percius, "You will pay for this," she hissed, and she stumbled out.

Percius came to me and hugged me, "I am sorry about her. Do not listen to her words, she is drunk. You are my love, my only love." He kissed me. "Let us have some wine." He grabbed my hand, pulled me over to the bed, and poured us both a glass of wine as we sat up in bed.

"Tell me about every woman you have been with," I say to Percius.

He looked at me with shock in his eyes. "Agnes…" he stammered.

"I am playing with you Percius!" I laughed.

"Oh, thank the gods," Percius answered, with relief in his eyes.

"I do not care about the women you have bedded, Percius. What I care about is how you feel here and now. And how I feel…and I love you, Percius."

"Those are the sweetest words in this world." He rolled over to kiss me. Then he took both of our wine glasses out of our hands, set them on the table beside the bed, and crawled on top of me. He unlatched both of my clasps, undid my belt, and pulled my doric off, leaving me exposed. He pulled his belt and his doric off as well. Grabbing his wine glass, he gave me a small drink and poured the rest of his wine from my throat to the tops of my thighs. Then he licked every drop of wine off me.

There wasn't one part of my body that didn't feel the passion and the explosion that this man created in me, over and over again. I wanted to sink my body into his, I wanted to devour this man.

We made love all night, stopping to catch our breath, and then talking some more. We loved what we each said and had so much fun that it always led to more love-making.

Eventually though, it was morning and time for the men to go. We all gathered at the gates, the soldiers already on their horses or standing guard waiting for their commands. All the women were bawling and saying good-bye to their respective men. I was saying good-bye to Percius. I had already said my good-bye to him at his house, as we knew Alexander wouldn't allow this to go on long because he didn't have a woman to say good-bye to.

Alexander gave the command and they were gone.

As is the custom, the women stood there watching the men go off to war until we could no longer see them, which I think is ridiculous, but whatever. Polly and I walked arm in arm back into the house to have our tea.

My Name is Agnes　　　157

"Where did you escape to last night?" Polly said.

"Percius was feeling down so I kept him company," I said, looking at her to see if that was going to be enough of an explanation.

Eunice came in just at that moment. "So are you and Percius getting married next?"

"What?" Polly asked, looking at me, shocked.

"Did you not see them saying good-bye today?" Eunice said, in her teasing voice.

"I must admit, I did not notice anyone else but Philip. Agnes, do tell!"

"There is not much to tell, we are in love," I said. "We just finally admitted it last night. Percius did not want to leave without telling me."

They both squealed and hugged me. "Oh, I could not be happier for you, Agnes!" Polly said, "Or for me! We are already like sisters, now this will connect us further!"

"We are all one happy family!" Eunice squealed again.

It took some time to adjust to the absence of the men, but they had spent most of their time in the war room so it wasn't that much of an adjustment. I found the nights to be lonely. Percius and I had just finally admitted our love and then he was taken away from me. I moved into his house. His smell reminded me of him so that was a comfort. Plus I didn't want Kordinia sneaking in anywhere. I swear, if I had seen her, I wouldn't have been able to control my magic. I wouldn't have killed her, but she might have accidentally succumbed to an unfortunate incident involving scissors, her hair, glue, and turkey bones.

We settled into a routine after a while and things became tedious so I was always trying to lighten the mood with harmless pranks. Eunice was easily shocked, so she was often the brunt of the joke.

On one particular morning, Eunice came down to the table to eat. She grabbed an olive, but I had replaced it with a cow's eye. Of course she screamed and threw it in the air as we all laughed. The only thing different this morning, as she had fallen for this particular joke many times, was that Polly went running for the bathroom.

I, of course, followed her.

I heard her retching. "Are you all right?"

When she was done, she came out with her face white as a ghost.

"Oh my, Polly. You look horrible."

"I did not sleep my usual slumber, that is all." She tried to smile. "I will just go back and rest. I am sure to be feeling myself in no time."

"I will accompany you." I walked with her, taking her arm in mine. "Once you are in bed, I will bring you some bread."

"Thank you, Agnes." Polly was asleep before her head hit the pillow. I checked on her later — the bread was gone but she was sleeping again. The next morning I sat at the table waiting for her. When she came down she didn't look like she'd had any sleep.

"Polly, you look like shit."

"Thank you, my friend," she looked at me annoyed. "I slept all day but I was up all night throwing up."

"Well sit down and have some bread and cheese," I said. Polly looked like she was going to hurl again. I smiled. "It is not like I offered you the olives."

"I am glad my ailment amuses you," she sneered at me.

"Sorry, I was just thinking of something."

"Olives?" Polly looked at me through narrowed eyes.

"Yeah," we both giggled.

Ina came in. "What are you girls giggling at?" she said down her nose.

"Nothing, ma'am," Polly said.

She looked at Polly. "Good. Are you feeling better then?"

"A bit, yes," Polly said.

"Well." Ina tried to look mean. "Just do not strain yourself." And she left the room.

"I am not sure why she feels she has to be so hard-nosed," Polly said, shaking her head. "I know she has a big heart, she just chooses not to show it."

"Strange, I get it!"

"Oh shit." Polly bolted for the bathroom.

I just let her be. Normally I would be giving her a special drink

My Name is Agnes　　　**159**

to get rid of her illness, but I had to make sure of something first. I walked to the bathroom Polly was exercising the right to puke in.

"Darling, you promise to make your way to bed after you are finished?"

"Ohhhh yesss. I promise!"

"All right, I am just going outside for the shortest amount of time. I will be back before you know it. I love you!" I made my way outside to the grain fields then back to Polly's room. Polly was resting.

"How are you feeling?" I asked.

"I feel the gods are punishing me, but for what I am not sure."

"Shall we start to make a list?" I asked her.

"Even when I am near death you can always make me smile. Seriously Agnes, if this is a grave illness I do not believe you should be near me."

"Oh Polly, I am not going anywhere, so you shall have to get used to my face right beside your bed. But do not be silly, you are not near death and I have a test to prove it."

"What?" Polly looked at me confused.

"Now, it may seem a bit unorthodox, but I need you to urinate on these barley and wheat seeds." I gave her the bowl of seeds.

"You want me to what now?"

"Oh just trust me and go urinate in this bowl. Or sit right there and relieve yourself, I really do not care, as long as these seeds become saturated with your urine it matters not to me." I shoved the bowl at her with a very serious face.

She looked at me for a moment until she realized I was serious, then she shrugged her shoulders, took the bowl to the bathroom and peed in it.

"Here you go," she said as she handed me to bowl. "Now what do we do?"

"We wait." I set the bowl on the other side of the room, came back and sat down. "How are you feeling? Can I get you anything?"

"Bread?" Polly said, confused as hell.

For the next four hours Polly napped and ate bread. I cooled off a cloth to place on her forehead. We talked. We laughed. I acted out

160   *Kelly Brookbank*

plays and stories that ran through my head. Any time she asked about the bowl of pee, I just said she would have to wait.

Finally after enough time had lapsed I walked over to the bowl and brought it to the bed.

"Well, as usual, I am right. You don't have a plague and you are not dying. The reason you have not been feeling well is because you are with child."

"I am what?"

"Pregnant. That means you are having a child. The usual amount of time is nine months; You see, a man and a woman meet and fall in love…geez, this conversation would have been fortuitous previous to the wedding…"

"I know what it means, you silly woman. I am shocked it happened so quickly! The gods have blessed me with a child! Oh thank you Priapus!" she said as she looked upwards. She jumped out of bed and hugged me. "I cannot believe it!! Wait, how do you know and what is with the seeds?"

"It is something my aunt taught me," I lied. "A woman soils the wheat and barley seeds with her dew. If either of them sprout than we know she is pregnant. If no sprouts — no pregnancy." The two different seeds actually mean the two different sexes, but I wasn't about to tell her if she was having a boy or girl.

"As long as it speaks the truth, it matters not to me! We need to go tell Ina and Andias. And Eunice! Oh my, they are going to be so excited!"

Things around the mansion were considerably more festive once the announcement that a baby was coming. At least it was something to keep our minds off the men.

One morning we were sitting around being fanned, as it was a particularly hot day, when we heard the horns start to blow. We all got up and started to run (Polly waddled, really) to the gates to see what was coming. We saw soldiers on horses making their way home!! The first to make it back was General Thracian (Robin), to advise us of what had happened so far. Our men would be back in the next couple of days as they were staying to make sure all of the wounded, etc. made

My Name is Agnes   **161**

it back.

We brought the general back to the house to get him some food and wine (all he really wanted was the wine) and he began his story:

"It was a long gruelling journey to Taves that took about five and half months. Once we got there and set up, we had to silently inch our way to see where the Aphlios army was situated and where King Plennsenous was. We had to strategize to determine where the most strategic place to attack would be.

"We had set up our army in a U-shape surrounding them; our army in the middle was the strongest on the field with our spears and shields. The Carnacias Army on the right flank was set up with archers and the left flank was the Army of Attica with their slingshot apparatuses; shooting various kinds of ammunition.

"Once the battle was at full tilt, the Army of Carnacias and the Army of Attica put down their bows and slingshots, picked up their spears and shields, and joined the battle.

"The battle was in the open field and in the Aphlios camp. The fighting was around and in tents. The soldiers were falling in fires and fighting around piles of wood stacks. The women were screaming and running for the hills."

Ina interrupted. "We must cease for the day. This talk is too much for delicate ears and we must wait for our men to tell us what happened."

Polly said, "I agree, this may be too much for me to hear in my condition."

Eunice looked terribly disappointed.

"True," I said, "let us hear this from the men. I believe I will go to Percius's house and freshen it up for his arrival."

General Thracian bowed to the ladies. "I will retreat to my quarters as well."

I could not get to Percius's house fast enough, and I filled my wine glass when I got there. "Ok, 'General.'" I rolled my eyes. "Let us see what happened." I took his hands and waited for the vision.

What a blood bath. Spears were being thrown everywhere. Shields were being used as weapons, axes, knives, hammers, whatever.

162   *Kelly Brookbank*

Anything you could pick up you used as a weapon. Robin was really good at this soldier stuff! He weaved and bobbed, slashed and gashed. Not bad for a newbie.

Then I saw Alexander, Philip, and Percius. They were beautiful to watch. Philip was strong and talented, and Alexander was capable and nimble, but Percius was extraordinary. He was masterful. It was like watching a finely tuned machine, yet he was always keeping an eye out for his brothers as well, especially Alexander, who was just a bit clumsy in his defenses. Alexander always seemed to be one step behind. And I think Alexander knew it.

Percius was usually relentless in teasing Alexander, but battle was one topic that was never brought up. I don't believe Alexander would have survived battle if it hadn't been for Percius, but this was just an understanding between them that they knew one looked out for brothers.

This battle was not going well for King Alexander's army. It was becoming clear that Plennsenous just had too many men and we were being out-manned. It was Alexander who first started looking around to assess the situation.

At this point Robin took off towards Aphlios' camp. What was he up to? He looked around into tents until he found one and rummaged around in it. Then he went out and hid behind it and watched what was happening from behind the tent. Just as I suspected, King Alexander retreated his men and Plennsenous and his men started shouting and celebrating as they made their way back to camp.

I saw Plennsenous coming closer and closer towards this tent, then he went inside. Robin went inside as well — and as soon as he did he poofed himself and Plennsenous to just outside of our camp. When they got there he punched Plennsenous out. "Fucked if we are not getting something out of this battle," he said and he spit on Plennsenous. He tied Plennsenous's hands up, tied him to a tree, and waited.

Once the men were back at camp and Robin thought enough time had passed, he went running into camp to find Alexander. "Sir, may I have a word?"

My Name is Agnes

"General, why do you not have a drink with us? You deserve it as well."

"I believe I have something you will all want to be a part of, sirs. Will you please come with me? It is somewhat of a time-sensitive matter."

"You have us intrigued, that is for sure," Alexander said.

They followed Robin to the tree where Plennsenous was tied up and just coming to.

"Well what do we have here?" Percius said.

"Well done, General. Well done." Philip smiled.

"This *is* time sensitive. They will notice he is gone soon and will want retaliation," Alexander said to Robin as he ran his knife up the side of Plennsenous's neck, "General, will you please go instruct the troops to pack up immediately and be off for home? We will deal with Plennsenous and be right behind you. Tell the women we lost the battle but won the war."

Chapter 23

The picnic was perfect. We ate, we drank, we talked, we laughed... we laughed a lot. We got along so well. I always had such a good time with Stuart, but I was starting to get really confused. This fire in my belly was growing and I was sure he felt the same way, but he wasn't making any moves. I wasn't putting any vibes out that I wasn't interested. Maybe he wasn't interested and I was reading everything wrong? I didn't know.

"So my driver has dropped the phone off with Detective Lester," Stuart said, looking at his phone.

"Is Lester his first name or last name?" I looked at Stuart.

He put his phone down. "You know what? I don't really know."

"I think Lester would be cool for a last name."

"What if Lester is both his first and last name?" Stuart said. "Detective Lester Lester." He laughed

I laughed too. "What if he turns out to be a molester? Lester Lester the molester." We both laughed.

Stuart wiped away a tear, finished his glass of wine, and picked up the bottle to pour some more. "Uh oh, wine is done."

"What should we do now?"

"How about a movie?"

"Great!" We packed up the picnic and his driver took us to a movie theater where we watched a comedy. It had some laugh-out-loud moments but could have been much better. We got some frozen yogurt and sat outside talking about the movie and engaging in other movie talk.

In between bites Stuart said, "The funeral is tomorrow morning, I'd like you to come with me."

"Oh, ok, sure. No problem. It'd be good to see who shows up anyway," I said, taken by surprise.

"Yeah, true, but I just want you to be there with me." He took another part of his yogurt.

Ok there — right there! Doesn't that mean he likes me? So why doesn't he make a move? "I'd be honoured," I said kind of quietly.

"Well." He stood up. "I guess we should get home if we have to be up early." He held out his hand to help me up.

Oh, ok… We walked to the car, NOT holding hands, if you're wondering.

"So what time is the funeral?"

"Ten o'clock," he said.

Seriously? Ten o'clock is early? I'm sooo confused. "I should probably text Bobbi, I don't know if she even knows yet." I texted Bobbi while my head was spinning, wondering what the hell this man was up to. When we got to my place I didn't even invite him up for a coffee in fear that he would reject me.

"I'll pick you up about 9:00," Stuart said as I peered into the car.

"I think I will go into the store for a couple of hours, can you pick me up there?"

"Lovely, see you there." He winked, waved, and sat back.

I walked into my complex and into the elevator still as confused as hell.

When I got into my condo I threw my keys in the dish.

"What's the deal with that?" Robin said.

"I do not know," I said as I fell into the couch, still dumbfounded.

"I would've taken you right there on the blanket at the park," Robin said.

"I know, right?" I sat up as I looked at him then fell back down. "Maybe I need to be more direct. More obvious." I stood up. "Stuart's gonna get Agnessified." I snapped my fingers and did my cat walk away, trying not to fall.

Monday morning, I was sitting in my favourite chair having my favourite coffee. *Ahhh, bliss.* I had a firm plan to seduce Stuart. But what if he didn't want to be seduced? What if he wasn't even attracted to me? What if we were such good friends he didn't want to mess that up? You know what? Fuck that. I'm all that and a bottle of wine and if he couldn't see that, then I would just have to make him see it. Self-doubt is so unattractive. Confidence is sexy. Humour is hot. I was going to Agnessify him right upside the head!!

I had picked out a sexy number for the funeral, but also brought a suit jacket to wear over top. I didn't want to show up looking like a hussy the first time I met Stuart's family. I had gotten the store all ready to go for the day by about 8:30, so I had about half an hour to get my sexy on before Stuart got there.

Jeremy came into the back room to let me know Stuart was there. "Damn girl. You are lookin' fine!"

"Thanks hun, that was the exact look I was going for!" I grabbed my coat and put it over my arm, put my purse over my shoulder, and headed out to meet Stuart.

I walked around the coffee bar where Stuart was standing up waiting for a coffee. I said to Bobbi, "I'll have a latte to go too, please."

Stuart turned to me, "Good morni…whoa." He looked me up and down, I pretended not to notice, but I could tell he definitely liked what he saw!

"Good morning, how are you doing today?" I put my hand on his arm and stood too close.

"Uhhhh, yeah, I'm…I'm good."

"Good." I kept my gaze on him a little too long.

"Here's your coffees, Agnes," Bobbi said.

"Thanks Bobbi." I put my suit jacket on. "Are you sure you don't want to come with us?" I asked her.

"No, I think that will be too awkward. Plus I don't want to be there if his family blames me."

"I don't blame you," I said.

My Name is Agnes   **167**

"Neither do I," Stuart said.

I looked at him funny.

"What? I'm just being honest. My family is bat-shit crazy."

I shrugged my shoulders in agreement. "Here's your coffee. Shall we go meet this lovely, loony family of yours?"

"Might as well rip the head off at some point." He extended his arm so I could take it and we left arm in arm. When we got outside he said, "Agnes, you look really great."

"Why thank you, sir." Stuart opened the Town Car's door for me. "Where is the service being held?" I asked as we got on the road.

"St. Mary Magdalene Catholic Church."

I just about choked on my coffee. I had known Mary Magdalene and she was no saint!

"Christ Agnes, are you ok?"

"Yes, I'm fine, thank you. I think my coffee must've gone down the wrong pipe," I lied. *Well, I guess the venue is fitting!* "So why there?" I said with a smirk.

"That is where my father was baptized and we kids were all baptized. In fact that is where Peter was baptized as well. I think the only thing that Thomas insisted on in his entire marriage was that church. They got married there, their kids were baptized there, and they went to church on the big holidays there. Everything else Angelina got her way, but not with that church — Thomas put his foot down with that."

"So they were religious?" I asked.

"Not especially but you have to put up appearances."

"True."

We pulled up to the church and for some reason, in my head I had pictured this tiny, kind of run-down, pathetic church, but this church was a massive, grand cathedral. Everything inside was red velour and gold. Gorgeous arches, beautiful candelabras, stained glass everywhere, hardwood floors...just magnificent!

"Holy shit!" I said. "Oops, I probably shouldn't say that in here, but this place is stupid stupendous!"

"Really?" Stuart looked around. "Yeah, I suppose it is. I guess you tend to lose appreciation when you grow up in a place."

168   *Kelly Brookbank*

The usher gave us a memorial card. Stuart had his hand on the small of my back. The front pews were marked off for family so Stuart purposefully sat one pew back. "I don't see anyone else except family here," Stuart said to me.

I looked around. "Not that I would know the difference but there isn't anyone sitting in the "non-family" section, you're right."

Since it was a funeral you felt obligated to be quiet so you just automatically whispered, which I took full advantage of. I whispered right into Stuart's ear. Hee hee. *Oh right, this is a funeral, dial down on the seduction.* All of a sudden there was this pretty little thing poking Stuart.

"Isabella."

"Uncle Stuart, what are you doing out here? You have to walk in with the family."

"Oh, I thought I would just sit out here…"

"Please Uncle Stuart, I could really use you to lean on today. Grandma is looking for you too." Isabella pleaded.

I punched him in the shoulder. "Get going, I'll be fine."

"You can come with me."

"Um, that's a hell to the nuh-uh. I'll see you after. Go on, get." I practically pushed him out of the seat.

I sat there looking around at the church for a second and then started to get the feeling that people were looking at me. I looked over and, sure enough, Stuart's ding-a-ling family were giving me the hairy eyeballs. I started to give them the hairy eyeball right back. Then I decided to have some fun. I turned my top teeth into dentures, took them out with my tongue and poked them at his family. They turned around immediately.

Then someone came and sat a couple of seats down from me. He had a lot of piercings and you could tell that he usually did his hair a lot different, but it probably wouldn't have been suitable for funerals.

I smiled at him, and he cautiously smiled back at me. You could tell that he was nervous.

"Hi," I said. He waved at me. "My name is Agnes. I am a friend of Peter's uncle." *And I helped to murder him.* "How did you know Peter?"

My Name is Agnes   **169**

"I'm Chuck. I went to rehab with him."

"Good for you. Were you still going to the centre that Peter went to?"

"Yeah. We were both mentors."

"That's really admirable and courageous. I'd like to make a donation there, what's it called?"

"All Acceptance. Here, I have a card." He handed me a card just as the processional music started to play and we all stood up.

I whispered, "Thank you, Chuck. And I hope you stay on track." I put his card in my pocket. Cool, another lead we could check out.

We all looked back to watch everyone come in and I noticed Detective Lester had snuck in and sat in the back. He nodded his head at me. I nodded my head back.

The family all walked in, and as Stuart went by with Isabella and his mom he gave me a wink. *That's right, he wants what I'm selling — and it's on sale, baby.*

The service started and I looked around. The only people who weren't family were me, Chuck, and Detective Lester.

The funeral was nice, very personal. They had a slideshow of Peter. You could tell he was a happy kid, then when he got to a certain age the pictures started to change. Facial expressions were different, his clothes changed, and his body language was different. Something had definitely happened to him.

When the family walked out Stuart grabbed me on the way. He introduced me to his mom and Isabella as soon as we were in the common area of the church. They were both very sweet. There was definitely an overload of crazy around there.

Stuart's family wore such flashy clothes I was thought I was back in Studio 54, except there was more bling in this church. I swear they were trying to match the volume of their voices to the volume that their clothes spoke.

Thank gourd Detective Lester needed to speak to us and we could excuse ourselves outside.

Going through those doors was like coming up for air after being held down under water against your will. We were almost out of breath

170   *Kelly Brookbank*

as we exited. Trying to escape all the crazy was exhausting. Lester waved us over by the side of the church, away from the front doors. "Maybe we should come over here a bit, just in case. Sorry for showing up here but I thought it was important to get this information to you right away," Lester said.

"No problem, Detective, we appreciate it," Stuart said. I nodded in agreement.

"Can we go grab some coffee somewhere?"

"Can we ever," I said.

"God yes," Stuart said. "I'll just quickly say good-bye to Isabella and Mom."

I nodded to Stuart.

Lester said to me, "There's a Dunkin' Donuts just around the corner to the south of us, can we meet there?"

"Yes, of course, we'll be there as soon as we can." I could have kissed that detective. I just about skipped to the Town car.

Stuart came to the car a little later and he was as excited as I was. "Phew, that couldn't have been better timing, hey?" he said.

"I know, right?" We were both giddy.

We got to the donut store and Lester was already there. We ordered a coffee and met him at the table. It was against my rules to have a black coffee without Baileys, but I guess I could break it this one time...

"I searched the numbers on Peter's phone and all the numbers except ten are KTP. Known to Police. Mostly drug associates. The others, except one, were businesses, like a maid service, a pizza joint, a candy shoppe, a pool cleaner, etc. The only one that didn't check out was an unknown named Charles Benson."

"Oh, that's probably Chuck. I just met him at the funeral." I pulled out his card. "Is this the same number?" I handed Lester the card. He pulled out the phone and compared it to the number.

"Affirmative, that's the number. All the numbers are accounted for. So other than the girl he stalked, all the associates he had, except one, are drug addicts or drug dealers," Lester confirmed.

"Sounds like it," Stuart said.

My Name is Agnes

"Right. Well that's not the most disturbing thing we found on his phone, Mr. Digion."

"Stuart."

"Uh huh, well I've printed them off here." He showed us pictures of grown women and men asleep in Peter's upstairs bedrooms in the Spiderman and Strawberry Shortcake blankets. Both Stuart and I went through them dumbfounded.

"Well I guess this is what he was doing with the kids' linens."

"Yeah, mystery solved," I said as we kept flipping through pictures. "Wait a minute! I recognize her." I pointed to a picture. "This is one of Bobbi's friends, Amanda."

* * * * *

I let go of Robin's hands. "What does this mean?" I said to him.

"In military terms it means that we failed to secure Aphlios but killing Plennsenous was a major military coup. He was the backbone of the Aphlios Army. I do not believe Trevario will be able to control the army the way Plennsenous did."

"So this is positive news then?" I asked.

"Better news would be that we secured Aphlios and killed Plennsenous, but this is the next best thing," Robin replied.

"And you know for sure that Plennsenous is dead?" I looked down at my feet then looked up sheepishly at Robin.

"Would you like to see?" Robin asked.

"No. Yes. I do not know. Yes. Wait. I thought they sent you to pack up with the others?" I asked knowing very well the answer.

"I sent the real General back to help pack up while I flew over to watch the torture killing. I can assure you he is very much dead and got exactly what he had coming to him. The man was one of the most gruesome creatures to ever live on this planet."

"I know that. But I must see for myself. Give me your hand."

Alexander slapped Plennsenous and they threw water in his face until he woke up and he realized where he was. Once he figured out he was tied to a tree he started to try to pull himself free and untie

172   *Kelly Brookbank*

the ropes. Of course the ropes and knots that Robin used would be impossible to break free of.

"What do you fools think you are doing? Do you not know what will happen to you? My men are noticing I am gone right now and are on their way to avenge me," Plennsenous growled at them.

The three looked at each other then burst out laughing. Alexander said, "Do you really believe the morons you keep in your company are wise enough to surmise you are missing?

Percius said, as the three walked around Plennsenous, "I keep wondering to myself, where do detestable pigs like you come from?" He punched Plennsenous in the face.

Plennsenous laughed and spit out blood.

"I hear this beast liked to rape children and defenseless women, did he not, brothers?" Philip asked. He kicked him in the nuts.

Plennsenous groaned.

"I believe he liked to watch others being tortured as well," Percius said as he punched Plennsenous in the stomach then punched him in the nose.

Plennsenous groaned again.

Alexander stepped in front. "Brothers, I believe we should see what this man is really made of." He started to punch him continuously in the face until Plennsenous passed out.

Alexander said, "We had better put this bastard out of his misery before his cavalry come to find him."

Something in Phillip snapped. His eyes had the look of a mad man. "This snake does not deserve to get away this easily," he snarled as he grabbed his knife. He cut out Plennsenous's tongue and eyes. He cut off his ears and penis. Then he grabbed his sword and opened Plennsenous up from his throat to where his penis used to be. Then finally, with one swift motion he cut of his head and stomped on it as Alexander and Percius looked on in shock.

I let go of Robin's hand and put my hand up to my mouth with a gasp. I could see something in Philip's eyes I hadn't seen before.

Robin put his arms around me. "You know in your heart he deserved to die."

My Name is Agnes   173

"I know he did, I know," but I was still shaken.

"Come have a drink," Robin said.

I laughed. "It is I who should be offering you a drink, you silly thing." I tried to get my mind off what I had seen. "The trip went well?"

"It was obviously a faster journey to return home as we had fewer men, less artillery, less everything. We were all anxious to return home as well. We stopped at every town to spread the word that Plennsenous was dead. People were so relieved and grateful — they fed us very well on the way home. I believe many political ties were made on the way home as well."

"It sounds as you had your fill of adventures. I have missed you, my friend." I gave Robin a hug. "I had better head back to the house to see if Polly needs anything. I hope your story has not stressed her at all. I doubt it has. I believe her baby is very strong, but I should go check on her anyway. Your "men" are probably expecting you. Or they will be expecting the General anyway. Are you going to be Robin for a while?"

"Yes, I think I will take a break for a bit and fly around. I miss hovering. I do not think I will stay too close to you once Percius gets back though," he teased me.

As I walked into the house, everyone was flying around trying to get ready for the men's arrival. Ina was furiously bossing people around and everyone else was furiously trying to avoid her. I thought I should probably jump in and defuse the situation, but decided I would just avoid the situation all together.

I sat next to Polly. "How are you?"

"Anxious, but fine." She smiled and rubbed her ever-expanding belly.

"Can I get you anything?"

"I am fine. Thank you, Agnes."

"If that is the case then I believe I am going to go for a walk into town, is that all right with you?" I took Polly's hand.

"Of course, truly I am fine."

I thought I would go to town and go by the medical centre. I wanted to alert them that the wounded soldiers were coming. As

174   *Kelly Brookbank*

I walked into the centre I could see that it was a calm evening and everyone was having such an ordinary day. Yet here I was, coming to throw a bomb on the place. I took a deep breath and pulled the pin...

"Excuse me," I said to the most "official" man I could find.

"Yes?" he said as he looked me up and down with an eyebrow raised.

"My name is Agnes. I am living at the House of Dracas, my best friend is married to Prince Philip. I am here to warn you of the impending wounded soldiers on their way back from war. They will be here forthwith."

As he registered what I was saying his eyes started to widen, he grabbed my arm and threw me in front of a cabinet. "Tear all those sheets in strips. Now!" And he was off. Preverbal pin had just been pulled. All of a sudden people came out of nowhere and were running everywhere doing everything at once. It was a complete madhouse.

Once my sheets were all torn into strips I decided I would try to tiptoe out. I was only going to be in the way. I made it to the main door when it crashed open and a bloody soldier fell into my arms. I looked behind him and it looked like the line-up of bloody soldiers was never ending. I put the soldier's arm around my neck and helped him back into the hospital, while I shouted for help.

The same doctor I'd seen before waved me over to a room, "Bring him in here."

"They are here! There are many more at the door." I shouted.

The doctor blew his whistle and what seemed like thousands ran by me to the door. He came to help me bring the soldier to the room. Then he pointed to a bowl and told me to fill it with water and start washing the soldier's wounds off while he examined him. I followed his orders and did the best that I could. I wished that I could just give the soldier my magic to make him and everyone else all better, but that would have raised too many questions and I would have to disappear. So I just did what I was told and hoped for the best.

"Thank you, Agnes." The doctor stopped what he was doing and looked at me. "I think you have done all you can here. Now I need you to go room to room and do the same for everyone else." And he went back to working on his patient.

My Name is Agnes

I was shocked, but yes, I could do that. I went to the next room and said to the doctor there, "My name is Agnes, I am here to help. May I help to clean off your patient?"

The doctor looked up at me, shocked, then relieved. "That is very much appreciated, thank you Agnes." I filled up the pan and started cleaning off the patient. Once I was done, the doctor stopped what he was doing and said, "I do not believe someone has ever done what you just did, Agnes. It is very nercessary. I mean very nercessary. I mean necessary. I do not know why I cannot say that. Very nercessary. Anyway, I believe I will speak to someone about this. Thank you Agnes."

"Maybe you should call your helpers nurses," I said with a wink.

I went to the next room and introduced myself to that doctor. "My name is Agnes, I am here to help. May I help to clean off your patient?"

The doctor looked at me, "Oh dear, I am sorry, you should not be in here, this patient has passed and it is quite a delicate matter." I could not help myself and quickly looked down at the patient. I only saw a part of his face but there was something familiar about it.

"Hold on please, Doctor, I believe I might know this patient."

The doctor tried to get me to leave.

"Agnes?"

I turned around to see Percius, forgot about everything, and ran into his arms. "What are you doing here?" I asked.

"Come on, let me get you out of here." He grabbed my hand.

"Hold on, Percius," I said. "I thought I recognized this patient." The doctor was still guarding the door, pushing me out.

Percius was pulling me out as well. "Let us get some wine, I have much to tell you," Percius said with a half smile. I thought he looked odd but felt he must have been feeling guilty about how they had tortured Plennsenous.

We found a tavern to get a bottle of wine and then a piece of grass to sit on.

Even though I knew what Percius was about to tell me about Plennsenous, I said, "What happened?"

Percius told me of the journey down to Aphlios; how they snuck

176   *Kelly Brookbank*

up on them, surrounded them in a U-shape, then were too clumsy to keep quiet so the Aphlios army found them out, the ambush didn't go as planned, and they retreated.

He even told me about the torture. "We left Plennsenous as he was. We wanted Trevario to see him like that. We wanted Trevario to know that we had tortured Plennsenous exactly as he had tortured countless others. We took off right away and helped get the injured soldiers carted up. The three of us were coming up behind, guarding the troops. We thought we were making good time but all of a sudden behind us we could see Trevario and his cronies coming fast on their horses."

"Oh my gods!" If only Robin had stayed behind he could have kept an eye on them.

"Phillip, Alexander, and I told most of the troops to take the injured ahead as planned, and we kept about fifteen of our most trusted comrades back with us. We hid in the trees on either side of the road. Trevario could still see our troops marching on ahead in front of them. All of a sudden we pulled up a rope and cut off Trevario and his men's horses, then ambushed them. They were quick to their feet and the fight was on.

"We were evenly matched as far as sparring goes. It seemed as soon as we killed one of their men they would kill one of ours. The fight felt like it went on for days, we were so closely matched. Our men were finally getting the upper hand when Trevario and I locked eyes."

Percius grabbed both of my hands and held them to his chest, looking into my eyes. "Oh Agnes, what happened next will be etched into my memory for the rest of my days. I do not know if I will ever stop thinking about it."

I put my hand on his cheek. "Whatever happened we will get through it together. Tell me what happened my love."

"We both started running towards each other, the hatred spewing out of our mouths, screaming at each other. We were no more than three meters apart when I felt something catch my foot. I could not move. I looked down and saw an injured enemy soldier had grabbed my foot. It only took a few seconds to cut off his hand, but in those

My Name is Agnes

few seconds so much happened.

"It all felt like it happened in slow motion. I heard someone yell "NO" as I looked up. I saw Trevario's axe leave his hand and as I was bringing my shield up to protect myself. I saw him come flying in front of me to protect me from the axe."

He put his head in his hands then grabbed me and hugged me. My head was swimming. Who had protected him? Why was he in the hospital? Oh no! The man in the room. I pushed Percius away from me.

"Percius, who was the man lying dead in that room?"

He took a deep breath. "King Alexander."

Chapter 24

"Hi Amanda. Thanks for meeting me here." I had asked Amanda to meet me at a coffee shop near her work. She was a hairdresser in Maricopa. I had already ordered her coffee and it was waiting for her at the table.

"Um, no prob. I have fifteen minutes so it'll have to be quick."

"Ok, then I'll get right to it. What can you tell me about Peter Digion?"

Amanda got fidgety. "Nothing, he was Bobbi's boyfriend and now he's dead. Other than that I don't know anything. Sorry you wasted a trip down here for nothing." She started to get up from the table.

I put my hand on her hand to stop her. "Amanda, it's ok. You can tell me." She hesitantly sat back down. "In fact I already know, I just want to know what happened."

She looked at me with bewilderment in her eyes. In a hushed voice she said, "How do you know?"

"Peter took pictures and we recovered them off his phone."

"Oh Jesus, that fucking creep," she said as she looked out the window and clenched her fists.

"That's an understatement," I said.

Amanda looked at me and knew she could trust me. She took a deep breath. "Ok...Bobbi and Peter had just started dating and he was obviously head over heels about her." She started fidgeting with the lid on her disposable coffee cup. "He had called me and asked me over to his place because he wanted to get Bobbi a surprise and he needed some advice. I was nervous but I thought that sounded innocent enough, and he was clearly infatuated with Bobbi so I agreed.

"He asked if I wanted a drink, so I just had one beer. He started asking me questions about Bobbi, like what her favourite flowers were, who her favourite band was, what her favourite color was, questions like that. I had asked him what the surprise was, but he didn't really have a specific answer; he just said that he liked to surprise his girl-friends all the time. I remember that I started to feel lightheaded and woozy and kind of nauseous.

"The next thing I know I wake up and I'm sleeping in a kid's bed with Strawberry Shortcake pyjamas on and in Strawberry Shortcake bedding. I didn't know where I was so I got up and looked around and in the next bedroom over, in a Spiderman room, was Peter...it was the weirdest fucking thing. I got the hell out of there and straight to the hospital to get a rape kit done."

She looked at her watch and took a drink of her coffee. "I wasn't really sure how to take it, but the rape kit was negative. So this asshole slips me the date rape drug just to dress me in kid's clothes so he can sleep in the room beside me in his own kid room? What kind of a fucked up cat is this?"

"A seriously fucked-up one," I said with an obvious look of disdain on my face, I mean I knew this guy was weird, but seriously?

"I was so embarrassed about the whole thing I never told anybody. It's not like I called the police or anything — what are they going to charge him with? Unlawfully dressing me up? I just tried to forget it. Turns out I should've told Bobbi...maybe that would've warned her off him, I don't know." She looked out the window.

"I think I probably would have been too embarrassed to tell anyone if I was in your shoes as well." I admitted to her.

She got up from the table. "Thanks for that. Listen, I have to get back to work but I actually feel better telling someone about this." She turned to walk away but then turned back again. "Why are you asking about Peter anyway?"

"Oh I'm doing some research on drug abuse for a book I'm writing," I lied.

"Gotcha, well I think there was more wrong with him than just the drugs. As far as I'm concerned the drugs were just an excuse for him to let the demons out."

I couldn't say I disagreed with her.

"Have a good day, Agnes. And thanks for taking us out on Friday, that was so much fun. I wish I had a boss like you."

I got up from the table. "No problem, thanks for opening up to me, Amanda. I know that had to be hard. If you ever need anything, just give me a call." I gave her a hug.

As I walked to my car I called Stuart. "You have got to hear this!" and I told Stuart what Amanda had told me.

"This guy just keeps getting weirder and weirder!" Stuart said.

"Just when you thought he couldn't get any weirder…BAM he smacks you right in the face with another weird-ball sandwich. So what's the plan Stan?"

"Well…I thought maybe we could become drug addicts today."

"I don't think it's that easy," I said. "Besides, there are so many drugs to choose from — how would we decide?"

"I'm pretty sure you could pick something; whatever is the prettiest, I'm sure."

"Or has the coolest name."

"Yeah, that must be high on the criteria list when deciding what your drug of choice is," Stuart said, his voice dripping with sarcasm. "Where are you? I'll come get you and we'll venture over to All Acceptance.

"I think I should change," I told him. "I feel Patty, the housewife, who is addicted to Percocet and vodka, wouldn't wear this. So you can pick me up at home. Text me when you're close."

All right, another step in my seduction plan is about to transpire, bwaa, haa, haa, haaaaaa.

I tried to half-ass do my hair in an up-do so it looked like I was a stay-at-home mom with a haphazard, throw-it up, sexy, "Don't really care" look. Not sure if I was pulling it off or if I just looked like I came

My Name is Agnes   **181**

out of a windstorm.

Stuart texted me that he was close, so I texted him that I wasn't ready yet and he should come up for a bit. I buzzed him in and when he came to the door I was wearing a silky little housecoat. I told him to have a seat on the couch.

When I came out a little bit later I was wearing cut-offs and holding my halter-top on with my hand. I sat in front of Stuart on the couch with my back towards him.

"Can you zip me up please?" I asked.

"Uh, sure… There you go."

"Thanks! I have this chunky necklace too, can you do it up for me?"

"Yeah, no problem," Stuart said shakily.

"Thank you." I turned around and put my hand on his knee. "Would you like a drink?"

"Ummm, no I'm, uh, no — fine."

"Yeah, you're right, we probably shouldn't go to a rehab smelling of booze!" I laughed and slapped his thigh. "So what did you do the rest of the morning?"

"What? What did I? Oh right. I was going to go back to Peter's house but then…"

I fixed my halter top. I looked at him. "You were saying?"

"Peter has a house. Er, I mean, so yeah I was going to Peter's house but then my dad's idiot side of the family upset Mother at the funeral so I ended up taking her home."

"How did they upset her?" I knew I should have spit my teeth at them at the funeral.

"Just as I suspected, someone said something about drugs. Mother defended Peter, then the idiots said, 'She might as well know. Blah, blah, blah." I put her in my car then I went back in and gave them a piece of my mind."

I picked up his hands and checked his knuckles. "What are you doing?" he said.

"Just looking for cuts or bruises on your knuckles. I don't see any so you mustn't have punched anyone, that's good."

He laughed. "No, I didn't go that far, but I sure felt like it. Why did

182   *Kelly Brookbank*

she need to know? One more day and that would have been it forever. They couldn't go one more day of keeping their fat selfish mouths closed. The poor old lady's memory of her grandson is now tarnished because of their immaturity and selfishness. As of that moment I disowned the lot of them."

"Good for you. But they're still your family, it's got to sting a little — are you sure you're ok?"

"You're very insightful, you know that?" We sat there looking at each other and sat there, I leaned in a little...All of a sudden Stuart got up and said, "Well we should probably get to the rehab center. You have your story, but I still have to make up mine."

Man this guy was frustrating! Good thing I don't give up easy...

"Ok, we can think of one on the way there."

We walked to the elevator in silence. Got into the elevator, still silent.

"Ever had sex in an elevator?" I asked.

Stuart looked shocked. "What? No."

I looked straight ahead. "Neither have I but it's on my bucket list." The doors opened and I walked out. I noticed Stuart took a moment before he exited.

"Ok, so we need a story for you." I said after we settled into the car. "How about you are my husband and you have taken to the bottle because you can't deal with my pill popping?"

"That's pretty boring," Stuart said.

"Yeah, you're right."

"Uh, all right, how about I'm a sex addict á la Tiger Woods?" Stuart suggested.

"Hence my penchant for pills and vodka?"

"Exactly!!"

Once we got to All Acceptance and I introduced us, for some reason I thought we should be Texans. I was Betty Lou Drainall and my husband Billy Joel. All Acceptance definitely lived up to their name. They welcomed us with open arms, literally. They showered us with pity and got us straight into a couples group.

I thought Robin could ham things up, but the Oscar goes to Stuart.

My Name is Agnes

He actually cried…or pretended to anyway. And the story he came up with — phew! Where he got the idea that we should live in a trailer court with no running water and a communal outhouse was nothing short of brilliant. I just sat there dumbfounded.

After the session, they gave us a group tour of the place, which was perfect because I caught a glimpse of Chuck and the other counsellors hanging out in the courtyard.

They had a vigil dedicated to all their fallen members, which was sadly a lot, and Peter's picture was there as the latest victim.

All Acceptance was pretty liberal as they let you walk around the place at your own will. They wanted you to feel comfortable. All the counselling rooms' windows were frosted so you couldn't see into those but otherwise everything was an open book.

We walked up to Chuck and I excused myself for interrupting. He looked at me with a bit of shock on his face and stood up immediately.

"Hi Chuck, do you remember me?"

"Yes, Agnes wasn't it? He looked at my outfit with a bit of confusion. "What are you doing here?"

"I was wondering if we could have a conversation in private, about Peter? This is Peter's uncle, Stuart."

Stuart stretched out his hand. "Hi Chuck, nice to meet you. I hear you were a friend of Peter's?"

"Uh, yes. Umm, sure let's go over here to this table." He kind of looked around and walked over to the other table and we followed him.

We sat down. I said, "Thanks for talking to us Peter. I'm a little confused. This place looks like it's a pretty tight community, I'm surprised more people weren't at Peter's funeral."

Stuart said in a quiet voice, "I really wasn't supposed to go, but I wanted to support him. We do our own vigil here. All Acceptance doesn't want to be held responsible, so we aren't allowed to attend the funeral services. I guess there've been some altercations in the past."

"I was wondering if you could tell me a bit more about my nephew…I kind of lost touch with him in the past few years." Stuart tried to look sad, and Chuck probably bought it but I knew better.

"What was your name again? Stuart? Uncle Stu…Yeah, he told me

184   *Kelly Brookbank*

about you. You were definitely his favourite uncle. You were more like a dad to him. He said you used to take him and Isabella all sorts of places every weekend when he was young. He loved you very much. He didn't even think his parents knew you did that, that's how much they paid attention to him and his sister."

"Ouch. Did you see that bug fly into my eye? That really hurt," Stuart said softly, as he wiped his eye.

Must explain why his eyes were watering. Yeah…that's it.

"I don't think his parents are getting any "parents of the year awards," that's for sure. Did he mention anything about something traumatic happening when he was young?" Stuart asked.

Chuck got antsy and started looking around. "I feel a little uncomfortable talking about this. I feel like I'm breaking a confidence or something."

"Listen, Chuck, we're only trying to get to the bottom of this. I feel bad for letting my nephew down. I should have seen that something happened to him when he was young. I was the only one he had and I gave up on him. If someone mistreated him when he was a defenseless kid, then we need to know who it was and that person needs to be dealt with." A tear fell down Stuart's cheek. "Besides, Peter is dead."

"Yeah, I guess. You're right. Well, one night Peter and I got pretty hammered." Stuart and I looked at each other then back at Chuck. "What? We're drug addicts, not alcoholics…anyway, I had told Peter all my demon stories a million times so I was pressuring him to tell me his story. He always said it was just a rich-kid-gone-bad thing but tonight he was in the mood to talk, I guess. Anyway, he said 'he absolutely loved his childhood and if he could go back to being a child with his sister he would. Then one day he took it all away.' "

Stuart and I were leaning in, listening intently. "Who?" I almost yelled. I am so not a patient witch!

"That's all he said."

"Oh, I see you've met Betty-Lou and Billy-Joe." Marilyn, the counsellor from our session came over to our table.

"Who?" Chuck said confused.

"Well, I think we've taken up enough of your time, Chuck." Stuart

My Name is Agnes   185

stood up and shook Chuck's hand.

"What's with your accents?" Chuck looked even more confused. Stuart stood in front of Chuck so Marilyn couldn't hear him.

I stood In front of him as well, "Yes, thank you so much, Chuck."

Stuart shook Marilyn's hand. "I'll leave a generous donation at the front desk."

"Oh, that would be greatly appreciated, Billy-Joe. We can use all the support we can get." Stuart took Marilyn's arm and started walking her toward the front desk. She smiled at Chuck, who was still looking very confused sitting at the table.

Funny how the word "donation" comes up and all questions get forgotten.

* * * * *

"Oh no! Percius, my love." I hugged him.

Percius pulled away and looked at me. "Something snapped inside of me when I saw Alexander take that axe for me. I looked at Trevario and I think he recognized it in my eyes. I believe he would have run if he could have. I crouched down in a twirling motion and swung my sword across his knees, below his shield, with one hand; pulled the axe out of Alexander with the other hand; and came around and sunk it in Trevario's skull. I pulled the axe out of Trevario's head and kept going, killing one after the other until every one of the Aphlios soldiers Trevario brought with him were dead. I picked up Alexander and we caught up to the rest of the crew without muttering a single word."

"I am so sorry."

"It feels like a bad dream. It does not feel real but every day I wake up to meet the sun I see his dead body again. That should have been me lying there. That axe was meant for me, not Alexander. I was his protector, not him for me."

"I do not know why this happened, but I am glad you are still here with me," I said as I looked down. He pulled up my chin. "I know I am selfish," I said with embarrassment.

"I am selfish as well." He kissed me. "And I am glad I am still here with you as well." We kissed again…a little longer this time.

Percius looked at me. "We need to get back to the estate. Philip and I agreed it was best if we both broke the news to everyone together."

We walked back to the house holding hands. As we walked in you could tell that Philip was clearly irritated by the women berating him for answers. We walked in and heard him saying, "Please, just wait. I said. Just. Wait. No. I am not saying anything. Just! Wait!" He saw us and bee-lined for Percius. "It is about time. I could not hold them off any longer." Philip gave Percius a glass of wine, then they went to the front of the room.

Percius said in a loud voice, "Please take a seat. Please. I am sure you have heard by now that we were not able to secure Aphlios, but we did make some gains by killing Plennsenous."

Ina said, "Where is Alexander?"

Philip said, "One moment, Mother," as he smiled at her, that seemed to calm her down.

Percius continued. "Also, we were able to kill Trevario as well." Some of the generals that had come back early sounded glad about that. "Unfortunately," he cleared his throat, "in that battle…well, when we killed Plennsenous, Trevario and some of his men came to take revenge and in that battle, Alexander saved…"

Philip cut him off, "Alexander lost his life fighting bravely in that battle when Trevario came to revenge his father." Percius and Philip had agreed not to tell everyone what really happened, in the event that some people might blame Percius.

A chorus of gasps and what?'s went off throughout the little crowd that had gathered.

Percius clinked his glass to get everyone to be quiet. "Settle down everyone, please. Hush. So if we could just have a moment of silence for King Alexander, who fought so bravely for his country and his family."

We all bowed our heads for a moment in complete silence. After an appropriate amount of time, Percius raised his glass and said, "To King Alexander." The crowd echoed, "King Alexander" as everyone took a drink of wine.

My Name is Agnes

Percius came to get me first and gave me a kiss on the cheek. He whispered in my ear, "I do not believe I could get through this without you." He kissed me on the lips this time.

"I would not be anywhere else but by your side." Wow, being in love makes you a real sap.

We made our way over to Eunice. I gave her a big, long hug as she cried on my shoulder. "I am truly sorry, Eunice."

"I just can not believe he is gone," she said as she wiped her eyes. She hugged Percius. "At least you were with him when he passed."

"That is true," Percius said as he held my hand.

"Oh there is Aspasia, I should go speak to her," and Eunice was off.

"Are you all right?" I asked Percius.

"I am fine but I am not going to want to stay here for long." He put his arm around my waist and pulled me close to him. "I need to lie with you."

"We need to see your mother and father." I poked his nose.

"Ugh, I suppose. But that will not relieve my stress the way I suggested will." I smiled at him and pulled him in his parents' direction.

We came up to Ina and she was crying into Philip's shoulder. She saw us and gave me a quick hug then hugged Percius a bit longer then went back to Philip. Percius stood by Andias. I saw Polly being ignored on the other side of everyone so I went and talked to her.

"What are you doing over here?" I asked.

"Oh Ina does not want to be consoled by anyone other than her precious baby so I am standing here by myself. I have hardly seen Philip at all since he has been back. I do not even know if he has noticed I am pregnant."

"Well you do not need to be standing here the whole time, why do you not come and sit down over here with me. Have you had anything to eat?"

"I am not sure, I really cannot remember. I believe I must have. My stomach feels full. I do not feel hungry anyway. Everything has crumbled around us, my mind is no longer thinking."

I took Polly's hand, "So you have not spoken to Philip at all?" I looked at her with obvious concern on my face.

188   *Kelly Brookbank*

"When he first came home he saw me, and he was on his way to come to me but Ina cut him off and took him the other direction, so he only waved at me."

"You would think Ina would want him to see that you were pregnant, would you not?" I said.

"I do not know. Ina does strange things. I have taught myself to not question them any longer, especially when it comes to her baby Philip. If I know Ina, I believe she would want to be the one to give him the good news," Polly said, matter of factly.

Shocked, I said, "What? Does that not anger you?"

She shrugged, "She can tell him if that is what she needs to do, I am the one that will give him his child."

"Oh Polly, you bitch." We laughed but tried to keep it quiet.

"Stop making me laugh, Agnes, you are going to make me piss myself." We started laughing again. Then I looked down. "Uh, Polly... did you piss yourself?" I looked up at her face and she looked as if she had seen a ghost. She was holding her stomach.

"I do not know!" She was obviously scared.

"No, Polly, I believe your water has broken. You are about to give Philip that child!"

I got up and grabbed Philip and Ina. "Ina, Polly is going into labour. Philip, if you did not know, Polly is pregnant and she is about to give birth. Can you go to her and give her support until I get back? She is over there." I glared at him and pointed to where she was sitting.

I went over to Percius. "Polly is going into labour, so I am afraid it will be a little while until I can relieve you of your stress." I kissed him and went back to Polly. "All right, honey, let us get you out of here and get you comfortable. Philip can you carry her to the room in the back we have set up, please?"

We had one of the rooms set up with a comfortable bed, lots of cloths, towels, bed pans, everything we needed to keep her comfortable while giving birth to her baby. Philip laid her on the bed and then he left. Usually the men would celebrate but with the sombre mood, the celebration was dampened a bit. Polly's contractions started almost immediately. The staff started bringing in the pans of hot water, cold water and wine. I was by Polly's side holding her hand the whole time. I cooled the cloths and kept her forehead wiped. Once the water got too warm I asked for another bowl, but most of the time I kept my attention on Polly. At one point I looked up and I could have sworn that Kordinia was dressed as one of the staff. There was so much going on I could have been mistaken, but I was pretty sure it was her. She caught my eye and immediately looked down and left the room. What in hell was she doing there? Oh well, a matter for a different time.

Polly was about the strongest person I had ever seen. She was in such pain yet you could see that she knew it was worth it. She didn't complain once. She never said she couldn't do it. She was completely exhausted yet once the contraction came she said, "Here it comes," and she started pushing again.

In between contractions I told her how strong and amazing she was, how lucky I was to have her, how lucky Philip was to have her. Every time I said Philip was lucky to have her, I snuck a look at Ina to make sure she could hear me. And if she was looking at me I added a bit of a glare also.

Finally, the doctor said he could see the head coming. I told Polly to push a little harder (I helped her out as well — Robin had been teaching me the spell without saying it out loud), and just like that Polly gave birth to a healthy, strong, big, baby boy. I gave her a hug. When the doctor cut the umbilical cord, I suggested that I wash the baby off. Ina came over and started to voice her contention, but I just looked at her and suggested that I wash the baby off. Magically she backed away. Man, I was getting better at these spells.

I took the baby over and washed all the guck off of him. He was a beautiful boy. As I washed him I spoke to him softly, telling him that he was going to be faithful and loyal, he was going to be strong and talented, and he was going to be intelligent and humorous. He would do great things and he would be a good man. I had him all washed up, then I got him wrapped up and took him over to Polly. She looked down at him adoringly with a big smile on her face. This was what she was meant to do.

She looked up at me, "He will be called Axle."

I smiled at her. "That is a fabulous name. You should rest. Do you want me to take him to Philip?"

"That is a good idea. I am exhausted. Just take him for a short while then bring him back please? He will need to feed soon." She lay back down as I took the baby.

Ina started to argue again as I took Axle, but I just glared at her and she stopped. We walked Axle down to the main room and all of the men were in there still, eagerly awaiting the news. As soon as they saw us they stood up.

"Philip, may I present your son, Axle." I handed him his son. He had tears in his eyes as he awkwardly took the baby. I guided his hands and arms into holding him the correct way until he had the hang of it.

Percius came behind me and put his arm around me. He looked down at me like he was a cat that had caught the mouse. He kissed my forehead then stepped in closer to get a look at Axle. Andias was standing on the other side. Ina was trying to sneak her way in there too. I stood to the outside, giving them their turn to see Axle. He was hard to resist looking at.

If it had been sombre until now, it turned more celebratory instantly. The next generation was here! Philip had the firstborn boy to carry on the family name! Axle was being such a good baby, he wasn't even fussing with all the passing around. Every single person wanted to hold him. Ina, of course, was glued to Axle's side, never letting him leave her sight.

Everyone wanted to toast Philip and share in a drink with him. I couldn't get that image of him out of my head when they tortured Plennsenous so I decided to study him. Percius was talking to some of his mates, looking back at me every few moments with a wink.

I heard Axle start making a fuss. "I have to take Axle back to Polly then we can go back to yours, does that sound good?"

"Mmmmm," Percius pulled me to him and said in my ear. "That sounds more than good." And he kissed the small of my neck. I licked and sucked his earlobe. I could feel his excitement. He took my head and gave me a passionate kiss.

"I will be as quick as possible." I flirted as I squeezed his ass. I saw

My Name is Agnes   **191**

him grinding his teeth.

I found Ina holding Axle. "Polly wanted me to bring him back so she could feed him."

"He is fine for a little while longer," Ina said.

I looked straight at her, "Ina, I need to bring Axle back to Polly, please." This time she agreed and gave me Axle back.

I went to find Philip. "I am taking Axle back to Polly in case you were interested."

"Thank you Agnes. I really appreciate you and all your help," he said with a smile. That confirmed it, he was changed — something in his eyes told me he was different. Exactly what had changed, I would have to find out.

Chapter 25

Stuart wrote the cheque and we got out of All Acceptance.

When we got in the car Stuart said, "I think we need to keep searching Peter's little apartment. This time we should stay away from the sweets."

"Agreed. I think I have a sugar hangover from yesterday. Hey Stuart," I said, "Did you mean what you said to Chuck back there?"

"You're going to have to be more specific, Agnes."

"Right, sorry. About feeling bad about letting Peter down?"

"In a way, yes. In a way, no. It's not like I didn't try to figure out what was wrong with him. Obviously I noticed a difference in him, but he completely shut me out. I offered help — not just from me, but from counsellors, psychologists, rehab, psychiatrists, whatever he needed — but he didn't want my help. So at some point I just gave up. I guess I should have tried harder but…"

"But what? I doubt anything you say is anything I haven't thought of already."

"Maybe this type of behaviour was already in his nature."

"What?" I grabbed my chest like I had been shot. "How can you even say something like…" I rolled my eyes. "I know, I've thought the same thing. At some point everyone has to take responsibility for themselves, right?"

"Exactly, kids can't always blame their mommy or daddy…Even if they are like Angelina or Thomas."

We got back to Peter's and tried to remember as much as we could through the sugar haze we'd been in the last time we were there.

"Ok, so I think we made it through the majority of the cupboards in the kitchen, right?" Stuart asked.

"Ummm, yeah — let's hope we don't have to go through those again. I'm getting the shakes just knowing those candies are in there."

"How about we go in, under, and through things? You found his cell phone in the couch last time, maybe we'll get lucky again," Stuart suggested.

"Good idea. Just be careful, you just never know what kind of needles there might be poking around. I suggest picking things up instead of just sticking your hands down. Why don't we work together — you pick stuff up and I'll look?"

"Once again, I'm getting the shitty end of the deal." Stuart pouted.

I rolled my eyes. "Oh suck it up, strong man. I'll help you out, I'll pick up the cushions on the couch, you just have to pick up the whole couch."

"Oh, gee...thanks."

"Anything for you, darlin'." I slapped his ass. I may have cupped my hand a little too. Hee hee. "All right, let's tear this bitch apart!"

I pulled the cushions off the couch. Nothing. Stuart lifted the couch. Nothing. I pulled the cushions off the loveseat. Nothing except $5.87, which we agreed to split. Stuart lifted the loveseat. Nothing. Stuart pulled the entertainment unit back. We found a dead goldfish, which was strange since Peter didn't have any fish, but that was it. We both felt around the walls to see if there was anything abnormal, like a hidden cupboard or something but we couldn't feel anything.

Stuart lifted the mattress on the bed. He put it on his shoulder and bent over a little. "Look, I have the weight of the world on my shoulder."

I laughed at him. "If you bent over a little more and rested your chin on your hand, you could be..."

All of a sudden a latch let way and a flat box fell out of the mattress, scaring the shit out of me. "Stuart, I believe we may have found

194 *Kelly Brookbank*

a missing piece to a puzzle."

"Well, for Christ's sakes, check to see if there's anything else in there — this mattress is getting heavy!"

I stuck my hand in the hole and sure enough there was a laptop in there also.

"You're so smart, Stuart," I said with a lisp. "I totally would have gone for the box and not even looked further into the hole."

"Well, what can I say? I'm a thorough kind of guy."

"Here, Mr. Thorough, you can do the honours." I gave him the metal box. It looked like an old security deposit box, but a wide, flat one. He opened it up. It had three tickets from a 1995 Arizona State Sun Devils baseball game, movie stubs from *Aladdin, Home Alone 2* and *Toys*, two ticket stubs from the Arizona State Fair, an old Bugs Bunny button in a clear case, a digital camera, a couple of patches from Boy Scouts, a napkin from Pistol Pete's Pizza, matchbooks from Arizona Inn and Buddy Ryan's Bar, some old money, Spiderman comic books, Spiderman stickers, a small Spiderman action toy, Spiderman keychain, Spiderman wallet, Spiderman watch, Spiderman trading cards, Spiderman toothbrush, lots of Spider-man stuff!!

"Holy, holy, holy. You might want to brace yourself for this, Agnes." Stuart handed me two envelopes. Inside were two one-way airplane tickets for himself and Bobbi to New Orleans, Louisiana, leaving five days from today. I'm pretty sure Bobbi was unaware of those plans.

"What is this? Why Louisiana? There's no way Bobbi would have agreed to go with him." I was dumbfounded. "What the fuck?" I looked at Stuart.

Stuart hugged me. "He was a seriously disturbed kid."

"He really was," I said into his chest. "Ok," I said as I tried to gain my composure, "Let's check out the camera."

"I think I'll get us a drink first though."

"Bring the bottle." I yelled after him.

We sat down with our drinks, turned on the camera, and tried to flip through the pictures. Nothing in the memory.

"Shit."

"Maybe the pictures are already downloaded onto his computer?"

My Name is Agnes   195

Stuart suggested.

"Did you take some smart pills today or something?" I asked him.

"That would suggest that I'm not this smart every day..."

I looked away from him. "So the power cords were with the computer and everything? I'll just plug those right in over here and we can have a looky loo!" I took a drink, avoiding his playful glare. "All righty, let's check out what creepy pictures Pete has on his laptop."

I clicked on his pictures icon. There were six different files, four with the names, Mary, Louise, Erin, and Maureen. One was titled "Emmie and me" and one was titled "Boating."

"Interesting," Stuart said. We both took a drink. "Let's take "Emmie and me" for 500, Alex."

I looked at Stuart like I should know that from somewhere, but couldn't quite place it.

"Oh right, you don't watch TV. It's a game show. *Jeopardy*?"

I was still looking at him.

"Oh never mind."

I clicked on the picture folder. There were over 300 pictures.

"He was quite the shutterbug!" Peter had obviously had a relationship with Emmie. There were all sorts of pictures of Peter and Emmie doing things together. They seemed very happy. Then the pictures started to change from happy to strange. It wasn't all of a sudden, it was a gradual change. Emmie's smile started to fade. She and Peter transitioned from doing things during the day to doing things at night. They started to wear darker clothes. Peter took more of a role behind the camera. You could see more skin blemishes appear on Emmie's skin. She started to lose weight and not taking care of herself or worrying about her appearance. Bags under her eyes became more pronounced. She was wearing the same clothes over and over again.

Then they started doing weird shit. Melting dolls. Throwing fast food hamburgers at people's houses. Emptying drinks onto cars off overpasses. Pushing grocery carts onto streets. But these escapades escalated also; they grew from immature acts into violent, disturbing behaviour. There were pictures of gang fights on homeless people, stabbings, holding heads under water, choking, etc. Emmie was always on the sidelines watching, with no expression on her face. There were lots of pictures of the two of them in different S&M scenarios also. Peter was always taking the picture so his head was never in the photos but Emmie was obviously consenting.

Then the pictures stopped. The date stamps on the pictures were 2007 – 2009.

We both finished our drinks. "I think my brain is about to explode," I said.

"What happened to Emmie?" Stuart was thinking out loud.

"I'm afraid to ask," I said. I filled our drinks. "I guess we should look at these other girls.

"Well, pick one," he said. I don't know why, but I picked Erin. The first picture was of a very skinny girl with straight, scraggly, shoulder-length brown hair, skin blemishes on her round face. She had a big smile on her face, but her teeth were brown and broken. She was wearing jean cut-offs that were too big for her tiny frame and a button-up dress shirt that was tied in a knot at the bottom, the pocket and sleeves torn off. She and Peter were at a park and she was sitting on a swing. In the next picture she was sitting on a teeter-totter wearing an old cowboy hat and old cowboy boots. Her feet were up in the air, and she was laughing.

In the next series of pictures, she was on the merry-go-round. She was laughing at first, then her smile was fading, and you could tell she was asking to stop. The next pictures were of her puking. One picture had a foot on her head while she was on the ground throwing up. The next picture she was in the garbage can.

Some pictures she was happy. Some pictures she was not. Some pictures she was shooting up. Some pictures she was being tortured. Some pictures she was having sex. Some involved S&M (not sure if it was consensual or not). None of the pictures had Peter's head in them, but he was obviously taking the pictures. These time stamps were all 2011.

All the other girls' pictures were basically the same, but the girls looked different; different hair color, different height and ages, but they were all clearly drug addicts/prostitutes. They hung out in different

My Name is Agnes

places and they were all tortured in different ways. We checked the time stamps of the pictures and it looked like Peter kept each of the girls around for about a year at a time. Mary was in 2009, Louise was 2010, and Maureen was 2012, all up to about two years before, which was the point Peter had supposedly gotten clean.

"You might have to go and get a second bottle," I said to Stuart as we sat there staring at the screen.

Stuart closed the laptop and looked at me. He took a drink. I took a drink. "Let's think about this. Peter is obviously using at this time."

"Obviously."

"He is dating one particular girl at a time."

"Another user." I threw in.

"Another user, and he uses and tortures her. Why?" Stuart says.

"He's probably her supplier." I suggested.

"That would make sense." Stuart nodded his head. "But then why does the relationship end?"

"Peter got bored? They wanted to get clean? Peter got too danger-ous?" I was just throwing out suggestions, but the last one kind of made sense to both of us. We both looked at each other... "Maybe we should check the computer to see if we can find anything more," I suggested.

"Ok," Stuart said as he opened up the laptop again. "Let's see if his emails have a story to tell." Stuart clicked on his email icon. "Nothing in his inbox."

"Check his trash."

Stuart looked at me. "Isn't that what we're doing?"

"His email deleted items...oh you're being funny. HA HA haaa. You should take your comedy act on the road.

"Ok, You're right. Peter wasn't very good at deleting his deleted items. Luckily he didn't have very many friends so he didn't have very many emails. Ummmm, ok let's see here, I'm going to scroll down to 2009 in August. Airline ticket reservations. Two tickets for Peter Digion and Mary Accont to New Orleans. One month later there's another reservation for Peter, but no Mary. September 2010, Two tickets for Peter Digion and Louise Perlisk to New Orleans, one month later Peter comes back alone. November 2011, Erin Tranio escorts Peter to New Orleans but five weeks later only Peter comes back. September 2012, Peter and Maureen Redwood go to New Orleans. Guess what?"

"They get married and live happily ever after?" I took a drink.

"Not exactly." Stuart sat back and took a drink. "I wonder why New Orleans?"

"Maybe they get lost easily in the party town?"

"You would think he would take them to Vegas then." Stuart thought as he took another drink.

I took another drink and turned the computer towards me. "That's true." I opened up the file titled, "Boating."

"This might explain it." I turned the computer to Stuart. The picture on the computer was a small houseboat with the body parts of Mary Accont spread out on the table and holding her decapitated head, smiling widely, was Peter Digion.

* * * * *

Percius and I lay exhausted in bed. "You were away far too long." I said as I ran my fingers along his abdominal muscles.

"Yes, I was. And we will have to leave again soon."

"What?" I sat up then lay down again. "Makes sense. Now the heads are cut off the snake you will need to go back to rip open the entire body."

"Exactly. I believe other lands will be more receptive to our ways as well. They were all so terrified of Plennsenous I believe they will be thankful to follow us. We will need to go and convince them to stand behind us."

"When will you leave?" I started to kiss his chest.

"Mmmmm," was all I heard.

"I do not believe that is a time." My hand started to tickle the crease where his thigh met his torso as I licked his nipple.

"I cannot think when you touch me." His eyes were closed.

"Then I will not stop touching you." I followed my finger along

My Name is Agnes   199

his pelvic hairline from side to side, barely touching it. I could hear him trying to catch his breath. I started to his kiss my way down the middle of his stomach. Then I kissed farther down until I noticed a birthmark. It was a C and a comma in the middle, kind of in a heart shape.

"Oh my queen, I missed you!" Percius said. I turned my body so we could pleasure each other. After the dizziness passed I climbed up the bed to lie beside Percius, after drinking some wine.

"Why did you call me your queen?"

"Because that is what you will be, my queen."

I sat straight up. "Percius, does this mean you are going to be king?"

"Truthfully, I already am."

"I do not understand."

He sat up. "With my father and Alexander it was different because my father stepped down — he bestowed the position on Alexander. When a king dies, the honour falls to the next in line, which is his son. Or if he has no son it is the next sibling."

"I had no idea. I thought it would go back to your father. Congratulations. What a horrible way to gain the throne, but..." I hugged him. Sparks. Skin on skin. We started kissing again and fell back on to the bed, then we pressed our whole bodies against each other. We just couldn't resist each other...

While we were in the shower and I was soaping Percius's back, I said, "So now what?"

He took the soap from me and started to soap my back. "We have a ceremony where we start with burying King Alexander and we follow by pronouncing me king, and end with a celebration feast."

He turned me around and I took the soap from him to soap his front.

"Hmmm, sounds very formal."

"It is very formal and beautiful. It is all quite natural." He took the soap from me to lather my front.

"Yes, I suppose it is. Nice that everyone does not stay sad," I said.

"You are such a beautiful soul."

"I love your birthmark," I circled my finger around it.

"I have always thought it a curse."

"Why would you think that?" I asked.

"I am not sure. From here it looks to be nothing."

"From where I can see, it is a heart. It just took you finding me to see it."

Percius put the soap down and got on his knees. "Let me see if I can find a birthmark on you anywhere."

We finally dressed. We hadn't slept all night, but I didn't need sleep anyway. Philip needed his wits about him so I put a potion in his tea that made him wide awake. Percius needed to go to the war room with Philip and their father to start making plans for their new takeover. I needed to go check on Polly first and then Ina to find out what needed to be done for the ceremony.

I walked into Polly's room and she was holding Axle in her arms, looking down at him, and smiling brightly. "Well you look amazingly fresh," I said.

"He slept most of the night. He woke up twice to feed and then went right back to sleep. He is just perfect."

"All right, all right. Do not monopolize him. Hand him over." She gave him to me reluctantly and he snuggled right into me. I could have sworn that he smiled at me.

"He is beautiful, is he not?" Polly asked.

"He is that and more," I said as I smiled back at him.

"How do you feel about being queen?" Polly asked me. I just about dropped Axle.

"What are you talking about? I am not queen!" Polly smiled an awkward smile. I could see that she was jealous. "Percius and I would have to be married for me to be queen and we are not, silly. I am just some tramp by his side." I snuck a glance at her.

She laughed at me. "You know you are no such thing. You are just as much married to Percius as Philip and I are…"

"But we are not, so there is no sense talking about it. Is Ina coming around every five minutes?"

"Oh, she is insufferable!" That took Polly's mind off the subject, and I was grateful for the distraction. I stayed with her for about an

My Name is Agnes

hour to talk and help out with Axle. I found out that Philip had not come back last night, thought it suited Polly just fine, he probably would have woken Axle anyway.

"I need to find Ina to find out what needs to be done for the ceremony. I will come check on you later." I gave both of them a kiss on the cheek.

Ina was trying to be strong but she was barely holding it together. She was trying to give orders, but she would break down crying instead. All the help was standing around confused. I felt sorry for her for the first time and I told everyone to leave us alone for ten minutes.

I took Ina's hand. "Ina, a mother should never have to bury a child. I cannot even imagine what you are going through. I just need you to be strong for a few minutes to tell me what needs to be done and I will look after everything. Then you can go grieve for your child, do you understand?"

She nodded her head.

"Now please tell me what I need to do and it will all be taken care of."

Ina explained all the details of the ceremony. She stood up and gave me a hug then left through a side door. I invited all the help back in. "Good morning, everyone. I need your help. We have lost a great man in King Alexander and it is up to you and me to send him off to the gods in the Spirit Release Ceremony. We also have the immense task of celebrating the next brilliant man to take the throne; Percius. Will you help me?"

Everyone nodded in agreement.

"Thank you."

I listed off things that needed to be done and asked who could help with what. Everyone was very helpful. I assumed this wasn't the way Ina went about organizing things…

In two days the ceremonies began. King Alexander was on display on a large wooden raft by the seashore, dressed in his king's attire. All the townspeople could come, say their good-byes, and leave a flower on the raft. By the time the ceremony began and we walked down, the flowers that surrounded him had piled so high you couldn't see his casket. King Alexander had been a well-liked and well-respected man.

The high priest said the prayers and the ceremonial words to the gods. Then the family threw our flowers into the casket with King Alexander. As the women stepped back, each of the men closest to King Alexander grabbed the lit torches that surrounded the body. As the high priest said the final words to the gods, the men lit the raft on fire. Someone turned the wheel and King Alexander's burning raft was sent out to sea and back to the gods.

Everyone stood there watching his body drift out to sea in a fiery good-bye surrounded by a fog that seemed like a hug from those who loved him. It was a grey and gloomy scene; the only color was the red flames that jumped above the fog far in the distance. We stood there until the carriages came to pick us up to take us back to the house. The bands were playing at the house, which we could hear as we got closer, seemingly changing our moods the nearer we reached the house.

We left the grey behind and emerged into the brightest light spectacle anyone had ever seen! I had fires all along the drive, and the house was all lit up; there were strings of candles everywhere. There was champagne as we exited the carriages and a band playing. Another band was playing in the back and another band in the house. I did not want anyone to go without drink or to ever be without sound.

When King Alexander had been pronounced king it was a small supper but this was to be very different. This was to be a grand affair! I had ice sculptures, fountains, mounds of food, and wine. I had people waiting in the wings specifically to keep food dishes full.

Percius could not stop thanking me. He took me around, introducing me to everyone and showing me off. I could not have been more proud of him. I was about to burst I was so proud of him.

The announcement was made for us to sit down for supper, which was being held out in the back yard. It was a beautiful setting; a huge tent with candles and flowers everywhere.

Percius and I sat in the middle of the table with Polly and Philip on one side and Ina and Andias on the other, then "General Thracian" and the rest of the commanders-in-chief. The help served the head table first and then the other tables.

My Name is Agnes

Supper was delicious. We'd had pigs roasting all day and the aroma had our mouths watering for hours. Everything was turning out wonderfully and I was delighted for Percius. I was so happy to see the smile on his face because I knew he still felt guilty.

"I do not know how you pulled all this off, my love. You are the best." He kissed me.

"You are worth it." I held his hand.

Stumbling a bit, Andias stood up and clinked his glass. "May I haz your attention please." The crowd settled down. Andias was clearly drunk. "First of all, I would like to thank my wife, Ina, for putting this ceremony together under short notice and under such heart-wrenching circumstances." He raised his glass to her. "Ina, my love, you never cease to amaze me." She smiled at him and bowed her head while everyone clapped for her.

Percius started to get up to say something. I put my hand on his arm. "It is all right Percius, really. It does not matter."

"Everyone should know it was you."

"I did this for you and no one else. I do not care that anyone else knows." I kissed his cheek.

He smiled at me and mouthed the words, "I love you."

Andias continued, "We said good-bye to my first-born today, who laid his heart down on the battlefield. I was proud of Alexander. He was destined to be a great leader. I also predicted he would die on the battlefield. Now I am no teller of fortunes and can not see into the future..." The crowd laughed a little. "I just knew my son. He knew everything about war. He knew strategies. He knew the risks. He knew rewards. He was meant to lead men into battle. He just was not meant to be in the battle. Ah, but he tried. He practiced day in and day out with his sword, but he just could not quite get the hang of it. He had perseverance, our Alexander did." Andias paused. Then he raised his glass. "To a great mind for war, King Alexander!"

Everyone raised a glass and kind of mumbled, "To King Alexander."

Then Andias turned to Percius. "Now Percius." He smiled as he raised his glass. "You want to see a warrior? That is our Percius. If you could take anyone into battle with you, you would want to take

Percius. He is a force. Brilliant with a sword. Just brilliant. I am so proud of Percius. He will be a brilliant king, brilliant." He wiped away a tear. "To King Percius."

Everyone shouted and raised their glass, "To King Percius!"

Andias put down his glass, took the crown from the servant behind him, who was holding it on a pillow, and placed it on Percius's head. Andias and Percius embraced.

Percius stayed standing as everyone clapped for him and he shouted, "Let us dance!!" People shouted and cleared the tables away to make a dance floor, the band started playing, and everyone got right back into the festive mood again. Percius grabbed my hand and we had a couple of dances. I kept having a look over to Polly and she seemed very happy. At least Philip was beside her and they seemed to be talking and being friendly.

After a couple of dances, Percius and I had to sit down. "Oh my heavens, I can not dance like that after having such a big meal!" I said after I took a drink of my wine.

"I know what you feel like!" Percius said as he finished his wine. He gave me a kiss. The servant filled Percius's glass again as he took another drink. I still had my glass in my hand so I did not need a top off. I had a strange feeling so I turned around to look behind me. The servant that was filling our wine was Kordinia, Philip's ex I found in his bed. "What in Hades' gates?" I said.

Percius started to choke.

I turned to him. "Gods in the heavens! No!"

I heard Kordinia behind me say, "I told you, you would pay." And I heard her fall and the glass break beside her.

Percius fell off his chair as his body spasmed and foam came out of his mouth. "Percius, no!" I tried to hold him up, but we both fell on the ground. "Percius, stay with me!" I was holding him on my lap. "No, Percius!" I slapped him. I hugged him. I knew he was going to die, so I whispered in his ear, "Percius, I love you, I love you."

I kept repeating it until I felt him take his last breath.

Chapter 26

All the other pictures in the boating file had Peter, smiling widely, holding the decapitated heads of Louise, Erin, and Maureen with their body parts spread out beside them on the same houseboat.

"Jesus," Stuart said.

"Faaaaaack," I said. We sat there staring at the screen, unable to take our eyes off it; like a car accident scene…you know you're not supposed to look but you just can't help it. After a while, eerily at the same time, we both grabbed our drinks and sat back and took a drink, still looking at the screen.

Philip's phone rang, and I jumped and spilled my drink. Philip yelled, "Get down!" as he sat up straight. I tried to wipe myself off and he picked up the phone and answered it. "Hey Thomas. Yeah, that was something, wasn't it? Are you glad it's over? I imagine. Yes, we're here right now. Ok, see you in a bit." He hung up. "Thomas is coming over."

"I gathered. I don't think we should show him the pictures, do you?" I asked.

"Hells no. We need to figure out who those girls were first. We'll call Lester after Thomas is gone. Then we need to figure out what we're going to do with the information."

"Yeah, I know." I closed up the computer. "All right Muscles, get this mattress up so I can put it back." I put it back in the hiding spot.

"What's with yelling, "Get down" when the phone rang?" I asked with a smile.

"I don't really know. I guess looking at those pictures kind of freaked me out."

"Not that I don't appreciate you saving me from the dead man on the computer screen..." I smiled, looked at him slyly, and started laughing.

"Oh you think that's funny, do you?" He poked me in the side. I pretended that I was ticklish, he kept poking me, I kept pretending. We were kind of wrestling standing up, our bodies pressed together, laughing together, our faces only an inch apart once we stopped laughing. We looked each other in the eyes, I was telling him to kiss me with my stare...he started to lean in to kiss me...then he pulled away.

"Why did you pull away? Why do you keep pulling away from me?" I asked.

"Stuart? Agnes? Where are you guys?" Thomas was yelling from the front of the house.

"We better go see Thomas." Stuart pointed at the door and hurried towards it to open it. He held it open for me.

I glared at him as I passed. "This is not over," I growled at him.

We met Thomas in the front room.

"Oh hey, there you guys are. Where were you?"

Stuart pointed back toward Peter's room. "Peter's little hideaway."

"His what?" Thomas looked confused.

"Oh, you didn't know about it..." Stuart looked at me.

"Follow us," I said.

We led Thomas into the apartment and he looked around. "What the fuck is this?"

"We're assuming this is where Peter spent most of his time."

"Huh. I guess this doesn't really surprise me. Did you find that pin of Angelina's I was telling you about?"

"No. Here is a box of keepsakes that we found though." Stuart put it on the counter in front of a chair, assuming that Thomas would want to sit down.

"Would you like a drink first?" I asked.

My Name is Agnes

"I'm fine," Thomas said as he poked through the box, obviously looking specifically for the pin and not giving a shit about anything else that was in the box. He slammed the box shut when he didn't find it. "Well it must be here somewhere." He turned around and went into the kitchen. He started looking in cupboards, slamming the doors shut as he went. "Have you looked in the rest of the house or have you only looked in here? Where else have you looked, exactly?"

Stuart and I both gave him a look. "We've looked pretty much everywhere, but please, search for yourself." Stuart gestured to him. Stuart and I sat down and poured ourselves a drink. "So you want to catch a movie later, Agnes, since we don't have anything better to do with our lives?" he asked me.

"That sounds great, Stuart, what kind of a movie would you like to see?" I played along with his game.

"Well, Agnes, I have not seen a good western in a long time, have you?"

"You know, Stuart, now that I think about it, I have not."

"Well then, Agnes…"

"Ok, ok, I get your point. I'm sorry I was being abrupt." Thomas said.

Abrupt? I thought. *A dick, more like it.*

"Shouldn't you be happy that Peter didn't steal it like you thought?" Stuart asked.

"Yeah, yeah, you're right. I'm just a bit stressed out right now." Thomas rubbed his temples.

"Worrying yourself ragged about an antique pin isn't really helping things, is it?" I asked. "Maybe Angelina just misplaced it."

"I hope so," Thomas said. "Well I better get back and leave you to it. If you find it, let me know."

"Take care," I said as Thomas and Stuart walked out. I gave Thomas the finger as they walked away.

When Stuart came back, I said, "Did Thomas ask you anything else as he was leaving?"

"Nope."

"Didn't ask you if we found anything else out in our investigating?"

208 *Kelly Brookbank*

"Nope."

"Don't you find that a bit odd?"

"Nope."

"You don't?"

"I find that a lot odd." Stuart had a sad but pissed off look on his face. "I have to call Lester to do a search on these girls of Peter's before I forget. He opened up the computer and dialled Detective Lester. "Yeah, hi Detective Lester, this is Stuart. I was wondering if you could do some background checks for me? This first one is Emmie Trumoo. T R U M O O. Second is Mary Accont. A C C O N T. The third is Louise Perlisk P E R L I S K. Fourth is Erin Tranio T R A N I O. Last is Maureen Redwood R E D W O O D. Do you need their pictures? Ok, I'll text them to you in that order. Thanks Detective." He took pictures of the screen and texted them to Lester.

I was deep in thought while Peter was on the phone. I probably looked like I was constipated.

"Penny for your thoughts?" Stuart said, sheepishly.

"Why would a penny be a fair trade for my thoughts?" I said as I snapped out of my trance.

"What the wha?" Stuart looked at me, shocked.

"As a matter of fact my thoughts are priceless, mister..." Peter didn't know which way to run. "Actually they are confusing even to me. Anyway, so Peter would take these "girlfriends" to Florida to murder them and then feed them to the gators, then he would stay for about a month after he did the deed, right?"

Once Stuart caught his breath again, he said, "According to the time stamps on his pictures and the flights on his emails, yes."

"Then he would come back here and start the process all over again. Find another drugged out "girlfriend," start a relationship, gradually become controlling and out of control, doing more and more danger-ous things, and eventually getting to the point that he wants to kill her — why does he want to kill them?"

"And what happened to Emmie?" Stuart thought out loud.

"Why kill her? They seemed to be a partnership." I asked.

"Maybe he didn't kill her, maybe she decided to get clean and got

My Name is Agnes   209

the hell away from him."

"Awww, you're such an optimist." I put my hand on his arm and gave him my, "I'm giving you the green light" eyes. Then I remembered about earlier and my plan to seduce him. "Oh right! About earlier…why do you…"

Stuart's phone rang. He picked it up faster than a gold coin in a group of homeless people and looked to see who was calling. "Oh, it's Lester, I better get this." He answered it immediately. "Hi Detective!" He sounded way too cheery. I glared at him. "What did you find out?" He smiled at me. I didn't think it would be a good idea to throat chop someone while they're on the phone with the police so I just rolled my eyes.

"Oh really? All four of them? Huh. Ok, and Emmie? What? Seriously? You've got to be kidding me. All right. Thank you, Detective. No, I'm not sure if we have anything or not. I'll let you know when I know for sure. Thank you again. Oh, of course. I will, you bet. Good bye." He hung up. "Well, that answers one mystery. Emmie Trumoo is dead. She died in 2009 from asphyxiation in the midst of a consensual sex act with Peter Digion. Of course Thomas got Peter off so he just received a slap on the wrist. She was a known drug addict and a ward of the state so there wasn't anyone to go to bat for her. Case was thrown out."

"Are you kidding me?" I said, stunned.

"Yup and all four of the other girls were known drug addicts/prostitutes, so they've all been listed as missing in the system, but that's about it." Stuart took a swig of his drink.

"So Peter was pretty much just re-enacting his relationship with Emmie?" I was trying to figure this out in my head.

"I suppose so. I guess Peter must have liked the killing part a little bit more than he thought he would." Stuart was surmising as well. "Then he was having a guilty conscience so he decided to try and get clean?"

"But as soon as he fell for someone and she put up a resistance, he couldn't handle it and was going to take Bobbi on a little trip to her final resting place in New Orleans as well. I guess he wasn't just using the Rohypnol for taking pictures of his freaky little kids' rooms, he would've had to use it on Bobbi to get her to New Orleans. What a sick bastard. I'm glad the drugs got to him before he got to Bobbi!"

Little fucker, I thought. When Robin and I had gone to Peter's house we enchanted him to tell us the truth and he admitted he was going to murder Bobbi, though he didn't say how. I thought it was going to be that night, I had no idea what a sick bastard he really was.

"Yeah, too bad it couldn't save the other girls though." We started flipping through the pictures of the victims. Emmie was wearing a Bugs Bunny t-shirt in a lot of her pictures.

"Wait a second," I said. "Go back." Stuart went back to the Bugs Bunny t-shirt. I looked at it for a second.

"What?" Stuart asked.

"I don't know." I went to the box with all the trinkets and rummaged around until I found the Bugs Bunny pin inside the case.

"If you had an antique pin, wouldn't you put it in something like this?"

"Probably," Stuart said with a quizzical look on his face.

"Does Bugs Bunny seem like something Peter would keep in this box?"

"Actually, now that you say that, it does seem a bit out of the ordinary in that box."

I opened the box and took the pin out. Nothing else was in the box or under the foam. I looked on the underside of the pin. There was a memory stick on its underside. "Hmmm, you think this might be what Thomas looking for?"

He put it into the computer. I guess we'll find out," he said. It was an audio file.

* * * * *

"General, Philip, can you please take Percius?" I asked them. As soon as they took Percius, I went to go make sure Kordinia was dead. I found the first member of the staff I could find and had them take all the wine away from the head table and replace it with fresh wine. I saw

My Name is Agnes   211

some of the help trying to pick up Kordinia and take her away and I rushed over there and said, "No! I will deal with her. Leave her!"

Polly came up to me. "Agnes, what are you doing? We must cancel the festivities."

I took her hand. "No Polly, we cannot. We are crowning a king tonight. No matter what, we need a king to lead us into battle to gain Aphlios' lands. This must be done soon. Percius has died therefore Philip is now king and you are his queen. This is what Percius would have wanted. If Philip suggests anything other than this, you must convince him, do you understand?"

"Yes, you are right. You would have made a wonderful queen." I nodded and smiled.

"Agnes?"

"Yes, Polly?"

"How are you not weeping?"

"I am not able. I have never wept, even as a babe," I lied. Truth is, witches can't cry. "Do you know who Kordinia is or who her family is?"

"I do not. I believe she is a commoner."

"Whomever she is, her family will not have a body to send to the gods." I turned and picked up Kordinia's body and took her out the back. I suspect it was a spectacle to see me picking up a body, as women don't do that sort of thing, but I didn't much care. I was given permission as I was in mourning.

I walked her into the woods until no one could see me any more. There was a familiar flutter of bat wings behind me. The wings grew and enveloped me.

"Thank you, Robin. I know I will always have you." We stayed there for a while. He was partly hugging me, partly holding me up. He not only had his wings around me, he was keeping my world together as he had many times in the past and would again many times in the future.

I took in a deep breath. "Is the coast clear?"

Robin looked around. "It is sweetheart."

"Let us burn this bitch." I laser-beamed the hell into this murderous skank. After she was burned to ashes I spit on her, and my spit covered the entire pile of ashes preventing any from going up to the gods. The rest of Kordinia sank into the earth and down to hell.

"All right, I am good. Let us go back and celebrate Philip and Polly."

Robin and I turned around and headed back to the House of Dracas. I probably seemed like I was a heartless bitch but witches' emotions worked differently than humans. We felt all the same emotions and felt them deeply, we just felt them in the moment. Once they were over, they were over. We did not linger. We felt them, dealt with them, locked them away, and moved on. Earth help them if they ever came out all at once.

When I got back to the house, understandably everyone was in a sombre mood, shocked by what had happened. I walked up to Polly, who was consoling Philip. I pulled her to the side.

"What is going on? I gave you strict instructions."

"He was not having it. He said this was a time to grieve for his brother." I looked around and, of course, Ina was sobbing in the corner with Andias trying to hug her. Everyone else was in a daze.

"Oh for the gods' sakes."

I walked up to Philip. "Philip, listen to me," I said with a stern voice. "You are now king. You need to lead these people, is this how you want to start out your reign? Showing them how weak you are? Look at them. They are in shock. They are in pain. They need direction and they need a leader. We will mourn Percius, but not right now. Now is the time to celebrate our new king and that is you. It should have been Percius, but it is not. If I could be queen and lead them I would, but I am not. So gain your strength, I am about to announce you as king." I knew what it was I saw in his eyes. He was losing his mind. I turned to the rest of the people.

In a loud and commanding voice, I said, "Everyone, please, settle down. May I have your attention, please? As you all know we have been dealt a terrible blow tonight with the loss of King Percius. I believe we have all dealt with enough loss these past few weeks to last us a lifetime. Later we will take the time to mourn our sweet Percius, but that time is not now. Tonight is about celebrating our new king. Today we thought we were only gaining a king but this night we gain

My Name is Agnes   213

a queen as well. Our king will not only lead us in battle, he will guide us into more prosperous times. The queen has just given birth to a grand young son, so we know the strong bloodline will go on forever. It is with great honour, on behalf of King Percius, to introduce King Philip and standing by his side, Queen Polly. Please raise your glasses and join me in a drink to them." I nodded to the band to start playing.

I gave Polly a hug and then gave one to Philip as well. He said in my ear, "I do not know where you find your strength."

"One of us had to find our balls." I pulled away and looked at him. He, all of a sudden, started laughing. Then I started laughing. Polly looked at us like we had lost our minds, which was true for one of us. Then she started laughing too. It was such a good stress reliever. Philip had tears streaming down his face by the time he stopped laughing. He wiped his face then grabbed me and hugged me again. "Thank you Agnes, I will never forget this."

"I hope you never will Philip, now you know the depths of my strength." I pulled away and let the line up of people come and congratulate Philip and Polly. I grabbed a drink of whiskey — I was off the wine for a bit, and went to hug Axle for a moment or two.

After a while, exhausted, Polly came to find us. She fell into the chair. "I cannot stand to keep this ridiculously fake smile on my face any longer."

"You will have to get used to that. I do not know how to build those particular muscles up, but one must have to practice somehow. I believe a mirror would be in order."

Polly snickered, "Maybe that is why Ina is such a sour puss, she could not stand all the fake smiling."

"Does not seem like a bad trade-off, actually. You get to be a bitch year round and your face doesn't hurt all the time. She is a wise old woman."

Polly laughed, "I had not thought of that." She cooed at Axle for a bit. "Agnes, may I ask what you did with Kordinia?"

"I took her out back and burned her. Why?"

I don't think Polly could tell if I was serious or not. I didn't let on that I was joking, so she was starting to believe I was serious.

"Wh-what d-do we tell her parents?"

"If her parents come to ask for her, you send them straight to me. I would like to meet the parents who raised that girl. I would be curious to know if they knew what their daughter was up to."

"What will you do to them?" she asked nervously.

"I will decide that if they come here. It will depend entirely on their attitude when they get here." Polly looked shocked. "Polly, these are the types of decisions you will have to make as queen now. Some decisions will be easy, but some will be extremely uncomfortable. I will be here to help you but the decisions will ultimately be yours. You are now in a position of power. People will want to harm you and your family. What would you do to someone who might want to harm Axle?"

The innocence faded from her face and the hardness crept in like a fire being snuffed out with the smoke remaining. The smoke swept up her throat, out through her mouth, in through her nostrils, and out her ears again like she was steaming. "There would be nothing left of them," she said in a voice I had never heard before.

"Now remember that feeling and apply it others when they implore you to help them, but also remember there are always two sides to every story. There is good and there is evil, but there is always in between. There are liars, there are truth tellers, there are those that are on your side and there are those you need to keep on your side because you would not want them on the other side. It is always a good idea to have someone on your side everywhere you go."

"Philip has lost two brothers, but they were also his partners…you are now going to have to fill that role, I will help you with this. You will have to help him with the strategic warfare planning. Let him think everything is his idea though."

"You should take this little one to bed, tomorrow will be a long day. Sneak him away, I will tell Ina you were not feeling well."

Polly's eyes welled up. "I fear I will do your weeping for you, Agnes. I cannot believe how strong you are. You are this family's rock, you know that? Even though you do not share our last name, you are one of us. I love you more than you will ever know."

My Name is Agnes   215

"I doubt that," I said as we embraced. "Now make yourself scarce before Ina tracks you down."

I went back to the celebrations to say my good-nights and told Ina Polly had taken Axle to bed. She was disappointed but she would get over it. She needed to learn she was the grandmother and not the mother. Polly was the new reign, Ina was the old. I was going to make sure of that.

As soon as I got home I could smell Percius. I saw him everywhere. I could feel him here. This house was going to keep him alive for me, I was going to remember him for as long as I lived here. I felt happy here. I almost felt like I could talk to him here. But, of course, it was Robin that I was talking to...Robin didn't need to know that though.

The next day I went to get Polly and she was already out of bed and ready to go. Axle was bundled up for us to take with us. "I am surprised, I was expecting to have to coax you a bit."

Polly finished getting ready while I played with Axle. "I did some thinking last night and you were correct about a lot of things. I need to step up and be more than just a wife to Philip. I need to be his partner."

"Good girl," I said, "but we have to have our wits about us. We cannot just barge in there and demand he listen to us. We have to be delicate. I suggest we take in some food for them, listen to what they are saying, then make some suggestions...work ourselves into the conversation."

"That is brilliant. I am starving myself. Let us go get a bite first, then we shall take them a plate. Philip can never resist pastries." I picked up Axle and we made our way to the dining room. After we had our breakfast we packed up some pastries and travelled down to the war room.

The men were deep in discussion when we entered. As soon as we stepped in they stopped, of course. Polly said, "Oh do not mind us, we thought we would bring you some pastries from the kitchen. We need our men to keep their strength up!" She kissed Philip on the cheek. We went to the back table to display the pastries. The men went back to their discussion.

Philip said, "I am just afraid we will be up against too strong an army in Aphlios and we will lose too many men again."

General Thracian said, "I do not believe they are a uniform army without their leaders. They will be scattered — they most certainly will be shaken."

"I am fearful of losing more soldiers," Philip said, defeated. I looked at Polly and gave her a nudge. She took a deep breath and took a plate over to the men.

"Here you go, men," she said. "I could not help but overhear, my love, but did I not hear you say when you came back from Aphlios, after telling the people that Plennsenous was dead, the people were so thrilled they all pledged their allegiance to you?"

"Well, yes, but…"

"Then, as you said before, now is the time to strike. On your way to Aphlios, you will gain the people who pledged their allegiance, growing your army as you go. By the time you get to Aphlios your army will be twice the size of theirs. Like General Thracian said, they do not have their monstrous leaders any longer to terrify them into following them."

Philip stood straight up. "We will go back to my original plan and strike Aphlios immediately." He kissed Polly. "Thank you my love, you have inspired me!" Polly and I went to the back of the room to play with Axle and keep an eye on the men.

"Here is the plan," Philip said to the men, "General Thracian, tell the soldiers we will depart in one week." He got out a map. "Here is the direction we are to follow," and he trailed his finger along the map. "Now, we are securing lands and men along here…" He continued, just as we suspected, like it was his plan all along. I stayed for a little while because it was amusing but then after a bit excused myself.

"You stay here and keep these boys in line, Polly, I have a Spirit Release Ceremony to plan. Unfortunately I have recent experience doing so." I gave Axle a kiss. Polly winked at me as I left.

Two days later we attended Percius's Spirit Release Ceremony. Everyone said good-bye to Percius but me. Then I went home, lay in his bed and breathed him in. I dreamed of every part of him. I missed him. I would never say good-bye.

Five days later, the ladies and children stood at the gates as the men left for battle. *So much has happened since the last time we did this, it seems like a lifetime ago,* I thought, as the men got smaller the farther they walked into the distance. *It seems as though we were children then and we have graduated to women now.*

Eleven months had gone by when the troops came back and we all went running down to the gates to meet them. Philip was extremely proud and could not wait to tell us everything that had happened. He beamed, "Where is my girl?" Polly ran to give him a kiss. "Now where is my boy?" I put Axle down and let him walk to Philip. He was actually walking to Polly, but Philip didn't know any better. Philip picked him up and gave him a big kiss. He grabbed Polly's hand, "Come on, girls. I have much to tell you."

We all sat down to listen to Philip's tale with Ina, Andias, and General Thracian, along with some other right-hand men and some wine.

"We started out the same as we did before, and followed the same path, which was a sombre task for me as I did not have my brothers by my side." He put his head down and Polly put her hand on his. I heard Ina sniffle.

Oh for the love of the heavens, is this the way this tale is going to be told? I thought. I had not thought Philip to be that dramatic a thespian, but apparently I was mistaken. I rolled my eyes as I took a drink of my wine. I had started to drink it again, not long after Percius had died. I figured, why not? — even if it was poisoned it wouldn't affect me — only witches can kill witches.

Percius continued after a long, cleansing, deep breath in…I was going to throw up soon. "The first township we came to that had pledged their allegiance to us was quite reserved still. I believe they were still in terror of Plennsenous. It took some convincing, but I was able to gain their confidence and persuade them to take allegiance with us. I was right in believing they would take up arms and follow us to Aphlios.

"Once we gained our first allegiance, every township after that

218   *Kelly Brookbank*

could see the merit and followed suit. Once again I was right, by the time we got to Aphlios our army was twice that of theirs. They conceded immediately. Aphlios was immediately under our siege." Polly hugged Philip and the rest of us started clapping. Philip continued to beam. We were raising our glasses to him. Oh my, he was sucking this up!

"Oh but hold! The tale does not end there!"

What? We all looked at each other. What could be better?

Philip had a sly grin on his face. "We immediately took over the House of Tracraud where Plennsenous's youngest son was ruling. He was only a young lad and very timid. It did not take much for him to reveal all the family secrets. It has been well known for many, many years that Aphlios lands are rich, but the secret has been well kept how they got rich...Well now we know." Philip threw a gold coin on the table.

As well as the rest of us, Polly was confused, "I do not understand, Philip."

Philip looked like the frog who had eaten the last fly on earth, "Gold swims under Aphlios."

Chapter 27

"Can you make out what they're saying?" I asked Stuart.

"No, it's too muffled. There are definitely voices though."

"Shit. Do you think Lester could clean it up with his police stuff?" I suggested.

"Yeah, but I think we've asked too much of Lester, and he might suspect that we know more than we're letting on. I know a computer guy who could probably help us out. I'll give him a call."

Stuart went out into the hallway to make his call. I went to the bathroom to fix my hair back to its normal state. When Stuart came back in he said, "No problem. He's got the equipment to fix the recording at home, so he said to go to the Tipsy Lounge and he'll come and meet us."

"Cool beans. I have no idea where Tipsy Lounge is, but it sounds groovy."

"I guess you'll just have to trust me."

"I guess I will. Should I change first?"

"Why would you do that? I like you just the way you are," he said with a stupid grin.

I just glared at him. "You're exhausting."

When we got in the car I said, "So New Orleans is because of the alligators, right?"

"Well New Orleans is known for quite a few things; there's Mardi

Gras, Fort Lauderdale, and spring break is quite popular, but yes — they have a swamp full of alligators."

"I'm about to dismember you and throw you to the alligators…"

"Oh, you mean why Peter took the girls there, yes I would assume that's why he took them to New Orleans." Stuart chuckled to himself.

"You think you're quite the comedian, don't you?"

"You think you're pretty funny too, don't you?" He looked at me accusingly.

"Yeah, but I'm actually funny." I stuck my tongue out at him. "Have you ever been there?"

"Yes."

"Do you think that kind of thing goes on all the time?" I gave him a serious look.

"I don't know. I hope not." We sat in silence for a few minutes.

"There's Tipsy's." Stuart pointed to the lounge. The parking lot was pretty full.

"Wow, looks pretty busy for a Monday night," I said.

"Monday night football."

"Right!" Duh, Agnes…

We walked in and found a table. The place was busy but luckily we could still get a table. We ordered some appetizers and drinks. It wasn't too long before Stuart's buddy was there. He was a big guy who looked like he could be playing some Monday night football himself. Stuart did the introductions. His friend's name was Max. We asked Max if he wanted to stay for a drink, but he said he would after he got the recording done. Fair enough.

"That is not what I pictured your "computer guy" to look like." I leaned in as I said it. I'm not sure why because Max had already left.

"Max isn't your typical computer geek."

"No he is not. How did you meet him?" I asked as I took a chicken wing.

"He works for me."

"At your pharmacy?"

"What pharmacy?" He asked, looking confused.

"I thought you said you were in pharmaceuticals," I said, looking

My Name is Agnes 221

confused back at him.

"You seriously don't know who I am?" Stuart asked.

"You are Stuart Digion. So?" I was even more confused now.

He looked a little bit relieved. "My name used to be Stuart Digion a long time ago, I changed it to Stuart Decker after I graduated high school because I didn't want to be associated with my brother."

"Ok, so you're Stuart Decker. If you're into pharmaceuticals and you don't have a pharmacy then what do you do? Are you a pharmaceutical rep or something? You sure keep weird hours." I was completely confused.

He looked relieved. "I am so glad to hear that, you have no idea." He got off his seat and came around the table, took my head in his hands, and kissed me. "I have been wanting to do that for months now."

"You are seriously the most confusing man I have ever known! I have been trying to get you to kiss me for two days now and you keep pulling away. You have been waiting to tell me your real but not-so real name first? I don't get it."

He kissed me again.

"Ok, I only let you do that because I really enjoyed the first kiss, now will you tell me what the hell is going on?" I said.

He laughed and sat back down. "I wasn't sure if you knew who I was or not. Most women around here know who I am and try to take advantage of that. I own a pharmaceutical company...among other things."

"Oh, so you have money? I don't care about that." I ate another chicken wing. "Wait a minute, so women have tried to target you because of your money? That's terrible. Wow, we can be real bitches, hey?"

"Yeah, it's made me fairly sceptical and mistrustful of women."

"I imagine. Well you don't have to worry about that with me." I told him.

We had a couple more drinks and kept flirting back and forth until Max came back. He didn't have a happy look on his face.

"Hey Max, could you get anything off the memory card?" Stuart asked.

"Yes, I got it cleaned up for you." Max waved the waitress over and ordered a drink. "I put it on this mini-cassette and brought a player for you. You can both listen on these headphones."

I went and stood beside Stuart. We put one ear-bud each in our ears and hit play. It was hard to tell what we were hearing at first, but then I could make out it was two people fighting — they were clearly drunk or something. Stuart mouthed to me, "It's Peter and Thomas."

Thomas: Why do you keep wasting your life away?

Peter: I don't have much to live for.

Thomas: What are you talking about? You're a young man, you can do anything you want.

Peter: You ruined my life.

Thomas: Come on Peter, don't start this again.

Peter: Why can't you admit it? There's no one here, it's just you and me, admit what you did to me.

Thomas: I didn't ruin your life, I made you a man.

Peter: I was a child, Dad. You took my childhood away.

Thomas: Don't be such a baby, it made you stronger.

Peter: How can molesting me make me stronger?

Thomas: It taught you to grow up, didn't it? Finally got you off your mother's tit. You were such a fucking momma's boy. Turned you into a man.

Peter: You turned me into a drug addict.

Thomas: (laughing) You did that to yourself, I didn't do that you.

Stuart turned it off. His hands were shaking. I put my arms around him and whispered in his ear, "I'm so sorry." After a minute or two I said, "We should get this to Detective Lester."

"Thanks for doing this for me, Max." Stuart stood up and shook Max's hand.

"I'm sorry for bringing you this news," Max said. He stood up, downed his drink, and then turned and left the lounge.

"Come on, let's get this and the computer to Detective Lester," I said as I put some money on the table. I grabbed Stuart's hand and the tape player and we walked out to the car.

When we got in the car Stuart grabbed me and sat me on his knee

My Name is Agnes

with his arms around me. We stayed like that, hugging in silence all the way to Peter's house and to the precinct.

We sat in silence in the waiting room of the precinct too. What a creepy place to just sit and wait when you're stressed out already. You just know there are germs everywhere. Who sat in my chair last? A murderer? Not that I should talk. A prostitute? In a short skirt? How short was her skirt? Did she have her legs crossed or uncrossed? Does that really matter? Was she wearing panties? Do they wear panties?

"Do prostitutes wear panties?"

"What?" Stuart asked me with a really weird look on his face.

"Never mind, there must be one around here I can ask." I looked around. "Oh, she must be one." I pointed to a woman in short shorts wearing a bra-type shirt. "I'll ask her." I started to get up.

"Sorry to make you wait," Detective Lester said as he came through the door.

I'd have to ask a prostitute some other time.

"I hear you have something I need to hear?"

"How often do these chairs get sanitized?" I asked Lester.

"I have no idea, but I would wash your shorts when you get home." I looked back at the chair as we walked to the door.

"Follow me."

We followed Lester into an interrogation room and Lester and Stuart sat down.

"I think I'll stand, thanks," I said.

We showed Lester the pictures and emails first. He sat back in his chair. "Well at least we can give the families some peace."

"This is what I would really like you to listen to." Stuart put the tape player on the table and pressed play. After it was done playing, Stuart said, "That was Peter and his father, Thomas."

"That is a terrible thing, man, just terrible. But we can't prosecute someone based on an audio-tape. I'm sorry. Plus the only person who can testify against Thomas is dead. Does Thomas know you have this?"

"No, when he came by we hadn't found it yet." Stuart answered.

"And where was it when you found it?"

"It was inside a box hidden in a compartment inside Peter's bed.

The memory file was taped behind a bug's bunny button in a case."

"So you don't think anyone had found it before you two discovered it?"

"No, I don't believe so. We found it by accident," Stuart said. "Why?"

"Well if Thomas had found this memory file then it would have been motive to kill Peter, but now we're back to square one. We still don't know who killed Peter, if anyone did. Maybe it was an overdose after all," Lester said, deflated. "This explains why Thomas wanted you two to snoop around the house though."

"So there's nothing you can do?" I asked.

"I'm afraid not. Audio files are just not good-enough evidence. That could be anyone on those tapes." He put his hand up before Stuart could say anything. "Not that I don't believe you, but that's what even a child pretending to be a lawyer would be smart enough to say."

I tried to cheer Stuart up when we got into the car. "At least we gave those families some peace, that's a silver lining."

Stuart knocked on the pane separating us from the driver, "To my brother's house, please."

"Ohhhh, this is not going to be good," I said. "Are you really sure you want to do this? I mean, you could wait a bit, settle down for the night, sleep on it? We could go for a drive or something? Look at all the stars out toni…seriously? It's Arizona, the one night I want to see stars and it's overcast. Well, it's still warm out, we could go for a walk? Do you want a drink? No, that will just make you angrier. I mean, I get it, he's a total douche and he deserves all that's coming to him, but maybe we should think of a plan?"

Silence.

"No? Ok, I probably just made things worse. We could go back to my place, huh? Now that we have all that silliness of you thinking I'm a gold-digger out of the way…" I snuggled up closer to him."

He turned to me, grabbed my legs so I was straddling him and pulled my head down to his, until our faces were about an inch apart. I opened my eyes to see his were still open. He had this look on his face that was just about the most sexy thing I had ever seen — this fire

My Name is Agnes   225

was in his eyes like he was about to devour me, yet he was wearing this sly little, crooked smile on his face. My head pulled away a bit and I'm pretty sure the look on my face changed from shock to "hummina, hummina, hummina."

He slowly brought my face down so our lips met, barely at first, then he traced my upper lip with his tongue. He kissed the corner of my mouth, under my chin, and then made small kisses tracing down the side of my neck and down my clavicle.

"We're here, sir."

"Thanks for getting my adrenaline pumping, babe." He kissed me on the lips and sat me on the seat beside him, then got out of the car.

"What the fuck?" I sat there in a daze. "Oh no you didn't, you son of a motherless goat!" I got out of the car and ran to meet him. "Ok, match point to you asshole, but I want it on record I don't think this is a good idea even though I'm still behind you."

He turned to me and kissed me again. "Thank you." He called Thomas. "Hey, I'm outside your house, we need to talk. Are you alone? Good, let me in." Thomas came and opened the door.

"Hello, good to see you again, come in." Stuart and I walked in without saying anything. Thomas shut the door. "Can I get you anyth…"

Stuart turned around and punched him, and the force of his punch threw Thomas into a table with a decorative vase, causing the vase to fall on the floor and break. It didn't look like a knock-off vase.

"What the hell, Stuart?"

Stuart punched him again and then picked him up. "We didn't find your precious pin, Thomas, but I think we found what you were really looking for." He pulled out the memory stick.

You could see the guilty look on Thomas's face. "Look, Stuart, I can explain that."

Stuart punched him in the stomach. "How the fuck can you explain that you molested your own kid, Thomas?"

Thomas started crying.

"Jesus Christ." Stuart dropped him on the floor. "You're pathetic."

"I know." Thomas sobbed. "I'm sick. I've been living with this guilt for the last twenty years. Looking over my shoulders, waiting for the police to come and arrest me. I just can't handle it any more. Please don't go to the police, Stuart. I would rather die than put my family through this shame, please Stuart. I'm begging of you."

"We did go to the police, asshole, they can't do anything with just the audio file," Stuart spit at him.

Thomas sat up a bit and stopped crying. "What about the video file?"

"There was no video file."

"That stupid imbecile never did a video confession?" Thomas started laughing. "Then there's nothing they can do!" He laughed harder.

Stuart picked up the memory file and knocked Stuart out with one more punch before we left.

* * * * *

"That is fantastic Philip, I had faith in you." Polly kissed Philip. "Gaining Aphlios is wonderful and the acquisition of the gold is a secondary bonus. We must celebrate!"

"Yes!" Ina stood up. "I will go tell the kitchen to get a feast prepared." And she was off, once again like it was her idea.

Polly and I just shook our heads, and she waved to the servants who were standing by. "Please bring wine for all of us and round up a band, will you?"

We partied late into the night, and I hung out with either Polly or General Thracian. I was very excited to have Robin back. I was always keeping my eye on Philip though, still not trusting him, somehow. Polly seemed happy to have him back and he seemed happy to be back and to have his family surrounding him again.

The next morning I came to get Axle up, have our morning time together, and get our breakfast for the day. Polly and Philip came down, not soon after, still happy; seemingly still in the honeymoon phase. We all had a nice breakfast together. Philip told us some funny war stories while we had some quiet moments together. He also told us that General Thracian had taken it upon himself to be his guardian,

My Name is Agnes   227

of sorts. Thracian wouldn't allow him to go into battle any longer. He'd explained that Philip's country needed him now more than ever so he wouldn't risk him going into battle. I made myself a mental note to ask Robin about that later.

When Philip was done with his breakfast, he stood up from the table and wiped his mouth with his napkin. "It is off to the war room. Can I expect to see you ladies in there shortly?"

Polly and I looked at each other. "Of course," I said.

"Yes, I just have to gather some things for Axle."

"Excellent. See you soon then." He gave Polly a kiss, turned and left.

Once he was definitely out of hearing range, we both smiled at each other. "Thank the heavens!" I said. "I was afraid he would not continue to keep us in his strategic planning."

"He would be a fool to not include us — look what we did for him last time!" Polly winked at me. "We must hurry before he makes any decisions without us."

I yelled over my shoulder as I started down the hall, "You go fetch some things for Axle, I will retrieve some food for him and arrange to have someone come with us in case he starts to get restless."

In less than ten minutes we were in the war room. The men hadn't started anything yet, they hadn't even finished their teas. We got Axle settled down and then poured ourselves tea and headed over to the maps. We thought we might as well first figure out what they needed to figure out before they needed to figure it out for themselves.

As we looked at the map, we saw there was a clear pattern of land that we had conquered over the years. It was obvious to us where they should go next and then after that. This next hurdle wasn't going to be easy but neither had Plennsenous been. Polly and I were looking into the future as well, not just the next battle.

After securing Aphlios, the best course of action was to attack two major cities coming down from Aphlios, separating and hitting them both from the centre, keeping the camp in the middle and the centre strong. It was risky but it could be done. Both armies could slowly retreat to the middle and when they got there, a fresh batch of cannons, sharp swords, shields, fire, etc. would be there for them.

"Let us get down to business, shall we?" Philip said. "Should we continue to acquire lands or should we stay put and try to reach out to our neighbours to the south?"

One of the other generals spoke up. "The lands to our south are still Molossian Lands. If we do not conquer them and stake them as Mathesdon, then we are at risk of war."

"I do not believe any king would hand over the key to his city," another general said, "The only way to gain lands is by force."

"I wish it was not this way, but I believe you are right," Philip sadly uttered. "Let us have a look at the map and choose a direction." He pointed west. "This is the area I think we should focus on first."

The generals thought out loud and talked about that, saying they thought this would be a good idea, etc. etc.

"General Thracian, could I speak to you a moment?" I asked him.

"Yes, Miss Agnes."

Polly and I showed him our map. "You see where we are here? And all the lands we have conquered on the way to Aphlios?" I traced the area with my finger. "What do you think of this idea? Come down from Aphlios here, set up camp here, and attack these two centers from the middle outwards?"

"That would be a bold move. Those are two very affluent cities," Robin said.

Polly interjected. "If both armies slowly retreated back to the middle, there could be fresh artillery in the form of cannons, sharp swords, shields, fire to shoot with arrows, etc."

"Brilliant, ladies, absolutely brilliant," Robin said. "King Philip, might I have a word over here, sir?"

"Yes, Thracian?"

"Well sir, I am embarrassed to even suggest this, as I am sure you would have proposed it anyway, but what about this idea?" He told Philip of our plan.

"I was just about to tell everyone I had changed my mind and we were going to do this exact plan. But I thought maybe we would not separate and attack both cities at the same time, but attack one city and once that is conquered come back and take the other."

My Name is Agnes   229

"Darling, I do not believe that would be as effective," Polly said. You could tell Philip was pouting. "I know, my love, why do you not pitch both ideas to the generals and they can choose which they believe to be the better plan?"

"Yes, I was going to suggest that as well. Our minds are so similar, Polly." He kissed her on the cheek. "Gentlemen." He walked over to the map the men were standing over. "I have had a change of plans. I need your help with the outcome though, I can not decide which is the best way to finish the battle." He presented both courses of action. Of course, the generals chose our way. Before Philip could start pouting again, I got his mind off the subject...

"Philip," I asked, "may I ask who you left in charge of all that gold in Aphlios?"

"What do you mean? I left twelve soldiers."

"Were they trusted soldiers?" I probed.

"Not terribly," he replied, becoming impatient with me.

I was wrong, Philip had completely lost his mind.

Robin interrupted. "I believe what she is trying to say is that we should probably think about what our plans are with Aphlios."

"Yes," Philip said, "that was on my agenda for today. What exactly are your concerns, Agnes?"

"Is the gold that is under Aphlios well known or was it kept under wraps by Plennsenous?"

"I do not believe anyone knew but the House of Tracraud," Philip replied.

"When do we move our belongings there, Philip?" I asked.

Everyone gasped when I asked the question. Even Polly was shocked and she was by far the sharpest one out of the lot, except for Robin, of course.

Robin jumped in. "I agree with Agnes, we do not want word getting out that there is gold in Aphlios. The sooner we get there, the better. If Russell has told anyone, it will not take much to overthrow twelve soldiers."

"We could leave Ina and Andias here to run things," Polly suggested.

"It would be better to have our home base there anyway," one of the generals threw in.

Nice. Getting the other generals on board was always good.

"I have made up my mind," announced Philip proudly. "We are to move to Aphlios immediately. Polly, you and I will go break the news to Mother and Father immediately.

Ina and Andias were not thrilled with the idea of their family leaving them, but they didn't have much choice in the matter. With Polly and I leading the charge on the move, it didn't take long to get it organized. Once we had it firmly in hand and were convinced everyone knew exactly what their jobs were, we left for Aphlios.

Luckily when we got there, we discovered that Russell (like another baby in the family) hadn't had enough experience or intelligence to think of overthrowing the twelve soldiers who were there. In fact, he was a great help in divulging all his secrets and helping us get set up. He became a great asset and was named advisor for the House of Dracas. What an idiot.

While we were waiting for the rest of the staff and soldiers to get there, Philip was busy training the new soldiers from Aphlios. Once the rest of the troops got there, they were off almost immediately to besiege Abuta and Morean.

Although it didn't seem like it, two years went by as we were busy getting the estate ready, looking after the daily business of the gold empire, watching Axle grow and anxiously awaiting the arrival of another baby, little Patricia. In fact, it was almost two years to the day, when Philip and General Thracian returned and came through our doors.

Philip's demeanour was decidedly different than it had been the last time he returned. He was certainly not beaming like the last time. He was beaten and bruised this time, mentally...not physically. It was obvious they had not won the war. Philip refused to talk about it. He went to his bedroom and closed the door.

I turned to Robin. "General Thracian, what happened? We knew the plan had risk, but it also showed promise!"

"Yes it did have promise and it probably would have worked, but at the last minute, King Philip changed the plans and chose his earlier

My Name is Agnes   231

plan. We did not split the army and invade both Abuta and Morean, we came around and attacked Morean only, leaving our camp and fresh artillery exposed in the middle. King Philip believed we would defeat Morean, pick up the fresh artillery, and continue on to Abuta. We were doing well, pushing Morean back, believing we were just about to defeat it when Abuta's army joined Morean, carrying our fresh artillery. We tried to fight on but they were just too much, we had to surrender."

I think if Philip had been in the room Polly would have slapped him.

Chapter 28

"Don't worry about Thomas, he's an ass. Obviously he's been an ass for a long time. You know that. Let's just forget about him. What about that walk I was talking about before? I wasn't completely joking." We were just sitting in the car. Neither of us really knew where to go or what to do.

"I can't believe he's going to get away with it. He always gets away with everything. He's such a snake," Stuart said through clenched teeth.

"Is that why he became a criminal lawyer? Just kidding. You don't think he's going to charge you with assault, do you?"

"Probably. Little bastard."

"Maybe you could play the tape for Angelina. I bet she would have a different view of it than the courts," I suggested.

I think I actually saw the light bulb go off above Stuart's head. "That's it, Agnes, you are brilliant!" He kissed me then grabbed his phone and texted Thomas.

"Ha! There — now the little fucker at least thinks I might tell Angelina. I have one up on him. He definitely won't be filing charges against me and he'll be keeping his nose clean from now on. I feel better now." He let out a sigh and took my hand. "Let's get away for a couple of days."

"What? What do you mean get away? Like on a holiday? I don't think I've ever been on a holiday."

"You've never been on a holiday? You've never been away from the store for more than one consecutive day in a row?"

"No, I don't think so."

I could tell by the look on his face that he couldn't believe it. "You do have people that can, if you were to leave said store for more than one day in a row, look after the place, right?"

"Oh, of course, I trust Sarah and Julia to look after the place. They're great."

"Perfect," said Stuart as he grabbed my phone and gave it to me. "Call them and let them know you won't be back until next Monday." He knocked on the windowpane, "We'll need to stop by Agnes's condo, please."

I got off the phone. "So are you going to tell me where we're going or is that going to be a surprise?"

"Oh, I was going to tell you, but now I think it should be a surprise."

"Fantastic, so how am I supposed to pack?"

"I will give you a couple of hints. It will be hot and you won't need to pack much." He gave me that sexy — hummina, hummina, hummina look again that made my stomach flutter instantly. He leaned into me and swung my legs around so I was under him.

"You know I'm going to get whiplash one of these times if you keep doing that to my legs."

"Don't worry, there are other things I am going to be doing to your legs next time we are in this position." He gently kissed me, turned his head and kissed me again harder. Sitting up he found my hands, holding them both in his left hand and putting them up above my head. He gently traced his finger down the right side of my neck, then followed the same trail with kisses. My whole body was shivering. He did the same thing down the left hand side of my neck. Then he lightly traced his finger just above my clavicle at the bottom of my neck and followed it with kisses. Shivers on top of shivers!! He started tickling his way up my shirt and kissing down my cleavage.

The car stopped. "We have arrived."

Stuart got up, "Let's go get you packed." He moved out the door. I was still lying there.

I sat up on my elbows. "Are you fucking kidding me?" But Stuart was already out the door. I slowly moved my legs down and sat up.

He poked his head in, "Are you coming or what?" I glared at him.

I met him at the elevator and smacked him on the arm. "You have got to stop doing that to me," I growled. He looked at me and winked. *Uh huh, two can play at this game,* I thought.

We walked into the elevator and happened to be by ourselves. Before the doors even closed I turned and pressed myself up against Stuart, planting my lips onto his face, kissing him wide, sticking my tongue in his mouth. I ground my pelvis against his. I put my hands under his shirt and gently dragged my fingertips up the small of his back and back down his sides, under his armpits. The elevator dinged as we passed each floor, so I knew where we were. Just before we got to our floor, I took my hands out from under his shirt, grabbed both sides of his face and finished kissing him slowly. I looked at him straight in the eyes. "Never start playing a game you can't win." I kissed him again as the elevator doors opened and I turned and walked out to my door. The doors to the elevator just about shut, but Stuart got a hand in between them at the last second.

He quickly snuck into my condo and shut the door. "Make yourself a drink, I won't be too long." I yelled from the bedroom. Stuart came in not very long after. "You win," he conceded.

"I know," I said. "I really don't know what to pack so I'm just packing a few bathing suits, shorts, shirts, dresses? Anything else?"

"That sounds perfect."

"Ok." I shrugged my shoulders. "Whatever."

We finished our drinks and headed out. We got into the elevator, looked at each other and started laughing. As we held hands, Stuart took my head with his other hand and kissed me. We kissed softly all the way down the elevator. I don't even know if anyone else was on with us.

Once we got to the airport, we immediately got onto Stuart's private jet. Everything of Stuart's was black and white or black and silver, it was absolutely gorgeous. "So you're, like, private-jet rich?"

My Name is Agnes   235

"Yup," Stuart said.

"Ohhhh. Oh well," I said, nonchalantly. "I guess there are people that have private jets."

"Yes, people do."

The flight was very short, we were only going to San Diego. Once we got off the jet we got into Stuart's car service, headed to the marina, and arrived at the docks. Stuart showed me to this absolutely huge, three-story yacht.

"This is our home for the week, honey," Stuart said as he gestured to the yacht, which was named Prescription for Paradise.

"Holy shit," I said. "So you're, like, fucking huge yacht rich?"

"Uh-huh."

"I guess there are people that have fucking huge yachts," I said, trying not be impressed.

"Yes, some people do."

"Okey dokey, let's check this bitch out," I said as we started up the walkway.

Once again, everything was black and white/silver. And stupid gorgeous. One of the living rooms had five couches and a grand piano. There were marble staircases, an exercise room, and a media room. The formal dining room had two ten-person tables with a full bar on each end. A huge hot tub was on the top deck, and there were fifteen cabins and twenty-one full time crew members. Every luxury you can imagine, this boat had it. Plus other boats were stored inside the yacht, so if we wanted to take a smaller boat out for a spin or water ski or something, we could do that too. Seemed a bit excessive for just the two of us.

I stopped asking, "Is this the master suite?" because all the bedrooms were so gorgeous, you just assumed they were the master suite.

"This is the master suite." Stuart opened the double doors. I walked in and it was absolutely breathtaking. The double king bed, or whatever you call that big-ass bed, was raised with beautiful, carved, dark wood surrounding it. There were two couches and large windows, which surrounded the whole bedroom. It had patio doors onto a surrounding deck. The bedroom was at the bow of the ship, so the view was unobstructed.

"This is absolutely magnificent. How do you ever leave this boat?" I went and stood by a window.

Stuart poured us some champagne and brought us each a huge strawberry. He handed me the champagne then gave me the strawberry. Gesturing to the couch in the middle of the room, he said, "Come sit here, this is my favourite place to sit in this room." He went and opened the patio doors. We sat on the couch, snuggled up, and looked out to the water and the stars, eating our strawberries and drinking our champagne.

"To answer your question, up until about six months ago I used to come on this boat a lot more."

"What happened six months ago?" I said dreamily, taking everything in.

"Someone told me about this coffee shop that made really good coffee. I had been meaning to stop in for a while, but for some reason hadn't, so one day I made a point to go in. I discovered that they did, in fact, make really good coffee. But something else happened to me that day."

"Go on."

"I saw the most beautiful woman I had ever seen in my life." Stuart looked at me.

I sat up.

"I couldn't stop thinking about her, so I had to go back every day just to see her. Some days she would talk to me, some days she wouldn't, but it didn't matter, I was just happy to see her every day, hear her voice, hear her laugh. I couldn't help it, I was falling in love with her."

I put my champagne glass down and turned to him. "Why didn't you say something to me?"

"Because of who I am. I don't get involved with women anymore, but with you it was different, I just couldn't help myself. I had to get to know you."

I grabbed the bottom of his legs — they didn't really move.

"What are you doing?" he asked.

My Name is Agnes   237

"I tried to swing your legs around so I could jump on you but it didn't work so good…"

"How about this?" He picked me up and took me over to the bed.

"Yes, that worked much better." I smiled at him. I tried to do his hummina hummina hummina look, but I probably should've tried it out in the mirror first.

"Are you ok?" he asked.

"Never mind," I said. "We need to switch this around — you're getting on the bed," I demanded of him as I stood up and he got on the bed.

"Uh, ok." He lay on the bed resting on his elbows.

I went and got our champagne glasses and put them on the side of the bed, and then I pounced on him, straddling him with my legs. "So let me get this straight, you came into the store every day just to see me?" He nodded. "But yet you never once asked me out?" He shook his head no. "Then I was practically throwing myself at you but you still resisted?" He nodded. "Hmmm, you must have a lot of restraint, huh? I think we should test that theory, what do you think?" He shook his head no.

I bent down so our noses were just about touching and whispered, "I think we should." He put his hands on my ass, and I took them off, "Oh, no touching Mr. Self-Discipline or I'll have to restrain you." I sat up again. I started gently rocking back and forth, "So this is what you came in to see every day?" I took off my shirt. He nodded. I started rocking back and forth a little harder. "Or maybe you came in to see this?" I took the left strap of my bra off my shoulder. Stuart groaned. I started rocking a little harder. "Or this?" I started to take the other strap off.

"Oh for fuck sakesl Agnes," Stuart reached up to grab me while bucking me off at the same time to roll over on top of me. I laughed as he did. "There's only so much one man can take!" Kissing me hard, he reached behind my back to undo my bra. He threw my bra to the side and looked down at my chest. He cupped my breast and kissed my nipple, then kissed his way up to my lips again.

I started to pull his shirt out of his pants, then up and over his head. "I have to be honest with you, Stuart."

He stopped. "What?"

"This belt of yours is going to get in the way, I think maybe we should take it off."

Relieved, he said, "That is true." He let me take it off.

"Well, if we're going to be completely honest, these buttons on your shorts are starting to jab into areas they shouldn't be jabbing." He traced his fingers on the buttons on my shorts.

"That could be just plain dangerous, we should probably get rid of those," I said, with deep concern in my voice. He ripped off my shorts.

"Your pants are probably going to give me a rash if you keep them on." I told him as I was already pulling them off.

I lay there as Stuart looked at my naked body, until he looked up at me and said, "Now this was worth the wait." He kissed me again on the lips then started kissing his way down my body and didn't stop until I was gripping the covers, throwing my head back and shivering from head to toe. He made the tingling sensations start from the top of stomach and the bottom of my thighs until they met in the middle with an eruption that didn't stop until he did, which was good because I don't think I could stand much more.

He grabbed the champagne glasses and we both took a drink, then he lay beside me again, pressing our bodies together, kissing at first and then sliding himself into me. He rolled on top of me and within minutes we were both on top of the world again, we just fit so well.

Exhausted we lay on the bed. "Good thing that didn't suck," Stuart said.

"It definitely did not suck," I said.

He grabbed the champagne glasses and handed one to me. "Have you ever had a relationship that you thought someone was absolutely great but then the sex just…"

"Sucked?" I said.

"Well…yeah," Stuart replied.

"No, actually, I was a virgin before tonight."

Stuart just about choked on his champagne. "What?"

"I'm just kidding. Yes I have, I mean there's only so much you can do yourself, right?"

Stuart put his champagne glass down. "I thought I had a good idea of who you were when I was visiting your store for six months…"

"You mean stalking me…"

"Whatever. But I had no idea what delightful things were going to come out of your face. I am never going to be bored with you, am I?"

"I haven't even started playing practical jokes on you yet." I poked his nose.

"Don't start a game you can't win, Agnes, my love."

"I accept that challenge, sir." I pinched his nipple.

"Ouch! Oh you're going to pay for that, missy!" I squealed and laughed as he started lightly biting me.

We made love again and then he fell asleep spooning me. It had been a long day and he needed to sleep. I stayed in that position for a while because it felt good to be in his arms, finally. After a while I slipped out of his arms and quietly went to the walk-in closet to see if there were housecoats in there. Sure enough, the softest housecoat I had ever put on was in there. I slipped it on and walked out.

I heard Stuart rustle so I turned around to look back at him. There it was, on the small of his back, just above his waistline, the heart birthmark. I could just make it out in the moonlight. I quietly snuck up closer to him…it was definitely the same birthmark — a c and a comma in the shape of a heart, the tails curved. I got some water out of the mini fridge and went out to the deck to lie on the deck chair.

He came back to me…again.

Stuart was right, I didn't need to pack much; we were either naked, in our bathing suits. or in our housecoats. Stuart and I had so much fun together, it was like we had known each other forever — which we kind of had.

The week went by so fast — I should take holidays more often! Even though I loved my store, I almost didn't want to go back. I could have gotten used to this life. I'm pretty sure every single one of the crew saw me naked, but I didn't really care. I pretty much forgot that they were there. We had sex just about every place we went on the yacht. Good thing witches can only get pregnant by other witches.

When we pulled into the marina it was getting dark, but it was taking longer than usual, not that I knew any different. Stuart was getting a bit anxious, so he thought we should go see what was going on. Just as we were getting up to see, Robin, who was our captain, came in.

"Sir, there seems to be a problem at our berth."

"Agnes, this is Captain Dibben."

"Nice to meet you, Captain Dibben." I shook his hand with my middle finger tickling his palm, he hates it when I do that!!

Stuart said annoyed, "Is someone parked there again? Just have them remove it."

"Ummm, no that's not it, I think maybe you should come take a look." Stuart shot me a confused look. We went down to the lower deck and Captain Dibben shone his flashlight over to the buoy on the dock. "There, do you see that?"

"Jesus, that looks like a body bag," Stuart said.

"Yes, that would be the problem," answered the captain.

* * * * *

"He will not come out of his room, it has been two weeks, what are we going to do, Agnes?"

"Come here." I grabbed her hand and took her to the window. I pointed out to the pasture. "You see those horses out there?"

"Yes," Polly said, looking outside.

"Do you see the smaller version of a horse?" Polly nodded. "That is called a donkey. The pitchfork behind it would make a better king than your Philip."

Polly made a face at me. "Agnes, be serious."

"All right, let us go down to the war room." I suggested.

Being in that room just put you in a better frame of mind for dealing with military coups and war strategy.

"I have asked General Thracian to meet us here too," I told Polly. "If Alexander and Percius were here, what would they do?"

Polly was the first to admit, "They would go back and conquer

My Name is Agnes

Abuta and Morean using our original plan."

"But we can not do that now because we are down too many men," Robin said.

"So we need to get more men, how do we do that?" I asked.

"That is the problem," both Polly and Robin said.

"Let us look at the map." We took out the map and I focused on the area directly around us. "Now see this area? This area is still mostly slave land because of our predecessor, correct?" Polly and Robin agreed. I branched out farther. "Now this area, these are slaves for Abuta and Morean?"

"Agnes, just spill what is floating around in that head of yours," Polly said, with a roll of her eyes.

"My thoughts are this, the three of us — and the children of course, with their tutors, travel around and make agreements with the people who live on these lands." I was trying to inch my way into the "big plan."

"What kind of agreements?" Robin asked.

"That they will join our army," I said.

Polly was sceptical. "You believe they will join our army just because we ask them to?"

"Not exactly..." I said sheepishly.

"Oh for Zeus's sake, just tell us your plan!" Robin said. If he had been in true form and Polly hadn't been there, I'm pretty sure he would have thrown something at me or slapped me with a wing.

"What do we have an abundance of here in Aphlios?" I asked them.

Robin scoffed, "Used to be patience, but that is running thin."

"Gold?" Polly answered.

"Yes, Polly." I shot a look at Robin. "We travel to all these homes and offer them gold to go back into trades or into the land in exchange for their allegiance to our army. They will no longer be slaves — they will be stronger and self-sufficient. They will be businessmen, but they will still work for the king and queen. While the men are away at war, the women will run the businesses." I paused. "What do you think?"

Robin and Polly sat for a minute thinking about it in silence. Robin was the first to say something. "I believe it would be grand if it works."

242   *Kelly Brookbank*

Polly said, "I do not think we really have any other choice."

"We had better get packing for a road trip," I said.

"Hey Zeus, she finally told us the plan!" Robin yelled up to the heavens, teasing me.

One great thing about being rich is that it doesn't take long to get things done. It's not quite as good as magic, but it's the next best thing. We were ready to go the next day. We had four carriages; one for the adults, one for the children and their tutors, and two for the paraphernalia.

We left the carriages with the House of Dracas colors on them. We wanted the people to know it was royalty coming to their house. It was probably very intimidating for them to see four royal carriages pulling up to their doors out of the blue, in fact, they were probably scared shitless.

Robin got out first and helped the two of us out of the carriage. The owners of the house were standing on the doorstep, shaking like leaves. When we came up to them, they bowed. "Hello there, I am Queen Polly, this is my most trusted advisor, Agnes, and this is General Thracian. What are your names?"

The man trembled. "Good morning, my queen, I am Anthony Bengbrill and this is my wife Ciarra. How can we be of service, my queen?"

"May we come in, Anthony? We would like to speak with you about something."

"Y-y-you would like to c-c-ome inside? Inside m-m-my home?" Ciarra asked.

"Yes, if that would be all right?" Polly said.

"Yes, yes of course," Anthony said, and he and his wife looked at each other before escorting us inside. They showed us to this tiny little table of a thing Anthony had obviously built from scrap wood. There was only one usable chair, which they obviously pulled out for Queen Polly.

I looked around the one room, obviously the remains of what used to be someone's house. From what I could see, Ciarra kept it very clean and tidy and did what she could with what she had. The couple looked like survivors and were very resourceful. I was very impressed.

My Name is Agnes   243

"Tell me Mr. Bengbrill, what did you do before you hit on hard times?" Polly asked.

"I was a farmer, my lady," he said as he bowed his head, looking ashamed.

"Have you looked at the soil around here, sir?" Robin asked. "Is it suitable for farming?"

"Oh yes, sir." Anthony perked up. "I go out to that soil every day and think to myself that it is such a shame there is nothing growing out of it. I miss farming so much, planting the seed, caring for it, nurturing it, watching it grow..."

Ciarra put her hand on his arm, "Anthony."

He looked at her, looked back at Queen Polly, and dropped his arms, "I am sorry, my lady, I just think about farming and it brings back such fond memories."

"I have a proposal for you, Mr. and Mrs. Bengbrill," Polly said. "I am going to give you the deed to this land — we will go out later and figure out the border. I am also going to give you some gold to help you get started in your new venture and get you back on your feet. There are a few things I ask in return: One is that you pledge your allegiance to the army of Aphlios. Two is that your first business is always to the Crown of Dracos. How do these terms suit you?"

Neither of them said anything.

"Do you need time to discuss it?" I asked, confused by their reaction.

They both started crying and laughing at the same time, hugging each other. "Time to discuss it? My lady, absolutely not! Yes we agree! Throw my robe to the heavens, I do not believe it! Thank you!"

Ciarra sunk down to the ground crying. I went over to get her and pick her up. "Are you ok?"

She hugged me. "I am overwhelmed. I have never experienced such kindness."

"I am glad," I said.

Through tears Ciarra said, "We used to be a complete community until Plennsenous took over and ruled," she told me.

"Are you telling me everyone around here has a role to play?" I asked. She nodded. "Do they live here today?" She nodded again.

"Polly, General. Ciarra tells me this used to be a fully functioning community before Plennsenous's rule, and everyone lives here still. Might we have a town meeting instead of going door to door?" I looked at Ciarra and Anthony. "Does that sound like a good idea?"

They stood up, "We will gather them in the town square."

We walked outside and watched the commotion starting as Anthony and Ciarra yelled into doorways and people came out of their homes confused.

"This is definitely a good start," Polly said. "I believe the children should join the party."

"These people would enjoy a good feast as well," Robin suggested.

"Brilliant idea!" Polly said. She had no idea how much we'd packed and would be oblivious to the fact that it would magically replenish itself. Robin went to tell one of the helpers to get the feast ready and another to bring the kids.

Once everyone had gathered in the town square, Polly announced the reason why we were there. Everyone was shocked and extremely excited. After the excitement died down, we figured out what role everyone played then got down to the business of signing contracts. Then we let the feast begin. These people were just so appreciative. Not one of them was dry-eyed by the end of the day and each of us got at least two hugs from every one of them. The kids had a grand time playing with each other and Axle and Patricia learned a great lesson in this.

When we left the next day we told them that we would be back for the men on our return but that they should have their businesses up and running by that time.

The three of us could not stop smiling as we pulled away. "I can only hope every town is that easy..." Polly said. And it was. Once we crossed over to Morean and Abuta lands we took the House of Dracas colors off so it wasn't so obvious that we were royalty. We went house to house and didn't have town meetings like we had on Aphlios land because we didn't want word to get out to the wrong people, but at each house they would tell us important information about the next house and so on. When we got to the end of the road we asked the men to come with us immediately — the women were fully capable of

My Name is Agnes   245

running the businesses on their own.

After a long and hard journey we finally made it back to the House of Dracas without really knowing what to expect on our return. We especially hadn't known what to expect of Philip, so we went down to the war room first. We assumed that he had snapped out of his depression at some point and was in there fuming (Polly had left a note for him). Or else he had given up on us and was trying to figure out his next pansy-ass move. When we walked in there was nothing. The map we'd had out was in the same place.

We walked into the house. Quiet. Polly looked at me. "You do not think?"

"There is only one way to find out." I shrugged my shoulders. We walked to his room, opened the door, and there he was, in bed with a fully grown beard.

Something in Polly changed when she saw him. She went straight over to the windows and pulled all the drapes to let the sunshine in. He groaned, then she went to the bed and pulled the covers off.

"Get up, Philip," she hissed at him.

He sat up. "What is going on?"

"You are getting up, that is what is going on," Polly sternly said.

"I do not want to," Philip said as he lay back down.

There was a jug of water beside the bed and Polly dumped it on him. "It was not a request." She stood by the bed with her arms folded.

He looked at her and could tell how serious she was. "All right, all right." He slowly started to get up. "I do not see what the point is, everyone is better off with me here in bed."

"That might be true," Polly said, "but unfortunately I cannot lead the men into battle or I would be doing that for you as well. Meet us in the war room in ten minutes." Polly grabbed the untouched note she'd left him and we left.

"So, no more coddling him then?" I said as we walked down the hallway.

She looked at me with fury in her eyes, "Did you see how pathetic he looked in there? And that is our king? Hopefully he can keep it together long enough for Axle to take over. We need Philip to secure

246   *Kelly Brookbank*

Abuta and Morean, after that we will be indestructible. Then it will be my job to raise Axle to be a great king, not a fool like his father."

I didn't disagree with her, Philip was an idiot, though he wasn't terrible to her...but there was still that feeling I had about him. Man, that was driving me crazy!!

In ten minutes on the dot Philip was in the war room, still wearing the beard, although at least it was trimmed. "General, will you please tell Philip what the next course of action is going to be?" Polly said, so annoyed that she couldn't look at Philip.

"Because I know you so well, I know that you will want your next plan of action to be,.." Robin started.

"Oh for Zeus's sake, we are not playing that game any more." Polly looked at Philip. "We are going to tell you what to do. You can take credit for it, but under no circumstances are you to deviate from the plan, do you understand?"

Philip nodded.

"Continue General."

"Uh-huh, well we are going back to set up camp between Abuta and Morean, split up and attack them from the middle. Same plan as we had before."

Philip looked like he was going to cry, "But we cannot." He dropped his head. "We do not have the manpower."

"Come with me." Polly gestured for Philip to follow, as we left the war room and went down to the pit where the soldiers trained. We held our breath until we got to the balcony. "Look," she said as she pointed to the men training — they barely had any room to move. Philip looked confused. "Now look over there." She pointed beyond the walls, where you could see men training as far as the eye could see. "We can not fit them all in here."

"Wha? How? I do not.... Where did they all come from?" Stuart asked after he picked his jaw up off the floor.

"I brought them here for you," Polly said.

"How many are there?"

"Twenty-five thousand."

My Name is Agnes   247

Chapter 29

Lights were flashing all over the place. Kinda looked pretty on the yacht.

"Under different circumstances we could totally have a disco," I said.

"We still could." Stuart looked around. "Throw some music on, get the juices flowing. You up for it, Captain?"

"Sure, yeah. I don't have to drive tonight," Robin said.

We all started laughing.

"I really want to see who is in that body bag," I said to Stuart, under my breath.

"I know, me too." He sat there thinking. "I've got it, follow me."

We went up to the top deck and he looked around one of the bars. "Here it is!" he said, pulling out a camera with a very long lens. I looked at him with an accusatory face. "What? One of the bartenders is a pervert." We went to the deck, lay down, and then inched our way to the edge. Stuart put the camera over the edge then focused it. He handed me the camera without saying a word. It was dark but I was pretty sure his face had lost all its color.

"What is it?" I took the camera, adjusted it and looked at the corpse. I had no idea who it was. I took a couple of pictures anyway and went to give the camera back to Stuart, but he was already gone. I took the memory chip out of the camera and then I inched my way back and met him at the bar. He had made himself a drink. I went behind the bar and put the camera away then went around to Stuart.

"Who was that?" I asked.

"That was the captain of the Arizona Wolverines NHL team."

"Oh. Are you a big fan or something?"

"Something. I own the team."

"What? The body of the captain of the NHL team that you own is in a body bag tied to the berth that you own?"

"Uh huh."

"Gee, do you think it's personal? Shit, we should probably get back down then."

"Yeah, we probably should, before they start piecing things together," Stuart said.

As we were just about to step onto the lower deck, Robin came to find us and handed us both drinks. "One of the detectives was looking for you. I told them you were somewhere having a drink."

"Thank you, Captain."

We sat back on the deck chairs with our drinks. A man came up to us wearing Nordstrom dress pants and a crinkled JC Penney dress shirt with a matching tie. He was very serious. He had his hand out to shake Stuart's. "Hello Mr. Decker, my name is Detective Nick Ray."

"This is my girlfriend, Agnes," Stuart introduced me to the detective. *Girlfriend, I like the sound of that.*

"I need to ask you a couple of questions," the detective said. He gestured to sit on the deck chairs. "How long have you two been away?"

"We left Monday night," Stuart said.

"And you haven't been back since then?"

"No, you can check the manifest."

"Thank you. We will have to look into some of your business assets, if that is all right with you, Mr. Decker. We will probably be contacting you in the next couple of days, so please don't leave the country again. Although if I had one of these I don't think I'd ever be on land again." He looked at the yacht.

"I'll have to take you out for a weekend sometime," Stuart said, shaking the detective's hand. The way he said it and the way he was

My Name is Agnes

looking into the detective's eyes he really meant it too.

"Wow," the detective blinked about a thousand times. "That would be amazing! Ok, I will be in touch. Thank you. Have a good night."

"Oh, Detective?" I said.

"Yeah?" He turned around, his face still flushed. "Any idea who the body is?"

"Sorry ma'am, I'm afraid I can't divulge that information until the family has been notified."

"Right. Have a good night." I waved to him. "Shit, you should've asked him that. I think he probably would've given you the keys to the precinct if you asked him."

"Maybe." He answered, obviously preoccupied. "Is it ok if we stay at your place tonight?"

"Of course. I don't think I have much in the refrigerator though and I am starved, should we go get a bite to eat?"

"Yes. I'm starved as well."

We went to this little seafood place off the beaten track and completely run-down, but it makes the best seafood you will ever eat. They only served ice-cold Corona. A cute Chinese couple ran it. I fucking loved this place. Cute couple that ran the place, serves awesome seafood, had ice cold Coronas, and played Elvis constantly. How could you not love this place? The owners would stop and dance every once in a while and sing the songs. You try not to laugh when a thickly accented Chinese woman sings *Blue Suede Shoes*. It's impossible. Stuart actually spit some crab out laughing when she first started singing. I suggested customers should wear safety glasses in there.

It took Stuart's mind off of things for a while, anyway. On the plane ride home he became subdued again. "Hey, are you ok?" I asked as I snuggled up to him on the car ride back from the airport.

"Yeah, I know someone is sending me a message, I just don't know what the message is."

"Not a very nice message, we know that," I said. I looked up at him. "I want to try something, ok? It might be blurring the edges of legal and not legal, if you're the kind of guy that worries about that sort of thing. I don't know, some people are, some people aren't. Some people say they are, but when it comes to a situation that they're involved in and they have a choice, they opt for the blurred line, which, in my opinion, is a bit hypocritical. It's kind of like having a strong opinion on a subject when you really haven't researched the other side of the subject, because that isn't doing your due dili…"

"Agnes!"

"Yeah?"

"What in Christ's sake are you talking about?" Stuart said, exhausted.

"Oh, right, so you remember when we were on the boat and we were looking at the corpse with the camera?"

"It was a whole couple of hours ago, but I do vaguely remember, yes," Stuart said impatiently.

"Well, I took a couple of pictures, 'cause I just do that kind of thing. And then I took the memory card, 'cause that's just another thing that I kind of do."

"So far, you haven't done anything that has shocked me, which is kind of shocking in itself."

"Thank you, I think? Anyway, so I know this reporter, sort of, that I send scoops that I happen upon. She has this amazing ability to get information before anyone else…"

"You think we should send this to her?" Stuart asked.

"I think it's worth a try."

"If you think we should, then we should." He kissed me. With an answer like that, I SO kissed him back.

"I'll send it to her when we get to my place."

"Why do you get newspaper scoops?" Stuart asked.

I looked at him. "I know, right?" Then snuggled up to him again.

We got into the elevator with a couple of other people. "I don't think I will ever be able to get into this elevator without thinking of what you did to me," Stuart said. We started giggling.

"I don't know what you're talking about," I said.

Once the other people got off, I said, "Don't forget about my bucket list though."

"What bucket list?" Stuart asked.

My Name is Agnes   251

"Having sex in an elevator." I turned and pressed myself up against him. "That will be another memory for this elevator." I kissed him. The door opened and I walked out.

He came out a bit later. "You have got to stop doing that to me!"

"I think we are about even now," I said and unlocked the door.

"At least I can do this now." He picked me up and whisked me to the bedroom.

After Stuart had fallen asleep I went to the living room and picked up my laptop. I put the memory card in my computer and clicked on the last two pictures. You could clearly make out that it was Drew McCarland. I opened up a server, logged on to an anonymous email website, and I typed the email address rittenwrdash@sundaily.com into the TO spot. I typed in "scoop 4 u" in the subject line. In the body of the email I typed, Captain of the Arizona Wolverines found dead in San Diego Bay. In the body of the email I typed: Do not run story until after game. I attached both pictures and hit send.

"What the hell are those other pictures on that memory card?" Robin said as he perched on my shoulder.

"I don't know," I said. "Wow, this bartender does not have a preference when it comes to women. He takes pictures of pretty much anything with a vagi…nope, never mind, doesn't matter if they have a vagina or not."

"They pretty much only need to be breathing…although these are pictures, how do we know if they're breathing or not?"

"That is a true story," I said. "Whoa, pervert does not suit this guy. I don't even think some of these pictures are legal." I shook my entire body.

I started surfing the web. "Let's check out this Drew McCarland guy. Hmmm, let's see. From Canada, of course. Born in 1987. Drafted first all around. Been with Arizona his entire career. Played with the Canadian Olympic team. Not married. Good looking guy."

Robin yawned, "I'm just going to have a nap over here. Come on Agnes, This is all boring."

"You're right, let's check out rag magazines on this guy. Ok, well, looks like he's done some growing up in the last little while. Did

his share of partying in the past, when he first got in the NHL —
understandable — but he has stayed out of the party scene the last six
months or so."

"Really?" Robin asked. "Why would he do that? Is he married or
with someone?"

"No, not that I can see."

"So he's only, what? Twenty-eight? He's rich, good looking, single,
young, and he stops partying? That doesn't make much sense."

He has a point, I thought. "What a shame, he was such a talent.
Someone kills a skilled kid like that just to send a message to Stuart?
But who? Could be anyone. Someone he does business with. Someone
jealous of him. Anyone in the hockey world. Thomas or anyone in his
family. Oh that's right!" I turned to look at Robin, and he had to fly off
my shoulder. "Sorry. He disowned them all when he left the funeral.
That didn't mean as much to me then as it does now. Of course they
would expect something in his will, but not if he disowns them. Grrrr,
why didn't I go over and smack them all with my teeth at the funeral?"

"What?" Robin asked.

"Oh yeah, you missed that. Never mind. Who else? I can't believe
I'm saying who else! I'm actually making a list of who all wants to kill
my boyfriend, for shit sakes."

"Calm down, Agnes. It's not like that's the first time you've
said that."

"You're right." I went back to the computer.

Stuart said, "Check out what else went on while we were gone.
Stuart's business dealings?"

"How the hell would I know? Besides, Stuart kept up with all that
while we were away."

"How about hockey? What are the standings?" Robin asked.

"Arizona is in first place in their division."

"Ok, is that unusual?"

"Let's see. Oh wow, they did not do very well last year. They were
third from the bottom, but somehow they got the top draft pick
because of this lottery thing. Ok, they got this superstar rookie this
year who is breaking all sorts of records. He's gelling really well with

My Name is Agnes   253

the team, especially the captain, and together they are unstoppable."

Robin's eyebrows raised. "Hmmm, that can't be good for the rest of the hockey teams. They gotta be pissed about that."

"That's a big ten to the little four, good buddy," I said with a big wink and the fake gun shape with my fingers pointed at him.

Robin shook his head at me.

"Why do people keep doing that to me?" I thought out loud.

"Let's see if Thomas has kept his nose clean," Robin said as he was still shaking his head.

I did a quick search. "Nothing. Good boy, Thomas." I got a ding in my fake email inbox. I saw it was a reply from Ashley Taylor and opened up the email.

"Thank you for the tip, this will be a huge story for me, I owe you. I made some inquiries and the police reports are saying murder by drowning."

* * * * *

"I do not believe it," Philip said.

"Believe it," Polly said. "Now, you need to come back to the war room so we can tell you what your plan is." She turned around and walked out. The rest of us followed her. I thought her red-haired temper was finally coming out again and I liked it! I was the last to follow and I realized Philip was still looking out at the men in the field.

"Philip!"

Shocked, he turned around, "Right, sorry." He followed me. "How did you two find all those men?"

"We just appealed to their better judgment and we came to an agreement that benefitted us mutually," I said.

"So you offered yourselves?" Philip said.

"Yes, Philip, that is exactly what your wife and I did — we had sex with 25,000 men. If you do not mind we are very exhausted, now listen to this plan so we can go have a nap." *Idiot.*

"Fair enough," he said.

I had to cover my eyes so I wouldn't disintegrate him right there. We went over the plan again for Philip and then again for good measure. "Now Philip, I want you to understand this clearly." I got very close to him. "General Thracian has strict instructions to use brute force on you if you deviate from these plans, are we clear?"

"Yes." Polly came closer as well. "And it will not matter whether you are behind closed doors or in front of your troops. Imagine what that would do to your already bruised ego."

"I understand. When shall we attack?"

"I do not see any reason to wait, do you General Thracian?" I asked Robin.

"I do not. All our weapons were being made while you were gone so everything is ready."

"I have everything under control — you girls should go have your nap," Philip said to us. He had seriously taken too many blows to the head in battle.

Polly looked at me funny.

"I will explain on the way to the house," I told her.

The invasions on Abuta and Morean were swift and victorious.

While Philip was gone Polly became absolutely devoted to her children. Axle was school age so she had him taught by Aristotle. He was exceptionally strong and athletic so he was being trained by Nicea, and of course he was battle training every day with a cousin of the family, the great Magesia.

Once the men were back there was definitely a change in the air. Philip was different. The soldiers were different. They came back accompanied by young men and women who worshipped the ground they walked on. Every night was a party in the barracks of the soldiers.

Philip came in to see his family and everyone else, especially his kids, who of course were excited to see their daddy. They went running to him and he picked them up and swung them around. He gave Polly the obligatory kiss. Everyone was there to hear the news so someone yelled out, "How did it go, King Philip?"

He yelled out in return, "Abuta and Morean are now ours!" Everyone cheered. "Now let us celebrate!!" And the party began.

There was something that was definitely different with Philip. I had

My Name is Agnes   255

been on this earth for thousands of years so I could tell a lot about men and what their body language reveals, but most telling is what their eyes tell you.

When men are only interested in one woman, in other words — taken — there's a certain way they "check-out" women. They will look at them and then look away, like they're saying, *Oh, yeah — she's hot* or *Yep, she's got a nice ass.* But if they are available or putting out the vibe that they are available, the way they "check-out" a woman is different; they will look at them but their stare will linger and they will look them up and down like they're saying, *I want to bed that,* or *What I wouldn't do to get that.* They are putting out the vibe that they are available, even if they are not.

I have seen those men with women to whom you just know they are completely devoted. You absolutely know that man would never cheat on his woman because he absolutely loves her. Yeah…Philip wasn't one of those men any more. I could see it in his eyes and I could see it in the way he was looking at the women around him. Philip was a changed man.

Polly came up to me then. "I am going to take the kids to bed before this gets out of hand." She kissed me on the cheek.

I grabbed her hand. "Wait. Have you seen all those people that came back with the soldiers? Is that not a bit strange?"

She held my other hand as well. "Agnes, when we conquered Abuta and Morean, it was a grand feat for us. We have become almost a super-power now. With that comes great prestige, almost like fame. The soldiers are going to take advantage of it."

"Just the soldiers?" I questioned.

"What are you saying?" She looked at me straight in the eye.

"Have you not noticed Philip has changed also?" I tried to sound as kind as I could.

"Of course he will lap up some of the fame as well, I do not know any man who would not. It is not my concern. My only concern is those two children of mine." She kissed me again. "Thank you for being my best friend. I really must get them to bed." She turned and headed to find her children.

She didn't mean what I thought she meant did she? She must have misunderstood what I was saying, right? I mean, I knew Philip was as smart as my used toilet paper but he was still her husband. She must have misunderstood what I was saying, of course.

I stood there, nonchalantly watching Philip for a while as I sipped on my drink. I noticed that as soon as Polly left a lot more of the young girls joined the party.

"Hey you." Robin came up behind, scaring me back into reality.

"Oh, hey!" I said, startled.

"Did I scare you?"

"Yes, in fact you did," I said, in my best mysterious voice.

"What were you thinking about so intently?" Robin said with concern in his voice.

I looked at him face to face, "Tell me the truth, does Philip do anything he should not while you go away to war?"

Robin looked shifty-eyed, "What do you mean, 'he should not?'"

He knew exactly what I meant, "With other women?"

"He may have strayed once or twice." He looked down at his feet.

"That fucker."

Robin tried to make excuses for him. "It is not that unusual when soldiers go off to war, it is just part of war. Women just ignore it, I guess."

"Did Percius?" I asked matter of factly.

"No, but..."

"There you go. I cannot believe you never told me."

"I have not even had a chance to talk to you yet! He only did it this time after we conquered Abuta and Morean. We are like a super-power now, you should see the girls falling all over us," Robin explained.

"Yeah, I hear. You are all god-like, blah blah blah. I bet you are just batting them away are you not?" I teased him

"I may have indulged. A general has to have his fun now and then."

We giggled and then I turned serious. "Anyway, that is no excuse for Philip. He is married to my best friend. Hey Zeus, look what he is doing right in front of everyone!" Philip had slipped his arm around the waist of one of the girls and pulled her in between his legs as he

My Name is Agnes   257

was sitting on the arm of a chair. He was kissing her neck. I had to stop myself from screaming at him. I started to walk over there but Robin stopped me.

"Now be smart about this," Robin said. "Wait until they are committing full adultery and then show Polly."

"Thank you again, Robin, my impatience gets the best of me too often."

Soon enough, Philip took the hand of the hussy and led her to one of the chambers. I followed them to see which room they were going in then went to go get Polly.

She was in Patricia's room telling her a story. I asked one of the help if they could take over. "Polly, you need to come with me."

"Where are we going?" she asked, with a silly grin on her face.

"Come on, you must see this." I took her to the room Philip and the trollop were in. "I am sorry you have to see this but I just could not stand by." I opened up the door a few inches so she could look inside. She looked inside and then looked back at me. "What?"

I was confused. "Are they not in there?" I looked inside the room. Sure enough, Philip and the tootsie roll were having sex. I pointed in the room. "That is Philip in there."

Polly started walking away. I grabbed her arm. "Polly, that is your husband in there!"

"I told you, that is none of my concern. My only concern now is my children. I do not give a shit how many bitches that idiot fucks, as long as he does not touch me."

I couldn't believe it. Is this the way it always works around here? You don't marry for love, you marry either for political reasons or you marry to have children and then it's over? I don't believe it. What Percius and I had was love and he was a real man — there had to be more to marriage than the two options. Besides, Philip was embarrassing my best friend and I wasn't about to stand for it.

I turned around and burst into Philip's room. I was so mad I don't even know what they were doing but I really didn't care.

They tore themselves apart. "Agnes, what are you doing?"

"Philip," whined the little floozy, "What is she…"

258   *Kelly Brookbank*

"Get. Out." I glared at her. She looked at Philip, and he nodded. The little slut pouted and left in a huff.

"Agnes, I do not think..."

"No, Philip, you do not think and you may not talk. I shall do the talking and you shall do the listening and the agreeing. Do you understand?" I grabbed a wine and took a seat on the chaise across from the bed. "I always had a bad feeling about you, Philip, but you took Polly's heart so I did not want to stand in her way of happiness. I could not understand this bad feeling about you. You seemed to be a good person. You treated Polly well. You came from a good family. You seemed to love her. But my bad feeling has never really gone away... until now."

"Agnes..."

I put my finger up. "Remember, no talking, if I remind again, my mood shall quickly change and believe me, Philip, you do not want that. Now where were we? Ah yes, bad feeling. I have recently come to learn that this may be typical for the men in the family to step out on the woman and the woman to be accepting of it, to devote her time to the children, etc."

Philip was nodding. I looked at him. "I am not in favour of this." I gave him a look that told him, *Holy shit, this chick is as serious as a branding iron up my ass*, or as I like to call it 'the look.'"

"Now," I sat back and crossed my legs, "I am not an unreasonable woman. I realize men have their needs." I stood up. "But you flaunting your philandering ways in front of the whole world does not sit well with me." I bent down so I was inches from his face. "In fact, Philip, it makes me very angry. Very, very angry." I stayed like that for about thirty seconds. A bead of sweat rolled down his forehead. I sat down again.

"I do not believe you have witnessed my anger, have you Philip?" He shook his head. He didn't speak...I guess he's not as stupid as I thought he was. "Do you believe I would be pleasant when I am angry?" Philip shook his head. "Would you like to be on the receiving end of my wrath, Philip?" He shook his head really hard. "Good, we are on the same page then." I downed my wine.

My Name is Agnes   259

"Here is what I am going to do for you Philip." I stood up. "You may have a girlfriend, but no one is to know about her. You are not to show affection to her outside of this room. She is not to tell anyone of this arrangement. If I see you winking at her, touching her inappropriately, looking at her too long, anything — you will experience my wrath. Do you understand?" He nodded. "Good King." I started to walk to the door. Just as I was about to open it, I turned to Philip. "Oh, and by the way, people love me around here and I talk to everyone, and I mean, everyone. If I hear any of the girls talking about your little relationship, she will no longer have a tongue to speak with, and you will no longer have a dick to fuck with. Have a nice night, King Philip."

I went back out to the party, found a glass of wine, and went to find Eunice. "You people have some strange customs," I said to her.

"What do you mean?" she said so innocently.

"Never mind. What is going on out here?" I asked.

"It is terribly disgusting. I do not know where all these girls came from." She looked around.

"Why do we not go for a walk?" I suggested.

"I would enjoy that." She smiled at me and picked up her wine.

"You know I feel as though you are my sister, do you not?" I asked her.

"I feel the same, Agnes." She smiled brightly at me.

"May I ask you something?" I asked her.

"Yes," she said sceptically.

"Why do you not have a suitor?" I asked her. I noticed her cheeks getting pink.

"What is your meaning?" I could tell I'd embarrassed her.

"If you look around, there are many good looking men in close proximity. Brave, good looking, honest. Plenty of them would have your hand in a heartbeat."

"I am waiting for the right one and none of the men around here are him. I see what you and Percius had and I want that. What Polly and Philip have is what I do not want. I do not want that to happen to me."

260 *Kelly Brookbank*

I stopped walking. "I have to apologize to you Eunice."

She looked at me, shocked. "What for?"

"When I met you, you were a young girl. In the past few years you have grown into a woman and I have not even noticed. I am so sorry I have not spent more time with you."

"Oh Agnes, I can not keep it in any longer." She looked as if she might burst. "I am in love!"

"And who might this fortunate man be?"

"Nefarius of Olympia."

Chapter 30

I had never been to an NHL game before, let alone to the owner's box. Stuart took me shopping first. Apparently what you wear when you meet the wives matters. I'm not one of those girls. I have a disposable income because I'm a witch. I can go into any store and buy whatever I want. I don't care what it is or what it costs, I just want it to be comfortable. And "don't care" are the operative words...I really don't care about brand names. I am not going to wear a so and so if it gives me blisters — that makes no sense. But if a "whatsa-ma-call-it" makes my ass look fantastic and doesn't give me a muffin top, you can bet I'm going to be buying a couple of those!

Stuart didn't want to throw me to the wolves right off the bat, so we met with the team's general manager and his wife first. Ryan and Liz were very nice and Liz and I got on instantly.

"I remember when I first came to the wives' lounge, I was scared shitless," Liz said. "Ryan had told me horror stories about them." We stood at the bar as we all made ourselves drinks. She shot him a look and he giggled. "Turns out it wasn't as bad as he made it out to be."

Ryan and Stuart went to go see what was going on on the ice while Liz and I stayed back. "Oh, I'm not too worried. I don't really care what people think of me."

"Good for you, Agnes." She clinked glasses with me. "I wish I could be more like that. It's tough when you're in this business. Some of them can be really nasty, but for the most part they're quite nice."

We chatted for a bit before I brought up the question I really wanted to ask.

"So how well do you know Drew McCarland?"

"I don't know him personally, but Ryan does, of course. Why do you ask?"

"I just heard he wasn't playing tonight for some reason so I was wondering if you knew anything about it," I lied.

"No, not me. Some of the wives might though. Do you think you're ready to go into the wolves den?"

"Bring it on! I'm just going to say good-bye to Stuart."

I patted Stuart's ass. "Hey, we are going to head to the den."

"You sure you want to do this?" Stuart genuinely looked afraid for me.

I laughed. "I think I can handle myself," I said as I gave him a kiss.

Liz opened the door for me and I walked into the lounge, Liz following behind me. I stopped, turned around, walked back outside and looked behind the door, then came back in. Liz said, "What are you doing?"

"I was just looking for the sign that said you must be six feet tall and stunning to enter this room." Liz started laughing.

A couple of the wives heard what I said and came over. "I like you already," they said. Liz introduced them as Sophie, the goalie's wife, and Ella, one of the defensemen's wives. I had asked Liz to just introduce me as Agnes — if I wanted to tell them I was Stuart's girlfriend I could, but for now I would just be Liz's friend Agnes.

The wives were dressed nicely but not like they were going to a soiree after. I wasn't really sure why some of them were dressed that way.

As I looked around I saw how some of them were looking at me, and I could definitely see who the bitches were. I was getting the stare-down from three in particular, so I gave them an enchantment curse that made them gain seven pounds that they would never ever lose, no matter what they tried. I felt like sticking my tongue out at them afterward too.

My Name is Agnes   263

Sophie and Ella took me around and introduced me to everyone including Chloe and Macey (the assistant captain's wife). They were obviously distracted by something.

"Is everything ok?" I asked.

"We are just wondering why the captain isn't playing tonight," Chloe said, almost consoling Macey.

"Yes, I heard he wasn't going to be playing tonight. I was wondering if anyone knew anything about it," I said.

Macey said to me, "Who are you again?"

"My name is Agnes, I'm a friend of Liz's. Do you know him very well?"

"I don't know if I would say, really that I know him, you know, all that well. Of course my husband knows him well, of course, because they're captain and assistant captain, so they know each other well, of course." Macey stammered.

"Of course," I said. *There's obviously something going on here*, I thought.

I asked some other ladies about him. He was definitely a partier, a drinker — no drugs. He was a womanizer, but had stopped a couple of months ago. Every time I asked why he'd stopped with the women everybody obviously knew the answer but wouldn't say. I thought I might have to get Sophie and Ella drunk and went up to get us more drinks when the three bitches, whose clothes looked really tight all of a sudden, "accidentally" bumped into me.

"Oh, excuse me, I don't think we've met. My name is Agnes."

"Right and who are you?" Bitch #1 said as she looked me up and down.

"I'm a friend of Liz's."

Bitch #2 said, "So you're just a friend of Liz's?" They looked at each other and rolled their eyes.

"I'm not sure I know what you mean by that."

Bitch #3 piped up. "You realize this is a WIVES' lounge?"

"Mm-hmm."

The bitches started walking away.

"Oh, ladies?"

You could just tell they rolled their eyes again as they turned around. "Yes?" Bitch #2 said.

"I'm also fucking Stuart Decker." You want to see someone's facial expression change? I should have taken the before and after pictures. Even the color drained from their faces.

"The owner, Stuart Decker?" Bitch #1 said.

"That's right, the man your husband works for. Have a great night, ladies."

I could hear them muttering, "Stuart has never been here before." "He has never brought anyone here either!" "What have we done?" "Fuck."

I had met pretty much everyone so I did my social butterfly thing and walked around getting to know everyone better, every once in a while looking back at the three bitches sulking in the corner and virtually "cheers"ing them with my drink. They just gave me half-assed smiles back. Sometimes I really really enjoy being Agnes the witch.

Eventually it was time to go to our seats to watch the game. Liz decided to watch it in the owner's box, but I asked to watch it with Sophie and Ella. They were thrilled to have me sit with them. The bitches? Not so much. We got to our seats and there wasn't a seat next to Sophie and Ella, obviously, because I'd just butted my way in there. I looked at the three bitches and what do you know? One of them offered me her seat! Awful nice. It wasn't a sold out game so she had to sit about ten rows up.

I had a steady stream of alcohol flowing the whole game and we were having a really fun time. Even the bitches were starting to loosen up. By the third period tongues were starting to wag, and I was hearing all sorts of things about the players and their wives!

I had to nudge just a little bit and kerblam! There it was: "So, what was Macey acting all sketchy about in the lounge for?" I asked Sophie.

"Oh that! She's been having an affair with Drew McCarland for a while now. You know Drew McCarland? He's the captain you know. And she's married to the assistant captain, so that's bad. That's really bad." She put her finger up to her lips.

Ella leaned over, "Do you know who else is having an affair?"

My Name is Agnes   265

"Who?" asked Sophie.

"Stephanie and Chloe."

"I don't even know who Stephanie is."

"Oh yeah, I mean Steven."

"You mean her husband?"

"That's right! But I don't know if it's true or not."

"I pinky-swear not to tell."

Hmmm, so that threw another link in the chain. The captain was sleeping with the assistant captain's wife? I had to tell Stuart and get this news to Ashley. The game was just about over, so I'd have to wait a couple of minutes.

After the game I got the ladies back to the lounge and got them all one more drink with an enchantment to sober them up and forget everything they had told me in the stands. I said my good-byes and excused myself before they started drinking their last drink.

"I have some pretty juicy gossip for you." I whispered in Stuart's ear when I got back to the owner's box.

"Did you enjoy the game, Agnes?" Ryan asked.

"Yes, it's a lot more entertaining live than it is on TV." I answered, not that I had ever watched it on TV.

"It was a great pleasure meeting you, Agnes." Liz gave me a hug. "You can come and watch the game with me any time. I always have to entertain such fuddy duddies." She rolled her eyes.

"I would like that," I said honestly.

"We have to go and meet with the press. Always a fun time," Ryan said sarcastically.

"Better you than me," Stuart said.

"That's not a bad idea. They would love to see you!" Ryan almost shouted.

"Not on your life. I can still fire you, Ryan."

"Ok, ok." He put his hands up and laughed. "You win!"

"Hopefully see you two more often." Liz said, and they left.

Stuart turned and gave me a kiss. "So what's this big juicy gossip?" He took my hand and led me to the seats at the table while he got me a drink.

"Well, Mr. Decker. Turns out our Mr. McCarland had been having relations with Mrs. Assistant Captain."

"Is that right?" He put my drink down and sat at the other seat. "Well, that would explain why he stopped all the partying then. He has a girlfriend after all."

"Yeah, she just happens to be a married woman. A married woman who is married to the guy who is the assistant to your cap...tainage? Damnit that was sounding so smooth in my head."

"Did it sound like Alec Baldwin in your head?"

"Yes! It totally did."

"I thought that was the voice you were going for. It started off sounding really good."

"It's too late." I took a drink. "I should probably get this scoop to Ashley. Is there a computer in here?"

"Yes, right here." He went to the cupboard and got it. Damn, him bending over sent sensations to parts of my body that instantly put a shit-eating grin on my face.

He handed me the computer. "Do you need glasses or something?" He asked me.

My eyes widened. "What? No, why?"

"Oh, it just looked like you were squinting."

"Right, squinting. Maybe I should get my eyes checked." I smiled. I opened up the computer and sent the information to Ashley. I looked up the headlines and there it was, all over the news.

"It's gone viral. Captain of the Coyotes found dead in San Diego Bay." I told Stuart and showed him the computer. He looked at the headlines and let out a big sigh.

He closed the computer and turned to me, grabbed my head with both hands and kissed me. "Let's just try to escape everyone for a little while, just be you and me...I have a feeling shit might be hitting the fan right outside this door..."

* * * * *

I hugged her. "Oh Eunice, I am so sorry." She looked at me in shock. "You are sorry? Why are you sorry?"

"I know I have not been paying as much attention to you as I should have been but I had not realized just how much. A lover? You have a lover and I did not know? How long has this been going on?"

"We started seeing each other not long after we moved to Aphlios."

"Are you happy?"

"Yes," she said with a big smile.

I hugged her again. "Then I am happy for you. Have you had a crush on Nefarious since before the Olympics?"

Her face went red and she looked at the ground. "Yes."

"I remember you acting strangely that day. I also remember Nefarius being a bit of an ass that day." I looked at her sideways.

"He has changed a lot since that day. He is not that boy any longer, he is a man, I can assure you."

"I trust you Eunice."

Because it was Eunice marrying Nefarius, we had to move to Olympia until the wedding. We had sent word to Ina and Andias but I was hoping they weren't going to be there until the wedding day. I didn't want her to show up and start bossing everyone around.

Polly had retreated more and more by the day. She had been isolating herself away from everyone else and focusing only on her children. She would still allow me to come and visit with her of course, but I was starting to think maybe even that would stop one day. She was refusing to come to Olympia until the wedding day saying that the childrens' tutors weren't able to come so she had to stay with them there. I was hoping getting her to the wedding would help break her out of her depression.

Nefarius's mother, Glykeria was nothing like Ina, she was actually charming. She wanted Eunice to decide what she wanted, not tell her what she wanted. Nefarius's father, Matthan was the typical war hero father. Nefarius's brother, Eldon was a big help with the wedding; he gave an opinion on everything from the napkins to the trivets. I have a feeling if it wasn't for Nefarius, the family name would not have carried on.

This wedding planning was such a non-stressful time, unlike

268   *Kelly Brookbank*

the last one. We were all getting along. There was no pending war. Nothing. It was strange to feel this way — I kept wondering what was going to happen and was looking over my shoulder all the time.

Then it happened. As I was going to bed, General Thracian came to get me.

"Excuse me, Agnes?"

"General Thracian. How can I help you?

"We have a situation that requires your attention, can you come with me, please?"

We walked out of the House of Prodicus until we were out of earshot. "What's going on?"

"King Philip is in town and he is drunk, falling all over women."

"Hades' gates. Ok, you change into a guard and we will go down there."

We went to the tavern and there was King Philip, drunk as a skunk, slobbering all over the women, kissing and fondling them.

I walked up to him. "Excuse me, King Philip?"

"Yess?" He looked up at me. "Agnes, my pretty, have you come to party with me?"

"Yes, Philip, that is right. I am your new drinking partner. But I can be your only drinking partner so your new little friends need to disappear."

One of the girls was so drunk she could only open one of her eyes, so she looked at me with that one, "I do not think so." One eye was enough once she could focus and see the glare I was giving her. "I am going over there, missus."

"That sounds like a great idea." I looked at the other one with my dead stare. "And what about you?" She couldn't even talk, she just put her hands up and stumbled off.

I pulled up a chair to sit beside Philip. "So what are we drinking tonight, Philip?"

"They have some fine ale, Agnes, fine ale." I looked at Robin. He brought us back two ales, one with a sobering enchantment.

Philip started drinking. "You are not too bad, Agnes, you know that?"

My Name is Agnes   269

"Is that right, Philip?" I took a drink. "You are an ass, Philip, you know that?"

He started laughing. He took another drink. "You are funny, Agnes. Funny Agnes."

I took a drink. "Yup, funny girl, I am."

He took a drink. "Yeah, funny. Ha. Ha." He looked at me. He looked around. He finished his drink. "Shit." He looked at the ground.

"I thought we had an agreement, Philip?"

He wiped his face. "I do not have my room here. She did not come with us."

I took a deep breath. "Oh Philip. I am really coming to hate you, do you understand that? It is because of those children I have not killed you. They need a father. Luckily Axle is turning into a fine young man." I sighed. "I will be right back. This gladiator here will babysit you." Robin grunted at him.

I went to speak to the man behind the bar. When I returned I said, "It is settled, just to avoid a repeat performance such as this one, I will rent you a room here. Again, you will find one girl. I repeat, one girl. She will never speak of this. Am I clear, Philip?"

"Yes, Agnes. Thank you."

"And you might want to restrict your booze consumption a bit?"

Philip nodded.

Robin and I walked back to the house of Prodicus, discussing how we'd gotten into this situation. "It is quite bizarre, is it not? I am doing this to avoid embarrassment and Polly does not even care."

"It is a weird one we have weaved."

"What have we weaved?"

"A web."

"I should write that down," I said as I pointed at Robin.

"You should."

"Good night, Robin."

I walked into the house and started thinking about what Robin had just said and how it could be said a bit more poetically. *A web is weaved? A web we've weaved? Oh that sounds good. A web we've weaved... Shit, where am I going? I've got myself all tangled up in this housed. Oh wait, a tangled web we've weaved! That sounds good! A tangled web we have weaved.* Here was my room. I opened the door and turned on the light.

"What in Hades' gates?" Two people were having sex — one was Nefarius's brother Eldon on all fours and the other was Jordan, the guy Polly had embarrassed with the snakes from school.

Chapter 31

Ahhhh, my favourite place, in my favourite chair, with my favourite drink. After the night before, I really needed this. We'd had about two minutes alone in the owner's box before Stuart's phone started going off and people started knocking on the door.

Somehow the media got word that Stuart was in the building, so trying to leave was a nightmare. If I could have used my powers I would have, but that would have raised way too many questions.

Ryan had Liz sent home and then come back to the owner's box. "Are you fucking serious? The whole time you knew and you didn't tell me?"

"We couldn't. We weren't allowed to until family had been notified," Stuart defended himself.

"Well obviously somebody has been notified because the press is all over it." He held his phone up. "This Ashley Taylor has his picture all over the news!"

Ummm, actually that's my picture, but I don't need the credit — go on with your tirade.

"I don't know how these media people get their sources. They probably pay cops off or something, I don't know. Maybe this Ashley Taylor is a cop. Whatever. Who gives a shit. The story is out. There's nothing we can do about it. What we can do is move forward," Stuart said.

"Ryan, do you maybe want to sit down and have a drink? Maybe you just need to deal with this news," I said.

He stood there, still fuming. Then he took a couple of deep breaths. "Yeah, maybe you're right. Ok. Yeah." He sat down and I went to go get him a drink. Ryan put his head in his hands. Then he slammed his fist down on the table. "Jesus, who would do this?"

I gave him his drink. "Here you go, get this down your neck."

"I don't know," Stuart said. "It's fucked up."

"I just don't understand it. Why would somebody do something like this?"

"It's hard for any of us to wrap our heads around," I said.

"The cops are saying murder by drowning," Stuart said.

"Jesus," Ryan said.

"Have you calmed down enough to talk to the coach and the team yet?" Stuart asked Ryan. "Otherwise I can. If we don't do it now they are going to be hearing about it soon."

They had a "no phone" policy in the dressing room until fifteen minutes after the game, and they were coming up to fifteen minutes soon.

"I'm ok. Let's go."

We all went down through the stadium's seating where there were hardly any fans any more and headed to the dressing room. Stuart and Ryan kicked all the media out — they weren't allowed any phones either, so they wouldn't have heard yet — and announced the captain's death to the team.

I wasn't going into the dressing room with a bunch of half-naked, emotional men so I stayed outside. Half of the media knew what had happened and the other half hadn't heard, so I watched the half who were in the dark, finding out for the first time. The reactions on their faces were priceless.

The news was already old to the other half, so now they started looking at me trying to figure out who I was. One of them looked at me so long, I actually said, "I'm nobody, really, I am literally no one." Once they figured I was no one they got bored with me and just hung out. To be polite they would introduce themselves to me and then walk away, so I started to introduce myself as funny characters from

My Name is Agnes

novels. I was Inigo Montoya, Angela Argo, Lady Jane Marie-France Tessier-Ashpool, Veruca Salt, Monroe Starr, Bucky Wunderlick, Ramona Quimby, Miss Havisham, and Mustapha Monde. Nobody even questioned that half of those names were male.

I was just about to see if I could find a bottle of tequila and start doing shots when Stuart and Ryan came out. The media swarmed and I felt like a McDonald's bag in an empty parking lot, while they were a bunch of shit-hawks. Luckily Stuart grabbed me before they started pecking and pulled me behind him. Some of the reporters saw him do that and started squawking. Ryan put up his hands and yelled, "Whoa, whoa, whoa! We will not be answering any questions tonight. We will be having a press conference tomorrow afternoon. Now please respect the players and leave them at this time. They have just learned of this development and need this time to let it sink in. They do not want to be answering any questions right now. Please respect them. Please do not ask them any questions. There will be a press conference tomorrow afternoon. Please, good night."

A couple of them still asked questions. Unfortunately, they were going to mysteriously wake up without voices the next day. Dumbasses.

We walked to the underground parking lot where Stuart's car was waiting. When we pulled out, the media was still there, flashing their cameras, almost right on top of the car, pushing and shoving one another. It felt like we were in a beehive and they were fighting to get in to see the queen. The plan was to go to Stuart's, but as soon as we got close we saw the media frenzy and headed straight to my place. Not that I minded, but I hadn't even seen his place yet.

I felt like I should be calling Sophie and Ella to see how they were doing. I really did feel a connection with them. They were fun and down to earth. If I was going to be with Stuart, I'd have to stay involved in his business life also. It was probably too early to call though. I always had to remind myself what time it was. Many times I had to stop myself from calling people at all hours of the morning, forgetting that they slept and I didn't.

Soak up this moment just a little while longer because pretty soon... beep, beep, beep, there's Giorgio. And my day began!

At about 8:00 Stuart walked in. "What are you doing here?" I asked after I gave him a kiss.

He gave me an exasperated look. "Media. Everywhere."

"Gotcha. Well, have a seat over there, I'll bring you over your favourite." I sat his drink down. "Did you have much work to catch up on?"

"Nothing that I can't do at home, but you know what home is like…"

"Agnes." Sarah blurted out.

"Sarah?"

"Right! I'm sorry to interrupt," she said a bit more quietly. "We have something that needs your attention with the delivery truck."

I turned to Stuart. "Might be one of those days! I'll be right back." I followed Sarah to the delivery truck out back.

Trevor the delivery guy was outside. "Hi Trevor. What seems to be the problem?"

"It's not that big of a deal."

Sarah interrupted. "Not that big of a deal? There is clearly a problem!"

"Ok, Sarah, just explain what the problem is."

"Well, you see right here." She pointed to Trevor's clipboard and as I bent to look at it, all of a sudden, my whole body and my head just started spinning. I barely heard Trevor saying, "Are you o…." as I started to fall. But what I could clearly hear and see was someone at the sandwich counter saying, "Hi, I'm Ashley Taylor. Are Agnes or Stuart Decker around?"

Bobbi replied, "Oh you're that reporter!! Yeah right!! Umm, Agnes is outside dealing with a book crisis, but Stuart is sitting right over there, and you're welcome to join him. Can I bring you anything to drink?"

"I would love a cappuccino, that would be great, thank you." She went over to Stuart who looked up.

"Hi my name is Ashley Taylor. Are you Stuart Decker?"

"Yes I am. Ashley? It's nice to meet you. Ummm, Agnes just went outside for a bit, she'll be right back."

My Name is Agnes   275

"Well, this is good that we get to talk for a bit first. Is that all right?" Stuart looked a bit confused. "Sure, yeah."

"Well I hate to be the one to break this to you, but I've been digging around and looking into the police records and toxicology reports from the coroner, both here and in San Diego. It's only a matter of time before they put it together, but your brother Thomas was the one who killed Drew McCarland.

"What? My brother killed Drew McCarland? How do you know for sure?"

"The same drug mixture that was found in your nephew Peter was found in Drew McCarland. Agnes said that the wives told her that Drew was no drug user. He was a drinker, but no drug user."

"I can't believe this. He must have taken some of the syringes from Peter's place, that's why they never recovered them. I never pegged Thomas for a killer."

"I bet you never pegged him for a child molester either."

"That's true. How are you able to get all this information? I know you're a journalist, but there are limits, aren't there?"

"Oh, I have my ways. I have an exceptional way of persuading people into giving me information." She took a drink. "Wow, this is a really good cappuccino."

"Yes, they make really great coffee here, but I am a bit biased."

"I hear you are dating the owner."

"That is true." He smiled and took another drink of his coffee. "Wait a minute. How in the hell did you know my brother was a child molester? We never put that in any computer anywhere."

"Stuart," I said as I walked up to the table, "This is my sister Ashley."

"What? I didn't know you had a sister!" Stuart looked at me, confused.

"Neither did I." I froze everyone in place.

"Hello Agnes," Ashley said. I was wondering if you would recognize me.

"I didn't until you came here. Why are you here?"

"Why do you think I would come for any reason other than to see my sister?"

I rolled my eyes. "Don't give me that shit. Winny told me a long time ago that everyone hates me, so just tell me why you're here."

Ashley laughed and gave me a hug. "Winny? You believed Winny? He's the only one left in Resempire because we all left to get away from him!

"You mean I've been thinking everyone hated me this whole time? That ass hole." I glared at nothing in particular. "Oh, I guess I should un-freeze everyone."

"What do you mean you didn't know you had a sister?" Stuart said confused.

"Oh, I just meant I didn't know Ashley Taylor was my sister because that's not her real name. And I haven't seen her since we were children so I didn't recognize her picture in the paper. I can't believe you're here, it's been such a long time." I looked at Ashley and had to pretend like we hadn't talked yet. "What are you doing here?"

"Well, I came to give Stuart the news and then when I saw you, I just couldn't believe it! Come here, give me a hug."

I gave Ashley a hug and as I did she whispered in my ear, "I also came to tell you, you're in danger."

* * * *

As soon as Polly arrived for the wedding, I told her that Nefarius's brother and Jordan from school were a couple. I didn't want the shock of seeing Jordan wandering around the estate sending her into a whirlwind of deeper depression. She didn't seem too bothered by it. It was almost like the memory of what we did to Jordan reminded her of what a sparkplug she used to be. Maybe this wedding was going to be good for her after all.

I was shocked to see the children. I couldn't believe how much they had grown. Axle was taller than me already, and Patricia was such a polite little young lady. Even though it was terrible for Polly, she was definitely bringing those two up right. I started to relax a little bit when it came to Polly. Maybe now that the two were getting older she would revert back to her old self.

My Name is Agnes   277

"Polly, do you want to go for a walk?" I asked.

She looked at the two children with a terrified look on her face. "Oh for Zeus's sake, Mother, I am sure you can leave us to ourselves," Patricia said.

"Hey Zeus, look! We are not children any longer!" Axle called to the heavens.

I took her arm and laughed, and she relaxed a bit but still seemed apprehensive. "They have your sense of humour," I said to her and gave her a bump with my hip.

"Oh, I know I am over-protective with them, Agnes, I am just terrified they will turn out like their father."

"You have every right to be nervous of that, but Philip was not always the man he is now. He was once a dazzling man, so you know that part of him will transfer to his children. And you know they will always have you to guide them. They have no choice but to succeed."

Polly stopped and took my hands. "Oh Agnes, I have missed you!" She gave me a big hug.

"And I you! You have to meet Eunice's new in-laws. Nefarius's mother is such a delight, you will be green with envy. And by the way, Ina got here almost a month ago and tried to undo almost everything we had accomplished. Luckily, Eldon's friend Garlas has discovered a way to weave baskets completely sideways from the way Ina does it so every afternoon he will completely undo what she does. Every morning he goes on a tirade about the baskets. Ina joins his campaign to figure out who is trying to make a mockery of this wedding...but not until these baskets are fixed. I think there are only three baskets involved, but it keeps her occupied. Poor thing, she is getting on in age but she has not forgotten that she is still in charge."

We had a good laugh. I missed having my best friend around.

The wedding was absolutely beautiful. Eunice was a blubbering mess. Good thing I planned two handkerchiefs for her to carry.

The supper was very grand. The family was all seated up front and I was honoured to be sitting up with them. I noticed that Philip was drinking more than he should have been. The kids sat in between Polly and Philip. Axle was trying to keep a handle on Philip and he was doing a pretty good job. The boy was definitely going to do well in politics. He was already more mature than his father.

Even the dedications didn't drone on for hours. Ina didn't get up and talk about herself this time, in fact she didn't get up at all. I think she was pretty upset she hadn't found the basket-weaving culprit. Andias's speech was eloquent as usual. Speeches about your sons are nice but speeches about your daughter are always special. His, of course, was a tear-jerker, Eunice being his only daughter.

The dancing and drinking started not long after everyone calmed down from the dedications and the crying. I had to go over and give Andias a hug because of his speech. He gave me an extra special hug because he'd never gotten to say a speech at Percius's and my wedding.

"I have always considered you my daughter, Agnes." He looked at me with a very serious tone. "I know you have done more for this family than most of the blood members. And whatever you do is in the family's best interest. Whatever happens, I want you to know I understand that." He nodded his head a bit.

I couldn't help but nod my head also. We had an understanding. I wasn't sure what it was just then, but I did later.

"Wow, I just had a really strange moment with your father-in-law," I said to Polly.

"Hmmm, I only have those moments with the mother-in-law," Polly said. She was completely relaxed after she'd had a couple of drinks. The kids were dancing and she actually looked like she wanted to dance. If Philip had asked her to dance she might have considered it. In the state of inebriation he was currently in, I don't think dancing was in his cards, though. He would probably have tripped over his feet. I would have liked to see that, actually.

Eunice and Nefarius looked so in love. It really made me think of Percius. He would have loved to see Eunice happy. They were both such free spirits. Happy and kind to everyone. Giving and generous. Loved deeply. Fiercely loyal. Weddings make me such a sap.

"What are you contemplating so deeply, Agnes?" Polly asked.

"Oh, I am just remembering Percius."

"I am sorry."

My Name is Agnes

"Do not be sorry. I was thinking how he and Eunice were so similar and how he would have loved to see her this happy," I said.

"Yes, I believe that is correct on all counts." She smiled that silly crooked smile at me. "I also believe I am drunk."

"I believe that is correct also. I also believe we should dance, but we are out of drink. Let us fill our glasses then shimmy to the dance floor."

She nodded her head and we danced our way to the drink table. We were having so much fun until we saw Philip acting suspicious around one of the curtains at the back of the room. He was looking around to see if anyone was watching him, then he snuck behind the curtain. "You have got to be kidding me, you son of a bitch," I muttered. "You are not going to screw some doxy at your sister's wedding."

"This really is distasteful, even for Philip," Polly said as she followed behind me.

I was marching over to the curtain and I almost ran right into Jordan. "Sorry." I said snottily.

"Look, I do not like you and you do not like me, but have you seen Eldon?" he said with some cheek.

"No I have not, you have lost your boyfriend, have you?" I chuckled a bit. "Listen, I would love nothing more than to track down your lover with you but I have another matter..." I looked towards the curtains.

As it sunk in what could actually, possibly be happening, I continued marching, Jordan following right behind me.

We stepped behind the curtain. There was Philip – he had Eldon bent over and he was giving it to him from behind. And there was Polly inches away from them with a knife in her hand.

Before either of us could say or do anything, Polly had sliced Philip's throat. Once she realized what she had done she took a few steps back and dropped the knife on the ground.

I immediately froze everyone in place. Robin flew in. Shit...what had she done? I looked at Robin.

"Fuck," He said as we stood there assessing the situation.

"I guess the cheating bothered her more than she let on...at least cheating with men," I observed.

"Or in public."

"Or at weddings."

"Perhaps she just did not like the man." Robin looked at Philip with his head sideways.

"Really, who could blame her?" I found myself looking at him with my head tilted also. Philip was half slumped over Eldon's back holding his throat with blood spewing out between his fingers. It was quite poetic, maybe I would sketch it one day, but I would probably change the heads to some sort of animal.

Once I snapped out of the trance, I said, "So how shall we fix this?"

"No one can find out that Polly killed Philip," Robin said as he crossed his wings.

"No they will not. Luckily we happen to have someone that we can blame for the entire thing." I looked at Jordan.

Robin retrieved the knife off the floor.

"Thank you." I enchanted Jordan to take the knife. When he woke up he would slice Eldon's throat as well. It would just be a nasty love triangle.

I gave Polly a kiss good-bye before sending her back onto the dance floor where she would wake up when I unfroze everyone, completely oblivious to what happened. This would be the last time I ever saw Polly.

I had used too much magic so it was time for us to move on. I would definitely miss them though. I heard that Polly didn't sink back into depression and married not long after Philip's death, which I am so grateful for.

Patricia went to school and studied medicine, she was actually a doctor, but because she was a woman they called her a nurse.

Axle took the throne, of course, and did great things. That's another thing that the history books got wrong, but I must admit, Alexander the Great has a much better ring to it.

About the Author

Kelly Brookbank will be the first to admit it...she gets her best ideas in the shower. She thinks everybody does, in fact. She's betting Edison spent most of his life in the bathtub. Must have to do with circulation or something...Kelly doesn't know, go ask someone smart.

So she got an idea in the shower, then fine-tuned it that one time she went on the treadmill. Somebody somewhere told her she was supposed to write down a timeline, so she sat down on her very comfortable couch and as her rear-end expanded, her fingers typed what her tornado of a brain told her to. Five months later the first wicked version of *My Name is Agnes* was born. In between her rear-end expansions and her brainstorms, Kelly is a hockey mom of two, a wife of three, and a gardener of one million weeds and five plants.

Printed in Canada